FRAMED IN GUILT

It didn't look good for Bob Stanton. The dead woman had been killed in his car—shot through the chest—and he didn't have an alibi. Several people were there at the club when Grace Turner had called him that evening. She had asked to meet him. But he hadn't kept the meeting. Or had he? After his drinking binge of the night before, he didn't really remember. But Inspector Treech is convinced that Stanton is guilty and is out to prove it. The murdered girl was English; Stanton had served in London during World War II. And new information suggests that he had been married to Grace's best friend, Eve. Now on the eve of his Hollywood marriage to movie star Joy Parnell, Grace could have ruined his plans. It all made sense—except that Stanton had never heard of Eve!

MY FLESH IS SWEET

Ad Connors is a down-on-his-luck pulp writer living in Mexico. But the day he witnesses Eleana Hayes run into General Estaban's car changes everything. It's not bad enough that Connors thinks he's killed the general defending Eleana's honor. It gets worse when he tries to help her find the Mexican lawyer who's been sending her money from her fugitive father—only to find his murdered body instead. Connors is in over his head fast, but there's something about Eleana that convinces him that she needs his help. Once he and Eleana escape back to America, the real mystery of just what she was really doing down in Mexico begins to haunt Connors—that and the fact that he's about to be extradited for murder! Is Eleana a damsel in distress, or is Connors just a pawn in her game?

DAY KEENE BIBLIOGRAPHY

This Murder, Mr. Herbert and Other Stories (1948)

Framed in Guilt [aka Evidence Most Blind] (1949)

Farewell to Passion [aka The Passion Murders] (1951)

Love Me—and Die [as by Keene, collaboration with Gil Brewer] (1951)

My Flesh is Sweet (1951)

To Kiss, or Kill (1951)

About Doctor Ferrel (1952)

Home is the Sailor (1952)

Hunt the Killer (1952)

If the Coffin Fits (1952)

Naked Fury (1952)

Wake Up to Murder (1952)

Mrs. Homicide (1953)

Strange Witness (1953)

The Big Kiss-Off (1954)

Death House Doll (1954)

His Father's Wife (1954)

Homicidal Lady (1954)

Joy House (1954)

Notorious (1954)

Sleep With the Devil [aka Sin With the Devil] (1954)

. There Was a Crooked Man (1954; revised 1963)

The Dangling Carrot (1955)

Who Has Wilma Lathrop? (1955)

Bring Him Back Dead (1956; revised 1963)

Flight by Night (1956)

Murder on the Side (1956)

Passage to Samoa (1958)

Dead Dolls Don't Talk (1959)

Dead in Bed (1959)*

Moran's Woman (1959)

So Dead My Lovely (1959)

Take a Step to Murder (1959)

Too Black for Heaven (1959)

Too Hot to Hold (1959)

The Brimstone Bed (1960)

Chautauqua [with Dwight Vincent] (1960)

Miami 59 (1960)

Payola (1960)*

World Without Women [with Leonard Pruyn] (1960)

Seed of Doubt (1961)

Bye, Bye Bunting (1963)

L.A. 46 [aka City of Angels] (1964)

Carnival of Death (1965)

Chicago 11 (1966)

Acapulco G.P.O. (1967)

Guns Along the Brazos (1967)

Live Again, Love Again (1970)

*Johnny Aloha series

As Lewis Dixon

Wild Girl [reprinted 1969 as by Keene] (1952)

As William Richards

Dead Man's Tide [reprinted 1958 as It's a Sin to Kill as by Keene] (1953)

As Daniel White

Southern Daughter [reprinted 1967 as by Keene] (1954)

Framed in GUILT
My Flesh is SWEET

BY DAY KEENE

STARK
HOUSE

Stark House Press • Eureka California

FRAMED IN GUILT / MY FLESH IS SWEET

Published by Stark House Press
1315 H Street
Eureka, CA 95501, USA
griffinskye3@sbcglobal.net
www.starkhousepress.com

FRAMED IN GUILT
Originally published by The M. S. Mill Co. and William Morrow
& Company and copyright © 1949 by Day Keene.

MY FLESH IS SWEET
Originally published by Lion Books and copyright © 1951 by Day
Keene.

Reprinted by permission of the Estate of Day Keene. All rights
reserved under International and Pan-American Copyright
Conventions.

"Introduction" copyright © 2005 by Ed Gorman.

ISBN: 0-9749438-8-6
ISBN: 978-0-9749438-8-6

Book design by Mark Shepard, WWW.SHEPGRAPHICS.COM

First Stark House Press Edition: August 2005

Contents

Day Keene

Someone once complained that "Day Keene" sounded "made up." Wouldn't you make up a name yourself if your true monicker was Gunard Hjertstedt?

Day Keene truly did it all. Radio, confession magazines, pulp magazines, semi-slick magazines, paperbacks, hardcovers and, I believe, a few movie treatments, maybe even a script or two.

We remember him, when we remember him at all, as a paperback writer, where he was generally at his best, with the exception of his truly fine hardcover novel, *Chautaqua*.

His greatest literary quality, for me, was the intimacy of his voice. And it was as intimate in third person as it was in first. He was a buddy telling you of his adventures, some of them pretty unlikely but all of them spellbinding.

His other greatest quality was his ability to write believably about the common man and the common woman. As much fun as Raymond Chandler's stories are, old Marlowe gets awfully noble in quite a few of those tales.

Keene knew never to make his protagonist noble. This was an average guy set upon by trouble not of his own making and forced to survive by acting in ways that were downright ignoble. In other words, he responded pretty much the same way you and I would. The way most people would. You are, after all, trying to save your life.

He did great bar scenes, great fight scenes, and great dread scenes—the dread frequently related to the amount of alcohol his protagonist has consumed. Keene used the alcoholic blackout scene as often and as well as Cornell Woolrich.

His men were, unlike so many paperback gents, far more interested in love than lust. He understood that love is the deadliest weapon of all. He also understood that only love offers us any real hope of redemption. Love, not only in Keene's books but in most of the classic novels as well, is the theme that fascinates us like no other.

Keene has yet to have the kind of rebirth that Harry Whittington enjoys today. I'm not sure why. I see them pretty much as equals in their skills and abilities. And where Whittington was often Southern and small-town,

Keene generally gave us Northern cities and the social forces of the Fifties and Sixties. Which makes him a wee bit more interesting to me as a Yankee. His two favorite urban landscapes were Chicago and Los Angeles. He did well by both of them.

A final Day Keene virtue—his sly sense of humor. He was a moralist but not a preachy one. He'd sneak in his feelings about a person or a social situation or a modern trend but he'd sugar-coat it as wit.

Finally, as most of us who write full-time will tell you, not all books turn out as you hoped they would. John D. MacDonald once remarked that "Unfortunately, it takes just as long to write a bad book as a good one." Of course, this is true of writers in general. James Jones wrote a number of novels but only one was a masterpiece. Same with Joseph Heller. Stendahl. Katherine Anne Porter. Probably even Hemingway. But it's especially true for people who write two or three books a year to make a living. You can't mass-produce masterpieces. Every once in a while one might sneak through—most writers can show a book that seems to exceed the normal restrictions of their talents—but that, as they say in the movie business, is generally a "happy accident."

Which is a warning for those of you who start collecting Keene. Not everything will be wonderful. Always readable as hell but sometimes spoiled by the obvious speed of its composition. In addition to the two novels in this book, you might start looking for *Joy House* (a French film adapted by Charles Williams no less!); *Home is The Sailor* (I wish, no kidding, that Edgar G. Ulmer had had this to direct instead of the "Detour" storyline—a wild blood-and-booze-soaked noir); *Sleep With The Devil* (as innovative a plot as was ever to appear as a paperback original); and (if you can find it) his 1946 collection of pulp stories *This is Murder, Mr. Herbert* (which shows you the kind of solid if not remarkable work he turned out magazines such as *Ace-G-Man Stories*, *Dime Detective* and *Black Mask*).

A long time ago I spoke to one of Keene's former agents. The man spoke fondly of Keene as a bright, modest, talented hard-worker who, despite a few drinks now and then, constantly tried to improve his material.

That's pretty much how I've always pictured him: good guy, good writer.
—Ed Gorman

Framed in GUILT

BY DAY KEENE

CHAPTER 1

If as is said, on occasion, coming events cast their shadows before them, Grace Turner was let down badly. No fiery writing appeared on her wall to warn her. No one blew a trumpet. There was nothing at all unusual about the night she died except, perhaps, the 'shooting' star she chanced to observe from the window of the hotel room she couldn't afford and from which she was to be evicted in the morning.

It was a night for love and softly whispered lies. A crescent moon hung low in a star-studded sky. Dreamy-eyed young couples, replete with hot dogs and Coca-Cola, strolled arm in arm down Vine Street, wishing they could afford to patronize the smart eating and drinking places. In the foyers and under the marquees of the smart eating and drinking places, middle-aged couples, replete with charcoal-broiled steaks and Chateau Rouge '29, belched politely at each other and wished they were young again.

Grace watched the brief stellar display. Then, turning from the window, she studied her reflection in the mirror of her dressing table. Perspiration had blotched the powder on her nose. The same wisp of untidy hair had escaped again to dangle damply under one ear. And for all the eight pounds she had spent on it in the hopes of impressing Arthur, her new, dull rose traveling suit fit her practically nowhere, except, perhaps, in the hemline.

Damn Arthur.

She tucked in the wisp of hair and re-powdered her nose, reflecting there were various degrees of foolishness. And the highest degree of all was usually awarded to an over-eager biped of the female sex confronted by a lusty, lying male who *claimed* to be in love.

"Just call me Art for short, kid."

Her cheeks hot, she returned to the window and its illusion of coolness. The thing to do was not to think of Arthur. She had to put Arthur out of her mind. Look at the people on the street below. Marvel at the lights. If this other matter went right tonight she could write Arthur off to experience. Of course what she intended to do would be wrong. It wasn't cricket. It was against the law. She could even go to prison for it. On the other hand there ought to be some lamb in every life. It shouldn't all be mutton. It wasn't as if she were concealing the information from Eve. Eve had a right to know and she'd told her. She had posted Eve an airmail letter within an hour after she'd read the item in the cinema chitchat column. This other idea had occurred to her later. She'd just glanced in through the window of the restaurant on Vine Street and there Robert was.

She looked for her purse and found it in a drawer. It contained a single one-dollar bill, seventy cents in silver, a comb, a compact, and the clipping—

...Of interest to the admirers of Joy Parnell is the rumor that Robert Stanton, author of the current best seller, *Men Back of Wire*, and top-flight Hollywood scenarist, is reputed to be edging out Lyle Ferris in the romantic race for mi-lady's hand....

There it was in black and white. Robert wasn't dead after all. He hadn't died in that crash over Bremen. He had merely allowed Eve to think so, allowed her to cry her eyes out for a man who didn't care one snap of his fingers for her.

Grace returned the clipping to her purse. The liar. The dirty mucking liar. He deserved no consideration. She hoped Eve sued him for fifty thousand pounds, and got it. Even at this late date it was difficult to decide which of them had been the bigger fool, herself or Eve. She was older, had been around. But in 1941, that was seven years ago, Eve had been a child.

"*Mocambo, the Coconut Grove, the Brown Derby, Ciro's, Malibu Beach, Palm Springs, Snow Valley. You'll see them all, baby,*" the bold bad wolf had promised her. "*Back home I have a big ranch, and servants, and cars, and a swimming pool. And they'll all belong to you.*"

And Eve, little pig, had believed him. Eve had allowed him to huff and puff and blow her defenses down. Eve had acted like a cheap little trollop. Color flooded Grace's cheeks. Well, not quite like a trollop. She was a fine one to throw stones. At least there had been a war going on. Eve *thought* she was in love. And she did have her marriage lines.

The more Grace thought over the situation the more certain she was of the firmness of the ground on which she intended to tread. First Lieutenant Robert Stanton hadn't been story telling about his wealth. He did have a big ranch. He was a Hollywood scenarist. It stood to reason he would have servants and cars and swimming pools.

She phoned the desk and asked the time. It was eleven-thirty. Thirty more minutes to go. She wished she could afford to buy a drink to brace her before she met Robert. Well, why not? The manager had been considerate but he had asked her either to pay up her bill or vacate her room in the morning. She might as well be completely stony. You couldn't get anywhere in Hollywood on one dollar and seventy cents.

As she slipped into her mustard-colored tweed coat her garnet ring caught in the worn sleeve lining. No matter. Tomorrow she would buy another coat. Tomorrow she would buy an entire new outfit. She would wallow in silken underthings. She would buy hats and hose and shoes. For all his fumbling around the point and pretending over the phone that he didn't remember her, Robert didn't dare not to meet her. He didn't dare refuse her anything she asked. She'd been a witness to his and Eve's wedding.

As she turned in her key the desk clerk said, "I beg your pardon, Miss Turner. But the manager—"

"I know," Grace interrupted him sweetly. "I have already spoken to the manager and made arrangements to take care of my statement in the morning."

The clerk shrugged and turned to wait on another guest. Across the lobby Shad Hanson got up from an over-stuffed chair and watched the girl enter the dimly lighted bar opening off the foyer. There might be something to the tip he'd had.

A middle-aged man of medium size with the freshly scrubbed complexion of some Scandinavians, his pink and white cheeks, blue eyes, and flaxen hair gave him a benign and naive appearance. In his case appearance was deceptive.

Ostensibly a lawyer, he maintained a luxurious Hollywood office. He even kept office hours. But he hadn't appeared in a courtroom for years. He didn't have to. He knew where too many bodies, male and female, had spent their lost weekends. His was a nasty business but he never had trouble with his conscience. There was a reason for that. He had none.

Seated on a padded bar stool, Grace counted out her seventy cents in silver and ordered a Scotch and soda.

"A nice night, eh?" Hanson said conversationally as he slid onto the stool beside her.

He might have been speaking to either the barman or her. Grace decided he was speaking to her. "Yes. It is a nice night," she agreed.

"And not unusual for this time of year," Hanson followed up his lead. "A marvelous state, California. You a native, Miss?"

Grace admitted she was English. It seemed so was he, that is on his mother's side. The bond, slight as it was, established, he insisted on buying a drink to cement it. He liked English girls, so he said. The incident, although trivial, restored Grace's self confidence somewhat. She might look like an English frump to Arthur but there were other men to whom she was not entirely unattractive. It was with difficulty she begged off a third drink, pleading a previous engagement. But out of gratitude she agreed to meet her new-found bar companion at one o'clock if her previous date petered out.

She was almost gay as she said good-bye. It was nice to be wanted. The night was warm. The walk was crowded. Grace struggled out of her coat and carried it over her arm, totally unconscious that Hanson had followed her from the bar.

Nearing the northwest corner of Vine Street (which she had appointed as a meeting place because she was familiar with it and because Robert had been in the Vine Street Silver Pheasant when she'd phoned him) Grace wondered how much to ask for, five or ten thousand dollars. Perhaps it would be more diplomatic to allow him to name the sum. She needn't accept it if it wasn't sufficient.

The drug store on the far corner of Vine was brightly lighted and well patronized. A few feet farther on, beginning with the Brown Derby and the Hollywood Plaza Hotel, the street was ablaze with light. But the windows of the large department store on the corner which she had chosen were unlighted. The manikins in the window looked slightly sinister. It might, Grace thought, have happened in a cinema play. Of all the brightly lighted corners she herself had named this one. Not that she had anything to fear. Or had she?

Her lips suddenly dry, she wet them with the tip of her tongue. The whiskey fire was dying out. She should have accepted a third drink. *Damn Arthur.* He'd gotten her into this. Gild the kettle as she might, this still was blackmail.

In mental panic her feet retraced their steps to the hotel and the friendly man in the bar. Then she thought of the single dollar in her purse and stood her ground.

She was expecting him on foot. The horn of the car at the curb tooted twice before she realized it was tooting for her. It was the type of car he would drive, a long, low convertible. He opened the door. "Is that you, Grace?"

Some of the fear gone out of her loins, Grace waggled her hips across the walk to the car. "Grace," she admitted. "I thought you didn't remember my name."

"It came back to me," he said. "I'm glad to see you, Grace. Get in."

Grace hesitated briefly. He must know what she wanted. Still he didn't sound a bit angry. And he'd said he was glad to see her. Nothing ventured, nothing gained. The seat was wide and low. In her relief there wasn't to be a brawl about this thing. She sprawled on it with sensuous pleasure as the car merged with the southbound traffic.

In a darkened doorway a few feet farther on, Shad Hanson lighted a cigarette as he stared after the car. "Well, I'll be damned," he admitted. "I will be damned."

A few blocks south of Vine Street the driver of the big car made a wide U-turn and headed north. "I thought," he suggested, "we would drive out somewhere and have a bite to eat and maybe a few drinks. Is that okay with you?"

Grace said she would enjoy that very much. In the faint light from the instrument panel Robert looked much as she remembered him except he had put on weight. He still wore a thin, almost hair-line, mustache. He had been drinking but wasn't drunk. "You're looking well," she made conversation.

He said he felt fine. "And you?"

She said she also felt fine. "You must have been surprised to hear my voice."

He said, "I was. Grace Turner. Hmm. It must be all of five or six years since I last saw you."

Grace pinned down the date. "Much more than that. It was in October of 1941."

They were out of the brightly lighted Hollywood business section now. For the length of a dozen blocks the only sound was the rush of passing traffic, the soft purr of the car motor, and the suck of the tires on the pavement. When he spoke again there was a new note in his voice. "All right. Let's have it, Grace. What are you doing in this country? And what was the idea of that 'meet me or else' business you pulled on the phone?"

"Well, it's a long story," she improvised.

Holding to the course she had charted, she began by telling him the story of Technical Sergeant Arthur Hale. It wasn't a pleasant thing to tell. It had happened after the war without even war hysteria for an excuse. She and Arthur had met at a dance and liked each other. He seemed genuinely in love with her but everything had been in such a tangle due to the ending of the war she had been forced to accept Arthur's word he would marry her in the States as soon as he was discharged. His father, he said, was an enormously wealthy man who owned a large and prosperous ranch near Van Nuys. He would be pleased, so Arthur said, to receive her as a daughter. The prospects had been inviting. She had always wanted to live in the States.

That had been over two years ago. It had also been the last she had heard from Arthur. She wrote into a seeming void. Finally, frantic, she had wangled a passport and using her own savings to purchase passage had come to California in an attempt to locate him.

"And you couldn't find him, eh? He'd pulled a fast one."

"No," Grace corrected. "I found him. Only his father's large and prosperous ranch turned out to be a quarter-acre tract in a scrubby sub-division. He was a nasty old man who swore at me and called me ever so vile names. More, Arthur was already married and had a simpering little blonde wife and three dirty-nosed children to prove it. He damn near fainted when he saw me. 'Get out of my life, you frowzy English frump,' he shouted. 'I thought you had sense enough to know it was only one of those things.'"

Overcome by shame and self-pity, she leaned against the door of the car and wept.

The lights of Santa Monica dropped behind them. Now they were descending a steep ramp leading to a broad highway built parallel with the shore line of the ocean. "I'm sorry, Grace." The man seemed sincere. "There are no two ways about it. You've had a bad deal. And if you're in a spot, if you need passage money back to London and a few hundred for expenses, I'll be glad to help you out." His eyes stayed glued to the ribbon of road unwinding under the wheels. There was a note of reproach in his voice. "But you shouldn't have pulled that 'or else' business. It is so old and corny we don't even use it in pictures any more. Besides, you haven't a thing on me."

Grace stopped crying. "No?" She said it defiantly.

"No."

"There's Eve."

"Yes. There is Eve," he admitted. He didn't sound so confident now.

"And Robin."

"Robin?"

He sounded genuinely puzzled. Gloating, Grace picked up her whip again. *He didn't know about Robin. He didn't know Eve had a child. He didn't know he had a son.* "Yes. Robin." Her mood was bright again. "So called for two reasons. One, because Robin is a diminutive of Robert. Two, because he came in the Spring."

The man at the wheel seemed to shrink. His coat was suddenly too large for his shoulders. It seemed difficult for him to breathe. "I didn't know there was a child. Believe me." He took a bottle from the glove compartment. "After that I need a drink."

"You might ask if I cared for one," Grace said.

He handed her the bottle. It was dimpled bottle Scotch and tasted as good as it smelled. Grace drank sparingly, then corked and returned the bottle to the glove compartment.

Her companion switched on the car's fog lights. His voice was meek. "If you don't mind, Grace, we'll get out of this fog by cutting through one of the canyons and eat at some spot in the Valley where I won't be so apt to be recognized. I'll have to have time to pull myself together. I don't mind saying what you've told me has been a shock."

Grace was smug about it. "I should imagine. Fun is fun. But when a wealthy man deserts a blind wife and six-year-old son for over seven years—"

"Blind?" His voice groped toward her through the barrier of fog. "Eve is blind?"

"She is, poor thing. It happened during the next to the last buzz-bomb raid. Or could it have been the one before that?"

"And this blindness is a permanent condition?"

"I don't know," Grace admitted. "Eve did mention the possibility an expensive operation *might* restore her sight. But there is no certainty about it. As I understand it, it has something to do with shock. A paralysis of the optic nerve."

The car swerved sharply to the right and for a moment Grace was afraid he intended to dash them both to pieces by crashing into what appeared to be a solid wall of stone. She barely stifled a scream as the wide mouth of what he called a canyon loomed out of the fog. Almost immediately the car began to climb. "That's too bad. Believe me I'm sorry to hear it," he said. "I had no idea there was a child. And I, of course, had no way of knowing Eve was blind."

"You would have known," Grace needled him, "if you had returned to England instead of allowing her to believe you died in that crash over Bremen. The London papers were filled with it."

"Believe me," he repeated. "As that heel of a sergeant told you, I thought it was one of those things. I thought Eve had forgotten me long ago and married someone else."

"Seeing you're alive, it's a good thing she didn't. After all, your marriage was legal."

"Yes. I suppose it was."

There was less fog here but Grace didn't like the canyon road. In spots it clung to the cliff on one side while the other ended precipitously on the edge of what appeared to be a black abyss. If there were any houses she could not see them.

He slackened his speed and seemed to be searching for a turnout. Grace was mildly amused. If Robert thought he could feed her drinks, then sweet-talk her out of the money she had coming, he was badly mistaken. She'd had enough of that sort of hanky-panky. From here on in little Gracie was looking out for number one. The car lost its momentum and instead of curving left with the road, he allowed it to roll out onto a large, dark, graveled turnout and up to within a few feet of a black and white striped guard rail. Theirs was the only car on the turnout but thirty feet away, faintly silver in the moonlight, Grace could see a large water tower and below it an unlighted metal building displaying a prominent sign—

HOT DOGS—SOFT DRINKS—SIZZLE-BURGERS

Then she discovered the valley. It was spread out far below them. Tiny, twinkling lights bejeweled the night as far as she could see.

He switched off the car lights. "Pretty, eh?"

"It is beautiful," Grace admitted.

She felt nervous, jumpy, though she couldn't have told just why. Robert had been a perfect gentleman. He had taken the bad news like a soldier.

He took out the bottle from the glove compartment and uncorked it. "How about another little drink?"

She wet her lips and handed him the bottle. He drained it and set it on the floor of the car just behind the seat. Then he wiped his lips on his hand. "Now let's get down to business. You want money, of course. Presumably a lot of money for, well, let's say not making public what you know about me."

"That would seem to sum it up," Grace said.

"How much?"

She named the first sum that came to her mind. "Fifteen thousand dollars." She held her breath at her own audacity, then was sorry she hadn't asked for more when he said softly, "Considering everything, that doesn't sound too unreasonable. And if I don't pay off, you'll contact Eve?"

"Also the newspapers and Miss Parnell." Grace was amused by the thought. "I don't presume you would wish Miss Parnell to know you have a wife and child in London?"

"No," he admitted. "I wouldn't. But now let me ask one more thing. You have kept this knowledge to yourself. You didn't confide in this sergeant?"

Grace dismissed Arthur with a contemptuous, "Him. I wouldn't tell Arthur the time."

"And you haven't contacted Eve? You haven't written or cabled her you saw me?"

Grace lied, "I have not."

A long silence followed the lie. Grace felt uncomfortable, then suddenly terrified. Except for the stars and a faint crescent moon, the night outside the car was a stifling sable cloak that seemed about to descend on her head and smother her. She wanted people and lights around her. She wanted to hear human voices. "Don't you try any of your tricks now, Robert. You start this car and drive me to some restaurant. I don't like this place. It frightens me."

He said he was sorry she was frightened but made no move to start the car. His voice was unutterably sad. "Believe me, Grace. I wish you hadn't made that phone call. I wish this didn't have to happen. But, damn it, I can't trust you. I can't afford to take the chance."

"You wish what didn't have to happen?" she asked evenly. But even as she asked, she knew.

Far below them, in the valley, the toy-like headlights of a car began the long climb to the summit. But it wouldn't reach them in time. Grace knew. Panic released her contracted throat muscles. "No!" she screamed. "No! I lied. Harming me won't do you a bit of good. Eve knows. I airmailed a letter to her two days ago."

"Even so," he said quietly, and lifting the gun in his hand he did what he had come to do if it seemed feasible. The two reports were loud inside the car, then swallowed by the night. Grace's chin dropped forward on her chest. A first, then a second stain, darkened the dull rose of her suit coat.

The gun held limply in his fingers, the man stared at the spreading stains. It was the first blood of his own drawing he had ever seen. But blood, like fur, it would appear was all one color in the dark....

The girl was dead. There was no question of that. She lay on her back, most of her body concealed by a clump of wild holly, about fifty feet below the turnout on the summit of the canyon road. One arm was flung over her eyes as if to ward off a blow. The holly had broken her fall. Had the body rolled five more feet it would have plunged over an almost sheer drop to lie hidden, perhaps for months, in the thick tangle of greasewood and live oak growing at the base of the cliff three hundred feet below.

A curious motorist seeing police cars on the turnout swung in to form the nucleus of a crowd. Three other cars followed in time to see prowl car officers McIntyre and Gleason of the Valley Station climb the low guard rail and make their way cautiously down the dew-slick slope. Inspector Treech of Los Angeles Homicide, who had picked up the call on his car radio enroute from his valley ranch to his downtown office, wanted to know who had discovered the body.

A stocky man with a broken nose wiped sweating palms on the skirt of a clean white apron. "I did," he admitted. He jerked his head at the hot dog stand. "I'm the day man, see? And almost every morning after I open up I walk out here to pick up the bottles folks throw out of their cars instead of please bringing 'em back to the stand like we ast 'em. And—" He waved one hand vaguely at the valley emerging in bright crazy-quilt-patch patterns from the morning fog. "Well, it's kinda pretty, see? So I always give it a look. But this morning the first thing I seen was her."

"You don't know her?"

"No, sir. I do not."

Still more cars pulled into the turnout. There was a blue and white car from the Malibu division of the sheriff's office, a fire warden in a red pickup truck, two cars with press stickers on their windshields, also a Los Angeles squad car carrying three of Inspector Treech's own men, Jack Gieger, Matt Kelly, and Bill Swen.

The sheriff's men were pleased. After looking over the guard rail, one of them crowed, "She's your baby, Inspector. The city line extends two hundred feet back from the summit."

Lou Saunders, in charge of one of the local press association offices, asked if the body had been identified.

"I just beat you here, Lou," Treech admitted. He could never quite make up his mind whether he liked Saunders or not. A former war correspondent, the reporter drank heavily and consistently but Treech had never seen him drunk. With all, or because of his failings, he was a good reporter. He called a spade a spade and viewed all humanity as copy.

A big man with slightly bloodshot eyes, Saunders stroked his pencil line mustache as he watched the two prowl car men. Treech looked out over the valley. Except for scattered clumps of live oak, wild holly, and mesquite, the hills were brown and would be until the first rain. The floor of the valley, however, most of it irrigated farms and groves, was lush and green. The whole was dotted with houses and barns and villages that from this distance looked like toys. His own small ranch was less than twelve miles away. A citrus grove blocked it from sight but he could see one corner of Bob Stanton's barn. The sight caused him to make a mental note to see if Hi Lo had remembered to have Eddie fix the back pasture fence. If Stanton's Palomino colts got into his young walnut trees again he intended to raise hell.

The two prowl car men reached the body. "She's been shot twice," Gleason called.

Treech asked if she had a purse. "I don't see one," McIntyre said. "You want we should bring her up?"

"You know better than that," Treech growled.

Gieger and Kelly were already descending the slope. A stocky man, well-padded with good living, Treech grunted his way over the guard rail and stood a moment, breathing heavily, holding on to the rail with one hand.

"Tough, eh?" Saunders asked pleasantly. "Corpses haven't any consideration. They insist on being found in the damnedest places."

Treech ignored him and joined the officers around the body. The girl was no longer in her first youth. Treech guessed her age at thirty. Her body was well-formed but too thin. Her face was long and slightly horsy. Her parted lips revealed bad teeth. Except for such snagging incident to the roll of the body down the cliff, her clothing was not disordered.

Gieger lighted a cigarette. "Not much to look at, is she?"

"No," Treech agreed.

Lifting the body with one hand, he felt under it with the other. The grass under the body was dry. That would seem to place the hour of its disposal sometime before the morning dew began to form. He got to his feet and stepped back as a police photographer, unbalanced by his equipment, half-skidded, half-scrambled, down the slope.

Kelly caught Treech's arm as he stepped back. "Careful, Chief. It's a long way down."

Treech leaned over the edge of the cliff. "A long way down," he agreed.

"Whoever dumped her must know this spot and figured she would roll right on over the edge. You and Jack better get down there and look around."

Kelly grinned. "Swen and Lieutenant Marble drew that cutie."

The photographer was still taking pictures when the medical examiner arrived. His on-the-spot examination was cursory. "Death has been absolute for six or seven hours. It was occasioned by two gunshot wounds in the left mammary gland. I would say, offhand, both slugs passed through her heart. I know they passed through the body."

There was no need for him to add that the gun had been held close to the girl's body. The powder stains on her dull rose suit coat were as visible as the clotted blood. At a nod from Treech the two prowl car men, assisted by Kelly and Gieger, carried the body up the slope. By the time Treech reached and climbed the guard rail the first echelon of fingerprint men and laboratory technicians had already taken over.

Working with dispassionate interest, they scraped the residue from under the dead girl's nails, examined her person, counted her teeth, inked and printed her fingers. There was, Treech thought, something very indecent about violent death. If death canceled all obligations it also revoked all privilege. The unidentified dead, on discovery, ceased to be one of we the people. They lost all right to privacy. They became wadded reports on a clip board; prowl car, lab, photo, fingerprint, Police Emergency, morgue; all pointing toward one end, the D.A.'s office.

The lab men, finished with their preliminary survey, told Treech all he wanted to know at the moment.

He knelt beside the body before allowing the wagon men to take it away and examined a garnet ring on the third finger of her left hand. The setting was rather unusual. Perhaps one of the boys could trace it. He slipped it off the finger and dropped it into one of his pockets.

As the wagon men put the body in a wicker basket, the lab man finished his oral report. "Say, twenty-nine or thirty. Slightly emaciated, or it could be chronic malnutrition. No skin or blood under her nails. No laundry marks and the store label in her suit coat is new to me."

Jack Gieger asked, "What was the name on the label?"

"Selfridge's," the lab man told him.

"That's a big store in London," Gieger said. "I thought that suit looked English."

Their trouser legs matted with beggar weed and cockle burrs, Bill Swen and Lieutenant Marble returned from searching the thicket at the base of the cliff. "There's nothing down there," Swen reported, "except one dead rattlesnake, a lot of broken bottles and tin cans, and the rusted body of a Model T. Whoever killed her must have glommed onto her purse. Any idea who she is?"

"Not so far," Inspector Treech admitted. "Jack thinks she might be English."

He considered the known facts. There weren't very many but he had no doubt they would be sufficient to identify the girl and, eventually, the man or woman who had killed her. The girl hadn't walked to the summit. Therefore she had come in a car. He didn't know the type, or make, or model. But someone did. Someone had seen her get into the car. The dead girl had lived somewhere, in a house, an apartment, a motor court, a hotel. Someone would miss and report her. Someone would recognize her picture in the newspapers or her body in the morgue. They would call in and say:

Why, that's the body of the girl I saw drinking in Johnny's Bar... standing in front of the Union bus station... getting into a Ford coupe on the corner of Lankershim and Ventura Boulevard... eating a chicken sandwich at the Owl....

A lot of specialists would ply their trades. They would take pictures and sprinkle powder. They would use scalpels and microscopes and test tubes. Still other specialists with tired feet would ring door bells and ask questions.

A youthful, lately arrived reporter pushed his way into the group of officers. "Have you any idea why the girl was killed, what the motive was, Inspector?"

"Well, I'll tell you, son," Inspector Treech said quietly. "And you may quote me. In my opinion someone didn't like her."

CHAPTER 2

The tree was old and gnarled. Time was when it was known as Hangman's Oak. That was a long time ago in the days when Tiburcio Vasques, Joaquin Murietta, Juan Flores, and Louis Bulvia rode the valley. In those days smart men declined the office of sheriff. They had reason. In those days California had more murders than the other twenty-one states combined, and the youthful, lusty *El Pueblo de Nuestra Señora, la Reina de los Angeles,* in its growing pains was responsible for a majority of them.

The road was built much later. In the interest of public safety the oak should have been cut down at that time. A sentimental road commissioner saved it by decreeing that the road be built around it. Now the only purpose it served was to make entering or leaving the driveway of the Rancho de los Alamitos a difficult feat of driving especially with a large car.

"Some day," Bob Stanton had sworn a dozen times, "I'm going to have that damn tree cut down."

He never had. He never would. "It's the poet in him," Hi Lo explained. "After he makes enough money to pay his back income taxes he is going to retire and write a sequel to *Trees.* It should be pleasant work."

The Rancho de los Alamitos was not the original twenty-six-thousand-acre-ranch of the same name. It was, however, in a section where any piece of ground over an acre constituted a ranch, considered large. There were, in all, some one hundred and forty acres. It lay on the far east side of the valley well under the long purple shadows of the San Susanna range. Two-thirds of the ranch was irrigated pasture and citrus and walnut grove. The balance, comprising the landscaped five acres around the house, the formal garden, the tile pool and cabanas, the guest house, and the stables, was enclosed by an eight-foot woven wire steel fence with two strands of barbed wire projecting from the top at an angle. But the fence kept few people out as the big front gates were never closed.

The main house was low and rambling, built of hand-hewn timbers and adobe. All of its rooms were large. They took their size and character from the beamed-ceilinged living room. Stanton's staff consisted of a cook, two maids, a gardener, a handyman, and two farm hands who lived out.

Then there was Hi Lo. At one o'clock in the afternoon he opened the door of Stanton's bedroom. The drapes on the windows were still drawn. Stanton still lay on his back fully clothed with the exception of his shoes. They had been thoughtfully placed on a highboy. An empty bottle of Scotch lay convenient to one hand.

This, Hi Lo thought, is a new phase. Ah, genius.... He had seen Stanton drunk before. He had been drunk with him. But this was the first time he had ever seen the other man drink himself into a stupor. His eyes becoming accustomed to the dim light, he noticed a smear of blood on the sleeping man's temple. Examination proved the wound to be minor. Either Stanton had been in a fight or he had fallen and struck his head on some sharp object. Wetting a rag at a tap in the bathroom, Hi Lo washed the blood and perspiration away without awakening the sleeper. Disgusted, he tossed the wet rag in the general direction of the bathroom. "Okay, you damn fool. It's your contract and your liver."

Closing the door softly behind him, he walked down the hall to the kitchen in time to hear Eddie tell Marta:

"Boy. Was the boss stewed last night! He roared in about four this morning taking the drive so sharp he gouged six inches of bark off the oak tree."

Hi Lo opened the kitchen door. "I'll eat lunch now, Marta. And you had better get at that back fence, Eddie. If those colts get in Inspector Treech's young trees again he—well, he won't be pleased about it."

Eddie gulped the last of his coffee. "Yes, sir, Mr. Hi Lo. That's the very first thing I planned to do this afternoon."

Retracing his steps to the living room, Hi Lo picked the mail from a silver salver and walked out onto the acacia tree-shaded patio. The table was laid with a bright cloth and gaily painted Mexican clay pottery. Swiss, big-bosomed, capable, Marta was never caught unprepared. Some mornings Mr. Stanton breakfasted early. Some mornings he breakfasted late. Some mornings he didn't breakfast at all. This would seem to be one of those mornings.

Hi Lo had two other names. One was George Wheary. The other was Little White Eagle. But no one in Hollywood, including his employer, ever called him anything but Hi Lo due to his preference for that form of poker. He seldom discussed his background or his antecedents. It was believed he was a graduate of Carlisle. It was rumored he had an Oxford Baccalaureate. It was known he was a full-blooded Sioux Indian and had been an Army infantry captain during the late unpleasantness with He Who Rides A White Horse and Man Who Smells His Mustache.

Six feet three inches tall, weighing two hundred and twenty pounds, the only race trouble he had ever known was attempting to pick the daily double at Santa Anita. Because he was self-admittedly lazy, and because he liked him, he had been Bob Stanton's combination friend, secretary, and paid companion for years. The work was light. The pay was good. He would, on occasion, buttle, but he drew the line at valeting. He reasoned, not illogically, that a writer earning three thousand dollars a week should have sense enough to put on his own trousers and know when he was aromatic enough to indicate a bath.

Marta made sounds like a mother hen as she served him. There were two men in her life, Mr. Stanton and Mr. Hi Lo. "Mr. Stanton will not be oudt?"

"He is out. Cold," Hi Lo told her. "I just looked in on him and he should be good for another hour or two."

Marta was quick in his defense. "Drink is a good man's failing."

In Hi Lo's opinion the allegation was open to dispute but one didn't dispute with Marta. Besides it didn't apply to Stanton. In the ten years he had known him this was the first real stinkeroo he had ever known him to pull.

He opened a four-page telegram from Marty Manson, the big shot producer at Consolidated, that began cordially—

...When the God deleted deleted heavens to Betsy am I going to get a shooting script of *Conquest* question mark exclamation. Who the deleted deleted deleted do you think you are exclamation question mark. And now with the cast all set and everything ready to roll you pull a binge on me. I am taking this up with J.V. this morning and if it were not for the fact your contract still has a year to run...

Holding the telegram gingerly between his thumb and forefinger, Hi Lo laid it on top of the other mail. He wondered what strange psychology always impelled drunks to pick the most public places in which to cut their didoes. Manson had seen Stanton last night. Now there would be hell to pay. It was good clean fun to laugh at the studios and talk about prostituting one's art but it was, after all, merely another form of writing, and a highly specialized one. You had to be good to do it and it paid much better than the true confession magazines or covering Mr. and Mrs. Herman Dillwaddy Drip's golden wedding anniversary for a newspaper.

Stanton's best seller was a fluke born of his own experience in a German prisoner-of-war camp. Taxes had taken most of the money. Hi Lo doubted if he would ever write another book. Pictures were his medium. Pictures had bought the ranch. But the golden spring wasn't bottomless. One picture could make or break you no matter how long you had been in the business. And Stanton had lost his grip. He had lost his sparkle and his perspective. Instead of writing entertainment, he was cutting in on Western Union by attempting to deliver a message. The finished pages of *Conquest* that he had proofread that morning might have been written by a librarian in Council Bluffs. Stanton was reaching for something—and missing it by a mile....

The room was hot. His collar was choking him. His belt was cutting into his middle. He could feel the squawking of the bluebird in the patio all the way down to his toes. Stanton wished the bird would shut up. He opened one eye cautiously to make certain he was home. He was, but he hadn't the least recollection of how he had gotten there or where he had been the night before. He wondered what he had been drinking.

He got up from the bed with an effort. His car was parked at an absurd angle on the apron of the car port. The left door was wide open. The left rear fender was mashed flat against the body of the car. *Maybe I'm crazy,* he thought.

It was common gossip around the studios that the years he had spent in a German prisoner-of-war camp had addled his brains. He actually insisted there must be more important things in life than dreaming up well-filled sweater variations of boy meets girl and Cinderella.

Clearing the table in the patio, Marta looked up and saw him. "Good morning, Mr. Stanton."

Stanton waggled his fingers at her and went back to bed, kicking the empty bottle as he did so. Now he had become a secret drinker. He even took bottles to bed with him. The next thing he knew he would be smoking cigarettes.

Happiness. That was what he was looking for. But he wouldn't find his answer in a bottle. You couldn't distill a bluebird.

Marta knocked on the door, then came in without waiting for an answer. She had two glasses on a tray. Stanton recognized one as iced tomato juice. "What's the other one?" he demanded.

"Oyster from the prairie," Marta beamed. "Raw egg, pepper, Worcester, and Tabasco sauce. Drink."

To purchase peace Stanton closed his eyes, gulped the obnoxious-looking mixture, then put out the fire in his stomach with the iced tomato juice.

Marta picked the empty Scotch bottle from the floor and put it on the tray with the glasses. "Now you feel better."

Surprisingly, Stanton did. Most of his nausea left him. Ten minutes later, stripping off his clothes, he was debating the merits of a shower against a plunge and decided in favor of the pool. The hot sun felt good on his bare back. The hot walk felt good to his feet. It was good to be alive.

Cutting the clear green water in a dive, he swam to the far end of the pool leisurely, then swam back in a fast crawl. Wearing a white linen suit that made his copper-colored skin seem even darker, Hi Lo watched him from a deck chair as he pulled himself dripping from the pool. "The master would seem to be himself again."

"Only in spots," Stanton assured him. "And one of them isn't my stomach. I must have pulled a beaut last night."

"So it would seem."

"What time did I get in?"

"Eddie says four o'clock. I didn't hear you."

Stanton sat on the edge of the pool and squeegeed the water from his thighs with his palm. "You read what I've done on the new script so far?"

"This morning."

"The tone indicating it's lousy."

"It isn't good. In fact it smells."

Stanton sighed. "I was afraid it did." He lowered himself into the pool and trod water. "Well, you can't write 'em out of a bottle. At least I can't." He held up one hand. "So help me."

"You won't ever blow out a candle again?"

"No. I mean it this time. Two-drink Stanton, that's me."

"Any idea where you were?"

Stanton turned on his back and floated. "Well, I had lunch at the Vine Street Silver Pheasant. Then I played a little poker over at the lot."

"And had a few drinks."

"And had a few drinks. From then on things become confused. I remember being in the Trocadero. I think I stopped in at the Blue Room. And I remember vaguely seeing Lyle Ferris and Marty and Lili sometime during the night."

"Speaking of Marty Manson," Hi Lo said. "He sent a wire this morning that would melt a tin G-string off a stripper."

"Hot, eh?"

Stanton was in the wrong. He knew it. Being human, he took refuge in anger. "He'll get his damned script. Just give me a little time."

A cream colored Lincoln Continental landau with the top down swung in through the wrought iron gateway and, standing up in the car, the girl at the wheel waved to the two men. Joy Parnell was of French ancestry. It showed in the volatile use of her hands, the flashing of her eyes, the sharp click of her heels on the crazy-paved walk. The man with her took off his dark glasses as they reached the pool. "Hi, stew bum," he greeted Stanton.

"Right back at you," Stanton grinned. He liked Lyle Ferris. Unlike so many Hollywood leading men, there was nothing phony about the actor. A fairly recent Broadway importation, with years of show business and a good war record behind him, Ferris had taken feminine Hollywood, including Joy Parnell until Stanton had cut him out, by storm.

"How's our girl?" Stanton asked her. "Mad at me?"

"I can't make up my mind," Joy said. "Marty tells me you're holding up production. But as long as he hasn't a shooting script I don't have to work." Her legs were bare. Painted nails peeped out of the open toes of her shoes. She was wearing a simple white pull-over dress that had cost two hundred dollars and was cut low enough in front to expose the hollow between her breasts. Her straw-colored hair, wound in twin braids around her head, was spun gold in the sun. Her only jewelry was a large emerald ring. "I thought you were going to drop over last night and grow some horns on Lyle."

Still treading water, Stanton apologized. "That would have been very pleasant. But it would seem that I got drunk."

Ferris pointed our, "The parties concerned have to be joined in holy wedlock before horns can be grown." He grinned at Joy. "That wouldn't by any chance be a proposal, would it?"

Hi Lo rolled out a portable bar and the petite star made a face. "Ugh. That nasty stuff again. Make mine water, Hi Lo. About a small eyedropper full. Then thin it down with two inches of gin."

Hi Lo looked at Stanton. The writer shuddered. "Just a very small hair." Pulling himself from the pool, he used the huge turkish towel Joy handed him, then kissed her. "Sorry."

"You should be," she said frankly. "There was a moon and stars. You can't tell what might have happened. We might be in Las Vegas by now. No. Not Las Vegas. I was married there the last time."

Ferris slapped her lightly where her dress fit the tightest. "How you run on, honey chile. You know you're in love with me."

"That could be," she admitted. "You are both fairly good-looking lugs and of a size. You both have two ears, two arms, two legs, and—"

"Careful."

"A mustache." Joy finished her drink, handed the glass to Hi Lo for a refill and sat on the edge of the diving board swinging her bare legs. Her eyes twinkling, she nibbled at one little finger, looking like a very lovely but very wicked little girl. Stanton wondered if he was in love with her. He had to make up his mind, and soon.

"Seriously," Ferris asked. "How's the script going, Bob?"

"It isn't," Stanton admitted. "I'm writing with two left hands. I guess that's why I got boiled last night. Did you see me anywhere, Lyle?"

"You came into Mocambo for a few minutes."

"Alone?"

Joy played with Stanton's fingers. "The answer better be yes."

"Alone," Ferris said. "You had one of those crying-in-your-rye jags, man's inhumanity to man and all that stuff." He admitted, "A lot of what you said made sense though. When I got home I wrote a hundred-dollar check to CARE."

Hi Lo mixed Ferris another drink. "He gets that way. You know, the sensitive writer."

Joy laughed, then turned around on the diving board to watch a car swing into the drive and park in back of hers. "Don't look now but I think the joint is pinched. If those guys aren't coppers, I wasn't born in Brooklyn."

"We've been having colt trouble," Hi Lo told her. "An Inspector Treech of the L.A. Police Department bought that little ranch adjoining Bob's pasture on the back road and it seems our colts got through the fence one night and into his young walnut trees."

Ferris nodded sagely. "Obviously a serious crime. What branch of the Force is the Inspector with?"

"I don't know," Hi Lo admitted. "But I think it's Homicide." He walked down the path to the police car to return almost immediately. "The Inspector wants to see you, Bob."

Stanton was annoyed. "Tell him I'm busy. Write him a check for any damage he claims the colts did and assure him it won't happen again."

"He says it doesn't concern the colts."

"Oh, oh," Joy exclaimed. "Were you driving last night?"

The sleeping butterflies in Stanton's stomach awakened and began to flutter. "Yes."

"You didn't hit anyone, did you?"

Stanton thought of the crumpled fender and winced. "I don't think so. I hope not." He got up from his chair and walked slowly toward the three men standing by the police car. A fourth man was examining a deep gouge in the oak tree. "You want to see me, Inspector?"

Treech said, "Yes," and left it there.

Bill Swen concluded his examination of the tree. "He must have hit it pretty hard. He gouged out six inches of bark and wood."

Joy had followed Stanton down the path. She snuggled her fingers into his. "How do you know Bob gouged the tree?"

Treech looked from Stanton to the crazily parked roadster. "Mind if we look at your car, Stanton?"

Stanton forced himself to say, "No." *I've torn it this time* he thought. *I ran over someone last night. That's why Treech is here.*

Hi Lo started for the house. "I'd better call Ernie Goetz."

Jack Gieger stopped him. "Easy makes it, chum. If anyone here needs a lawyer there'll be plenty of time to call one later on."

Swen and Kelly continued down the path to the car port. Gieger asked, "Where are the clothes you were wearing last night, Stanton?"

Stanton pointed to the French windows opening off the patio into his room. "In there." He turned back to Inspector Treech. "Why the mental third degree? What have I done? What am I supposed to have done?" he corrected himself.

Inspector Treech relighted his cigar and watched a lizard scuttle up the trunk of the acacia tree before he answered. "Did you ever hear of a girl by the name of Grace Turner, Stanton?"

The name was vaguely familiar but Stanton couldn't place it. He started to say, "No," and Ferris asked, "Wasn't that the name of the girl who phoned you at the Silver Pheasant, Bob?"

"Yes," Stanton said. "It was. That's where I heard the name. That was the name she gave."

Inspector Treech took a notebook from his pocket and thumbed through a dozen pages before he found the one he wanted. Then, looking at Ferris, he said, "You must be Lyle Ferris."

"That's right."

"You were at Stanton's table when this call was made?"

"I was."

"Who else was there?"

The actor thought a moment. "Bob, Lou Saunders, Johnny Hass, Ed Wilcox." He added in explanation, "We're all old friends."

"That checks with the list I have," Treech said. He closed his notebook and returned it to his pocket. "You do admit the phone call, Stanton?"

Before Stanton could answer, Hi Lo said hotly, "I don't know what you are trying to prove or disprove, Inspector. But Bob isn't admitting a thing, not even his own name, until we have more information. If you want some intelligent conversation, tell us what the charge is and allow me to phone his lawyer."

"Who is his lawyer?"

"Ernie Goetz."

"Goetz is good," Treech admitted. "Okay. Go ahead and call him if you want to."

"And the charge?"

Inspector Treech ignored the question. "This phone call. Just what did the girl say, Mr. Stanton?"

The *Mr.* Stanton grated on Stanton's nerves. It was the first time the Inspector had used it. Whether he meant it that way or not, it sounded like irony. He ran a palm over his forehead. What *had* the girl said? Stanton forced himself to think. "She said her name was Grace Turner. And when I said I couldn't place it she laughed and said I had bloody well better place it if I knew what was good for me. Then she told me to meet her on the corner of Hollywood Boulevard and Vine Street at midnight or she would blow her top."

"Blow her top?"

"That's what she said."

Inspector Treech asked Ferris, "Was that about how the conversation went?"

"I would say that was almost verbatim."

"How do you know?"

Ferris explained, "I couldn't very well help overhear everything she said.

We were all sitting in one booth when the waiter plugged in the phone and the girl's voice was quite shrill."

Joy's fingernails dug deeply into Stanton's forearm. "Who is this Grace Turner and why should she call you?"

"I don't know," Stanton said.

"You didn't meet her as she requested?"

"Of course I didn't. I thought it was a gag." Stanton realized he was talking too loudly and lowered his voice. "I thought someone was ribbing me."

"So what did you do about it?"

"I didn't do anything about it."

Gieger appeared in the open French window. "The suit he says he wore last night seems clean. But there's quite a bit of blood on the shirt he was wearing."

Hi Lo said, "There was blood on his forehead this morning. I wiped it off while he was still asleep. You can see the bruise. He either got in a fight or fell down and hurt his head."

Treech looked at Stanton's forehead. The skin was broken. The wound undoubtedly had bled. He didn't know how badly. He didn't particularly care. That was out of his department. That was up to the test tube boys.

Stanton touched the bruised spot on his forehead. He hadn't known it was there.

"How did you get it, Bob?" Joy asked.

He said, "I don't know."

Kelly and Swen came back up the path. Their faces were grave. "His car," Kelly reported, "is a mess. There is clotted blood on the seat and the floor mat and two big tears in the leather upholstery I imagine were made by the missing slugs. We'd better get the lab boys out here." He walked into the house in search of a phone.

Joy's fingers dug even deeper into the flesh of Stanton's arm. "What are they talking about? Don't stand there gaping like a fool, Bob. Tell me. What are they talking about?"

"I don't know," he said. "Believe me."

He turned and walked down the path to the car port. Treech made a movement as if to stop him, then changed his mind and followed close behind Joy who was still clinging to Stanton's arm, taking three steps to his one in order to keep up with him. Hi Lo walked into the house. Ferris hesitated briefly, then followed Stanton and Joy and the two detectives.

Stanton looked first at the crumpled rear fender of his car. His first blind panic over, his mind was beginning to function. This wasn't a hit and run case. He hadn't hit anyone with the fender. He'd hit the tree with that. He had gouged, or so one of the detectives said, six inches of bark and wood out of the oak. But neither the tree nor the fender had anything to do with the blood on the seat or the tears in the upholstery.

The seat of his car looked as if someone had stuck a pig in it. A dozen blue bottle flies were buzzing noisily over the pools of clotted blood. The two holes in the back of the seat could have been made by soft-nosed bullets that had already been flattened by smashing through flesh or bone. He had seen such tears before, in human flesh.

"Who did this to my car?" he asked Treech. "And how does it concern me?"

Looking under his arm, Joy whimpered, "Oh, Bob. It's blood."

It seemed suddenly imperative to Stanton to spare Joy any further possible revelations. "Take her home, will you, Lyle?" he asked the actor.

"No," Joy said. "I won't go home. I want to know what's happened."

Inspector Treech took off his hat and wiped the sweatband with his handkerchief. "A girl has been murdered, Miss Parnell. A girl by the name of Grace Turner. An English girl. You may have seen the headlines in this afternoon's paper."

"I saw the headline," Ferris said, "but I didn't bother to read the story. I wish I had." He touched Joy's arm. "Come on, Joy. Bob asked me to take you home."

Tears brimming in her eyes, the blonde star pulled away from him fiercely. "No. I tell you I won't go home. I won't leave Bob if he's in trouble." She clung to Stanton. "You didn't do it, did you, Bob? You didn't kill any girl."

Stanton rested his forehead briefly on her shining hair. "I don't know, Joy," he said finally. "I don't think so. But then, on the other hand, I don't know what I did last night."

"You had better get some clothes on, Stanton," Inspector Treech suggested. "And while I don't advise it, Miss Parnell, if you want to ride into town with us—"

"I do. I do," Joy said.

Stanton dressed, with Swen and Gieger waiting on him, watching every move he made. Out on the patio Marta was arguing hotly with Treech. "But Mr. Stanton cannot go away. He has not yet eaten breakfast."

Stanton could not hear Inspector Treech's reply but Hi Lo said something to Marta that caused her to subside. A moment later Hi Lo came into the room. "I still haven't been able to get ahold of Goetz. His secretary is ringing every place he might be and so am I. I'll keep on trying for another fifteen minutes. Then if we can't get ahold of him, I'll get some other lawyer."

"You do that," Stanton said.

Dressed, he walked out onto the patio accompanied by Gieger and Swen. Marta was standing by the acacia tree, her full face working and the hem of her apron to her eyes. Joy was already seated in the back seat of the squad car completely ignoring whatever it was Ferris was attempting to tell her. Kelly slid in back of the wheel.

"Ready to go?" Treech asked.

"Ready to go," Stanton said.

He rode holding Joy's hand in his. She had never been so near or dear to him. Public opinion was vitally important to her career. One burst of bad publicity could tumble her out of the high income tax brackets and the constellation of the great in the Hollywood firmament. Yet she was taking that risk to be with him. He squeezed her hand. "You're nice."

"Shh. Don't talk," she told him. "This is just a bad dream. We'll wake up pretty soon."

There were no reporters or cameramen at the morgue. Inspector Treech insisted Joy wait in the car as he handcuffed Stanton to his left wrist. "Not that I think you'll attempt to make a break. But regulations are regulations."

"I know," Stanton said. "It says in the book. I got that in the Army."

"We want to see the Turner dame," Treech informed the attendant. "Have the M.E. and the lab finished with her yet?"

"Two hours ago," the attendant told him. "There's not much to them gunshot cases." He slid out a lower drawer in the cold room as he asked, incuriously, "Is this the lad who killed her?"

"We intend charging him with it," Treech said.

Stanton looked down at the girl. She had a thin, unattractive face made even more unattractive by death. A wisp of hair hung untidily under one ear. Her shrunken lips revealed bad teeth. She had mere nubbins of breasts. Her nude body was so thin he could count her ribs. He didn't know whether to laugh or cry, and suddenly wanted to do both. Something was terribly screwball somewhere. The name on the drawer was plain—Grace Turner. This was the girl with whose murder he was presently to be charged. But to the best of his sober, or intoxicated, knowledge he had never seen her before.

CHAPTER 3

Five hours had passed. Stanton lay on the bunk in his cell blowing smoke rings at the ceiling and wondering if Hi Lo had been able to contact Ernie Goetz. As yet he had not been formally charged with murder. He had seen the complaint on the charge sheet when Inspector Treech had taken him up to the cell block. He was booked for investigation. That could be a good or a bad sign.

He lighted a fresh cigarette from the butt of the one he was smoking and snuffing the butt out on the floor he attempted to recall the exact words spoken in the morgue.

He had said, "I don't suppose you would believe me if I told you I never saw the girl before."

"No," Treech had said. "I would not."

The steel webbing of the bunk cutting into his back through the thin blanket, Stanton sat up and stared glumly at the floor. He couldn't take too much of this. He had spent too much time in confinement. The steel door at the end of the short corridor banged open and Stanton looked up hopefully.

Jack Gieger was with the fat turnkey. He took a pair of handcuffs from his pocket as the fat man unlocked the cell door and shot the bolt. "How are you doing, Stanton?"

Stanton said he was doing all right. He wished the detective sergeant wouldn't be so damn casual about it.

"We're going downstairs," Gieger said. "Most of the reports are in, including those from the lab. But there are one or two little matters you may be able to straighten out for us."

This wasn't Inspector Treech's office. Treech occupied a glorified broom closet less than one-fourth as large as the ante-room of this one. Lyle Ferris, Lou Saunders, and Johnny Hass were standing in one corner of the ante-room. All three raised their hands in greeting. Marta and Eddie were sitting stiffly in straight-backed chairs against the wall. On the verge of tears but trying to smile, Marta wiggled her fingers at him. Hi Lo was talking to a blond man Stanton didn't know. The copper-skinned giant cut short what he was saying and crossed the room to him. "Ernie is inside," he informed him. "Are you all right, Bob?"

Stanton nodded. "Yeah. I guess so. Outside of the butterflies."

Barely five feet two inches tall, Ernie Goetz might have posed as a miniature man of distinction. He had the look. He wore the clothes. He drank the right brand of whiskey. More important, he had brains. He got to his feet as Stanton entered the main office with Sergeant Gieger and shook one of his manacled hands. "I'm sorry I couldn't get here sooner, Bob. But it wouldn't have made much difference if I had. These things have to run their normal course."

Stanton looked around the office. Inspector Treech was sitting on the edge of a glass-topped desk skimming through a clip board fat with reports. Jim Reisler of the D.A.'s office was looking out the window. Saul Meyers, a deputy chief, was seated back of the desk. Both Meyers and Reisler were second-level brass. Reisler was being groomed to step into the D.A.'s shoes when he moved up to Attorney General. Meyers was slated to replace the Chief when he retired. Their presence could only mean one thing. Treech had a good case against him but the big brass wanted to be certain he wasn't unnecessarily embarrassing the politically and financially powerful motion picture industry. Stanton knew Meyers well. Meyers had been a lieutenant of detectives when he had covered a police beat.

Reisler inclined his head in greeting. Meyers said, "Hello, Bob. I'm sorry to see you in a jam like this." He added, to Gieger, "You can remove those handcuffs, Sergeant."

"Thanks. Thanks a lot, Saul," Stanton said.

Reisler suggested, "Well, suppose we get started. You have filed a formal complaint against this man, Inspector Treech?"

"No," Treech admitted. "I haven't. As I explained to you before, sir, it is a rather unusual case and in view of the prominence of the people involved I, frankly, don't want to kick up any stink until I am certain of my ground." He was careful not to look at Ernie Goetz. "I have had the five-hundred-dollar-a-day-boys representing the picture industry breathing down my neck before."

Goetz fingered the four-carat diamond in his tie but said nothing.

"It is because of that," Treech continued, "and because of your request, Mr. Deputy Chief, that I would like to check over the evidence we have with you gentlemen before I file a formal charge." He nodded to Gieger. "Let's have Shad Hanson first."

Goetz raised his eyebrows slightly. Hanson came in smiling, nodding to each man in turn. "Mr. Reisler. Mr. Deputy Chief. Inspector Treech."

Treech consulted his clip board. "You were in the bar of the Hollywood-Highland Hotel at approximately eleven-forty-five last night, Mr. Hanson?"

"I was."

Treech detached a newspaper cut from his clip board and handed it to Hanson. "Did you see this girl in there?"

"I did. In fact I talked to her. I bought her a drink. I tried to buy her two drinks. But she told me she had a previous engagement."

"With whom?"

"She didn't say. But when she left to keep this other date I followed her."

"Why?" Meyers asked.

Hanson grinned at him. "Because she told me if her other date petered out she would meet me back in the bar at one o'clock and I wanted to see what my chances were. So I followed her down to the corner of Hollywood and Vine. She stood around in front of the Broadway for a few moments and I thought maybe her date had stood her up. But a few minutes later she got into a '47 black Caddy convertible coupe. And I said to myself, that's that."

Inspector Treech asked him if Sergeant Gieger had shown him a car in the police garage. Hanson said Gieger had. "Was it the same car you saw this girl get into?"

Goetz opened his mouth to say something, closed it as Hanson said, "That I couldn't say, Inspector. It was the same make and year and model. But I didn't write down the license number."

"A man was driving this car the girl got into?"

"That's right."

"Can you identify him?"

"No, sir. I cannot. I didn't see his face."

After Hanson had left the office, Inspector Treech told Reisler, "It was Hanson who put us on the trail so quickly. He saw the dead girl's picture in one of the early editions and told us about meeting her in the bar. It was a push-over after that. She had only made the one phone call from her room, and that to the Silver Pheasant."

The waiter from the Silver Pheasant was next. He said he had been on duty at one o'clock the previous afternoon. A few minutes after one a girl giving her name as Grace Turner of the Hollywood-Highland Hotel had phoned and asked to speak to Mr. Robert Stanton. He had plugged in a portable phone to complete the connection and that was all he knew about it.

Gieger returned from escorting him out of the office to report two men who said they were executives from Consolidated Pictures but who refused to give their names were waiting in the ante room. "Let them wait," Treech said. He consulted his clip board. "Next we'll have Hass, Saunders, Ferris, and Wilcox."

Gieger said, "The others are here but we couldn't reach Wilcox. He's the flesh agent and his secretary told Bill he left on the seven o'clock T.W.A. for New York this morning."

Meyers wanted to know what the three men did. Treech said, "Hass is a free-lance cameraman. Saunders is the local head of one of the press associations. Ferris is an actor."

Treech looked at the three men. "I've talked to you fellows before. All of you were at the table when the dead English girl phoned Stanton. Now all I want to know is if any of you have anything to add to what you have already told me."

"I haven't," Ferris said.

"How did he act after this phone call? I mean did Stanton seem worried or depressed?"

"No. He thought it was a gag. We all did."

Unimpressed by the brass, Saunders lighted a cigarette. "I think you're barking up the wrong tree, Treech. I don't think Bob killed her."

"Who did?"

"How the hell do I know? I'm a reporter. You're the cop. But that blood in his car and the bullet holes, plus the phone call-no. That's laying it on too thick. I've known Stanton for years. And while we have never been particularly intimate I think I know him well enough to know he wouldn't be so stupid as to send himself to the lethal chamber for lack of a little common sense."

"He was drunk."

Saunders shrugged. "Have it your own way. But I haven't named him in any of the stories I've sent out."

"Thanks, Lou," Stanton said.

"Thanks for nothing," the reporter jeered. "I'm probably missing a damn good bonus by not nailing you to the cross. That's what friendship gets you."

Goetz got up from his chair. "I wonder," he asked Meyers, "if I might talk to my client privately a moment?"

Meyers nodded at a door. "Use the john if you want to, Ernie."

Stanton leaned against the wash bowl in the men's room. Goetz used one of the facilities. "Boy, am I glad to get in here! I've been out all afternoon drinking beer with a bimbo from Gary. And could she put it away. Did you do it, Bob? Did you kill this Grace Turner?"

"I don't know. But I don't see why I should have. I'm not particularly vicious when I'm drinking. I don't even know the girl. I never saw her before in my life. But I don't remember anything I did."

The lawyer thought a moment. "Are you willing to take a gamble?"

"What sort of a gamble?"

"Sodium pentathol. I won't pull it on them unless I have to. I don't think they are prepared to administer it if I do. But it makes a swell talking point. I can pound on desks, insist you *want* to prove your innocence and are willing to cooperate with the police in *any* way. That throws the onus back on them. And if I can keep you from being booked and out of the jug until we have time to investigate this thing we are that much farther ahead."

Stanton said he was willing to chance the truth serum. "I don't think I killed her."

"Fine," Goetz told him. "Fine. You're practically home and in your own bed right now."

Hass, Ferris and Saunders were gone when they returned to the office. Inspector Treech continued, "As yet we haven't found the gun with which Miss Turner was killed but we have recovered the slugs. In the upholstery of Stanton's car."

Goetz asked if the slugs were in a condition to be submitted to ballistics for comparison if and when the death weapon was found. Ignoring the question, Inspector Treech looked at still another report on his clip board. "The blood on the seat and floor mat of Stanton's car has been typed and found to be the same as that of the deceased. Blood was also found in the trunk of the car, not much, just a smear."

"This blood, too, was of the same type as that of the deceased?"

Again Treech ignored the lawyer. "The girl wore a mustard-colored tweed coat over her suit coat when she left the hotel. That hasn't turned up yet, nor has the white cloth purse witnesses say she was carrying."

"How about her background?" Meyers asked.

"So far we don't know a thing about her except she was English. Her passport was visaed in London on October eighth. That's three weeks ago. I've contacted both the London police and our immigration authorities, requesting any information about her that may be in their files."

"How about the clothes Stanton was wearing?" This from Reisler.

Treech said there was blood on his shirt. "Of the same type as his own," he admitted.

"You have attempted to trace his movements last night?"

"We have traced them to Sherry's out on the Strip. We have a witness who places him there between eleven and eleven-thirty."

"And the M.E. established the time of death at what hour?"

"Twelve-thirty, give or take a half hour either way."

"No sex angle?"

Treech grinned. "No. And it isn't likely with Stanton practically engaged to Miss Parnell. You should see the dead kid, Mr. Reisler. She's homely. Her clothes are cheap. And she looks like she hasn't had a square meal in five years."

Stanton lighted a cigarette he didn't want, took one puff and snuffed it out. Reisler asked him, "Have you ever been in London, Stanton?"

"Yes. I was in London during the war."

"What year of the war?"

"The summer and fall of 1941. I rode out of London as an observer in an English bomber in November of that year, was shot down over Bremen, and spent the rest of the war in a German prison camp."

"But you have been in England since?"

"No. That was the only time I was ever there."

Reisler spread his hands in defeat. "I don't get it. Assuming for the sake of logic that Stanton somehow was involved with this Miss Turner in London many years ago, she would hardly wait all this time to make trouble for him."

Goetz got to his feet. "We are interested in only one thing, serving the best interests of justice. Is that correct?"

Meyers said it was.

"I would be the last man," Goetz continued, "to deny there is a lot here that needs explaining. The Inspector can't explain it. I can't explain it. My client can't explain it. But I'll tell you what we'll do."

Reisler eyed him warily.

"Because," Goetz said, "while my client cannot explain why the dead girl phoned him, how her blood got in his car, or where he was at the time, he feels so guiltless in this matter, he will gladly submit to," Goetz pounded softly on Meyers' desk, "in fact we insist upon an immediate so-called truth serum or sodium pentathol test."

Meyers pushed back his chair from his desk. "And there goes your ball game, Inspector."

"Not necessarily," Inspector Treech said hotly. "Goetz is just pulling one of his usual fast ones. We're damned if we do and we're damned if we don't. He knows some men are constitutionally immune to the effects of sodium pentathol. They can beat it just like some lads can beat a lie detector. That's probably why he took Stanton in the john. He wanted to know if they had ever shot him full of joy juice in the Army and what effect it had."

Goetz fingered the diamond in his tie. "Okay. Then book my client, Inspector." He didn't raise his voice but it filled the room. "Charge him with murder. And when I get you on the stand you'll wish you had never been born."

A flat, newspaper-wrapped object under his arm, Matt Kelly entered the office without knocking and taking Treech by the elbow walked the red-faced Inspector to one of the far corners where they stood with their backs to the others. Jack Gieger leaned against the door jamb. "Those two big shots from Consolidated are still out here."

Treech turned, no longer red-faced, a shabby white cloth purse in his hand. "Stall them or tell them to go to hell, Jack. I don't care which." He handed the purse to Meyers. "It's all right to handle it. It has already been processed by both our own and the fingerprint men in the sheriff's office. It is Miss Turner's purse. A fire warden found it in the brush not far from where we found the body." He looked at Stanton. "You about had me fooled with that 'I never saw her before' and willingness to co-operate business, Mr. Stanton. But you should have looked in Miss Turner's purse before you threw it away."

Taking the purse back from Meyers, Inspector Treech opened it and took out a comb, a compact, a one-dollar bill, and a torn piece of newspaper. He unfolded the news-clipping. "Here is a clipping from Leatrice May's movie column in the L.A. *Times* as of a week ago. Listen. *Of interest to the admirers of Joy Parnell is the rumor that Robert Stanton, author of the current best seller,* Men Back of Wire, *and top-flight Hollywood scenarist, is reputed to be edging out Lyle Ferris in the romantic race for mi-lady's hand.*"

Meyers and Reisler lost their apathy. Goetz looked thoughtful.

"How about that, Mr. Goetz?" Treech asked. "Your client says he was so drunk he didn't know what he was doing, yet with one minor mishap he managed to drive his car from the Sunset Strip where he was last seen to his home in the Valley some forty miles away. He drank so much he can't remember what happened. But when I showed up at his place this after-noon, was he sitting on the edge of his bed nursing a hangover? No. He was stripped down to a pair of bathing trunks and dawdling around his pool with Miss Parnell, both of them with highball glasses in their hands. He didn't know Grace Turner. He didn't recognize her in the morgue. Yet she carried a clipping in her purse concerning his attentions to another woman, a woman as beautiful as *she* was unattractive. I don't know what she was in his past. We'll know that when we hear from London. But I do know there was something between them. I know she phoned him by name at the Silver Pheasant, recalled herself to him, and threatened to expose him if he didn't meet her. And he did. We have a witness who saw her get into his car."

Goetz corrected him. "Get into a *similar* car."

Treech rubbed it in. "She was seen getting into Stanton's car by one of your brother lawyers. But of course Shad Hanson couldn't identify Stan-ton as the man he saw at the wheel of the car. I was stupid not to think of that before. Why should Shad identify him and take the cake right out of his own mouth? There have never been any formal complaints so there is nothing we can do about him, but every man in this room knows as well as I do that Hanson derives his income almost entirely from blackmail."

Goetz looked thoughtfully at Stanton. *That does it,* Stanton thought. *Even Ernie thinks I killed her.* All his own doubt returned and the dormant but-terflies in his stomach swarmed. *Perhaps I did.*

Treech nodded at Kelly. "Put your cuffs on him, Matt. We'll take him up and book him correctly this time. We haven't any better case now than we had before but since this clipping has turned up I'm willing to stick my neck out. We'll have a case when we hear from London."

Tugging his handcuffs from his pocket, Kelly crossed the office to Stan-

ton but before he could snap them in place the office door opened again
and J. V. Mercer stood in the open doorway waving aside Sergeant Gieger's
protests with a long, platinum-banded ebony cigarette holder and the simple statement, "I am not accustomed to being kept waiting."

His hair still jet black at seventy, his expensive suit molded to a still
active and slim torso, only the parchment-like quality of his skin and his
bony hands betraying his age, the motion picture potentate looked exactly what he was, trouble for anyone who crossed his will.

One of the last of the early day picture barons, rumor had it he had been
born in the Levantine. It was true. His baptismal name wasn't Mercer. His
mother had been Syrian, his father Greek. When he had reached the
mature age of seven he had emigrated to the United States of America, via
the stow-away route.

That had been many years ago. He had lived through three major
depressions. But, unaided by W.P.A., unemployment compensation, a
union card, or hope of security from the cradle to the grave, he had somehow managed to survive. Now, along with some sixty or seventy motion
picture palaces scattered across the nation of his choice, he owned, and for
years had owned, Consolidated Pictures, lot, stock, and bare-legged stars.

Deputy Chief Meyers got to his feet hastily. "I'm sorry, Mr. Mercer," he
apologized. "I had no idea *you* were waiting. If you had only given your
name to the detective at the door—"

Mercer waved him silent with his holder. "I prefer not to have my name
or the name of my studio mentioned in connection with this affair. There
was a time when it wouldn't have mattered. But in this day of censorship
and purity leagues, when actors and actresses have to keep themselves, like
Caesar's wife, above suspicion, sex and murder have become far nastier
words than spit." The old man scowled at Stanton. "And the name of one
of my most highly paid stars is closely linked with that of the man whom
you, unjustly, thank God, are holding." He inclined his holder at Marty
Manson waiting patiently beside him. "Tell them, Marty."

His son-in-law cleared his throat. "I don't know just how to begin," he
began. He ran a finger along his hair-line mustache. "I wouldn't have
known a thing about this, Bob, if Joy hadn't phoned the house in tears,
wanting to know if there wasn't something J.V. or I could do to help you."

A brief silence followed his words. Stanton studied the producer's face
wondering what he was about to say. He liked old man Mercer. J.V. was a
bloody old pirate. He made no pretense about it. But Stanton could take
Marty and Lili, or he could leave them alone. He preferred, when sober, to
avoid them. Lili was no startling beauty or vestal virgin by many moons.
Manson was a social climber. He had been a failure as a writer, an actor, an
assistant director, and a yes man. His marriage to Lili Mercer had raised

him in four years to full producer's status. To give him his just due, he capably filled the shoes into which he had stepped and had turned out three smash hit pictures.

Manson turned to Inspector Treech. "Whether I can be of any assistance in this case, or nor, depends on the time this girl was murdered. What was the time of death, Inspector?"

Treech said, "Twelve-thirty, give or take a half hour either way."

"You're a lucky dog, Bob," Manson chuckled. "Look. If I save you from the gas chamber will you, please, for the love of little green apples, give me a shooting script on *Conquest* as fast as you can turn one out?" Without waiting for an answer, he looked back at Inspector Treech. "You have the wrong man, Inspector. Bob couldn't have killed the girl."

Manson's story was simple and to the point. He and Mrs. Manson had dropped into Sherry's for a bite to eat and a drink at approximately eleven o'clock on the preceding night. They had immediately noted Stanton standing at the bar in bad condition. The barman, in fact, was refusing to serve him.

"So that's where I saw you and Lili," Stanton said.

Nodding brightly, Manson continued. Worried about the script on which Stanton was currently working, a new picture starring Joy Parnell and Lyle Ferris, he explained to Meyers and Reisler, he had thought it best to attempt to get Stanton home and into bed. After seating his wife at a table he had gone to the bar and asked Stanton if he didn't think he had better call it a night. But Stanton hadn't taken kindly to the suggestion. Finally realizing the writer was in no condition to make decisions or to drive his own car, he had put Mrs. Manson in a cab and returning to the bar he had done the expedient thing. He had persuaded the barman to give Stanton three double shots in quick succession in order to knock him out and make it easier to handle him. The treatment hadn't been entirely successful but it had lessened Stanton's truculence to a point where he agreed to allow Manson to drive him home. Manson concluded, "So I did. In my own car."

"This was what time?"

The producer shook his head. "I don't know just what time it was when we did leave Sherry's. Possibly eleven-thirty. I imagine the barman can tell you. I do know that because of the fog last night I was forced to drive rather slowly and it was twelve forty-five by the clock on my dashboard when we reached his ranch." He chuckled. "I remember looking at the clock because I was worried that Mrs. Manson would be annoyed at me for spending so much time on a drunk. And she was."

Treech clutched at straws. "Stanton was fairly sober by the time you reached his ranch? He was able to walk?"

Manson laughed. "No. I'm sorry to disappoint you, Inspector, but the three double shots had caught up with him by the time we reached his place. He was out cold. I've always hated that large oak in front of his drive. And with the fog last night I was afraid I might mash a fender on it so I parked in front of the gate and carried Bob in fireman fashion. I dumped him on his bed, drew the shades, then took off his shoes and, as a rather crude joke, placed them on his highboy."

"Then?"

"Then I went home and made my peace with Mrs. Manson. But before retiring I phoned in a night letter to Western Union I hoped would burn Stanton's ears off and possibly shock some sense into him. You see, this heavy drinking on his part is something new and Consolidated Pictures still believes him to be a clever and a capable writer."

"And where was his car all this time?"

"That I wouldn't know. I imagine it was parked along the Strip somewhere. I suppose I should have asked him if he had his keys but frankly I never thought of it."

Inspector Treech walked over to the window of the office. There seemed no way, at the moment, he could prove it but he had a very strong suspicion he was being diddled, that murder was being countenanced and abetted for the sake of the Consolidated Pictures' payroll. Young Manson wouldn't dare to concoct such a story but J. V. Mercer would. And Manson was no fool. He knew on which side his bread was spread with dollar-a-pound butter. Turning from the window, he asked Gieger if Stanton's household was still waiting in the anteroom. When Gieger said they were he told him to bring them in.

Marta, frightened by her surroundings, but loyal, smiled timidly at Stanton. After identifying her for Attorney Reisler's and Deputy Chief Meyers' information, Treech asked the buxom housekeeper if she knew what time Mr. Stanton had returned home the night before. She looked at her employer for guidance. Stanton told her to tell the truth.

"No. I do not," she answered Treech's question. "Is both Mr. Stanton and Mr. Hi Lo oudt. I am tired. So on the table in the dining room I put night lunch, cold sliced chicken, pastrami, rye bread, cheese. Is coffee on the stove and cold beer in the ice box so I go in by mine bed at ten o'clock."

"How about you, Hi Lo?"

Hi Lo said, "If I thought lying would help Bob, I'd lie. But not having heard the preface to this, I have no choice but to tell the truth. It was two o'clock or better when I got in. And Bob wasn't home then. At least his car wasn't in the car port."

"You didn't look in his room?"

"I had no occasion to."

"Then tell me this. When was the last time he had a communication from Mr. Manson?"

"This morning," Hi Lo said promptly. "It was a night letter written on asbestos and beating his ears in because so far he has failed to turn in an acceptable shooting script for the new picture on which he is currently engaged."

Treech made one last attempt. He stabbed a finger at Eddie. "You. Tell me. What time did your employer return home last night?"

Eddie gulped but stood his ground. "Jeez, I don't know, Inspector. I heard a hell of a crash about four o'clock this morning when someone nicks the big oak and when I come down to breakfast I think it is the boss on account of his car has a crumpled left fender. But I didn't get up to see if it was the boss kissing his car off the tree. It ain't none of my business. I ain't paid to keep track of when he comes and when he goes."

Goetz adjusted the knot in his tie. "I don't know what I'm doing here. I might as well have kept on drinking beer with that bimbo from Gary." There was regret in his voice. "She should be pretty high by now."

Aromatic smoke curling toward the ceiling from the cigarette in his long holder, J.V. tapped Stanton's shoulder with a bony finger. "I want a shooting script the day after tomorrow, young man. See that it is on Marty's desk." So saying, he left the office.

Goetz's car, a big chauffeur-driven Packard, was parked in a no-parking zone. Leaning against one of its fenders, the lawyer asked, "I don't suppose you remember whether you left your keys in your car or not, Bob?"

Stanton admitted he did not. "You think Marty was telling the truth? Or did J.V. scheme up that one?"

Hi Lo said, "Never look a gift horse in the mouth. Outside of it being unsanitary, it might bite you."

"Treech will check and doublecheck," Goetz said. "He released you with plenty of mental reservations and if there are any flaws in Marty's story he'll find them. Either way you're still in the woods, I'm telling you that not as a friend but as your lawyer. If you didn't kill the girl someone tailed you to Sherry's and pinched your car in an attempt to pin the murder on you. Someone who knows you very well."

Stanton lighted a cigarette and savored the smoke a moment before replying. "Then if Marty's story shouldn't stand up, if it's just some of old J.V.'s attempted legerdemain to get his precious cameras rolling, we had better find out who is framing me before he makes this damn thing stick."

Goetz said he thought it was a good idea. "You and Hi Lo drop into the office tomorrow afternoon. I'll have a private agency man there and we'll try to outline something." He said good night, got into his car, and the big

Packard pulled away from the curb. Stanton and Hi Lo walked slowly toward Hi Lo's Ford. Eddie and Marta were already in the back seat. Hi Lo took the wheel and Stanton slipped in beside him.

"*Ja*. This is better," Marta beamed. "You eadt yet, Mr. Stanton?"

Stanton said he had. "They fed me about five o'clock. But I can sure go for some more when we get home."

"Is plenty," Marta assured him. "I am making a big meat loaf for cold sliced meat for night lunch when the detective came after the bottle that proved you didn't do it."

Stanton puzzled, "When the detective came after the bottle?"

"*Ja*," Marta said placidly. "*Jawohl*. Is nice little man. So polite. And when he told me what he is come for I am glad to give him the empty Scotch bottle I picked up off your floor this morning."

The big Indian shook his head. "Your guess is as good as mine." He sighed. "You know, sometimes I think I should have stayed on the reservation and punched Uncle Sam for my meals. Of course we didn't have indoor plumbing but life, in the main, was simpler."

CHAPTER 4

Heat lay in a long prickly strip from Cahuenga Pass to Calabasas. People and palms drooped limply under the beating they were taking from the sun. Wearing slacks and a light weight sport shirt open at the neck, his eyes red-rimmed with fatigue, Stanton got out of the Ford and looked at the cars in the used car lot while he waited for Hi Lo to join him. There were twenty-six cars in all, most of them the more expensive models, none of them with over twenty-five miles on their speedometers, and all of them priced from five hundred to two thousand dollars over list price. Stanton had done business with the lot before. Barney was pleased to see him. Stanton decided, finally, on a '48 Packard convertible and wrote out a check for payment in full, explaining, "The police impounded my car last night. You probably read of the mess in the paper."

"Yes," the used car dealer admitted, "I did." He added diplomatically, "But I knew there was nothing to it, that is, as far as you were concerned, Mr. Stanton."

Stanton transferred his driver's license from his wallet to the leather and glassine case on the steering wheel rod. "Take care of the white and pink slip and the insurance for me, will you, Barney? I want to use the car right now."

It was hot. Stanton was tired. He still had fifteen or twenty hours of hard work ahead of him. As he transferred his portable typewriter and director's case from Hi Lo's Ford to his new car, he grunted that he would catch up with him later at Goetz's office.

The big Indian shrugged, got into his car and drove off. Stanton went into the office, signed the necessary papers, griped about the gas tank only being a quarter full, then drove, too fast, to the Consolidated lot. After parking his car in the executive building parking space, he asked Manson's secretary if the great man was too busy to see him. Smiling, she said she thought not. He wasn't.

Manson was cordial but wary. "Don't tell me you've brought me a script?"

"I have it all outlined," Stanton said. "And half of the dialogue written. And this time I'm off on the right foot. I worked on it all night. I'd still be working but my joint is so lousy with reporters, ringing telephones, and sympathetic friends, they crowded me out of the house. I'm on my way up to the hideout to do the polishing and write-thirty. You'll have your shooting script tomorrow night."

"Good."

"I just dropped in to say thanks. Thanks a lot, Marty, both for taking me home and for coming forward when I needed you."

Manson made light of it. "Forget it, Bob. You can do as much for me some time."

"And J.V. isn't *too* sore?"

The producer grinned. "He isn't pleased. But if we gross as much with *Conquest* as we did with your last picture I don't think you'll have to worry about your contract."

"And that story you told Inspector Treech last night was on the up and up? You weren't just sticking out your neck for the studio?"

"For heaven's sake," Manson laughed, "stop worrying, Bob. You didn't kill the dame. And if Inspector Treech has checked on what I told him he knows as much by now. Three barmen, five waiters, one manager, and perhaps fifty customers saw me leading you out of Sherry's so blind you couldn't have shot the Pacific Ocean with a machine gun at five yards."

Stanton smiled wryly. "Thanks again, Marty. Thanks a million."

Leaving his car where it was, he walked to the writers' building and went directly to his own elaborately furnished office. He seldom used it, preferring to work at home. Finding the carbons of his three previous attempts to make a good picture of *Conquest* in his files, he transferred them to his director's case. Some of the dialogue was fairly clever and he could use it in the final copy.

Out on the lot again, he noted they were re-shooting the wedding scene from the picture Joy had just finished and on impulse he made his way to her dressing room and knocked on the closed door.

She called, "Just a minute." When she opened the door a moment later she was wearing an almost diaphanous silk shantung dressing gown. The white gardenia in her hair, plus the fact there was nothing under the dressing gown but Joy, made her look charmingly wanton.

"Sweetheart." Ignoring the certain damage to her make-up and elaborate seventeenth-century hair-do, she pulled his face to hers and kissed him. "I've been so worried about you, honey. And if you hadn't phoned me last night after Marty and J.V. got you out of that awful place I wouldn't have slept a wink. But why didn't you come over?"

Stanton drummed on the directors case. "I'm writing a picture, remember? And last night J.V. gave me until tomorrow to turn it in or face a firing squad."

She lifted her lips to be kissed. "But you do love me?"

He kissed her in evasion of the question. He liked Joy. She excited him. He thought she was a grand person. But he couldn't make up his mind whether or not he loved her. In his book there was more to marriage than excitement. It was a meeting of minds and social concepts as well as bodies.

"There is nothing new on the other, is there, Bob?" she asked.

He told her, "Not as far as I know. I'm on my way down to Ernie Goetz's office now. We decided last night it might be a smart idea for him to engage a private agency man to try and find out if my car was used accidentally or if someone doesn't like me. Bringing the car back to my garage after the murder would seem to substantiate the latter theory."

"And then? I mean, from Ernie's office."

"Then I am going up to the hide-out and put the finishing touches on the script."

"Oh." Joy sounded disappointed.

Stanton explained. "My joint is as bad as Union Station. Some enterprising punk even ran a rubber-neck tour out there this morning. You know, one of those guys who sit under an umbrella out on the Strip in front of a big sign reading—'See the Homes of the Stars in Your Own Car for Five Dollars.' It was all Hi Lo and Marta could do to keep them from camping on the lawn until I showed."

"You know you're welcome to use my place any time you want to, Bob."

Stanton wished Joy wouldn't pursue him quite so openly. It made him feel as if he were being stalked. "I'll tell you what, baby," he compromised. "I'll be through with the script tomorrow night, maybe tomorrow morning. And the moment I finish it I'll come straight over to your place and we'll do some serious talking about us."

She clung to him, kissing him again and again. Neither of them was aware for a moment that Ferris was standing in the open doorway. "Very touching," the actor said casually. "They're ready to do the re-take whenever you are, Joy."

Unembarrassed, Joy muttered, "Hell. Do I have to put that damn wedding gown back on?" She called loudly for her maid. "Beulah."

Stepping aside to allow Joy's maid to enter, Stanton said, "I'll see you later," and left the dressing room with Ferris. Ignoring him, the leading man stalked off stiff-legged toward the sound stage.

Lyle has it bad; Stanton thought. *His chickens have come home to roost. He is really in love this time....*

The private agency man's name was Patton. A well-dressed, wiry, gray-haired man of indeterminable age, he shook hands cordially with Stanton as Goetz introduced them. "This is a pleasure, Mr. Stanton. I read your book. And it's okay."

Stanton said he was glad he liked the book and waved a greeting to Hi Lo. The lawyer quickly got down to business. "Look. Here's how it stands, fellows. After leaving you last night I got to thinking this thing over. And acting on the theory there is no time like the present, I gave Patton a ring, outlined the known facts to him, and asked him to bring over what he could to this first talk."

Patton took a small notebook from his pocket and laid it open on one knee. "In the first place," he began without preamble, "while the facts, undoubtedly, are as Mr. Manson outlined them to Inspector Treech last night, from the time angle, the alibi he gave Mr. Stanton isn't so hot. The boys on the bar were pretty busy. You were just another drunk to them, Mr. Stanton. None of them particularly noted the time when you came in or when Mr. Manson waltzed you out. They remember the incident but that's all. The manager refuses to stick out his neck one way or another. As you know, Sherry's is one of those joints that pulls the shades, locks the door, and keeps its bar open long after the legal closing hour. And the management doesn't want to get mixed up in anything that might call attention to that fact. On the other hand, despite any accurate time check, from what I hear, Inspector Treech is satisfied Mr. Manson's story is the McCoy and has written you off as chief suspect."

Patton continued. "The rest of the picture is equally as good. Treech has heard from both the London police and the immigration authorities and there was nothing in either reply to connect you with the girl or even intimate she knew you."

"Good," Goetz said. "Good."

The agency man glanced at his notebook. "Boiled down, London reported Miss Grace Turner was twenty-nine years old, five feet six inches tall, and weighed approximately seven and one-half stone. Formerly a millinery apprentice, she served in the English equivalent of our Women's Army Corps from 1939 up until she was demobilized in March of 1945. After that she worked in an office except for a brief period of about four months when she resided with American Army Technical Sergeant Arthur Hale, presumably without benefit of clergy. They report Hale's present address is unknown to them but he was embarked for the States on or about June fifteenth, 1946. On September twenty-fifth, 1948, said Grace Turner applied for and was granted a passport, her stated reason for wanting a passport being she intended marrying said Arthur Hale in Los Angeles, California. And according to Lieutenant Marble of the Valley Station an Arthur Hale, formerly an Army tech sergeant, now a punk gambler of sorts, lives with his wife, three children and his father, not far from Van Nuys."

"Oh, oh," Hi Lo said. "That sounds like a good lead. Unless the sergeant's children are triplets, or at least one pair of twins, he must have already been married during the London episode."

Patton closed his notebook. "I haven't a thing on Hale and neither had Treech the last time I tapped in. Bill Swen and Matt Kelly were scheduled to bring him in for questioning this afternoon if they can find him. If he is the right Hale he lines up as our hottest suspect, the dead girl having told the immigration authorities anticipated marriage to him was her purpose for entering the country."

"But why should he pinch my car to do the job in?" Stanton asked. "And after he pinched it, why didn't he just stash it somewhere instead of driving it out to the ranch and giving me a headache? I never did anything to this Hale. I don't even know him."

"We don't know Hale did it," Patton said.

"And that leaves us—where?" Goetz asked.

Stanton said, "With the exception of Hale, right where we started. Someone doesn't like me. If the killer needed a car, pinched mine, then ditched it after he cut his caper, that would be one thing. But bringing it back to my garage makes it personal."

Saying that was the way he saw it, Patton asked Stanton if he knew of anyone who disliked him to the point of attempting to frame him for murder. Stanton said he did not.

"No one has ever tried to blackmail you? You have never received any threatening letters in your mail?"

Stanton shook his head. "Not that I know of."

"None. Period," Hi Lo said. "And I ought to know. I open the mail."

The agency man consulted his notebook again. "How about these four men with whom you were lunching when you got the phone call, Johnny Hass, Lyle Ferris, Ed Wilcox, and Lou Saunders?"

"What do you mean, how about them?"

"Have you ever quarreled with any of them? Are there any, or one, of them who might have reason to hate you?"

Hi Lo suggested, "Lyle Ferris."

"No," Stanton said. "I doubt it. Right now, because of Joy, Lyle isn't very fond of me. But I can't see Lyle in this. When he reaches the boiling point he'll punch me in the nose. But he isn't the kind of a man who would attempt to get revenge by harming an innocent third party."

"That can be as you say," Patton said. "But Treech isn't missing a bet. He has checked on all four men and not one of them has an alibi for the approximate time of death. Lyle Ferris *claims* to have been in the company of a woman whom he refuses to name. Hass *says* he was developing pictures in his dark room but admits he has no way of proving it. Saunders told Treech in so many words to go to hell. He said if Treech wanted to know where he was he should try to find out and give the taxpayers a little service for their money. Wilcox it seems is a member of Alcoholics

Anonymous and when Treech's office talked to him long distance to New York he *said* that at the approximate time of the murder he was combing Main Street for some stew bum who'd had a slip."

"How about the Shad Hanson angle?" Hi Lo asked. "If Hanson followed Miss Turner from the Hollywood-Highland Hotel and saw her get into a car, the odds are if he didn't know who was driving it he, contrary to what he told Inspector Treech, wrote down the license number in the hope of being able to put on a bite. And as it was Bob's car and he hasn't attempted to contact Bob he must have recognized the driver."

"That," Goetz said, "is good reasoning and a good angle. But even if he knows, will Hanson talk?"

Patton shook his head. "The answer is he will not. I have worked on other cases involving Shad. He plays a lone hand and he plays it tight to his belt buckle. Why should he talk? He'd only be upsetting his own gravy. train. No. If Hanson knows who was driving Mr. Stanton's car he'll keep the information between Hanson and Hanson's bank account."

Stanton told Parson of the man who, posing as a detective, had asked Marta for the empty whiskey bottle.

"Your housekeeper can describe this man?" Patton asked.

"Vaguely. He was small. He was a man. He was polite. Beyond that Marta doesn't remember."

"You brought the bottle home with you?"

"I don't know. I do remember seeing it."

"So do I," Hi Lo said. "It was pinch-bottle Scotch, and empty."

"Inspector Treech knows about it?"

"No. We didn't know about it until after I had been released and we were on our way home. But the lad, whoever he was, to get the bottle, sold Marta on the idea it would prove I hadn't killed the girl."

Patton shrugged. "Well, I guess that's about all for now. It's footwork from here on and I'd better get out and hustle." He got to his feet and shaped his hat to his head.

Stanton followed suit. "This party being on me, I'd better get up in the hills and raise the scratch. I turn in a shooting script tomorrow night or walk the plank. J.V. so informed me."

Hi Lo remained to talk to Goetz and make out a check for the retaining fee. Stanton rode down in the elevator with Patton. In the lobby he asked if he could drop him anywhere and Patton said, "No thanks. I have my own car, Mr. Stanton. But a word of advice. Watch yourself. If you have a permit to do so, carry a gun. If not, buy a gun and apply for a permit."

"What makes you think I'm in danger?"

"A girl is dead," the private agency man said quietly. "Someone made a more or less clever attempt to lay her murder at your door. He would have succeeded. You would be facing a grand jury right now with Reisler thundering for an indictment if Mr. Manson and his wife hadn't happened to stumble on you. You never know. Maybe the lad behind this was waiting outside of Sherry's to bat you over the head and louse you up proper with fingerprints and things. When Mr. Manson drove you home, that was out. So he did the next best thing. After shooting the girl, he returned your car. And if he didn't love you before, now you have wiggled out of the tight he isn't going to be any fonder of you. Take the advice of a man who has lost clients before. Play it close to the belt. Look both ways before you cross the street. And don't take any candy from strangers."

They parted in the parking lot. Sighing, Stanton drove south on Main Street toward the freeway and Riverside Drive.

He was forced to stop for a red light and an over-painted girl standing on the corner smiled at him. Her dress was cheap. The seams of her stockings were crooked. Her face was pinched. When he failed to smile in return she lost interest and appraised an approaching sailor. Just before the light turned green a hollow-eyed drunk in once decent clothes, still trying to assume a semblance of self-respect, staggered in front of the car. He looked a little like a re-write man with whom Stanton had worked in Kansas City.

There, Stanton thought, *but for the grace of God et cetera.*

He wasn't looking for anything. He had it. Having too much he was merely fed up with what he had. But from now on he would try to appreciate his own good fortune and use it to the best advantage. Instead of bemoaning the fact that life seemed to have no meaning, he would live it to the best of his ability. It was the only life he would ever have. Instead of crying in his beer about man's inhumanity to man he would write a check when he was called upon but leave the solution of the foreign situation to more astute minds than his. There was plenty right in the Valley for him to do. And the bottle was out from now on. A social drink was one thing. A two-week drunk was another. That was how you wound up on Main Street. From now on he would go back to his old rule. When he felt he *needed a* drink he wouldn't take one.

He angled onto the freeway and turned left on Riverside. The hide-out had been Hi Lo's idea. Previously, when parties at the ranch had grown too hectic and guests had lingered on for days, and he had work to do, it had been like working in a mad house. He knew too many people. Too many people knew him. But only a handful of his intimates knew of the hide-out. A crude cabin built on the top of a high knoll in a wooded section of the mountains rimming the valley, there was no road within a half mile of it. The nearest cabin was a quarter of a mile away.

He left the Drive to angle down a maze of streets that led eventually to a graveled road winding up into the hills. The road, rutted badly now, and dirt, continued a mile beyond the last house and ended at the natural barrier of a huge pepper tree. Locking his car, Stanton took his portable typewriter and director's case and continued on foot.

After crossing the dry bed of a creek that was a roaring torrent during the rainy season, the narrow foot trail began to climb. Here the underbrush was thick and tinder dry. Halting for a breather, Stanton started to light a cigarette, and stopped himself just in time. This was a posted area. It had burned over some dozen years before, destroying he didn't recall how many houses and cabins spotted through the hills. Most of them had never been rebuilt.

The path grew even steeper. The underbrush met over the path. There was a slithering in the leaves that could only be a snake. Stanton didn't know what kind. He didn't care. He was completely winded when he reached the cabin.

It consisted of one large room with a fireplace, a sleeping alcove, and a kitchen nook equipped with a gasoline pressure stove. No one had broken in. Nothing had been touched since he had been here. There was a single-shot .22-caliber rifle hanging over the fireplace. Thinking of what Patton had said, Stanton took it down and made certain that it was loaded. Not that it would do him much good. If someone was really out to get him he would be well-equipped. He should have stopped at the ranch and picked up a gun. Popping away with a .22-caliber single-shot gun at a man desperate enough to commit murder would be equivalent to trying to bring down an elephant with a pea shooter.

Dismissing the thought from his mind, he hung the gun back on its pegs and opened all the doors and windows. Then he pumped up the gasoline stove and put a huge pot of coffee on to boil. So Marty wanted another smash hit. He'd get it.

There was no one here to see him. Stripping off his clothes, Stanton padded out into the small stone wall-enclosed back yard and turned on the outdoor shower. Refreshed, he put on his shorts again. Then, still barefooted, he set up his machine on a plain deal table, spread the work he had done the night before and the carbons of previous attempts fan wise around the typewriter, poured a cup of coffee, and sitting down at his machine inserted a fresh sheet of paper.

A long minute of silence followed. Then the keys began to click and clicked steadily from then on except for the several brief breaks that he allowed himself.

The dialogue unrolled like ribbon. He'd had the story a long time. It was a natural for Joy. All he had needed was quiet and mental peace and time enough between parties and drinks to put it down on paper. It grew dark and he lighted a lamp. Midnight came and passed. It was early morning when he finally wrote thirty. He sat a moment sipping the dregs of the cold coffee in his cup, physically and mentally exhausted.

Stanton got stiffly to his feet and walked to the open door. The night was still studded with stars but the crescent moon was on the wane. There was a fresh smell to the air. Dawn wasn't far away. He considered packing his things, attempting to negotiate the path, and driving straight to Joy's Beverly Hills home. She would welcome him with open arms. And after he had turned over the script to Marty they could jump into a plane and—

No. That was out. Inspector Treech had told him to stick around. And Joy had been married in Las Vegas the last time. Stanton tried to remember whether he would be her fourth or her fifth husband. Or did it matter? Joy was a beautiful little mink.

He wasn't quite certain just when he realized he wasn't alone, or how he knew. The small pulse in his throat beat a trifle faster at an unidentified sound—he had a feeling of being watched. Then a sleepy squirrel began to scold. Stanton shifted his weight from his heels to the balls of his feet and stood away from the door jamb, remembering Patton's warning.

The squirrel was awake and really angry now. The short hairs on the back of his neck tingling, Stanton tardily turned out the lamp and crossing to the fireplace lifted the small gun from its pegs. It gave no feeling of security. It felt like a child's toy in his hands.

The door was a lighter blob of gray against the black of the room. Stepping out of his shoes, he tiptoed to the door and peered out. He could see nothing. The screen hampered his vision. He opened the screen door and stepped warily out onto the small stoop. It was a bad mistake. His body spread-eagled against the outer wall of the cabin, the waiting man brought down the club in his hands. Stanton sensed the blur of movement and turned. But before he could trigger his gun the vicious blow on his head knocked him to his knees.

Blind with pain, he got to his feet and the other man swung his weapon again. Stanton stumbled off the stoop, staggered a few steps, then pitched forward on his face.

CHAPTER 5

Stanton was conscious that he was warm. He was conscious his head ached. But neither sensation was acute. He opened his eyes and closed them. He tried to tear open the already open neck of his sport shirt the better to breathe in the hot air that was torturing his lungs.

Nausea doubled him into a knot. He sat up retching and realized he wasn't outside the cabin. He was in the sleeping alcove. The living room was bright with light. The sun must be high in the sky to generate so much heat.

He sat looking through the arch of the alcove at his typewriter and the neatly piled script beside it. Then he saw the .22-calibered rifle. Whoever had slugged him had hung it back on its pegs over the fireplace.

The heat grew more intense. Getting to his feet, he walked into the living room. It wasn't morning. The windows were still black with night. The cabin was on fire. Originating in the gasoline pressure stove, the whole west wall of the cabin was in flames. He realized as he stood staring stupidly at the fire that his shirt was sodden with whiskey and his head was light. Whiskey had been poured in and on him. But whoever had done the pouring had defeated his own purpose. He hadn't poured enough into him and he had recovered consciousness too soon.

He considered the situation. The flames had too great a head start to allow him to attempt to fight the fire with the small trickle of water available. All he could do was get out. Slipping into his shoes, but not taking time to lace them, he snatched the completed script from the table, stuffed it into his shirt, and tugged at the closed front door. It refused to give. Both the front and the back doors were bolted. In a bold attempt to cover his own guilt and write the death as misadventure on the police report, whoever had slugged him and started the fire had bolted both doors on the inside and left by one of the now closed windows. Only that fact had saved him from certain cremation. With all draft shut off, except that afforded by the fireplace, the fire had spread much more slowly than it would have if the doors and windows had been left open. As Stanton watched, the flame licked at the curtains of the alcove. The curtains caught fire and flame leaped from them to the bed. The rumpled and spotted chenille spread burned with the clear blue of an object well-soaked in alcohol.

First there had been an empty bottle. Now a full one. The slugger was hell on whiskey. Stanton decided against using either door and forming a perfect target for a possibly waiting marksman. Instead he opened one of the high side windows on the wall not yet on fire. The flames stimulated by the draft licked up at the unfinished ceiling and began to poke fiery tongues through the dry shingles.

The grass was wet with dew, the morning cold. Hugging the ground with his heat-fevered body, Stanton lay for long minutes sucking in lungs-ful of cool air. Partially recovered, but still gagging and choking on the smoke he had swallowed, he circled the cabin cautiously. He saw no one. He heard no one. No one tried to stop him. But his retreat from the knoll was cut off. Whoever had fired the cabin had also ignited a practical barrier. Four hundred feet down the slope a long semi-circle of flaming greasewood, whipped on by a brisk morning wind, was showering explod-ing sparks into the air that set still more greasewood, sage, and live-oak on fire.

In the far distance a siren wailed faintly. A look-out had spotted the fire. Men and equipment were already on their way. More men and more equipment would follow but the flames would reach him long before the first fire truck could possibly reach the end of the road. Fire traveled rap-idly up a slope. It was moving toward him as fast as an angry man might walk. Against the mounting crackle of the flames he heard, or thought he heard, a man's voice calling, "Bob!"

It sounded like Hi Lo's voice. He yelled in answer. But if the other man called again his voice was drowned out by the growing roar of the fire and the crackle and popping of the exploding greasewood. Stanton retreated a few steps and looked at the black wall of trees behind the burning cabin. He had never bothered to explore them. He hadn't the least idea what lay on the other side. He had no choice but to run for whatever dubious safe-ty they might provide.

One of his untied shoe laces tripped him and he sprawled his full length on the ground. Cursing, he tied the laces of both shoes and ran on. The pre-dawn was no longer cool. Each puff of wind on his back was hotter than the one preceding it. He reached the trees and entered them, thank-ful the ground was fairly level. But here there was no light. He stumbled over unseen roots, was whipped by low-hanging branches.

Finally he emerged in a small clearing from which he could see the cabin. A large portion of the roof had fallen in. The walls were sheets of flame. Even as he watched, the wind tore a flaming shingle from the intact portion of the roof and hurled it into the trees. The crown of a pine burst into flame and the flames licked from it to other trees. The fire was on his side of the clearing now. The race was on again.

He ran on doggedly in the growing dawn. Five hundred feet farther on, the knoll ended in a steep cut-bank. He had no choice. Plunging over the edge, he half-fell, half-scrambled down the slope, snatching at out-cropping clumps of brush and purple sage that held only long enough to break his fall before they came free in his hands. Small pieces of shale loosened by his feet hurtled by his head. A miniature slide carried him thirty feet before it stopped. He was relieved to reach level ground and still more relieved to find a faintly defined trail leading away from the base of the cut-bank.

Fifteen minutes later he emerged on a secondary road. A half dozen drivers ignored his thumb before he caught a ride from a curious motorist going to the fire. Relaxing on the seat, attempting to breathe normally, he rode looking out the window of the car. He could see the cut-bank. Above and below it now the whole side of the mountain was on fire.

"It's a honey, eh?" the driver of the car enthused.

"Yeah It's a honey," Stanton agreed. He was completely beat. His body was bruised sore by the roots over which he had tripped and the trees he had run into in the dark. They were forced by the jam of cars and the insistence of a state trooper to park two blocks from the end of the road. Losing his enthusiastic host in the press of curious onlookers, Stanton walked the two blocks thinking of the voice he had heard and wondering if it possibly could have been Hi Lo.

When he and Hi Lo had entered the Army they had made wills in each other's favor. He had the ranch and a substantial bank account. Hi Lo had nothing but his salary which he spent as soon as he got it. Hi Lo could have conspired with the girl, instructed her what to say over the phone, then, doublecrossing her, picked her up in his, Stanton's car, and left her corpse on the summit of the canyon road plainly labeled.

On the other hand, Hi Lo didn't seem to care that much about money. As the big Indian himself sometimes clowned—

"*Ugh. White man heap much foolish. Get up six o'clock every morning for twenty, twenty-five year and rush downtown to office to work hard and pile up heap much money so he won't have to get up six o'clock every morning and rush downtown to office. He want to live with squaw in tepee on a river, do nothing but smoke and fish. Indian he much smarter. Indian start out in tepee in first place. Save twenty, twenty-five year. Not forgetting to mention, he has heap much more time for squaw.*"

It was a problem and a knotty one. Stanton's car was where he had left it but it was hemmed in by three fire trucks, a police car, and an ambulance. Still thinking about Hi Lo, he walked on up the path to where two perspiring volunteers were attempting to hold back the crowd and asked a passing mountain patrolman if he had seen a big Indian around, hoping he would say he had not. "Yes. I did," the patrolman answered. He pointed to a cluster of men under a tree. "I think he is over there."

The corners of his mouth turned down, Stanton walked toward the tree.

One man was stretched out on the ground with an intern kneeling beside him. A gray-haired man with his back to Stanton was talking to a battalion chief. He chanced to turn as Stanton neared the group. "Holy smoke, Mr. Stanton. Am I glad to see you! We thought you were a goner."

"What are you doing here, Patton?" Stanton asked. "And tell me this. Where's Hi Lo?"

The private agency man stepped to one side so Stanton could see the man on the ground. "He tried to get through the brush when we first saw the flames and damned near burned his pants off. Then he tried it again with his clothes soaked with water and a wet gunnysack wrapped around his head and almost shot the works. I had to knock him out with my sap to keep him from committing suttee."

"From the Sanskrit word *sati* meaning true wife," the man on the ground said weakly. "And it's base calumny. I'm no wife to Robert Stanton. I just wanted to get him out of the joint. Was that your voice I heard, Bob? How's the climate, hot or cold?"

Stanton squatted in the space the intern had vacated. "Why, you damn fool crazy Indian. You know this is still California. The devil doesn't want the likes of us. We'd be too hot to handle." He looked at Patton. "But what are you and Hi Lo doing here?"

"Keeping an eye on you, or so we thought," the agency man admitted wryly. "I called your place last night about nine o'clock to give you some information concerning that fellow Hale and when Hi Lo told me where you were I hit the ceiling. What was the last thing I told you yesterday?"

"I know. But—"

"No buts about it. When you mentioned a hide-out I thought you meant someplace on your ranch, not a joint tucked away up here in the hills where anyone could get at you. So after I talked to Hi Lo I told him I thought we had better come up here and keep an eye on you. So we did."

"You and Hi Lo have been here all night?"

"Not right here. We were down at the road end sitting in my car. We walked up the trail when we first got here, looked in through a window, saw you batting away in a trance, and went back to the car. We figured anyone coming in would have to pass us. Then just before dawn we spotted the flames and the big Indian went nuts."

"And you were together when you saw the flames?"

Patton looked at him thoughtfully. "We weren't two feet away from each other all night. Why?"

Instead of answering his question, Stanton said, "I ought to have my mind sprayed with D.D.T."

Hi Lo sat up and leaned his back against the trunk of the tree. "How did you get out of there?"

"Out the back way and over a cut-bank," Stanton told him. "And the fire wasn't an accident. About five o'clock this morning, just after I had finished my stint, I was standing looking out the screen door when I realized I wasn't alone. So, like a fool, I took that pea shooter off its pegs, stepped outside to investigate, and someone dropped a load of bricks on my head. When I came to I was back inside the cabin on the bed, both doors were bolted on the inside, the windows were closed, someone had anointed the about-to-be burnt offering with essence of Old Grandmother, and all one end of the joint was on fire."

Patton said, "Now maybe you'll listen to me."

"I don't see," Hi Lo sighed, "how he could have gotten past us."

The battalion chief, who had been lingering in the background, listening open-mouthed, offered, "There is a trail in from the other side. It's a sort of bridle path but it was closed off during the war because of the fire hazard. Is that true what you just said, Mr. Stanton? That fire was set? It wasn't an accident?"

"It was no accident."

The intern returned with a stretcher and two bearers. His bandaged legs looking grotesque under the charred remaining fragments of his trousers, a lump the size of a turtle's egg back of one ear, and still coughing from the smoke which he had swallowed, Hi Lo got to his feet with as much dignity as he could muster under the circumstances. "What's that thing for?" He waved one hand imperiously. "Be gone with thanks. When the first Model T came in I promised my great grandfather, Sitting Bull, I would never ride on another travois."

"It's your funeral, Tonto," the intern grinned. "But maybe you'll do okay at that."

Stanton, the big Indian and Patton walked slowly down the trail to the road-end trailing a tail of whispers. *"That's Robert Stanton, the writer... That's the fellow who was supposed to have been in the cabin... Sure you've heard of him. He's the man the police picked up the other night accused of murdering that English girl...."*

It was almost nine when they reached the ranch. Stanton phoned Manson's office immediately, told him the script was completed and asked him to send a studio messenger out to the ranch for it. Manson said he would be pleased to. The producer evidently hadn't heard of the fire and Stanton didn't bother to tell him the story. He was too much in need of sleep.

Patton took his departure shortly. "I have some scouting around to do but I'll be here when you wake up. I'd like to lay out a plan of action. I traded a tip on that bottle you told me about for the information that when Kelly and Swen went out to pick up Hale yesterday someone had tipped him they were coming and he took a powder. However, using some of my own wires, I have found out that on occasion he works as a stick-man for Rodney Childs. It may just be Childs can tell us something about him if we drive out there tonight. Does that sound all right to you?"

Stanton said it did, refused to eat the eggs Marta insisted on preparing for him, drank the orange juice on the tray, then, after bathing his bruised body, stretched out on his bed. His eyes almost closed in sleep, he thought of his promise to Joy and dialed her number. Beulah said she was still asleep but offered to awaken her.

"That won't be necessary, Beulah," Stanton said. "Just tell her our date is still on for tonight and I said for her to wear something particularly sinful as we may drop out to Rodney Child's place and give the wheels a whirl."

"I'll do that, Mr. Stanton," Beulah chuckled. "I'll tell her the very first thing when she wakes up. She going to be pleased you called."

Stanton's own sleep was heavy but troubled and peopled by faintly familiar faces peering at him through flaming veils. But every time he was about to recognize a face it faded back into the fire. With the cool of late afternoon the fires and the faces faded and when the tinkle of one of the phones on his bed table awakened him at five o'clock it interrupted an *au naturel* swim he and Joy were enjoying in a cool green bottomless pool.

"Robert Stanton speaking," he said into the mouthpiece.

It was Marty Manson on the wire. The producer raved for a full ten minutes about the script. It was, he said, the best thing that Stanton had ever done. He and J.V. had spent the day reading it and J.V. would probably phone him later. "I knew you would come through, Bob."

"That's more than I did," Stanton said. "Well, thanks for liking it. And thanks for calling, Marty."

He had barely hung up the one phone when the house phone tinkled. It was Hi Lo this time. "I put Marty through because I think you'd better get up, Bob," he said. "Inspector Treech is here and he's been here most of the afternoon."

"What's new with him?"

"The bottle Marta gave to the phony detective. He's trying to find out who he was and where the bottle fits in."

As he dressed Stanton was suddenly ravenously hungry and he realized the last meal he had eaten was a cold can of beans almost twenty-four hours before. Seeing the table was set in the patio, he walked out and sat down. Inspector Treech, examining the big palomino stud in the box stall, saw him leave his room and walking back to the table he sat down across from Stanton.

"You live here now?" Stanton asked politely.

Treech shook his head. "No. I still live in the same place. I just dropped in to get a little information about a bottle. You wouldn't know anything about it, I suppose?"

"Not what happened to it. I remember seeing it on the floor and being horrified by the thought I must be turning into a secret drinker who took bottles to bed with him. And I mean that. Hi Lo said it was pinch bottle. But, as I recall it, it was dimpled bottle Scotch."

"The same brand that you drink?"

"Not me. I'm strictly a rum and rye man."

Marta brought a silver pot of coffee and a tray heavy with eggs, pork sausage, toast, and hash-fried potatoes. "Now eat, Mr. Stanton," she urged.

Stanton noted her eyes were red-rimmed as if she had been crying and looked angrily at Treech. "What have they been doing to you, Marta?"

She tried to smile. "Not a thing, Mr. Stanton. Just showing me some pictures." She pressed the heels of her palms to her forehead, then thrust them out in a short-armed gesture. "But I am such a *dumkopf* when it comes to faces. He was shorter as I am. He was polite. This is all I know."

Treech took a handful of pictures from his pocket and spread them on the table in front of Stanton. "These are the ones I showed her."

There was a picture of Ed Wilcox, one of Johnny Hass, Shad Hanson, Lou Saunders, Lyle Ferris, and a ferret-faced youth he didn't know. "Who's he?" Stanton asked.

"His name is Hale, Arthur Hale," Treech answered. "He is the lad who, according to London and the immigration authorities, Miss Turner *thought* she was going to marry."

"And Marta picked his picture?"

"No. She either couldn't or wouldn't put the finger on any of them." Inspector Treech sorted Shad Hanson's picture from the others. "The nearest thing to an identification I could get from her was an admission that Shad looked 'something' like the man as she remembered him. Gieger has gone for him now. They should be here any minute."

"How nice," Stanton enthused. "I'll tell Marta to set two extra places for dinner."

Hi Lo came out on the patio carrying a portable phone. He set it at Stanton's elbow, plugged it into its socket, then salaamed to the phone three times. "Pharaoh is calling, my lord. But he refuses to state whether Birnam Wood has come to Dunsinane or whether the plasterers working on the pyramids are asking for time-and-a-half for overtime and doubletime on Sundays."

J.V. was far more modest in his praise than Manson but he said he had glanced through the script and the dialogue seemed to be up to par. What he chiefly wanted to know was whether it was historically correct? Was there ever an authenticated instance where a wealthy French nobleman of that period, sailing under a Letter of Marque, whatever the hell that was, had fallen in love with a penniless indentured bond-maiden.

"Dozens of instances, Mr. Mercer," Stanton lied glibly. "Naturally, I did a lot of research."

"Naturally," J.V. agreed. "Well, I guess we'll shoot it. Costume pictures are hot right now." He still sounded a trifle dubious as he hung up.

Hi Lo unplugged the phone and asked Stanton if he wanted to see Lou Saunders. "He says he wants a statement from you on the fire."

Stanton poured a fresh cup of coffee. "Why not? The more the merrier. But whatever you do, don't forget to remind me I have a date with Joy tonight. If I stand her up just once more I'll lose out with her completely."

Hi Lo said he wouldn't forget and returned to the living room.

Inspector Treech was almost sympathetic. "This sort of thing, I mean phone calls and interruptions while you are eating, goes on all the time?"

"A good share of it," Stanton said. "That's why I have—" He corrected himself. "That's why I *had* a hide-out."

Saunders rounded the corner of the house. "What's the idea of locking the front gate? You afraid someone is going to steal you?"

Stanton said he hadn't known it was locked.

"Well, it is. And Hi Lo has Eddie doing guard duty with a shotgun. You have to state your name and business. Then he goes into the living room and confers with Hi Lo before he'll open up."

"I'm glad to hear it," Stanton said. "Someone tried to snag me this morning."

Inspector Treech looked thoughtfully at the end of his cigar. Saunders said, "That's what I want to talk to you about."

Stanton told him the story in detail. When he had finished, the reporter looked at Treech. "What do you think of that yarn, Inspector?"

"Not much," Treech admitted.

"I lean the same way," Saunders said. "To put it mildly, in one of my famous coast-to-coast-relished gems of understatement, it sounds highly improbable. Why should anyone want to knock you off?"

"Why should anyone want to frame me for murder?" Before Stanton could say more, Sergeant Gieger rounded the corner of the house with Hanson. The lawyer was smiling and seemingly unperturbed. He nodded cordially to Stanton. "A nice place you have here, Mr. Stanton. I've heard a lot about it but what I heard didn't do it justice."

Treech took the cigar from his mouth. "You've never been here before, I suppose?"

"No. I have never had that honor."

"Get the housekeeper," Treech ordered Gieger. "I want her to take a look at this guy."

"I seem to have come at the right time," Saunders said. "Don't be coy. Put out. What gives here, Inspector?"

"Just checking a theory of mine."

Gieger returned with Marta. Her hands were floured to the wrists. She wiped them with a towel as she looked from Inspector Treech to her employer. "*Ja*. You want Marta?"

Indicating Gieger, Inspector Treech asked her, "Is this the man who posed as a detective, Marta? Is this the man to whom you gave the bottle?"

"No," she said scornfully. "He is real detective. He show me his badge in kitchen and is different from other man's. His was like star with little round balls on the end."

"Probably a sheriff's posse star," Gieger said. "Those riding-club guys are always losing their buzzers. Besides, you can buy one almost anywhere."

Treech pointed at Hanson. "How about this man, Marta? Is *he* the man you gave the bottle to?"

Indecision patent in her eyes, Marta studied Hanson's face. Inspector Treech jabbed Hanson's thigh with his thumb. "Say something."

"Hi, baby," Hanson said.

Marta shook her head. "No. Other man is polite. He is not call me baby. Besides I think is fatter in the cheeks and wear not such nice clothes, also a derby hat." She seemed on the verge of tears.

Stanton got to his feet, furious. "Damn it, Treech," he shouted, "leave her alone. You either stop badgering Marta or Inspector or no Inspector I'll punch your teeth down your throat."

"Okay. That's all Marta," Inspector Treech admitted defeat. "And that's all for you, Hanson. For now."

Marta fled to her kitchen. Hanson stood his ground. Then, looking at Saunders and Stanton he asked, "I wonder if one of you gentlemen would enlighten me. Just what is this about?"

"A bottle," Stanton said. "You know. Bottle bottle. Who has the bottle?"

Saunders put down his cup. "Well, who has?" he asked cheerfully. "Did I say no to a drink? I much prefer whiskey to coffee."

Looking at Hanson, Treech jerked his thumb over his shoulder. "Scram." He added to Gieger, "Take it back wherever you picked it up."

Smirking, Hanson left with Gieger. Stanton got a bottle of whiskey and set it at Saunders' elbow. "From me to you. Go ahead. Drink yourself into a stupor, Lou. I read the papers while I was dressing and you're the only newsman in L.A. who is giving me a break."

"I don't see how you could have killed the girl."

Inspector Treech said, "I do. I thought from the first you were guilty, Stanton. Then, after Manson told his story, I didn't see how you could be. Now I think I know how it was done."

"You mean you think Marty lied for me?"

"No. Except for a small variation in time, Mr. Manson's story checks in every detail. But facts are facts. The dead girl seems to have been otherwise romantically inclined but it was *you* whom she phoned. It was *you* she asked to meet her at midnight or she would blow her top. *But how do we know it was midnight when you met her? How do we know you didn't contact her that afternoon and set the time up an hour?* We have only a known blackmailer's word it was midnight when she got into a car driven by a man. And between the time the dead girl's picture was printed in the papers and Hanson came forward to identify her he had plenty of time to contact you and for the two of you to get together on your stories."

Saunders said, "I still don't see how he could have killed the girl."

Treech told him. "He was supposed to meet the girl at midnight. He met her at eleven instead and killed her shortly thereafter. The M.E. says there was little but alcohol in her stomach and he could easily be off an hour on his original estimate as to the time of death. After shooting her somewhere along the Strip where the shots would pass as backfires, he put her into the trunk of his car and drove on to Sherry's where he was reasonably certain there would be someone he knew. There was. Mr. and Mrs. Manson came in. Mr. Manson fell for his drunk act. He liked Stanton. He wanted the scenario for the new picture. He didn't want him to get into trouble. So like a good Samaritan, and just as Stanton had reasoned someone would, Manson brought him out here in his own car and dumped Stanton on his bed, giving him an almost fool-proof alibi for the hour he was *supposed* to meet Miss Turner. All Stanton had to do after that was to wait until Manson had gone, sneak out of the house, take a cab back to where he had parked his car, drive home via the canyon road, stop to dump the girl's body over the summit, roar in here at four o'clock, go to bed, and then pretend he had been so drunk he didn't remember a thing that happened. But, unfortunately, for him, Shad Hanson saw the girl enter his car an hour earlier than she was supposed to."

"It sounds, Inspector," the reporter admitted. "You give me a motive and I'll buy it."

"I can't, yet," Treech said. "But I think I'll be able to after I talk to this lad Hale. If the Turner dame had something on Stanton, and it is obvious she did, she undoubtedly told her boyfriend all about it."

Stanton lighted a cigarette with fingers that shook slightly despite his effort to control them. "You're crazy, Treech. You're out of your mind. I suppose I slugged myself and set that fire this morning?"

"That is just what I do think," Inspector Treech said coldly.

"And the bottle?"

Inspector Treech was truthful. "I don't know where the bottle comes in.

It could be a red herring. Or it could be a slip on your part. It could be it had the girl's fingerprints on it and after you were arrested you thought of it and had Hanson come out here or send someone to pick it up before we got our hands on it. Naturally Shad wouldn't want to lose his golden goose." Treech snuffed his cigar in a saucer and got to his feet, "Well, that's all for now, Mr. Stanton. I just wanted to see you and Hanson together. And Hanson was so scared his knees were shaking. I could arrest you but there wouldn't be much sense in that until I dig up the motive. Goetz would spring you on some technicality. And the next time I get you in back of bars I mean to keep you there. Good night. Pleasant dreams."

Stanton half expected Saunders to follow the detective. The reporter sat fondling the bottle instead. "A motive," he said finally. "That's all it needs, a motive. And what a story."

Stanton continued to try to eat but his food was cold and sawdust in his mouth. His mouth was dry. His hands and cheeks were feverish. He had never felt so futile or so helpless. Each new facet of the case merely added another stone to the wall against which he was beating his head. Even Lou thought he was guilty. He could tell by the way the other man refused to meet his eyes.

CHAPTER 6

T he man in the booking office was kind and very helpful. Everyone had been kind. Everyone had been simply splendid. Finished with the filling in of forms and stamping and tearing of perforated papers, the man told Eve cheerfully, "And there you are. Second-class cabin from Southampton on the Moravia. You sail the morning of the second."

Robin, standing stiffly beside his mother, almost breathless with the wonder of it, unbent to hug Winston Churchill with all the strength of his six years. "You hear that?" he whispered. "You and Mother and I are going to the States." He added, "On a big ship with real live sailors."

The dog, inured to such ardent affection, yawned. It was hot and stuffy in the office. He looked wistfully out the window at the street. Then, as his mistress moved back from the counter to put the papers in her purse, he gently disentangled his neck from Robin's arms and padding a step closer to Eve stood, protectively, against her skirt....

There was some fog in the canyon, a lot of fog on the coast road, but none in Beverly Hills. Talking to Hanson, attempting to bluff the truth out of him had been Patton's idea. But Hanson hadn't been in his suite at the Hollywood-Highland Hotel. The clerk thought he might be at his newly purchased Malibu Hills home but the lawyer hadn't been there either although a Japanese house boy said he was expecting him later.

"I wonder," Hi Lo asked, "just when he bought that classy joint?"

Patton said, "I'll check the real estate transfers in the morning but the clerk said Shad had been contemplating such a purchase for some time. He probably bought it completely furnished."

The weather, for the time of year, continued warm but it was cooler near the coast than it had been in the valley. Riding in an open car, Stanton was glad he had worn his topcoat. It was shortly after ten when he braked his car in front of the massive closed gates in the high, ivy-covered stone wall that enclosed Joy Parnell's five-acre hilltop estate.

The gates were opened by remote control as soon as he telephoned the house on the phone set in a niche in the archway.

The house, set well back from the road in an incongruous planting of tall palms, had been a castle, complete with towers, merlons, crenels, and machicolations. It, with the ground on which it was built, had been a gift of one of Joy's former admirers, and she hated it, repeatedly threatening to sell it. She said it gave her the creeps. But no one but another star of her own magnitude could possibly support it.

Patton had never seen the house before. "Well, quite a prefab," he admired. "How many rooms exclusive of the towers and battlements, Mr. Stanton?"

"Thirty, I think," Stanton said. "Or maybe it's fifty. Joy has told me but I don't remember."

"Tish," Hi Lo depreciated. "Think nothing of it. What's twenty rooms between friends?"

Leaving them sitting in the car, Stanton banged the brass gargoyle knocker. Beulah opened the door. "It's about time you got here, Mr. Stanton," she reproved him. "Miss Joy almost give you up. You didn't get in no more trouble with the police, did you?"

He said, "No," and keeping his hat and coat on walked down the long entrance hall complete with lances and maces and suits of armor and great heraldic shields emblazoned with someone's family crest. Everything about the house was massive. Stanton suspected Joy secretly liked it that way because it accentuated her own tininess and gave her an illusion of youth. Joy had been around a long time.

He found her waiting in front of a crackling open fire that shot threads of red through her straw-colored hair and silhouetted her lower body. Her gown was white, strapless, backless, cut in front to the round of her breasts. The large emerald gleamed on one hand. Her toenails were scarlet ovals between the thin straps of her Grecian sandals. If she was wearing much of anything under the gown it wasn't apparent as she stood in front of the fire.

"Is this sinful enough?" she asked as she lifted her lips to be kissed.

Stanton kissed her hungrily. "You're a hussy. But you look marvelous to me. You always do." He pulled her to him and kissed her again.

She snuggled into his arms contentedly. "This is more like it. Do we *have* to go out tonight? Do we *have* to give the wheels a whirl? Can't we just stay here and talk? And maybe have a few drinks?"

He released her reluctantly. "I'd like to. But I'm afraid we can't. And I'm not being coy. Being here with you, having a serious talk about us, was how I planned the evening. But something new has been added. I thought I had Inspector Treech out of my hair but he turned up this afternoon with a brand new theory of how I could have killed Grace Turner, involving collusion with Shad Hanson. I tried to see Shad. I want to try again. Because with this new theory of his, if Inspector Treech can connect me with the dead girl in *any* way, well, I might not do too well with a jury."

"Even though you didn't kill her? Even though you'd never seen her before?"

"Treech doesn't believe that. He thinks she had something on me." All of Stanton's former depression returned. "Even Lou Saunders thinks I did it although he's given me a break so far." He sat on the arm of an uncomfortable looking love seat and ran his fingers through his hair. "They've got me going in circles. Maybe they're right and I'm wrong. Maybe I did kill her. Maybe I'm out of my mind."

Joy leaned her thigh against his and stroked his cheek.

He started to tell her of the fire and decided it would keep. "Anyway I want to try to see Shad. And I want to go out to Childs' and talk to Rodney. It seems this Arthur Hale whom Miss Turner thought she was going to marry has worked for Rod. He may know where he is. And if we can we want to locate Hale and talk to him before Inspector Treech does."

"We? You and I?" Joy asked.

"Yes," Stanton said. "And Hi Lo and a private agency man named Patton. They're waiting outside in the car."

The light went out of Joy's eyes. Her face looked older and drawn. Tiny wrinkles showed around the corners of her mouth. "Oh. I see. A foursome. Well, I'll have Beulah get me a coat." She took his chin between her thumb and forefinger and turned his face to hers. "What's the matter with me, Bob? What am I doing wrong? Don't I put the right perfume back of my ears? Should I use some other kind of soap? Won't my best friends tell me? Or what?"

He told her not to be so foolish. "It's just—"

"I know," she said quietly. "There's always something just a little more important. A week's drunk. A poker game. The races at Santa Anita. One of your Palominos about to foal. You have a new picture to write. And now—a murder. But I want one thing understood right now, Mr. Stanton."

"Yes?"

"If, and when, we ever do go on a honeymoon—no Hi Lo."

He laughed. "Okay. No Hi Lo. I may even come back here tonight and discuss the matter of wedding bells. How would that be?"

"I have heard that before," she told him. Kissing his cheek, she left, calling, "Beulah. Get me a coat. Better make it the sable. We're going out to Childs' and I may have to leave it behind to get us off the hook. I lost five thousand dollars the last time I was in the joint."

Stanton watched her walk from the room. Joy was pretty. Joy was people. She had the gift of lust for life. So their marriage did blow up. It would be fun while it lasted. She reappeared in a sable wrap that made her look like a bad little girl wearing a starlet's reward for erasing the word "no" from her vocabulary. "Whenever you are, Bob...."

The Childs establishment was in the hill back of Chatsworth. The landscaped grounds were extensive. The house was pseudo-Moorish, huge, and built in a square around a large courtyard. Except for the lighted windows, heavily draped, passers-by would never know the building was occupied unless they chanced to glance in at the well-filled parking space. Childs ran an orderly place. The play was high. The terms were cash. Evening dress was obligatory. If you couldn't afford to gamble, Childs didn't want your money. Rather, he didn't want the squawks such a situation might engender. A former two-bit dice hustler who had pulled himself up by the skin of his knees and the liberal use of switch dice, he knew his business. You were a lady or a gentleman while you were in his place. If you got drunk or boisterous you were asked for your card and were never admitted again. The usual hoodlum element germane to such a place was conspicuous by its absence.

The doorman was pleased to see Stanton and Hi Lo and Miss Parnell but regretted he could not admit Patton on two counts. He had no card. He was not in evening dress. However, if the gentleman cared to return in proper evening attire the apologetic doorman was certain the matter of a card could be arranged.

"Skip it," Patton said. "You can handle the question routine as well as I can, Mr. Stanton. I'll wait in the car."

The play for a Wednesday night was heavy. Joy knew everyone. Everyone knew her. Stanton bought her a thousand dollars' worth of chips, lighted her cigarette, got her a drink, and found a chair for her at one of the roulette tables next to a former Follies girl who had been smart enough to marry an oil field with a bad heart and distinct dipsomaniac possibilities. Then he asked a floorman if he might see Childs. The floorman returned with the information that Mr. Childs would be pleased to see him and Hi Lo.

"Ah. The trouble twins," the gambler greeted them cordially. "Here go the profits." A man of medium size, Childs played up his resemblance to a Mississippi river boat gambler in faultless modern evening dress. It was an act. He admitted it. But the public wanted front. It was much easier to lose a thousand dollars to a lad who looked like Rhett Butler than it was to lose the same amount of money to Jake Irving, a former dice game hustler. Front they wanted. Front they got.

Stanton said they were there on business and to ask a favor. "You've read about the jam I'm in, Rod?"

"We're in," Childs corrected him. "The police must have released you or you wouldn't be here."

"They're just giving me rope. Treech has me pegged for the fall guy. And what I want from you is this."

"Yes?"

"The present address of one of your former stick-men, an Arthur Hale."

"What has Hale to do with the case?"

"He's the reason for Grace Turner coming to this country. She thought she was going to marry him."

"Oh," Childs said. "I see." He pushed one of the buttons on his desk. "Well, in that case I'll do better than give you his address. I'll let you talk to him. He's running one of the dice tables tonight.... Put someone else on his table and send Hale in," he told the man who answered the summons. The gambler turned back to Stanton. "You say she thought she was going to marry Hale?"

"That's what she told the immigration authorities."

Childs shook his head. "Treech must be playing this one close to his belt. That hasn't come out in the papers so far."

"No," Stanton said. "It hasn't." Lighting a cigarette, he looked thoughtfully at the man who had just entered.

Hale looked like his picture. It wasn't saying much for him. A thin man in his early thirties, with small eyes and an oversized Adam's apple that jutted over the stiff wing collar of his dress shirt, he addressed himself to the gambling house owner. "You wanted to see me, Mr. Childs?"

The situation seemed to amuse the gambler. "No. But Mr. Stanton does. Mr. Stanton, Mr. Hale."

Stanton nodded but did not offer to shake hands.

Hale broke the awkward silence that followed. "I know Mr. Stanton by reputation. And, of course, I've read the papers." Tiny beads of perspiration appeared on his cheeks and forehead.

"What are you sweating about?" Childs asked

Hale said hotly, "If you were in my shoes you'd sweat, too, Mr. Childs. I knew the dead girl in England. In fact we were quite close for a few months and I guess she got some wrong ideas. Anyway, she showed up at my place the other day and raised all holy hell because I was already married. She made an awful scene right in front of my wife and father. I thought she had sense enough to know it was just one of those things, that I was handing her a line." He admitted, "I may have laid it on a bit thick to make the grade. But I was lonely. And, well, you know how those things go."

"No," Stanton said. "I don't. And I'm not interested. When did you last see her, Hale?"

"The day she came to my father's place. The next I heard of her was two days later when I read in the newspaper that someone had killed her and dumped her over the summit on the canyon road."

"Knowing her, why didn't you come forward?" Hi Lo asked.

Hale shrugged. "Why should I come forward? I didn't have anything to do with it. I was running a game right here that night. I can account for every minute of my time from nine o'clock until four o'clock in the morning. As it is, my wife won't even talk to me and I don't dare go home because two L.A. fly-cops are staked out across the street, wanting to ask questions that I don't know the answer to. And I have been through that mill before. They use gloves on a guy like Mr. Stanton because he has enough money to hire a high-price lawyer to sit in. But with a guy like me, it's different." Hale appealed to the gambling house owner. "You know how it goes, Mr. Childs."

"Yes," Childs admitted. "I do."

Stanton said, "This is all beside the point, Hale. I'm not accusing you of killing the girl. I don't think the police will. They're too eager to pin it on me. But it is possible you can help me. Think. During your relationship with Miss Turner, did you ever hear her mention my name?"

Hale shook his head. "No. I didn't, Mr. Stanton. And I was very surprised when I read in the paper that she had called you on the phone. To the best of my recollection she never mentioned you, although I will admit she did a lot of talking I didn't listen to most of it 'gimme—can't you get me' stuff. That dame would have swiped the whole supply depot if I'd let her have her way."

Taking his check book from his pocket, Stanton said, "Look. How much will you take to do me a favor?"

Hale was wary. "How big a favor?"

"I want you to tell Inspector Treech what you've told me. No more, no less. They may hold you for a few days. They may not. If they do I'll hire Ernie Goetz to pry you out as soon as he can. And I'll pay you fifty dollars a day for every day you spend in the pokey, plus any reasonable sum you name. It will be worth it to me to stop Treech from breathing down my neck."

The stick-man looked at his employer.

"It's up to you, Hale," Childs said. "You can strike a bargain with Stanton, or not, just as you please. But because he's been a good customer and I've known him for years, I'll throw this much in the kitty. I'll keep you on the payroll and hold your job open for two weeks."

Hale asked for a thousand dollars. For that much money he would go to Inspector Treech's office in the morning and make a clean breast of what little he knew of the affair. "My story may help you, it may not," he told Stanton. "But it can't get you in any more Dutch. Because the more I think about it the more positive I am that Grace never mentioned your name."

Stanton wrote a check for a thousand dollars and left the office slightly buoyed up by the turn of affairs.

More people had come in. Stanton saw a director whom he knew and turning to wave at him almost knocked down Johnny Hass. The camera-man was with a curvaceous chorus girl who had come to Hollywood to make good in pictures and her luck was holding. She had a house, a car, and a mink coat. Now if she could only get a part.

The girl grinned at him vacuously. Johnny said, "Hi ya, Bob. I see they haven't got you in the gas chamber yet."

Stanton assured him, "It's strictly an oversight on Inspector Treech's part. Keep your eyes on the obit column." He walked on with Hi Lo toward the table at which Joy was sitting. Joy was drinking, winning, and happy. She had almost tripled her chips. More, she was no longer alone. Lyle Ferris was hovering at her elbow.

At the table, Stanton asked, "How are you doing, honey?"

Her grin was gamin. "Fine. I almost have my five thousand back."

"And you?" Stanton asked the actor. "What are you doing out here, Lyle?"

"Looking for you," the actor said. "I dropped by Joy's place to talk over the new script with her and when Beulah said you had gone to Childs' in a foursome I figured it wouldn't be too much of an intrusion if I tagged along. Frankly, I'd like to talk to you about the script. Marty let me read it this afternoon. And I've read worse."

"Thank you," Stanton said. "Your words of praise overwhelm me. What have I done to deserve all this?"

"Bob!" Joy reproved him without taking her eyes from the wheel. "Don't be like that. Lyle likes the script. He said so."

"That wasn't the way I tuned him in."

Coloring slightly, the leading man admitted, "Perhaps my choice of words was unfortunate. I do like the script. I like the story. I like the dialogue. There's a punch in every line."

"Then what's your beef?"

"Simply this. I think you weaken the whole picture by giving all those good lines in the capture scene to a secondary character instead of giving them to the chief protagonist."

Stanton was in no mood to discuss the niceties of writing. Tapping Ferris' dress shirt with a forefinger, he told him, "Look, Lyle. You're paid to do one thing. I'm paid to do another. I'll write. You act. Okay? And if that isn't satisfactory, take it up with J.V."

"I may do that," Ferris said. "This is my first starring picture. It can mean a lot to me. And just because you're afraid I may yet cut you out with Joy I don't see why punch lines that rightfully belong to me should be parceled out to secondary characters."

"Oh, so I let my personal feelings enter into my writing?"

"I think you have in this case."

Neither man realized their voices had risen to a pitch that was causing everyone in the room to turn and stare at them. A suave houseman clapped a friendly palm to both their backs. "Gentlemen. Please. Let's keep our voices down. And let's not mention ladies' names."

Stanton shrugged the hand off his back. "Why, you two-bit, penny-pinching, tab-show leading man. When you can cut me out with anyone, let alone Joy—"

"Bob!" Hi Lo said sharply.

Stanton didn't even hear him. Thrusting his face closer to Stanton's, Ferris said, "Oh. Now I'm a two-bit, penny-pinching, tab-show leading man, am I? Well, let me tell you something, you swollen-headed, illiterate literary ape. I was a leading man on Broadway when you—"

Later, no one was certain who had struck the first blow. Some said it was Stanton. Others said it was Ferris. One minute they were yelling at each other. The next Ferris spun off balance into a group of men at the next table while blood spurted from Stanton's nose. Recovering quickly, the leading man returned to the attack.

After that things were confused. The housemen joined the melee. Ferris punched at Stanton when he could and at any houseman in between them when he couldn't. Stanton did the same. A happy smile on his face, Hi Lo battled housemen exclusively. It was the houseman with the sap who finally got to him. Hi Lo's grin expanded as Stanton landed a second hard blow to the leading man's already closing eye, contracted sharply as Ferris came back with a right to Stanton's jaw that caused his knees to sag and his eyes to glaze. Then the houseman, seeing his chance, swung the sap in a vicious arc that ended behind one of Hi Lo's ears.

Stanton knew he was sitting in the open door of a car on what would have been a running board if his new Packard had had running boards. He vaguely remembered Joy standing in front of him and cursing him up one side and down the other in pure, unexpurgated, Five-Points Brooklynese. But he didn't remember leaving the gambling room.

He dropped his hand to his lap and picking it up, Patton guided his finger back up under his nose again. "No. Keep it there, Mr. Stanton. It will stop bleeding soon."

From the back seat of the car Hi Lo, still slightly fogged, quoted, "Venus, Saturn, Jupiter, Mars. Holy smoke, Mother, look at the stars."

One of the group of housemen waiting in the shadows of the shrubbery bordering the parking space stepped forward and tapped Patton's shoulder. "Okay. They're both conscious. Get 'em in the car and get 'em out of here. You drive."

Patton helped Stanton to his feet and into the car. The doorman called and said Childs said to get their cards. "I already did," the houseman said. "I made the private eye fish 'em out of their wallets." He added, as Patton slipped behind the wheel and sat a moment familiarizing himself with the controls, "Come on. Get going, chum. And when they're awake enough to understand you, you tell Mr. Stanton and the big Indian not to come back, that they ain't welcome."

Hi Lo sat erect. "Ah. A ray of brightness in the gloom. That should save me a lot of money. What happened to Ferris?"

"He got the same dose," Patton said as he eased the car out of the drive and onto the highway. "They took his card away from him and told him not to come back any more. He drove off under his own power but I don't see how he did it. He had an eye on him that stuck out like a purple plum."

Stanton moaned. "And Marty starts shooting tomorrow."

"Marty intended to start shooting tomorrow," Hi Lo corrected him. "Lyle won't look normal for two weeks."

Stanton waggled his jaw experimentally. "I'm a cream puff alongside of him. Can that guy punch! What branch of the Army was Lyle in?"

"He was a Ranger, I think."

"I don't doubt that at all." Stanton asked Patton if Joy had left in Lyle's car.

"No," Patton said. "She gave him the same dose she gave you. Only he was conscious and could hear her. She blistered him front and back. Then she asked a stocky guy with a blackhaired bimbo with over-size bazooms if she could ride home with them."

"Probably Johnny Hass," Stanton decided. "He was there with that Stillson moron. Well, I guess this really tears it as far as the studio is concerned. Think we can make a living raising horses, Hi Lo?"

Patton wanted to know what the fight was about.

"I don't know," Stanton admitted. "Ferris said something nasty to me. I said something nastier to him. And the next thing I knew we were trading punches. How did you get into it, Hi Lo?"

"One of the housemen pulled a sap."

"But how about Hale?" Patton asked. "Did you get his address?"

"We did better than that. He was there. We talked to him." Stanton told Patton what Hale had said and what he had paid him a thousand dollars to do.

The cold wind felt good on Stanton's battered face. Low in the sky an elongated cloud formed a handle for the crescent moon and transformed it into a sickle. The speeding wheels gave him a feeling of suspension, of living on borrowed time.

Hi Lo turned around on the seat. "We're being followed."

Patton glanced in the rear-vision mirror. "It's probably Bill Swen and Matt Kelly. I saw them parked down the road a ways from Childs'. It being out of their jurisdiction, I imagine it's just a fishing tail Inspector Treech has put on Mr. Stanton."

"A fishing tail?" Stanton puzzled

"Yes. Treech is hoping you'll lead him to something. But it doesn't mean a thing. And I wouldn't let it worry me if I were you."

"Oh. You wouldn't. Well, that's nice. But it worries me." Stanton rode, scowling at the landscape, and trying to review the situation in the light of the night's brawl. Had Lyle deliberately picked a fight or was it just one of those things where two hot tempers ignited spontaneously? Had Lyle reason to fear or hate him? Lyle had no alibi for the night Grace Turner had been murdered. He *said* he was with some woman whom he refused to name. And Lyle had been in London. He could have known the dead girl. But so could Johnny Hass. He remembered seeing a whole spread in *Life* or *Look* or some similar magazine of the bomb destruction of London as photographed by Johnny Hass. Johnny was a chaser and not delicate in his tastes. Both men had been at the table when Grace Turner had phoned him. But so had Lou Saunders and Ed Wilcox. Their alibis for the murder night were just as weak. One had been looking for a drunk he couldn't find. The other refused to say where he had been. Both Lou and Ed had also been in London. Wilcox imported a lot of English talent. Lou had been a war correspondent. Stanton, reluctantly, put the thought aside that one of them might have killed the girl. The dead girl had known him. She had called him by name. She had prefaced her threat by saying she had seen him enter the Silver Pheasant. In an attempt to think for whom the dead girl might have mistaken him, he tried to recall who had been in the restaurant that day and gave it up as hopeless. Almost all of the gang at Consolidated ate at the Silver Pheasant from the lowest paid director up to Marty Manson and J.V.

He sighed and Patton, slowing the car, asked if they wanted him to stop at a bar so they could take a few drinks to perk them up before they headed into the hills.

"The hills?" Stanton asked stupidly.

"To see Hanson," Patton explained. "I presume you still want to see him."

"Oh, yes, Hanson," Stanton said. "Of course I want to see Hanson. But I don't need a drink. How about you, Hi Lo?"

Hi Lo said he believed he could wait until they got home. "In fact I would prefer to," he admitted. "I want to look in a mirror before I take a drink to make certain it won't run out the back of my head...."

There was a light in Hanson's living room this time. Hanson wearing a dressing gown and slippers, admitted them. "Good grief! What happened to you fellows? And not that I'm not glad to see you, but what's the idea of calling at this time of night? Sato said you were here earlier, Mr. Stanton, and I called your ranch to find out what you wanted. But all the information I could get from your housekeeper was that you were 'oudt.'"

"And how I was!" Stanton said. "Look, Hanson. I'll be brief. Inspector Treech has cooked up a new theory. He claims we're acting in collusion. He claims I picked up the girl at eleven instead of twelve o'clock and that I had her body in the trunk of my car when I 'put on' a drunk act at Sherry's. His theory is that you saw her get into my car at the earlier hour and I am laying plenty on the line for you to set up the hour."

"But that is preposterous," Hanson said. "The girl was alive and drinking with me at eleven forty-five. Both the desk clerk and the barman at the Hollywood-Highland should be able to so testify. I *know*, it was midnight when she got into the car. And I'll kiss the Bible on that in any court from a justice of the peace up to the Appellate."

"And the man driving my car?"

"Could have been you," Hanson lied. "I didn't see his face. But Inspector Treech hasn't a blade of grass to stand on. He's just trying to pull a fast one on you, Mr. Stanton. If you were in Mr. Manson's car at midnight you *couldn't* have killed the girl." Hanson apologized. "But I am forgetting my duties as host. I am sure you gentlemen would like a drink."

It was easier to accept one than refuse. Stanton sipped his highball, listening to the lawyer babble about the view, the construction, and the furnishings of his new home. Hanson stroked an expensive combination radio and record changer lovingly. "Living in a hotel all my life, I have always dreamed of a place like this. And now I have it."

"When did you buy it?" Hi Lo asked.

"Yesterday," Hanson told him. "And I moved into it today." He chuckled. "I suppose that is one of the reasons Inspector Treech thinks I am putting the bite on Stanton. But the fact of the matter is I've looked for a place like this for a long time. I like to know it was once owned by a star. I like to walk out on the terrace and see stars both above and below me. It gives me a comfortable feeling."

"It should," Patton needled him. "You have lived off stars for years."

Hanson wasn't insulted. "What's the matter, Patton? Jealous? There is nothing wrong with star dust. It spends just the same as any other kind. Believe me." He grinned. "Besides, I would rather—"

Stanton got to his feet and put his half-emptied glass on a coaster. "Yes. I know. We've all heard that boast before."

"Well, thanks anyway," Stanton said. "I'm glad you were on that corner when you were."

Hanson's words, silky, oily, somehow vividly indecent, followed them out the door. "Yes. So am I."

CHAPTER 7

For a time the weather was so bad it was thought all flights would have to be canceled. The sky was low and ugly and spiked on the uneven spires of the taller buildings of Manhattan. Toward plane time, however, the ceiling lifted and the sun shining through a rift in the clouds dissipated most of the fog and burnished the silver wings and body of the four-motored transport plane that had been jockeyed out onto the runway.

There was so much to see, so much to do. His eyes shining, Robin raced from the barrier to where Eve sat in the waiting room and back to the barrier again so many times Eve had lost count.

She and Winston Churchill were alone when the loud speaker announced the nine o'clock flight for Los Angeles would take off as scheduled, almost simultaneously with the same announcement concerning the first morning plane for Miami.

There was an immediate and audible stir and bustle in the waiting room. The sweet-voiced stewardess had promised to come for them. But would she? Would she remember? And where was Robin? Eve pleated her handkerchief nervously. She had come so far. Everything was so strange and new. Everything was in such a hurry. Even Winston Churchill, for once, had lost his usual aplomb and self-sufficiency and seemed confused.

She sat a moment longer in indecision. then got to her feet and one hand gripping Winston Churchill's harness, moved away from the bench on which she had been sitting only to collide with a stout woman hurrying for the Miami plane.

"Why don't you watch where you're going?" the woman snapped. "What's the matter? Are you blind?"

"Yes," Eve said quietly. "I am."

The voice was no longer harsh. It was liquid with swift tears and very contrite. "Oh, my dear. I am so sorry. I didn't know. I didn't notice your dog...."

Emerging from the cool green water of the pool, Stanton toweled vigorously and combed his hair in one of the poolside cabanas. Then, putting on a shantung robe with a large red dragon embroidered on its back, he padded barefooted to the patio and ate a substantial breakfast while Maria beamed approval. The past two weeks had been unproductive as far as new light being cast on the Grace Turner affair but Stanton had lost some of the feeling of having a sword suspended over his head by a hair. He was still being shadowed. Bill Swen and Matt Kelly, working in eight-hour shifts with four other detectives whose names he did not know, went everywhere he did. There was a twenty-four-hour stake-out on the front

gate of the ranch. But so far, at least, Inspector Treech seemed content to
let it go at that.

Stanton was satisfied with the status quo. If Inspector Treech hoped to
wear his nerves thin to the point of confession by constant surveillance,
the attempt was doomed to failure. He couldn't confess. He hadn't killed
the girl. He didn't even know her. The one and only time that he had seen
her had been in the morgue.

Finished with his breakfast, Hi Lo began opening the morning mail,
throwing most of it into the waste basket and neatly stacking the remain-
der.

"Anything new or important?" Stanton asked.

Hi Lo said, "At long last, among other things, your obituary." He handed
Stanton a sheet of expensive bond typewriter paper bearing the embossed
letter-head—

CONSOLIDATED PICTURES
Office of the President

"After letting you stew in your own juice these past two weeks, J.V.
wouldst have the pleasure of a tête-à-tête with you at three o'clock this
afternoon. The service will be private. P.O.E."

"Please omit flowers," Stanton sighed.

"No," Hi Lo corrected him. "Practically out. Fired. But why take it so
hard? You knew it was coming. You knew that after the dressing down he
gave Lyle, the old man would get to you when he had cooled down enough
to talk coherently. By hanging that shiner on Lyle and holding up production you committed the unpardonable sin. You cost him a chamber pot full
of money."

"Okay," Stanton growled. "Don't rub it in. I'm sorry I clipped Lyle. Believe
it or not, I like the guy. And he was right about those punch lines in the
capture scene. They do belong to him and I've sent Marty a revised shooting script."

Hi Lo poured the last of the coffee in his cup. "You have a good friend in
Marty. He likes you and he'll go to bat for you. He told me so yesterday. But
if I were you I would make my peace with Joy and take her with me to the
interview with J.V. Marty is only the old man's son-in-law. But Joy is his
biggest box-office draw and if she crosses that pretty padding over her
heart and promises that you will be a good boy from now on, J.V. will
think two or three times before getting in wrong with her by canceling
your contract. Do you want me to see if I can get her on the phone?"

Stanton thought for a moment, then shook his head. "No. I would rather
you didn't. I like Joy. I can't think of anything more wonderful than hav-

ing an affair with her." He got up and paced the patio. "But stars don't have affairs any more. It says so right in their contracts. And being married to Joy, well, it's not even marriage as I see it. When I do get married I want children, and a wife who isn't mentally sizing up every good-looking lug she sees as my possible successor. No. I'd rather you didn't phone her."

"Okay. Joy is out." Hi Lo slit another envelope, skimmed through the report it contained, then glanced at the attached bill. "But one more thing before you dress. How long do you intend paying the James R. Patton Agency forty dollars a day plus expenses for sending us rehashes of the previous day's report?"

"I wouldn't say that," Stanton defended Patton. "At least he keeps us informed as to what is going on in Inspector Treech's office. And he's moving around. He may turn up something. And I'm not out of this thing yet. I don't know why I'm worrying about a contract with a murder rap hanging over my head."

"It's your money. But plus the fifty dollars a day you promised Hale for every day the police held him it adds up to better than one hundred dollars a day. I thought Ernie was going to spring Hale."

Stanton sighed. "He has been trying to. But every time he gets a writ Inspector Treech or Jim Reisler persuades the judge that the retention of Hale is necessary to their investigation and the writ is denied. Treech is just stalling of course in the hope that Hale will get his belly so full of jail that in order to get out he will manage to remember something connecting me with the dead girl."

Reading Patton's report, Hi Lo admitted, "You may be right about Patton. He has established the fact that Jimmy the waiter at the Silver Pheasant is one of Hanson's stooges. According to this, Hanson has them spotted all around town, waiters, doormen, cab drivers, desk clerks, bellboys. He pays a standard fee of a ten-spot for any information he may consider worth looking into."

"Shad knew about the phone call then?"

"So it would seem. And, in that case, Shad was deliberately waiting in the lobby or the bar of the Hollywood-Highland for the Turner girl to come downstairs and keep her date. He undoubtedly figured by the way she talked over the phone that she must have something on you he could use."

"That damn phone call."

"It seems to be the crux of the whole affair." The big Indian massaged his right fist with the palm of his left hand. "Maybe I ought to beat the hell out of Shad. He knows plenty. And he's getting plenty from someone."

Stanton said he doubted force would get them anywhere but in a detention cell at the Malibu Sheriff's Sub-Station. They couldn't prove Shad was lying when he said he hadn't recognized the man at the wheel of the car. True, he was a rat. But he wasn't a physical coward. A beating would be nothing new in his life. More, Shad knew if he did talk and blackmail could be proven against him he would face a long prison term. If he *had* recognized the man, if he knew who had murdered Grace Turner, he was guilty not only of blackmail but also of being an active accessory after the fact of murder. Besides, it was only Hanson's insistence that it had been midnight when Grace Turner had gotten into the car later identified as his that was restraining the District Attorney's office from indicting him...

Later events of the day were to prove Stanton's summation of Hanson's character correct. Patton was in Goetz's office when he reached it and the private agency man had two fresh tidbits of information. One was that Inspector Treech, unable to tap Hanson's phone or keep a constant shadow on him, had plucked the lawyer out of his office the preceding afternoon and had starred him in a twenty-hour back room questioning bee. However, the long session of intensive grilling, using all known modern methods of interrogation, and some methods not quite so modern, had failed to shake the lawyer's story. There had been nothing Inspector Treech could do but release him.

"Shad is one tough little cookie," Patton summed him up. "His story could be on the level but I doubt it. *I know* the waiter who plugged in that phone call at the Silver Pheasant is one of his stooges. And I can't forget his voice the night you said you were glad he was on the corner when he was and he said, 'Yes. So am I.'"

Goetz asked, "And this other information?"

Patton looked at Stanton. "It isn't so hot for our side. You were in the Army, weren't you, Mr. Stanton?"

"I was."

"You were a commissioned officer?"

"Yes. Because of my previous civilian flight experience I was commissioned a First Lieutenant in the Air Forces and was assigned to a British wing to observe their operational methods."

"This was when we first got into the war?"

"It was in the fall of 1941, three months before we officially entered the war. Why?"

The wrapper on Patton's cigar was loose. He sealed it with his tongue. "You would be surprised, Mr. Stanton," he said finally, "how a steady diet of bologna sausage and macaroni stewed in watery tomatoes can stimulate a man's memory. I'm afraid you made a mistake in paying Hale to surrender. He is beginning to remember things. Just this morning he recollected the story of some girl-friend of Grace who married an American Army officer early in the war and how Grace said his getting killed was a tough break for her friend because this officer was *very* wealthy and had promised to bring her to California where he had a big ranch and a swimming pool and all that went with it."

Goetz thought over the statement. "That doesn't sound so good."

Stanton felt his cheeks get hot. "Stop looking at me that way, Ernie. I never married anyone. I've spent most of my life trying not to get married." He asked Patton if Hale knew the name of the officer.

"He says not," Patton said. "He says it was just a casual reference by Grace one night when she was beefing about the difference in subsistence pay between officers and enlisted men and how her friend could have had such a nice life if the officer hadn't gotten killed."

"If he was killed," Stanton said, "that would seem to let me out."

"That was my first thought," Patton said. "But on checking through a collection of clippings on you in one of the newspaper morgues, I see you were shot down over Bremen in the fall of the same year and spent the rest of the war as a P.W. If you didn't or couldn't, write, this unnamed friend of Grace would naturally assume you had been killed. In fact, according to one of the clippings, you were officially listed as dead for six months."

"Look," Stanton said hotly. "Get this. And get it straight. I was never married to any English girl."

Patton was patient with him. "I am not saying you were. I am merely trying to reason the way Inspector Treech will reason. And here is the spot you are in. Hale says he doesn't remember this officer's name. That probably is the truth. But another week of bologna sausage and macaroni, no woman, fifty dollars a day piling up to his credit, a thousand dollars cash in his kick, and the outside world just filled with kosher corned beef, sirloin steaks, and blondes, and it is reasonable to assume his memory may receive another stimulus and he suddenly remembers the officer's name was Manton, or Danton, or possibly even Stanton."

Stanton ran his fingers through his hair. "And I paid that louse a thousand dollars to give himself up. So now what?"

"So now," Patton said, "all we can do is wait. But even if Hale does name you, before Inspector Treech can pin anything on you he will have to locate this other English girl and prove you were the lad who married her."

Stanton slumped back on his spine and tilted his hat over his eyes. "Nuts. How did I ever get into such a thing? There I was with my nose in my own bottle, minding my own business, and now—" He lay on the back of his neck scowling and blowing smoke at the ceiling.

Patton left shortly thereafter and Stanton's conversation with Goetz concerning the possible cancellation of his contract failed to brighten his mood. The lawyer could tell him little he didn't already know. In Goetz's opinion, his fight with Lyle Ferris and the subsequent holding-up of the shooting schedule until the actor's eye returned to its normal state did not constitute a breach of contract. However, J. V. Mercer was a law unto himself. If he decided to arbitrarily abrogate the contract he would do so, regardless of the legality of his action. Any legal fight thereafter would be both drawn out and expensive. Goetz's opinion was that the best thing Stanton could do was to eat humble pie and throw himself on J.V.'s mercy. The old man had been content to let Ferris off with a tongue-lashing that had reddened his ears but left him in possession of his contract. And if Stanton's new picture grossed an amount of money equal to that grossed by the last picture he had written, the chances were that his sin or sins would be forgiven. Goetz, too, advised him to ask Joy Parnell to intervene for him with Mercer.

"She'd do it in a minute, Bob. Joy is crazy about you. You should have seen the way she carried on the day you were arrested."

"You should have heard her cuss me out the other night."

"I suppose she had no reason to."

"Well," Stanton admitted, "possibly she did. But on due and sober and considerable reflection, I would rather not become further obligated to her."

"That's not a very nice remark to make."

"It's the way I feel."

Goetz asked, "What's the matter with you, Bob? Are you in love with some other dame or have you joined a male nunnery, or what? Eleven million G.I.s voted Joy the girl of their dreams. But who is Joy's pin-up boy? You are. At the moment Joy thinks you—"

"That's right. Right there," Stanton stopped him. "Those are the three fatal words—*at the moment.*" He walked to the door of the office. "Well, thanks for everything, Ernie. Put the advice and the lecture on my bill. And you had better send in your bill while I'm still able to pay it."

"Don't be juvenile," Goetz said. "You'll still be in the big sugar when I'm a broken down police court shyster."

Stanton sighed and closed the door behind him. His head ached. The interview had settled nothing. He looked sourly up and down the street and located Bill Swen and Matt Kelly reading a racing form in a police car parked in a loading zone. Then, realizing he was hungry, he got his own car from the parking lot and drove to the Vine Street Silver Pheasant, the police car loafing along behind him.

The Silver Pheasant, as usual, was crowded. Most of its clientele were radio and picture people who ate and met there regularly. Most of the picture people were from the Consolidated lot. As he crossed the walk, Stanton could see Marty Manson in a booth flanked by two minor studio executives. Ed Wilcox and Johnny Hass were holding down another booth arguing vehemently about something.

It was the first time Stanton had been in the restaurant since the day of Grace Turner's phone call. Sarah, the hat check girl, was the first to see him. Instead of greeting him with one of her flip witticisms and reaching for his hat, a slight frown crinkled her forehead, a pink tongue tip moistened her lips as if in indecision. Her silence proved infectious.

Stanton felt like a fool. "What's the matter?" he asked hotly. "Am I suddenly poison?"

Johnny Hass heard his voice and called, "Hi, ya, Bob. Come on over. I was hoping you'd drive into town today."

Wilcox seconded the invitation. Still the hush continued. Then Manson looked up from his plate and waving cordially called, "Don't go away until I see you, Bob. I'll be with you in a minute."

The spell was broken. God's right hand had spoken. Stanton was still a curly white lamb and in the fold. They could afford to know him. A dozen men and women greeted him cordially. Smiling now, Sarah reached for his hat but Stanton refused to give it up. "No, thank you. I'll sit on it and save a dollar. But your tipster must be slipping, Sarah. You want to get a more accurate Hooper rating before you put on the freeze next time." A sour taste in his mouth, he crossed to the booth where Johnny Hass and Wilcox were sitting.

"So you're back from the big town, eh?" he asked Wilcox.

The agent nodded, amused. "How do you like coventry, Bob?"

"Spelled with a capital C, I like it fine," Stanton said. "As a social exercise it has its drawbacks. Either the boys and girls have me confused with Jack The Ripper or someone has been reading J.V.'s outgoing mail."

Hass asked, "Why? You scheduled to go on the carpet?"

"This afternoon at three o'clock. But if you don't think the condemned man is going to eat a hearty meal, you're crazy." He ordered soup and a salad with corned beef and cabbage to follow.

Jimmy the waiter wanted to know what he was drinking.

"Ice water," Stanton told him. "That is my beverage at the Silver Pheasant from now on. I drank rye the last time I was in here and look what happened to me. And how is Shad today, Jimmy?"

The waiter shook his head. "I am sorry, Mr. Stanton, but I am not acquainted with anyone by that name."

Hass asked if there was anything new on the case.

"Not a thing," Stanton lied. "But while I think of it, Johnny. Thanks for taking Joy home the other night."

The cameraman laughed. "Think nothing of it. But you did play a dirty trick on me. I was doing all right with that Stillson babe until I had Joy dropped in my lap. But after she heard Joy curse you, and all other men, from one end of Laurel Canyon to the other, all I got out of the date was, 'Oh, I *do* thank you *so* much, Mr. Hass, for *a very* wonderful time.'"

Stanton finished his soup and began on his corned beef and cabbage. "Well, who knows? I may have saved you from getting shot."

"Who knows?" Hass laughed. "But what a wonderful way to die."

Lou Saunders slid into the booth across from Stanton. "Hello, killer. You still at large. Tch-tch. Such an ineffective police department."

"Cut it, Lou," Stanton said sharply. "That isn't funny."

He continued to eat but his appetite was gone. There was an undercurrent at the table he didn't like. There was a strained look in Ed Wilcox's eyes. Johnny's laughter was too loud. There was an edge to Lou Saunders' voice. Either they weren't too certain of his innocence or they had axes of their own to grind. He looked up to see Lyle Ferris standing at the table.

Again the babble of voices had died away. Manson was on his feet, a frown creasing his forehead as he looked apprehensively their way. Stanton got to his feet slowly. He knew what the others expected. He didn't intend it to happen even if the actor was still angry. "Hello, Lyle," he said quietly. "It was all my fault. Believe me, fellow. I'm sorry. And I apologize." He offered the actor his hand. For a moment he thought that Ferris was going to refuse it.

Instead, his own hand gripping Stanton's, Ferris smiled. "I'll be damned if you haven't done it again, Bob. Those were my lines. I rehearsed them all the way to the table. I, too, am sorry it happened. And if I hadn't been such a hot head—"

"Forget it," Stanton grinned. "Forget it, Lyle. Sit down."

Patting the perspiration from his forehead, Manson resumed his chair. Saunders wadded his napkin into a ball. "A love feast. A lousy love feast," he snorted. "And here I was all primed to see the second round. Couldn't I induce you fellows to take at least one punch at each other?" he tempted. "I'll put both your names in the paper."

"Not mine," Ferris said. "Not after that star chamber session I had with J. V. I don't ever want to have to go through anything like that again. I'm lucky to still be in Hollywood, let alone have a contract. What did he say to you, Bob?"

"He hasn't said it yet. I'm due to face the firing squad at three o'clock."

Hass scoffed. "Aw. J.V. isn't going to fire you. You've made too much money for the studio. You—"

He stopped talking as Marty Manson walked up to the table. Manson admitted, "Was that a relief to see you two fellows shake hands!" He picked up Stanton's glass of ice water and took a sip. "But the suspense was enough to give me heartburn. Anything new on the other matter, Bob?"

Stanton said there was not. "How about the old man? I'm out?"

Manson admitted, "You were the last time I talked to him. I tried to plead your past successful pictures, this new honey that you've written, and the enormous amount of money you have made for the studio. But, as you know, the old man is bull-headed, and he's all set to throw you off the lot and let you sue us for the balance of the money still due you on your contract. He says he can excuse Lyle because every actor or actress he has ever known had been emotionally, if not mentally, unbalanced. But he claims you should know better. Then, of course, there is the matter of the English girl and the amount of unfavorable publicity the studio has received because of her. In giving you your alibi I had to tell the truth about your condition. And that's another point against you. J.V. says he can't see what in the world a man in good health with a ranch like yours, a best seller to his credit, and a salary check of three thousand dollars a week, has to get drunk about. At least that drunk."

"It was the first time in my life I was ever that drunk," Stanton said. "But I don't suppose there is any use trying to tell him that."

"I would," Manson said. "Frankly, I don't quite get the old man's attitude. But if I were you, I'd put up every argument and the best fight that I could. You've been in the racket too long to quit it now. You need the studio. The studio needs you." He glanced at his watch. "Well, I have to be on my way." He looked around the restaurant to make certain he was observed, then offered Stanton his hand. "But just so I go on record. I'm still in there punching for you, Bob. And I have a few more angles I intend to try."

Stanton shook hands gracefully. "Thanks. Thanks a lot, Marty."

The producer chuckled. "Think nothing of it. It may at least keep some of the minor snipers away." He looked at the cameraman. "And I'll see you in a half hour, Hass."

When Manson had gone, Hass explained, "He wants me to take over the cameras on *Conquest*. But I don't know if I want the job or not. I'm none too fond of technicolor work."

Wilcox said, "I'm sorry it's to be that way, Bob. But, if it is, do you want me to put out some feelers to the other studios?"

Stanton shrugged. "I doubt that it would do any good, Ed. Once J.V. puts his knife in you the other boys are afraid to pull it out. He owns too many theatres. He has too many stars under contract. But it was damn white of Marty to go on record the way he did."

Saunders belittled the gesture. "You've made money for the studio and Marty is worried about his percentage. I hear that when they were married, Lili talked her old man into giving Marty ten per cent off the top so he could support her in the manner to which she has been accustomed since she was a punk with braces on her teeth. He didn't have a dime. He didn't even have a job. All he had was a good line."

Wilcox chuckled. "It must be slipping as far as Lili is concerned. You know when she was supposed to have flown to Miami last week?"

Hass was interested. "Yes?"

The agent confided, "Well, I'm not saying there was anything wrong. Maybe Marty knew all about her change of plans. But I happened to be in New York that week. And I saw her down in a little bistro in the Village with that new juvenile man who is going over so well at Metro."

Saunders said he would be damned and the conversation degenerated into an intimate discussion of Lili Mercer's love life and affairs before she had married Marty Manson.

Keeping out of the conversation, Stanton ordered his first drink of the day. *They act,* he thought, *like small boys back of a barn. And I have been just as bad.* He sat sipping his drink, studying the faces of the four men, an ugly thought tapping at his mind, a thought so basic and simple he wondered why he hadn't entertained it before.

Three of the men, at least, were promiscuous in their relationships with women. Wilcox was reputed to be in love with his wife, a charming and lovable woman. But all four men were familiar with London. During the war all four had worn a uniform of one sort or another. Three of them were wealthy. Two of them had small ranches. Besides, wealth was an easy thing for almost any European, accustomed to their own meager scale of living, to attribute to any American.

In her phone call Grace Turner had said she had seen him enter the Silver Pheasant. *What if it were a case of mistaken identity, not of person but of name? What if Hale's recently remembered story was fact? What if one of the four men sitting at the table, unwilling or unable to use his own name, had borrowed his name to consummate a marriage of convenience with some, as yet unidentified, English girl?*

Wilcox was married. Ferris was in love with Joy. Hass valued his freedom and boasted of the fact. Saunders—Saunders was a problem. Somewhere in his life there was some deep tragedy that gnawed constantly at his liver.

Stanton's mind raced on. *All four men had enough money to attract Shad Hanson's professional attention. All of them knew he was drinking. All of them had heard the phone call. None of them had alibis for the night on which Grace Turner had died. Any one of them could have followed him to Sherry's. Any one of them could have used his car to meet the girl. Any one of them could have killed her.*

Carrying a portable phone, Jimmy the waiter interrupted Stanton's train of thought. "Pardon me, Mr. Stanton, but you have a call." He reached across the table to plug in the phone.

Johnny Hass got to his feet, looking at his watch. "If I am to see Marty

I'll have to scram. Holy smoke! Where does time go?"

The words sounded vaguely familiar. As Stanton accepted the phone from the waiter be wondered where he had heard them. Then he remembered. This was where he had come in. Business, page, and direction, the scene was identical with that of the afternoon preceding the midnight murder. It might have been a retake. He said, "Bob Stanton," into the phone, half-expecting a ghostly voice to answer.

There was nothing ghostly about it. Joy's voice, warm and intimate, plainly audible to the other men at the table, oozed out of the receiver and wrapped itself around him.

"Oh, my poor dear," she sympathized. "You poor darling boy. Marty just phoned and told me what J.V. intends to do. But I'm not going to allow it. I'll meet you in J.V.'s office at three."

Before he could protest she blew a kiss into the phone and hung up.

Saunders slumped lower on his spine. "Come home, darling. All is forgiven. I'll be damned if some guys don't have all the luck."

Ferris sat scowling at his coffee cup.

"Fine," Hass enthused. "That's fine. If Joy lays down the law, J.V. won't dare to fire you. That ought to make you feel pretty good, eh?"

"Yeah," Stanton said. "Sure. I feel fine."

But he didn't. He felt trapped.

CHAPTER 8

It was fifteen minutes of three when Flora, Marty Manson's secretary, was getting a drink at the water cooler in the hall. She said, "You look quite composed for a man on his way to the guillotine, Mr. Stanton."

"I am a firm believer in last minute reprieves," he told her. "And I hear there may be one in this case."

She smiled. "I've heard a similar rumor. But it hasn't gotten out of this office so far."

"Joy isn't here yet?"

"Not yet, Mr. Stanton. I believe Miss Parnell was in her pool when Mr. Manson phoned her. Mr. Manson talked and talked to J.V. without it doing a bit of good. Then he thought of phoning Miss Parnell."

His self-assurance fading, Stanton walked up the short flight of Carrara marble stairs to the door of J. V. Mercer's outer office wishing that Marty Manson had kept his nose in his own business. He had been reconciled to losing his contract. He had been going to do big things—some day. Now he was back in the same old rut, he hoped.

Miss Benson, J.V.'s confidential secretary, looked up from her desk as he entered the sparsely furnished ante-room.

"Oh, yes, Mr. Stanton," she said pleasantly. "Mr. Mercer will see you shortly."

Stanton sat in a chair by the window and picked a late edition newspaper from the tidy small pile on the table. Another psychopath had confessed to the murder of Grace Turner. This was the fourth youth to confess. Unfortunately this one, like the others, could not have killed the girl. On the night she had been murdered he had been serving the last of a thirty-day sentence for vagrancy in a cell in Lincoln Heights.

He got up from the chair, looked out the window for a moment, then began to pace the ante-room slowly. At the end of one of his turns, Miss Benson asked, "Remarkable how it stays so warm, isn't it?"

"Yes. Isn't it?" Stanton agreed.

He felt put upon. He was facing the lethal chamber and she talked about the weather. Fearful Miss Benson might think nervousness over his coming interview with J.V. was motivating his pacing, he returned to his chair. So J.V. fired him. So what? He wasn't particularly concerned what happened in that direction. He didn't care if Joy didn't show up. As a matter of fact, the more he thought about allowing Joy to front for him, the less he liked it. It would be the first time he had ever hidden behind a woman's skirts. He got up and asked Miss Benson, "I wonder if I could see Mr. Mercer right away? "

She looked at the clock on her desk. "But it's only four minutes of three, Mr. Stanton. Your appointment is at three. Besides, I believe Mr. Mercer is speaking with the manager of our branch office in Manila."

His hand on the knob of the inner office door, Stanton promised, "I'll wait quiet like a mouse right inside the door until he finishes his conversation. And if Miss Parnell should show up before I come out again—"

"Yes?" Miss Benson asked uncertainly.

"Tell her I haven't gotten here yet. Tell her anything you want but keep her out of the office. Savvy?"

Miss Benson got to her feet. "No. I don't, Mr. Stanton. And this is very irregular. Really, I can't allow—"

Stanton put a finger of one hand to his lips as he turned the door knob with his other hand. "Shh. Remember he is talking to Manila."

Closing the door quietly behind him, he leaned against it. He had been in the inner sanctum, often. It never failed to impress him. On the lot, on the street, behind a board of directors' table, at a story conference, Mercer, as far as appearance was concerned, could be a thin-lipped, successful, down-East banker who had pyramided a codfish and a pint of maple syrup into untold millions. But here a tasseled red tarboosh topped his two hundred-dollar custom-tailored suits.

The furnishings smacked of his Syrian mother and her boasted Persian blood. There were priceless gold-hilted scimitars. Ewers of chased and complicated silverware stood in frescoed niches beside rainbow-colored glazed earthenware vessels from Persia, enigmatic icons of Byzantium, and ancient Korans of intricate calligraphy. The furnishings were fat silk pads and great round elongated double pillows.

Mercer was speaking into one of the phones on his desk. As Stanton listened he said, "Yes... Yes... Yes... Yes... No," and hung up. Then, after glancing at his watch, he became aware of Stanton's presence. "You are a minute and three-quarters early, Stanton. Miss Parnell is in the anteroom?"

"What made you think that?"

Loading his ebony and silver cigarette holder, Mercer lighted the cigarette in a small flame burning in a copper bowl on his desk. "I have ways of hearing things. Well?"

Stanton walked slowly toward the desk. This wasn't going to be too pleasant. He had always liked and admired the old pirate. "Well, about my contract, J.V.," he began. "I don't want there to be any hard words or hard feelings about it. Outside of this last debacle that held up the shooting schedule I think you have had your money's worth out of me. For my part, I feel you have always been very generous."

The old man seemed slightly surprised. "Oh."

"I was wrong," Stanton continued. "After the years I have been in the game I should have known better than to clip an actor scheduled to begin a new picture in the morning."

"You were drunk?"

"No. I haven't even that excuse. I just got mad. My only excuse, if it is one, is that everything has been at sixes and sevens with me lately."

"Meaning the affair of the English girl?"

Mercer allowed twin spirals of smoke to curl upward from his thin nostrils. "Oh, yes. I dined with Marty and Lili the other night and Marty said the police have a new theory. That Inspector—"

"Treech, " Stanton offered.

"Yes. That's the name. Marty says the Inspector now claims you shot the girl at an earlier hour and had concealed the body in the trunk of your car before you simulated being so intoxicated Marty had to drive you home."

Stanton grinned. "I wasn't simulating intoxication. I was stinking drunk, Mr. Mercer. I was never so drunk in my life. I hope never to be so drunk again."

Mercer sucked at his holder. "The Grace Turner affair, of course, hasn't done the studio any good. Then there is this present instance, your fight with Ferris. I assume from what you have said, however, that you feel and acknowledge your guilt and that if the studio does abrogate your contract you have no intention of suing us for any movies you may feel due you."

"That is correct."

"You admit full responsibility for the fight and disfigurement of Ferris that cost the studio thousands and thousands of dollars in time lost and additional salaries?"

"I do."

"And that is all you have to say?"

"I don't know what else I can say."

"Then I'll do the talking," Mercer said. He came out from behind his desk, pausing briefly to finger a silk cushion. "In the first place, let me say this. If you had walked in that door with Joy Parnell beside you to intercede and beg and plead for you, you would have walked right out again even if Joy had walked with you. I don't like men who use their women's minds, or bodies, or prestige, to shield them. It smacks too much of the harlot's bully, a trade always abhorrent to men of my blood line. And I'm glad it didn't happen. Because I like you, Stanton."

"Thank you, sir."

The producer walked slowly to the far end of the office before turning. "In fact, I once had great hopes of you. May I speak candidly?"

"I wish you would, sir."

"As I used to say as a spieler for a carnival with which I was once connected, the following information is for your entertainment, edification, and amusement. My decision to drop you from the Consolidated payroll was not concerned with either the Grace Turner affair nor your fight with Lyle Ferris. The unfavorable publicity attached to your name means nothing. Who the hell ever looks to see who wrote anything? They like it, or they don't.

"As to the hopes I had for you," Mercer continued. "You are no great intellect. You are no genius. Both you and I know that. But we also know you have an earthy, lovable quality to your writing, a feeling for fundamentals. You know both story and human values. You haven't written one picture for me on which we haven't grossed a considerable amount of money." He puffed softly at his holder, continued. "For years I have said to myself, 'Stanton is going to do it but he isn't quite ready yet. He's young. He has to live. He has to learn. He has to be hurt. But some day he is going to write me a story.'" He made a disdainful gesture with his holder. "Not this, pardon it, crap, that you seemingly can turn out of a typewriter as fast as you can hit the keys." His voice took on an almost mystical quality. "But a story. A real story. *The* story. The story I have dreamed for years that one of my writers would write and I would produce and we might make a million dollars or we might not make a dime and we wouldn't care because we had created something real and beautiful that had helped the world and justified our existence.

"When you came out of the Army and published your book, *Men Back of Wire*, I said to myself as I read it, 'He's grown up. He's beginning to think. It won't be too long now before he writes *the* story.'" The aged producer picked a carbon copy of the shooting script of *Conquest* from his desk and thumbed through it with distaste. "And what do I get from you? Robin Hood in French pants panting after Cinderella the umpteenth on a mythical Spanish Main." He dropped the script back on his desk. "Maybe I'll fire you yet. I would if I didn't think that some day you might write that picture."

Holding his thumb and forefinger an inch apart, Stanton said soberly, "I feel about that big, J.V. But I would like to have a whack at that picture. That's been a part of my trouble, and the reason for my drinking. I have been groping for something, a sense of reality, a reason for living."

"Good. Good," the producer nodded. "Those are growing pains. You stay on the payroll. You—" He stopped as the door of the office opened.

Joy was indignant with Miss Benson. "Why, you deceitful thing, I *thought* I heard Bob's voice."

She posed a moment, her demure, long black faille skirt and long-sleeved, high-necked, wasp-waisted white shirtwaist counter-balanced by her flushed face and still slightly wet and hastily combed hair. Together, they gave her a charming, if somewhat wanton, appearance. Then, crossing the office to Stanton, she put her arms around his neck and stood on tiptoe to kiss him. "I'm sorry, so sorry, honey. I didn't mean to say the nasty things I said the other night. And I didn't mean to be late in getting here. I started in plenty of time." Indignation almost overcame her. "But a nasty old motorcycle policeman was just perfectly horrid to me on Wilshire Boulevard because, hurrying as I was, I didn't happen to look at my speedometer and notice I was doing ninety."

Mercer held out his hand. "Come. Give J.V. the ticket."

"I haven't any ticket," Joy said scornfully. "After the officer refused to take the fifty dollars I offered him to be sensible about it, I told him what I thought of him and tore the ticket up and threw it in his face. Then he tried to get tough, and I kicked him."

Sighing, J.V. walked to the office door. "Will you contact the legal department, Miss Benson, and ask them to find out just what the charges against Miss Parnell are and where she will need to be represented?"

Ignoring the certain damage to the primly starched ruffles on her shirtwaist, Joy snuggled closer to Stanton's chest. "Were you worried because I didn't get here, sweetheart?"

Looking over her head at Mercer, he said, "Well, I—I wondered."

Mercer winked.

"Well, it's all right now," Joy said. "At least it had better be. Bob is awfully sorry. Really he is, J.V. And he won't ever do it again." Her eyes narrowed slightly. "Besides, if he goes, so do I. You can take your old contract and you know what you can do with it."

"Oh, now, Joy," Mercer played out the game. "You mustn't even think a thing like that. But if you feel *that* strongly about it—"

"I do."

"Well, in that case," Mercer conceded, "I suppose there is only one thing I can do."

"See?" Joy turned triumphantly to Stanton. "I knew I could fix it." Slipping out of his arms, she kissed the producer's cheek. "You are a darling, J.V., and I love you. Of course not as much as I do Bob." She beamed at him. "Because Bob and I are going to be married just as soon as we can, aren't we, Bob?"

The little blackmailer, he thought. *She is as bad in her way as Shad Hanson.* "Yeah. Sure. Just as soon as we can," he agreed. "And when we leave here it might be a smart idea to drive down to Inspector Treech's office and see if we can't get his permission to fly to Phoenix, even if I have to pay the plane fare of a couple of his watch dogs."

Joy thought it a splendid idea. "And don't you worry, J.V. I'll be back in plenty of time to start the new picture Monday morning. We'll spend our honeymoon at home. And everything *is* all right?"

"You aren't angry with Bob any more for fighting with Lyle?"

"No. I'm not angry," he said. "But keep in mind what I told you about that next picture, Stanton."

Stanton insisted on shaking hands. "I will. And thanks a million."

"Don't mention it," Mercer said dryly. "I'm always glad to do Joy a favor."

When they had gone, he walked to the window of the ante-room, waited until they appeared in the parking lot, argued briefly over which car to use, then drove off in Joy's car. "Stanton's all right," he told Miss Benson. "He's sound. He's going to write me that picture yet."

Miss Benson was skeptical. "When?"

"A month from now. Two months. Not more than six. That's as long as Joy's marriages ever last."

Miss Benson answered the ring of her phone, then cupping her hand over the mouthpiece, she said, "It's the legal department calling back. Joy has been cited for speeding, reckless driving, blocking traffic, using profane language to an officer, attempting to bribe an officer, and they think the would-be arresting officer is holding back a resisting an arrest charge because he intends to file civil suit against Joy for feloniously and maliciously, and without due provocation, kicking him in a, well, an indelicate portion of his anatomy."

Leaning his head against the window frame, Mercer swore softly in Greek, switched to Syrian, added a few choice tidbits in Arabic and Yiddish, then appealed to the cloudless sky in English. "How did I ever get into such a business?"

Swinging back to Miss Benson, he leveled his cigarette holder at her. "Well, why are you just sitting there? Tell the legal department to get busy. Do you want Joy to be arrested?"

The office was small and hot. The straight-backed chairs were uncomfortable. They were told Inspector Treech was expected to return any moment but they had waited for an hour when he finally appeared, the inevitable clip board in one hand. He asked pleasantly if Stanton had dropped in to dictate a confession but didn't seem greatly disappointed when Stanton pooh-poohed the idea.

Joy smiled dazzlingly. "It's just that we want to be married. And we want to take a night plane for Phoenix. It is all right with you, isn't it, Inspector?"

"No," Inspector Treech told her.

Joy wanted to know why not. "We'll be back by tomorrow night. We don't intend to stay in Phoenix. Not that it isn't a very nice town. It is. But

I have to be on the lot Monday morning and I thought it would be a nice idea if we did come back tomorrow night and throw a big party out at Bob's ranch and have all our friends be happy with us. And of course we would want you and Mrs. Treech to come."

Seating himself at his desk, Inspector Treech said he appreciated the invitation but he and Mrs. Treech seldom went out nights, and then only to the home of immediate friends.

"Why keep riding me, Treech?" Stanton asked. "You know I didn't kill the girl. Your theory is all cockeyed. I'm not paying Hanson a dime."

"Someone is," Treech said. "He didn't buy that new house of his with what he had in the bank before Miss Turner was murdered. And, by the way, Stanton. Thanks for paying young Hale to turn himself in. He doesn't know much but what he does know is apt to prove quite helpful."

Stanton asked, "What happens if I try to leave town?"

"I'll have you arrested."

"On what charge?"

Inspector Treech pointed out he wouldn't need any specific charge to pick him up for further investigation. He slipped a warrant from his clip board. "But I could change the John Doe to Robert Stanton and use this one if I had to." He tossed the warrant across his desk.

Stanton protested, "But this is a warrant for arson. What did I ever torch off?"

"Read the warrant," Treech said. "It specifically mentions your mountain hide-out and quite a portion of the Oak-Ridge mountainside. Working with the Mountain Patrol, the boys on the Arson Squad have proven that fire to be of a definite incendiary nature."

"Of course it was," Stanton said. "I've explained how that happened a dozen times."

"Yeah. Sure. I know. Toward morning you heard a noise. You stepped outside to investigate. Someone slugged you. When you regained consciousness the cabin was on fire."

"That's the truth."

Treech retrieved the warrant and returned it to his clip board. "So you say. But go ahead. Try to leave town. However, I don't see why you can't be patient. If Hale keeps on remembering things the way he has, we should arrive at a motive for the murder of Grace Turner and have this case wrapped up in a few more days."

"Pretty please, Inspector," Joy made one last attempt. "Won't you let Bob fly to Phoenix if we take two of your detectives with us?"

Inspector Treech remained courteous but unrelenting. He had, as he frankly admitted, no legal jurisdiction over Stanton's movements. But he preferred that he didn't leave town.

"But what new developments could there possibly be?" Joy asked.

Treech was very vague. "Oh, let's say certain information that has come into our possession from a certain source."

Stanton took the bull by the horns. "Look, Treech. I won't tell you how I know. But I do know what Hale has remembered. He has remembered Grace Turner once told him that some unnamed friend of hers was married during the early days of the war to some unnamed American officer who was reputed to be wealthy and who was killed shortly thereafter. But I wasn't that officer."

Inspector Treech shrugged. Then, his phone ringing, he excused himself and ignoring Stanton and Joy, he talked at length to someone concerning a man named Eposita who allegedly had knifed a man named Garcia during a card game. The lengthening afternoon shadows brought no coolness to the office. It was hot and sticky. Joy's freshly laundered shirtwaist was limp and wilted. She began to drum her fingers on the desk. Recognizing the danger signals, Stanton got her out of the office. "The hell with it," he said. "Come on. We'll figure out some other way to get married." In the lobby of the building he suggested, "Why don't we get married right here in town?"

"Yes. Six days from now," Joy said hotly. "There's a three-day wait for the license. And a three-day wait after that. Besides, you have to take a lot of silly blood tests and get certificates and things. This is the damndest state to get married or divorced in. I know."

Stanton wished Joy wouldn't refer so frequently to her former marriages. He was intensely grateful but he certainly wasn't in love. And, in this instance, the holy bonds of matrimony would be little more than a membership card in a very exclusive club.

Joy was hot and irritated by what she considered the stupidity of Inspector Treech. "Well, you don't need to look so sour about it. I can leave the state. No one would try to stop me. I'm not accused of anything."

"I'm sorry," he apologized. "I didn't realize I was looking sour. But, naturally, I'm disappointed."

She was immediately contrite. "And I'm sorry I was cross. I didn't mean to be. We won't fight like other couples, will we, Bob?"

He assured her they would not.

"Not ever. Not even once." Joy sealed the assurance with a kiss, much to the amusement of the passers-by. "We'll just always be in love, forever and forever."

If Stanton understood her mind, and he thought he did, she meant it. But she had meant it the other times, too. Joy wasn't immoral. She merely had no other yardstick with which to measure emotion than her own five senses. As shrewd as it was in some matters, her mind hadn't kept pace with her body. She still believed in Prince Charming. He could be the next man she met, and very frequently was.

It was cooler on the steps of the building. He suggested at least applying for a license. They would be that much closer toward their goal. Joy vetoed the suggestion. "No. I have a much better idea. Let's go somewhere and have a drink and I'll explain it to you. They can't do this to us...."

It was, Stanton decided later, about what Joy would figure out. Still, there was an excellent possibility her idea would succeed. It was hopeless to think of attempting to board a plane. But Las Vegas was only two hundred and ninety miles from Los Angeles. They had waited so long, one more night wouldn't matter. She would drive back to the lot so he could pick up his car. There they would separate, she to go directly home, he out to the ranch. Both would immediately get busy on their phones and invite everyone they knew to a big engagement announcement party at his ranch the following night. Dozens, hundreds of people, were bound to come. The road would be black with cars, too many for Inspector Treech's detectives to keep track of. They would previously spot a car some distance from the ranch. And while the party was at its height he and she would slip away and drive to Las Vegas. They wouldn't be missed in the confusion. By the time they were missed it would be too late for Inspector Treech to do anything about it. They would be in Las Vegas by morning and could be married immediately. After a few hours of rest they could return the same day. Thus propriety, Inspector Treech, and themselves would all be satisfied.

"I do love you, Bob, I do." Joy kissed him tenderly in parting. "And everything is going to be just wonderful for both of us from now on."

It was dark by the time Stanton reached the ranch and an early rising moon was balanced on the ridge pole of the barn. Hi Lo was slumped in a patio chair, his feet higher than his head, and a frosty sun-downer convenient to his hand. "Well?" he asked.

"It has been a long day," Stanton said, "but I'm still on the Consolidated payroll." He unscrewed the cap from the bottle of rye on the table. "And, by the way, we are giving a big engagement announcement party tomorrow night. And sometime while it is going on, Joy and I are going to slip away and drive to Las Vegas and be married."

"Oh," Hi Lo said. Sensing the other man's mood, he made no further comment. "Well, I had better tell Marta and check the liquor supply." He got to his feet. "A party for how many people?"

Stanton admitted, "I'll be damned if I know. Every leech in Hollywood will probably be here." He drank from the neck of the bottle. "But Joy and I are going to be very happy and everything is going to be just wonderful for both of us from now on."

"I hope so," Hi Lo said, quietly.

"Of course it will be." Stanton drank from the bottle again. "What are a few former husbands and lovers between friends?"

"You're drunk, Bob."

"No," Stanton said. "Not yet. But just give me time. I will be...."

Eve wanted to be certain and asked Robin to read the sign. He spelled it out painstakingly. "This is the hotel, Mother. First it says Hollywood. Then there is a little squiggle. Then Highland. Then Hotel."

The doorman carried their bags into the lobby. Guided by Winston Churchill and an occasional, almost imperceptible, nudge from Robin, Eve made her way to the desk. There, releasing her hold on the dog's harness, she removed her gloves as she announced, "I would like to engage a room with bath, please. There are the two of us, myself and son. And a very well-behaved Seeing Eye dog."

The clerk moved the registry card so it touched the fingers of her left hand and put a pen in her right. "Yes, Ma'am." He handed a bellboy a key. "Show the lady up to three twentyfour, George."

Finding her gloves again, Eve asked the clerk, "And would you please tell me the room number of Miss Grace Turner?"

The clerk checked the room list. "I'm very sorry, Mrs."—he glanced at the registry card—"Stanton, but we have no one by that name registered."

"Oh," Eve said. "I see. Well, thanks. I had hoped she might still be here."

Grasping the harness again, she followed Winston Churchill, the dog sagely following in the wake of the bellboy who had their bags. The clerk watched her into the elevator cage, then shook his head. "A dirty shame. A pretty young dame like that, and blind."

He started to file the registry card, looked at it again, and a fine film of perspiration formed on his forehead. The blind girl had asked for Grace Turner. That was the name of the English dame who had walked out one night and wound up with two slugs in her on the summit of the canyon road. The newspapers had been filled, still were, with the name of Robert Stanton, the big shot movie writer who was suspected of killing her.

The clerk's fingers trembled as he inserted the card in the file. This could be big stuff. This wasn't any ten-spot tip on a pair of lush-up cheaters. This was the big time.

"Hello, Shad. I've got a hot one for you," he would say. "But don't give me that sawbuck stuff. This is worth a C-note. Who do you think just checked in? A blind dame, a boy, and a dog. And what name do you think she signed? Na. It wasn't Smith. This is a young boy, see, maybe about six years of age. And the name that she signed on her card is, Mrs. Robert Stanton and son, 44 Westbury Lane, London, England."

CHAPTER 9

A t nine o'clock, wine-mellowed, his dinner fitting his waistcoat well, Hanson rose from the table, telling Sato to take the rest of the evening off and lighting a cigar strolled out onto the flagged terrace. It was nice to have money, a lot of it. He meant to have a lot more. If the fish had been hooked before, he was gaffed and boated now. He didn't dare refuse him *anything* he asked.

The star-lighted vista was lovely. Pleased with the night and Hanson, Hanson stood fingering the locket in his pocket. His luck was holding. Of the hundreds of ethical lawyers in the state of California to whom the girl might have taken her case, he had gotten to her first. He wondered how much he dared ask for this new information he possessed and realized there was no limit.

Trailing a plume of fragrant cigar smoke, he walked back into the house to make certain the master recording of the dictaphone discs he had cut in his office was in place on the machine. He flicked the switch and listened-—

"My name is Eve Stanton of London, England. I have come to this country to ask my husband, Robert Stanton, the cinema writer and novelist, to take over the responsibility of his son's care and education and I would like to have you represent me in this matter...."

He switched off the machine. And there it was. The depths to which some members of the human race would stoop were, thank God, incredible. As an afterthought, purely as a precautionary measure and not because he expected violence, he transferred a blue steel revolver from a table drawer to the right-hand pocket of his dinner jacket. Infrequently, very infrequently, sheep became hysterically violent before they realized their only choice was to allow themselves to be sheared.

Sato had been gone half an hour when his expected caller arrived, not by the front door but, to Hanson's slight surprise, by the faint trail that led up the hillside from a lower road.

Tall, bare-headed, both hands plunged deep into the pockets of the slightly soiled trench coat he wore over his dinner jacket, the other man stopped well inside the shadows of a wind-deformed live oak growing on the very edge of the terrace. "Well? You said you wanted to see me. I'm here."

Hanson relighted his cigar. "Yes. I had a client in my office this afternoon. A client who makes this other affair make sense. She and her son arrived

in Los Angeles last night and, through one of my connections, I was fortunate enough to get in touch with her and offer her my services."

The other man called him a foul name.

Unperturbed, Hanson continued, "Her maiden name, as you may recall,
was Eve Shannon. Marriage changed her name but not the initial."

Hanson was amused. "So I want more money. A lot more money."

"And just why should an English girl named Eve Shannon mean anything to me?"

"You're here, aren't you?"

A moment of silence followed. Then the man under the oak took his
hands from his pockets and lighted a cigarette. "Yes. I'm here," he admitted. "You say she has the boy with her?"

Hanson chuckled. "A boy of six by the name of Robin."

The man under the oak swore softly. Taking a small gold locket from his
pocket, Hanson dangled it by its chain. "You may perhaps recognize this, a
small gift you once gave her." He chuckled. "I know you will recognize the
picture. I had quite a time convincing her she should give me this as proof
she was who she said she was. And you should be very grateful to me. If
this had gotten into Inspector Treech's hands—" He left it there.

Leaving the shelter of the tree, the other man took the locket in his fingers and snapping it open, studied the dime-sized picture it contained.

Hanson retrieved the locket. "It is your picture?"

"You know it is." He snuffed out his cigarette nervously. "Now what's
this about a dog?"

Hanson explained, "His name is Winston Churchill. He is, I imagine, the
British version of our Seeing Eye dog."

"Then Eve is totally blind."

"Totally. Just how permanently I don't know, but her optical nerves are
paralyzed. It happened during one of the last buzz-bomb raids and she
was, so she told me, very fortunate to escape from the bombed building
with your child."

They had moved into the living room. Amused, Hanson flicked the
switch of the turn-table and the record began to revolve—

*"My name is Eve Stanton of London, England. I have come to this country to
ask my husband, Robert Stanton, the cinema writer and novelist, to take over the
responsibility of his son's care and education and I would like to have you represent me in this matter...."*

"Stop that damn thing!"

Hanson shut off the machine and stood swinging the locket by its chain.
"Myself, I think she is being very reasonable. She doesn't ask a dime for
herself, not even enough to pay for the operation she says might restore
her sight. All she asks is her boy be raised as the son of a wealthy man."

"Have you called Bob?"

"No. Why should I?"

"Because, you damn fool," the other man explained, "I am entitled to some protection for the money this is going to cost me. There can't help but be a big stink over this when she finds out the eminent Robert Stanton disclaims all knowledge of the marriage. And just how are you going to explain to Inspector Treech that you didn't even bother to contact him when you undoubtedly told the girl you would?"

"I hadn't thought of that,' Hanson admitted.

"No. You were too greedy for the pay-off. Get him on the phone. Get him out here, now, tonight."

Hanson dialed Stanton's number. "And what am I supposed to tell him when he does get here?"

"Play it straight. Tell him what the girl told you. That way you are in the clear." He added, bitterly, "And if you're worried about your hold on me, well, you have the locket."

"Yes. That's right," Hanson said. "I have the locket." Connected with Stanton, he spoke earnestly into the phone for a few minutes then, hanging up, reported, "He kicked like a steer. It seems he's throwing a big party at his house tonight."

"Yes. I know. I'm invited to it. He said he would come?"

"Under protest."

Hanson dry-washed his hands in anticipation. "Now, about this pay-off that you mentioned—"

"You fool. You utter fool!" the other man cut him short. "Thanks a lot for everything. But I'm not paying you another dime." His face white and strained in the harsh light of the living room, he tugged a gun from the pocket of his trench coat. "See what I mean, Hanson?"

Hanson laughed at him. "Grow up. Don't be a juvenile delinquent all your life. Shooting me won't get you anywhere." He nodded at the platter on the turntable. "I have the whole story on wax. And, disregarding that, even if I were out of your way the girl can still identify you."

"How?"

"How?" Hanson laughed. "Why—" He stopped short, swallowing hard, the locket still dangling from his fingers grown suddenly so heavy his arm could scarcely support it.

"Yes. How?" the other man demanded. "How will she identify me? You told me yourself Eve is blind."

Hanson backed from him, terrified, fumbling, too late, for his own gun. A first, a second, and then a third, red bud-boutonniere sprouted, then blossomed, on his dress shirt front. He touched them gingerly with his fingertips, then kneeled, as in prayer, and fell forward slowly on his face.

His gun hand hanging limply at his side, the killer eyed the body without emotion. *Once you have killed,* he thought, *it isn't quite so difficult the second time.* Then, taking the chain and locket from Hanson's fingers and the record from the turntable, he turned off the lights and left by the same path he had ascended....

In London the night was cold and filled with fog. Here, too, there was fog. The sea wasn't far away. But the American boys she had met hadn't been pulling her leg. California November *was* warm.

The stored up hurt and loneliness and recent anger of the past seven years uncorked in that afternoon's exhausting interview with Attorney Hanson, Eve lay motionless in the dark room, listening to the night sounds on the street, waiting for the phone to ring.

What a fool she had been at seventeen. She might have known. Still, she wasn't too much to blame. Robert had been kind, and considerate, and thoughtful. He had brought her sweets and flowers. And *Mocambo, Ciro's Malibu Beach, ranches, swimming pools, servants* were magic words with which to dazzle the mind of a naive girl who had known only the genteel poverty of a village cleric's home.

If only she hadn't gone to London to aid in the war effort. No. She was glad she had gone. She would always be glad because of Robin. Robin was worth everything. She had no reason to reproach herself. She hadn't been bad. As dazzled as she was, she had insisted on marriage. It was fortunate she had. Attorney Hanson seemed to think her marriage lines should be worth a pretty penny. She hoped so, for Robin's sake.

Eve massaged her aching temples with her fingertips. Now she was actually in Los Angeles it seemed incredible she had been able to screw up the nerve to do what she had done. It had taken a bit of doing but she had known from the moment she read Grace's letter that she was going to do it. Robert wasn't dead. He had merely allowed her to think so, allowed her to cry her eyes out for a man to whom she represented only a bit of a fling.

Well, so be it. For herself she wanted nothing. She had made that clear to Attorney Hanson. But Robin must have the best. Now he was six it was only fair that his wealthy father should begin to support him in a manner to which Robin was as yet unaccustomed.

From the window, one arm around Winston Churchill's neck, Robin broke his long silence. "It's beautiful, Mother. The fronts of all the buildings are covered with colored lights and there are ever so many people on the walks." His voice was wistful. "You don't suppose, do you, that Roy Rogers might ride by on Trigger?"

Eve said she doubted he would at that hour.

"Of course not," Robin agreed. "Trigger is home in his stable eating hay.

But I will see a cowboy, won't I, Mother? A real live cowboy riding a real live horse?"

Eve promised he would.

"And an Indian?"

Eve said she didn't know about an Indian. *Why didn't the phone ring?* It had been five hours since she had talked to Attorney Hanson. A new and frightening thought crept into her consciousness. *What if Robert refused to see her? What if he denied Robin was his son?*

Her nails bit into her palms but she refused to cry. The tears were over and done with. Robert wasn't worth crying about.

From the window Robin said, "I'm glad we came. Aren't you, Mother?"

Eve said she was. But at the moment she wasn't so certain. At the rate her money was melting it would be gone in two days. Every one had been grand to her but everything was so frightfully expensive. After giving Attorney Hanson the two hundred-dollar retaining fee he had suggested as proper, she had less than forty American dollars left. Nor had she anything to pawn. She had given Attorney Hanson her only piece of jewelry with the exception of her wedding ring. *Why didn't the phone ring? Attorney Hanson had promised to phone her as soon as be had contacted Robert.*

Nothing ventured, nothing gained. She would wait until ten o'clock. If, by then, neither Robert nor Mr. Hanson had phoned her she would contact Robert in person, now, tonight, if it took the last shilling of her small reserve. She hadn't traveled five thousand miles to be kept waiting in a hotel room she couldn't afford....

Posted by Hi Lo, Patton was waiting at the gate when Stanton returned. "Where in the name of time did you go to?" he demanded. "Hi Lo and I have been having one sweet time with Miss Parnell. She thinks you got boiled and took a powder without her."

"I had a phone call from Shad," Stanton told him. "He said it was imperative that he see me at once, and alone; he had something important to tell me."

"And?"

"It turned out to be a false alarm. His place was dark and no one answered the bell. He either changed his mind or was called out suddenly."

"I don't like it," Patton said. "I don't like it at all."

Stanton shrugged. "The ride didn't hurt me. Have you got that car spotted on the back road?"

"I have. But how about Swen and Kelly?"

Stanton indicated the road. Cars unable to get into the small inside parking space reserved for the elite were parked solid on both sides of the road for a quarter of a mile in both directions. "They would have had to stand in the middle of the road and yell before I'd have seen them in that mob. I don't even know whose car I used. I just picked the first one I came to with the keys in the ignition. Where's Joy?"

"Down near the pool, I think. She was."

Stanton walked down the crazy-paved path leading around the wing of the house containing the rumpus room. The garden was gay with colored lanterns. Couples were dancing on an improvised floor in the garden and on the edge of the pool. Still others were in the pool and in the rumpus room. All the portable bars were doing business. He didn't know one-fifth of his guests. He doubted he would like them if he did. On the other hand, nine-tenths of them didn't give a damn about him or whether he and Joy would be happy or unhappy.

He looked for Lyle Ferris in the crowd and couldn't find him. Then he looked for Joy and saw her sitting on a bench near the pool, one toe tapping ominously as she talked to the Metro juvenile man with whom Ed Wilcox said he had seen Lili Manson.

Fortifying himself with a double rye, he made a Tom Collins for Joy and joined them. "And where have you been?" Joy demanded.

Sitting down beside her, Stanton handed her the glass. "It wasn't to London to see the queen. Scram, will you, Bobby? I wouldst talk with my betrothed."

Her toe still tapping, Joy repeated, "Where have you been?"

Stanton considered telling her the truth and decided it would serve no purpose. "I went down to make certain the car was spotted. You ready to take off for Las Vegas, baby?"

Joy was immediately contrite and insisted on kissing him wetly. "You had me worried, you, Mr. Man, you."

Lili Manson, with Marty hovering at her side, stopped in front of the bench. "Good luck, Joy," she miaowed. "If at first you don't succeed, try and try again."

Manson shook Stanton's hand warmly. "I can't tell you how happy I am for both of you, Bob. The best of luck."

Lili, too, was half seas over and Marty had to keep a strong grip on her arm as they strolled on. Everyone, Stanton decided, but himself, seemed to be having a wonderful time. He had either had too much or not enough to drink. "What say we take off?" he asked Joy.

She handed him her empty glass. "After one more drink. We can't go without a stirrup cup, can we?"

"Of course not," Stanton agreed.

The portable bar he had used before was ringed with couples. He walked on toward the bar in the rumpus room where Eddie should be on duty. As he reached the parking lot, Lyle Ferris was expertly nosing his low-slung, expensive, foreign-made car into the last open space.

"Hi, fellow. Congratulations, and all that sort of thing," the actor greeted him. He stripped off the trench coat he was wearing over his dinner jacket. "Sorry I'm late. I'd have been here sooner if I hadn't had a little business to attend to."

"Male or female?" Stanton grinned.

Ferris lost some of his cordiality. "You're getting Joy. What do you care? Where is Joy, by the way?"

Stanton said he would find her near the pool.

"Not swimming, I trust," Ferris said. "I much prefer my women wet on the inside. And that even applies to your woman, said he, being noble. But if I thought I still had a chance, boy, would I cut your throat!"

Stanton watched the actor stride down the path. He didn't doubt the statement. Lyle and Joy were well-matched. Both of them were unscrupulous where what they imagined to be their own happiness was concerned. He walked on, wishing there was some way he could back out and leave the field to Lyle. Rounding the rumpus room, he started in through the door only to pause mildly interested as a Los Angeles taxicab skirted the big oak expertly and swinging into the drive, parked as close as it could get to the front door.

A slim-faced, Eton-jacketed little boy who looked like a fugitive from *Good-bye, Mr. Chips* was the first to get out of the cab. He was followed by a huge Doberman pinscher and a stunning dark-haired girl who looked as if she might be the boy's sister. The *damnedest* people came to his parties.

He started toward the cab to ask them if they had the right address, then saw Hi Lo, omnipresent, walk out the front door to greet them. Stanton turned back toward the rumpus room, turned again, chuckling, as the boy's sharp eyes saw through Hi Lo's dinner jacket and cummerbund to his hereditary clout and elk tooth necklace. "You're an Indian," the boy accused.

"That's right," Hi Lo grinned. "Me heap big chief Hi Lo Jack." He turned to the girl in the smart traveling suit and just then Leatrice May, spotting Stanton in the doorway, dragged him inside the rumpus room and up to the bar.

...When did he and Joy intend to be married? Would they live at the ranch or in Joy's home? Did he think their marriage would last? Did they intend to have any children?

Stanton said he didn't know to all four questions and asked Eddie to fix him a double-rye high and a Tom Collins. While he waited for the Collins, he drained the double rye and Eddie had to mix him another. He had finally gotten rid of Leatrice and was picking up Joy's drink when Hi Lo whispered in his ear, "Eve's here."

"Who's here?"

"Eve."

The name didn't register in Stanton's mind. "Well, that's fine," he said pleasantly. "Tell her to have a good time. But now, if you will excuse me, I have to take a last drink to Joy before we you-know-what."

No double-entendre was intended but the remark was overheard and repeated and the room bulged with laughter.

Stanton reached for the drink again and Hi Lo blocked his hand. "Don't be a complete heel, Bob. This is the last time I'm telling you. Eve is here."

"So what?" Stanton demanded. "Is that supposed to mean something to me? I'm not being a heel. I just don't know any Eve. So Eve is here. Buy her a drink. Buy her two drinks. Tell her to get stinking drunk."

Neither man realized their voices had risen until they were almost shouting. "So," Hi Lo said sarcastically, "you don't know Eve Shannon?"

Thoroughly angered by what he considered an unwarranted interference in his personal affairs, Stanton lifted the other man's hand off his shoulder. "No. I don't know Eve Shannon. I don't particularly want to know her. What's the matter with you? Are you drunk?"

"Oh," Hi Lo said, "I see. So that's the way you're going to play it. Well, we've been friends for a long time, Bob. But I don't know you any more. In my book you're a skunk and a louse unfit to associate with even a Main Street wino."

The silence that followed his pronouncement was complete except for the tinkling of the battered player-piano. It continued to grind out the nasal voice of some long dead tenor.

Shaking his head to clear it, Stanton said, "Now wait. *Un momento*, Hi Lo. What's this all about?"

"You wouldn't know?"

"I would not."

The big Indian slapped his face first with the palm, then with the back of his hand. "But you do know what this means?"

White with anger, Stanton let fly a punch aimed at Hi Lo's jaw. Hi Lo rolled with the punch. Then, driving a hard left into Stanton's stomach that bent the writer double, he straightened him again with a right to the point of the jaw that left Stanton glassy-eyed and rubber-kneed. His face still expressionless, Hi Lo watched his employer crumple to the floor. Then he told the others, "Clear out. The party is over."

Leatrice May began a protest. "But—"

"You heard what I said," Hi Lo told her. "Clear out. All of you..."

CHAPTER 10

With returning consciousness, Stanton became aware first of a *slap slap slapping* noise, then of Leatrice May's face. Her back to the bar, a glass in her hand, the gossip columnist was waiting patiently for him to come to his senses. Except for Eddie they were alone in the rumpus room.

Stanton got to his feet and walking in back of the bar poured himself a stiff drink. "Where's everyone?" he asked Leatrice.

"Hi Lo ordered them off the grounds," she told him. "He ordered me out, too. But I thought I'd stick around. What's the story, Bob?"

Stanton felt his jaw. It was tender to the touch and swollen. "You tell me. I think the big Indian must have gone nuts."

The gossip columnist laughed. "I don't think I'll buy that. Why are you a skunk and a louse? Who is this Eve Shannon? Hi Lo said she was English. Would that relate her to the Grace Turner case?"

A sick sinking feeling in his stomach, Stanton set his glass on the bar. He hadn't considered that angle. He hadn't had time.

"I wouldn't know," Stanton told her. "Why don't you go ask Hi Lo?"

"I think I will," she said.

He followed her to the door. The band in the garden had stopped playing. The musicians were packing their instruments. The caterer's men were rounding up the portable bars and locking them in the cabanas. There was no laughter and no shouting. Those of his guests who still remained stood in small whispering clusters or moved slowly toward the gate.

He tried to locate Joy and saw her with Lyle on the edge of the pool engaged in animated conversation with Hi Lo. They talked for a long time, then Hi Lo nodded in the general direction of the house. Lyle and Joy turned and came toward him. Stanton thought they were headed for the rumpus room. They weren't. When they reached the acacia tree they turned and entered the house through the living room windows opening on the patio.

"You wouldn't know what this is all about, would you?" Stanton asked Eddie.

"No. Honest, Mr. Stanton," the handyman said. "I hear you and Mr. Hi Lo talking hot but I am mixing a drink and don't pay much attention."

Stanton walked slowly back to the bar wishing he knew the score. The more he thought about it, the angrier he got. Who did Hi Lo think he was?

Suppose he had known some girl named Eve. What was all the fuss about? He would beat the big Indian to a pulp. That's what he would do. If he couldn't do it with his fists he would use a baseball bat.

Eddie cleared his throat. "I beg your pardon, Mr. Stanton. But Mr. Hi Lo said as soon as you come to that I should shut up the bar and tell you to go in the house."

"Oh, he did."

"Yes, sir."

"Well, you're working for me, not Hi Lo. You take your orders from me."

"Yes, sir."

Stanton walked back to the door of the rumpus room. It was darker in the garden now. One by one the gaily colored lanterns were winking out. He considered looking up Hi Lo, and decided to wait until he had cooled off. On impulse he turned down the unlighted path leading to the stables. Day and early evening had been warm but a cool wind had sprung up within the last half hour. Too much had happened to him too fast. He had been under too great a strain. Clenching his teeth against a sudden nervous chill, Stanton considered returning to the rumpus room, then stopping in at the tack room, took a soiled trench coat from a peg and slipped into it instead. He had been building too many whiskey fires lately.

A slight movement in front of Danny Deever's stall caught his attention. Then the moon sailing out from behind a cloud revealed the small boy he had seen get out of the cab. Unaware he was not alone, his hands clasped behind his back, his legs spread for better balance, his neck thrust forward in interest, the small fugitive from *Good-bye, Mr. Chips* was regarding the horse with a light in his eyes that bordered on worship.

"Like him?" Stanton asked.

Slightly startled, Robin looked up, smiling. "Oh, yes, sir. I think he's wonderful. It's all right for me to look at him, isn't it? I mean, at such close quarters?"

Stanton looked at the child to see if he was being ribbed. He didn't seem to be. As big as a minute, with an intonation and a broad A decidedly British, the six-year-old handled words with the ease of a Caltech professor. "Of course it is," Stanton assured him. "You like horses?"

"Very much," Robin said. He explained, "I've seen lots of them in the cinema but this is the first time I've ever been so close to a real live one."

"Why don't you pet him?" Stanton suggested.

Robin was beside himself with joy. "May I? May I give him a piece of sugar?" He grubbed in the pocket of his jacket and came up with a sugar cube. "I saved mine from tea this evening just in case I might meet a horse."

Stanton passed a hand over his eyes. Everything happened to him. Only this wasn't happening. It couldn't.

Attracted by the timidly offered cube of sugar, Danny Deever lowered his head, nibbled the sugar off Robin's palm, then nuzzled him for more as Robin squealed happily. "He likes me."

Amused, Stanton picked him up so the boy could pet the big Palomino's high-arched neck and well-curried withers. "What's your name, son?"

"Robin."

"You're British, aren't you?"

"No, sir," Robin said promptly. "My mother is English. I am an American. My father was an American aviator."

He stroked Danny Deever's nose. Stanton studied the boy's happy face in tardy suspicion. "Your mother's name wouldn't by any chance be Eve, would it?"

"Mmm-hmmh. Do you know her?"

"N-no."

Fond of his new friend, Robin confided, "There's been some trouble between my mother and father and we've come to straighten it out. His name is Robert Stanton and he writes wonderful stories for the cinema and makes a lot of money. Do you know him?"

"I'm beginning to wonder," Stanton said. This was a new approach to something, just what he didn't know. But whatever the girl's story was, it was good. It would have to be good to fool Hi Lo. The big Indian liked a good time but he believed a man should meet his obligations. A supposedly deserted wife and child would explain the punch in the jaw. His mouth suddenly dry, Stanton thought of Hale's remembered story concerning the wealthy American officer who had married an English girl. It was true then. And Grace Turner had written or cabled the girl before she died.

Robin squirmed in his arms. "You're holding me too tight."

"I'm sorry," Stanton said. He felt better than he had felt in weeks. This, then, was the pay-off to the whole affair. Once the girl had gone on record that he wasn't the Robert Stanton she had married, Inspector Treech's wanted motive would blow up in his face. No possible suspicion in the death of the Turner girl would remain attached to his name. "So your father is Robert Stanton, eh?"

"Yes, sir." Robin wasn't too certain. "I think this is his ranch. But I was asleep when Mother woke me up and told me to get dressed. My, she was angry."

"She was, eh?"

"Oh, yes." Robin slipped one arm around the neck of his new friend. "It wasn't nice of Father not to even phone after we came such a long way, was it?"

The question baffled Stanton. "What sort of a person is your mother?"

"She's nice."

It was natural the boy should think so. It was very possibly true. The girl wasn't to blame if someone had played a shabby trick on her. "And as soon as you reached the ranch you came out here all by yourself to see the horses?"

Robin shook his head. "No. Mr. Chief Hi Lo Jack brought me out here." He confided, "He's a real Indian."

"And your mother?"

"I beg your pardon?"

"I mean, where is your mother now?"

"I think she's in the house. A Miss Marta took charge of her. Both Miss Marta and Chief Hi Lo seemed quite shocked when they found out who we were."

"Yeah. I can imagine," Stanton said. Still carrying Robin, he walked back up the path. "That bunch of boozers should be cleared out by now. Let's you and I go see your mother."

There were a few stragglers in the garden but most of the crowd had gone. Stanton checked the remaining cars in the parking lot. Ferris' foreign job was still there as was the Manson Cadillac. He thought the new Chrysler belonged to Johnny Hass and the big Buick to Ed Wilcox. He was pleased they had refused to leave. He wanted witnesses to this.

Marta was standing in the kitchen doorway. She took Robin from his arms, spluttering, "This time of night and a baby his age not yedt in bed after traveling five thousand miles to see his father." She glowered at Stanton as her Swiss indignation overwhelmed her. "Ach, Mein Gott! A father to deny his own son. What yedt is this world coming to?"

"Now, just a minute, Marta," Stanton attempted to defend himself. "Don't go off the deep end until—"

He stopped. Marta was no longer paying any attention to him. Robin cradled in her lap, she unbuttoned his collar, stripped off his coat and shoes, and began work on his stockings. "Gives it a hot bath, a cup of hot chocolate, and bed for you, young man."

"Real chocolate or cocoa?" Robin bargained.

Feeling like a fool, Stanton shifted from one foot to the other. Then, shrugging, he walked on down the long hall into the high-beamed, sunken living room.

Manson was sitting closest to the door. In the short interval since Stanton had last seen him, the producer had picked up quite a package. He rose unsteadily as Stanton entered the room and gripped his arm as if to assure him he was standing by.

His plump face red with indignation, Johnny Hass said, "Hi, heel."

Sitting next to his wife, a beautiful white-haired woman, Ed Wilcox looked at Stanton thoughtfully, but said nothing.

Joy was standing with Ferris in front of a roaring log fire that one of the group had built. Her eyes were hard and accusing. The corners of her mouth turned down. "So there was a reason why Romeo lagged in his courtship. You weren't quite heel enough to make love to me with a wife and child living in England. Yet you would have married me. We would have been on our way to Las Vegas if she hadn't shown up. And wouldn't that have been a pretty mess?"

"I ought to punch your face in," Ferris said. "I may attempt it yet. God knows I'm no angel. I've cut a pretty wide swath. But that is a single man's prerogative. I can't begin to tell you the extent of my contempt for—"

"Nix," Patton said from the window. "You folks don't know what you're doing to Mr. Stanton. If he is married to this dame he's in one hell of a spot."

"Please." The black-haired girl sitting in the high-backed wing chair by the fireplace stood up. "This is, after all, my show. And with the exception of Miss Parnell who is also vitally concerned, I wish you would all clear out as Mr. Hi Lo suggested."

No one moved. She continued:

"This is a personal matter between my boy's father and myself. And if my temper hadn't made such a fool of me—"

"So you are Eve," Stanton said. He crossed the floor and Winston Churchill lying beside the chair stood up to form a barrier between him and his mistress. "So you are Eve," Stanton repeated.

The girl turned toward his voice, a wry smile on her lips.

"Why the note of doubt? Surely I haven't changed so much that you don't recognize me. I am merely seven years older and no end wiser. Hello, Bob. Or should I call you Lieutenant Stanton? Just how does a deserted wife greet her husband? You are a writer. You should know."

An angry retort on his lips, Stanton realized for the first time the significance of the dog. There was no sight in the girl's blue eyes. The knowledge made him somehow very sad. This was the first time to his sober, or intoxicated, knowledge that he had ever seen her. But he had seldom, if ever, been so drawn to a woman as he was drawn to the blind girl. It was as though he had looked for her all his life—and here she was. It was almost a physical pain not to take her in his arms and tell her so.

"Well, why don't you kiss your wife?" Joy asked.

"If you try to I'll slap you," Eve said. "I didn't come here to be kissed. All I want is what is rightfully due Robin."

Stanton lied. "I wouldn't think of kissing you." The English girl was obviously proud. He didn't want to hurt her in front of the others by telling her that while she might have married a Robert Stanton, he wasn't the man to whom she was married. "But, as you say, this is a personal affair and I wonder if we couldn't discuss it better privately."

She shook her head, much to Leatrice May's relief. Stanton watched her bobbing curls, enchanted. He wanted to take them in his hand and never let go again. *It must be the Lennie complex in me,* he thought. *But this is the girl. This is it.*

"No," Eve said. "That was the way I meant it to be. But my temper spoiled that. I couldn't help it. I slopped over when I heard laughter and music and smelled perfume and good things to eat and drink and Robin told me there was a pool and people in evening dress were dancing in a lantern-lighted garden." She wasn't asking for pity. She was merely making a statement. "Life isn't very pleasant in England these days, you know. And despite his pint of milk and a hot lunch at the school every day, there were times when Robin didn't have enough to eat. And then when I thought of how you had promised me that—" Her sightless eyes were wet with angry tears. "But no matter. That's past. I really blew my top when I learned the party was being given to celebrate your engagement to another woman." She asked if Robin were in the room.

Stanton said he was not.

Eve continued. "I'm sorry I made a scene. I apologize. But I couldn't help telling your aborigine servant I thought it wasn't cricket for a man to allow his son to be deprived of the very necessities of life while he lived like a virtual nabob."

His face dark with concern, Hi Lo entered the room through one of the French windows opening on the patio. "The boy isn't where I left him. He—" Seeing Stanton, he glowered.

"Come in. Come right on in, my good aborigine servant," Stanton said. "And don't worry about the boy. I found Robin admiring Danny Deever and he is now in Marta's hands."

Hi Lo swept the room with his eyes. "I thought I told you folks to clear out."

"Not a chance," Joy said. "No man, not even the great Robert Stanton, is going to make a fool of me. If what this girl has told us is true, Bob, I'll run you out of Hollywood and pictures if it's the last thing I do."

Stanton wished her luck, then said, "All right. If we must wash our soiled linen in public, let's be at it. Here is my story, Eve. I never saw you before."

Wilcox called, "Shame."

Hass said angrily, "You really mean that, Bob?"

"I do. She may be married to some Robert Stanton but I'm not that Robert Stanton. I never saw her before."

Her cheeks flaming, Eve asked, "But you do admit your name is Robert Stanton?"

"I do."

"You are a cinema writer?"

"I write for the movies."

"And you were a first lieutenant in the United States Army Air Forces?"

"I was."

"And you were shot down over Bremen while flying as an observer with a British wing?"

"That also is true."

Eve was positive. "Then you are the Robert Stanton to whom I am married and I will thank you not to deny me. If it is Robin who is worrying you, I'm sorry. I would have told you of Robin before but I thought you were dead. You were so officially listed."

Stanton sighed, perplexed as how to straighten out the matter. It was far more serious than anyone in the room, with the exception of Patton and a tardily mentally awakened Hi Lo, realized. He asked Eve, "How did you learn I was still alive?"

Eve said, "Grace Turner wrote me a letter. She saw a clipping concerning you and Miss Parnell in one of the papers and sent it along. You remember Grace. She was a witness at our wedding."

"That does it," Stanton said. "That fixes everything just fine."

In the ominous silence that followed, Eve wondered what she had said that was so wrong. Her other senses quickened by her blindness heightened her perception of the tension.

"Well, I'll be damned," Wilcox said finally. "I think we'll take Hi Lo's suggestion and clear out. I don't want to become involved in this."

Puzzled but determined, Eve said, "You might have written, Bob."

"Now look, honey," Stanton protested. "You don't realize what you're doing to me." He laid his hand on her arm and she brushed it away angrily.

"Stop calling me honey. And don't you dare touch me."

Ferris stepped away from the fireplace. "Stop badgering the girl, Bob. Haven't you any common decency?"

"No. It would seem I'm fresh out," Stanton admitted wearily. "I don't know how I'm going to prove it but I have to. This girl is a stranger to me."

"Oh, but I'm not," Eve protested. "I'm your wife." Hot tears trickled down her cheeks and she made no effort to wipe them away. She might have known it would be like this. If Robert hadn't cared enough to let her know he was alive, it was only natural that he would deny her. He didn't want a dowdy little blind girl for a wife. He wanted Joy Parnell. She should never have come in the first place. She had no proof of anything she said except her marriage license and Robin's birth certificate naming him as father. He could deny them, too, claim they were forgeries. He had money, standing, and connections. She had nothing. And because he was ashamed, because he wanted to marry another woman, he was willing to throw her and Robin to the lions.

"Don't honey," Stanton pleaded. "Please don't cry. We'll get this figured out somehow."

Eve clutched at straws. Still, Robert didn't sound like that sort of a man. His voice was richer, fuller, more gentle than she remembered it.

Stanton studied the weeping face. If it weren't for the Grace Turner angle it would be easy to admit she was his wife. He liked her. He liked the boy. Emotion fought with reason. *Maybe she was his wife. Maybe he did know her. Maybe he had married her on one of his few drunken sprees snatched in the face of almost certain death during those early days of the war.*

He asked her, "Where were we married?"

Eve said promptly, "Lychester Chapel, Mayfair."

"On what date?"

"October tenth, 1941."

"I was sober?"

"You were sober."

Ferris said, "I'm afraid you can't wiggle out of this one, Bob. You were in London in the fall of 1941. I know you were because I saw you there. That was before I went into the Army. I was doing a play with Madge Gare and you and I got drunk at the Crillon bar."

"That's right," Stanton recalled the incident. "I was there then." He turned back to Eve. "Now tell me this, honey. You have our alleged marriage license with my signature on it?"

"I have."

"The original or a reasonable facsimile?"

"The original."

"Fine. My signature should settle this thing one way or the other." He looked at Joy and from her to Johnny Hass and Hi Lo. "To everyone's satisfaction including, I hope, Inspector Treech." He turned back to Eve. "And we lived together for how long?"

The girl's sightless face lifted. "Please don't misunderstand me. I am not asking for charity."

Eve's chin lifted still higher. "My blindness makes no difference. You aren't responsible for that. But we did spend a month together. And fortunately, or unfortunately, however one cares to view the matter, that month produced Robin." Her smile was wry. "Children are, after all, one of the main byproducts of marriage. But *do* have this straight in your mind. For myself I ask nothing. And I told Attorney Hanson so this afternoon."

Stanton said, "Hanson? You don't by any chance mean Shad Hanson, with offices in the Guarantee Building in Hollywood?"

Eve sensed the ugly something re-enter the room. "Y-yes, I believe that was the address. I asked the clerk at my hotel for the name of an attorney familiar with picture folk and he recommended Attorney Hanson. I conferred with him this afternoon and he promised to contact you at once."

"But he didn't," Stanton said quietly. "He didn't call me until nine-thirty tonight. Then when I drove up to his place in the hills he wasn't there."

Bulking large in one of the French windows, Inspector Treech asked, "Are you positive of that, Stanton?"

This is it, Stanton thought. *As soon as Treech learns who Eve is and that Grace wrote her a letter I'm on my way.* He attempted to bluff it out with little hope of success. "What are you doing here? Where do you come in on this, Treech?"

Inspector Treech said, "Where Homicide usually comes in, after the body is found."

Joy gasped, "The body?"

Leatrice May was sitting near the living room phone. Lifting it from the cradle, she dialed a number, the scratch of the revolving dial unnaturally loud in the hushed room.

"What body?" Joy demanded.

"Shad Hanson's, Miss Parnell." Treech took the phone from the gossip columnist's fingers and returned it to its cradle. "And if you don't mind, Miss May, let's keep this right here in this room for a while. When the news gets out that Hanson is dead and his records are open for inspection, there are apt to be quite a few Hollywood big shots packing bags and demanding plane and steamship reservations." His eyes settled on the blind girl's face. "Yes, at long last Shad is dead and, dying, left behind him quite an interesting story." He looked at Stanton. "And it would seem you are tagged for this one, too, Mr. Stanton."

Stanton told him not to be silly.

"I don't think I'm being silly," Treech said. "You were fairly lucky on the first murder, having Mr. Manson alibi you as he did. But if you really hoped to get away with killing Hanson you should have taken the time to go down to his office and destroy the original dictaphone records of his conversation with your wife." He asked Eve, "You are Mrs. Stanton?"

"Yes. I am Mrs. Stanton."

Stanton looked from Inspector Treech to the girl. It was, all in all, quite some evening. First a blind girl in claiming to be his wife practically convicted him of the murder of a girl who she claimed had been a witness to their marriage. Now Treech was accusing him of a second murder.

Across the room, Treech's announcement concerning Hanson finally having pierced her alcoholic fog, Lili Manson got to her feet. "Did I hear you correctly, Inspector? Did you say Shad Hanson was dead?"

"Murdered," Inspector Treech told her. "He was shot three times through the chest with the same calibered gun that was used to kill Grace Turner."

"Oh, dear God," Lili gasped. She turned as if to leave the room-and fainted in her husband's arms....

It had been two. Then it was three. Now it was four. A mental clock chimed the time distinctly. The fire in the fireplace had burned down. Someone had opened a window. There was a smell of morning in the air, of fresh green growing things. Still the nightmare continued. Her small oval face white with strain, Eve sat perched on the edge of her chair.

Inspector Treech, calm, unhurried, deadly patient, polished a new facet of the case. "I'll tell you what I will do, Mr. Stanton. We'll forget the Grace Turner angle for a while and concentrate on Hanson. Now we all know that Hanson was a rat." He appealed to Marty Manson. "Isn't that right, Mr. Manson?"

Manson nodded agreement.

"His death," Inspector Treech continued, "is no great loss to the community. I, myself, found a gun in the dead man's pocket. And if you will admit you shot him so we can hush this up as fast as we can and not have to drag his records into court and harm a lot of innocent people, I can almost guarantee that the District Attorney's office will accept a plea of self-defense. Mrs. Stanton went to Hanson and told him her story. Instead of trying to help her, he wanted a lot of money from you. You went there to protest. You quarreled. He attempted to draw his gun. You shot him. How's that?"

Stanton was torn between two desires. One was to punch Inspector Treech in the nose. The other was to aid Eve and Robin in any way he could.

"Don't do it, Mr. Stanton," Patton warned him.

"You stay out of this," Treech told Patton.

"I don't intend to," Stanton said. "In the first place I didn't kill Shad. He must have been dead by the time I punched his door bell. But even if I did confess to something I didn't do in the hope of getting a fair break from the D.A.'s office, I wouldn't get any break. They would immediately turn around and indict me for the Turner girl's murder, claiming I had two strings to my bow in killing Hanson, the other being Inspector Treech's theory I was paying Shad to set up the hour he saw Grace enter my car. No. I'm sorry," he told Treech. "Your concern for a lot of innocent people who were laying it on the line to Shad is very touching. But I'm afraid I can't accept your offer. This is another frame."

Inspector Treech was unruffled. "Don't give me that, Mr. Stanton." He explained as to a child. "You were planning on marrying Miss Parnell. You came to my office yesterday asking for permission to leave the state for that purpose. I don't know what you decided to do. It is none of my business. But I do know you threw a big party here tonight to announce your engagement. But naturally, a newly arrived deserted wife and child would upset your bridal cart. So when Hanson phoned you that your wife had arrived in Los Angeles in response to a letter sent her by the Turner girl, but had been blinded during the end of the war, you reasoned that with Hanson out of the way and the record he had made of their interview destroyed, you could deny the girl was your wife, which is exactly what you're doing. It wasn't a bad try. But you forgot that Hanson always kept the original dictaphone discs from which he cut his master records."

"Say. That's a honey," Stanton admired it. "That's even better than your Grace Turner theory. Consolidated could use you. With your imagination you could be a wow as a writer of mystery pictures."

Inspector Treech shrugged and returned to a well-traveled path. They had been over it a dozen times before. "But you do admit Shad Hanson phoned you about nine-thirty tonight?"

"I do. He said it was imperative he see me at once, and alone. He said he had something important to tell me."

"So, leaving your fiancée, you drove to his Malibu Hills home."

"That's right."

"And it is your contention that the lights were out and no one answered the door bell so you got back in your car and returned here without even seeing Hanson."

"That is my contention." Stanton squatted on his haunches beside the girl in the wing chair. "Look, Eve."

"Yes?"

"Can you positively swear I am your husband?"

"If you are Robert Stanton you are."

"Describe me."

Eve drew his picture from memory. "You are six feet tall. You weigh about fourteen stone. You dress well. You have rather light hair and brown eyes. And you wear a thin mustache."

"That would seem to sum you up pretty well, Stanton," Inspector Treech said. He appealed to the producer again. "Wouldn't you say so, Mr. Manson?"

As though against his will, the producer nodded.

"Okay. She drew my picture," Stanton said. "But Eve's description would fit a lot of men. You couldn't swing a cat on the corner of Hollywood and Vine and not knock down ten well-dressed guys, six feet tall, weighing around one hundred and ninety pounds and wearing thin mustaches. Take Lyle there, for example. Eve's description fits him as well as it does me."

"Please," the actor protested. "Don't try to pin your sins on me. I have enough of my own."

"I'm not trying to pin anything on anyone," Stanton said. "I am merely pointing out an indisputable fact. Eve's description also fits Johnny Hass, Ed Wilcox, and Lou Saunders. And all four of you were at the table with me when Grace Turner phoned. All of you have been in London. How do I know it wasn't one of you Grace Turner saw? How do I know it wasn't one of you using my name who married Eve?"

Eve began to cry softly and Stanton patted her knee. "I'm sorry. But my neck is at stake. If I am your husband, I'm guilty of two murders. If I'm not your husband, someone has played a dirty trick on you and the boy."

"Don't look at me," Hass said. "I didn't marry them."

"I wouldn't boast about it," Stanton said. Traveling on, his eyes stopped on Marty Manson and Lili. This thing had meant trouble for everyone. The producer sat glowering at his whitefaced wife who broke into violent spells of weeping from time to time. Instinctively he cautioned, "Don't be too hard on her, Marty. We all make mistakes."

Inspector Treech was thoughtful. "That wasn't a bad try, Stanton, but I doubt if you can pin either of these murders on any of the men who were with you when Grace Turner phoned." He addressed himself to Eve. "This locket of which you told me, Mrs. Stanton, the one containing your husband's picture that you gave to Attorney Hanson as proof you were who you said. Would you describe it again?"

"Of course. It was round, and gold, and inexpensive, about the size of a guinea, perfectly plain except for my initial, a block letter E."

"And the picture it contained?"

"I don't quite understand you."

"It was a professional photograph? I mean if Stanton continues to deny you are his wife, would it be possible for me to send to London for the negative?"

Eve shook her head. "No. It was just a face cut from a snapshot I took of Robert. And I imagine the film was lost with my other things when my lodgings in London were bombed."

Inspector Treech asked, "It was a picture of Lieutenant Stanton in uniform?"

"No," Eve said. "It was not. He was in mufti. Robert didn't wear his uniform except on duty. In fact, I never saw him in uniform. You see, that was just before America entered the war and he said his uniform made him feel self-conscious and somewhat ashamed, there being so few American soldiers in England at the time."

"I see," Inspector Treech said.

Hi Lo crossed the room and offered his hand to Stanton, saying, "That tears it. Apologies and all of that."

Stanton shook hands grinning. "Relax, my good aborigine. It was a natural assumption on your part. But next time either wear boxing gloves or don't jump to such hasty conclusions."

His eyes still thoughtful, Inspector Treech asked Stanton if he had a dictaphone is his study. When Stanton said he did, the Inspector dispatched Jack Gieger and Matt Kelly to get the machine and sent Bill Swen to get the confiscated dictaphone original from the police car. A few minutes later Eve's recorded voice filled the room

"My name is Eve Stanton of London, England. I have come to this country to ask my husband, Robert Stanton, the cinema writer and novelist, to take over the responsibility of his son's care and education and I would like to have you represent me in this matter...."

Inspector Treech stopped the machine. "You were familiar with Shad Hanson's methods, Mr. Stanton? I mean you knew he always made recordings of his conversations with prospective clients and quite frequently cut a master sales record from those recordings?"

"I did. I even used the gag in a picture."

"Then after you shot Hanson, why didn't you take his keys and go down to his office and destroy these originals?"

Stanton complained, "You have a one track mind, Inspector. The reason I didn't is because I didn't shoot Hanson and I didn't know such a record existed."

"So you say," the Inspector sighed. "If true, that bolsters your contention of having been framed on both murders. If false, these records were a bad slip-up on your part. Most murderers make one mistake. However, unless you can prove you aren't this girl's husband, I am afraid these records are going to send you to the gas chamber."

"I thought we had compromised on self-defense."

Inspector Treech shrugged. "That was just a proposition concerning Hanson only, and you didn't seem inclined to play ball. As I see it, the situation remains just about where it was before Hanson was killed. I could arrest you. I may before the day is over. But, because there is some doubt in my mind on certain points, and because Hanson was a rat whose death is a blessing to a great number of people, I am going to hold off for a few more hours."

"Thank you. The guilty man was given plenty of rope, eh?"

"Something like that," Inspector Treech admitted. "But you don't need to hang yourself. In fact I would rather you wouldn't. Just give us a little more time and we'll find both the gun and the locket. You thought you were playing it smart there, and you were. If you had left that locket on Hanson with your picture in it, it would have been the same as pleading guilty to both murders." Treech laid his hand on Eve's shoulder. "For the last time, Mrs. Stanton. Do you still refuse to make a positive identification of this man as your husband?"

"I can't make a positive identification," Eve said unhappily.

"You should know his voice."

Eve intertwined her fingers in indecision. Strange new doubts were creeping into her mind. Was it possible she had been imposed upon? Was the man they called Robert Stanton her Robert? She pleaded, "I can't identify him by his voice, Inspector. It has been a long time since I've heard it. Then we were together for so short a time and I was so young and—confused."

"Now I've heard all the names for it," Joy said dryly.

"Good girl," Stanton said. "You won't regret it." He didn't intend she should. She was as good as she was pretty. And she had courage. Using Winston Churchill for eyes, she had traveled a fourth of the way around the world to insist on her son's rights. And now, involved in a double murder, not even a strange police officer in a strange country could swerve her from her sense of what was right. In the morning, or rather, later in the day, he would have Dr. Schaeffer look at her eyes. He was reputedly tops in his line. Money would be no object. *Who* had fooled her didn't matter. Unless he went to the gas chamber he would spend the rest of his life making it up to her.

Outside the big front door a car, traveling fast, turned in the drive, kissed off the oak, and braked in a crunching of gravel. A second, a third, a fourth, a fifth, and a sixth car turned in behind it. Winston Churchill got to his feet and looked inquiringly at the door as Jack Gieger came in swearing. "Every damn reporter in Los Angeles just drove up."

Inspector Treech looked accusingly at Leatrice May. She smiled back brightly over the lipstick she was applying. "The freedom of the press and all that sort of thing, old pip-pip. If the police department wanted to keep Shad's demise hush-hush until they had beaten a confession out of their chief suspect, you shouldn't have allowed me to go to the girl's room."

Lou Saunders and Ben Morris, a photographer, were already arguing with Gieger who was attempting to keep them out.

Ignoring Stanton completely, Joy drew her wrap around her shoulders. "I presume that means we are free to go." When Inspector Treech nodded, she added, "Would you please see me home, Lyle?"

The actor said he would be glad to and asked Treech, "And just what does happen to Hanson's confidential records?"

Treech spread his hands in a futile gesture. "That's up to the State's Attorney's office. This is out of my hands now."

Marty Manson got to his feet and assisted Lili to hers. He had to guide her to the French windows that led to the patio.

They reached the French windows only to be engulfed in a wave of reporters, male and female, as Lou Saunders, tired of arguing with Gieger, and familiar with the house, spear-headed the invasion of human locusts.

After one quick glance at Stanton and the blind girl, Saunders immediately buttonholed Inspector Treech. Leatrice May picked up the living room phone to embroider a few more clichés on the story she had already phoned in.

There was a blinding flash as a half dozen press photographers shot Joy and Ferris in the windows. Partially shielded by the high back of the wing chair, Stanton seized the unobserved moment to kneel beside Eve and take one of her hands in both of his. "Now, just take it easy, honey," he counseled her. "Tell the whole truth, the full truth, and nothing but the truth. And don't let the reporters rattle or frighten you. You haven't a thing to worry about. Everything is going to be just fine for you and Robin. I swear it." He touched the tips of her fingers to his hair, his eyes, his nose, his cheeks, his lips. "But play fair with me, honey. Please. So I can help you. *Am I the man you knew as Robert Stanton?*"

Eve brushed away a tear. She wanted him to be Robert. She had never wanted anything so desperately. She wanted him to be Robert and love her and for things to be as Robert had promised they would be. This man was kind and good and gentle. She could tell it by his voice, his touch. But if he were Robert he couldn't be kind and good and gentle. If he were Robert he had killed Grace Turner and Attorney Hanson. Inspector Treech said so. She really had little choice. If she said he was Robert the police would take him away to be punished. She would never see him again. If she denied that he was Robert she would be branding Robin and depriving him of his rightful patrimony. "I don't know," she sobbed quietly. "I don't know. Oh, if only I could see."

Stanton stood up to find Hi Lo standing beside him. "I'm sorry," Hi Lo said. "If I hadn't lost my temper a lot of this could have been avoided. I might have known there was some mix-up. I did know as soon as she made that crack about mufti. The guy must have been in the Swiss Navy."

"Could be," Stanton agreed. "But don't let Marta hear you say that."

Finished with Inspector Treech, Lou Saunders stood looking down at Eve. "So this is the motive, eh, Bob? Not bad. When English girls are pretty they're superb. And she's a honey. A shame your happy reunion will be so short. The good Inspector informs me he is about to swing the ax."

"Which side of the nose would you rather be punched on?" Hi Lo asked him.

Saunders was cheerful about it. "Either or both. It's immaterial to me as long as I get a good story. And I have one. Oh, Mr. Robert Stanton, you stuffed-shirt Hollywood Babbitt. Just you wait until you read me in the morning papers. I'll make your name a hissing and a by-word from shining sea to shining sea."

Then the main body of reporters and cameramen, finished with Joy Parnell and Lyle Ferris and Marty and Lili Manson, engulfed that corner of the room.

Flash bulbs popping in his face, words whirling around his head, Stanton reached in the pocket of his dinner jacket for a cigarette, found he had none and remembered there was a freshly opened package in a pocket of the trench coat he had discarded shortly after entering the living room. He picked the coat from a chair and thrust his hand into a pocket. The package of cigarettes was there. But so was something else. To his startled fingers it felt small, and round, and smooth, about the size of an English guinea with a block initial E engraved on one side....

All was going splendidly. Astride Danny Deever with Roy Rogers on Trigger beside him, Robin was listening with rapt attention to Gene Autry singing *Ride, Ranger, Ride* when the Indians swooped down from the painted buttes, and in attempting to draw both of his pearl-handled revolvers at once, Robin grew panicky as his arms refused to move.

Then he sleepily realized what had happened. Marta had tucked him in too tightly. He removed his arms from under the covers and was preparing to remount when he saw the face over his bed.

Robin knew the man immediately. He should. He had seen his face often enough in the locket his mother wore suspended from her neck by a chain. So this *was* his father's ranch. He lay waiting for him to speak And his father could jolly well speak first after the way he had treated them. The least he could have done was phone their hotel and say he was pleased they had come.

His sleep-drugged lids grew heavier. Perhaps he should speak first. Robin meant to, he really did. But before his lips could form words a very amazing thing happened. Roy Rogers, who had missed him, came galloping back and Trigger, rearing on his hind legs, kicked sand in Robin's eyes.

The man stooped over the bed shuddered. The life of a child was so fragile. It took so little to extinguish it. A palm clamped over a mouth and nose and held there. A quick twist of a small neck. If only he could do it.

Blissfully unaware Death stood beside his bed, self-interest battling revulsion, Robin climbed up on Danny Deever's broad, safe back again and jogged on happily toward the distant painted mountains.

CHAPTER 11

The bedroom was large and beautifully furnished. Eve could sense it. Wearing a pair of Stanton's silk pajamas, the legs and sleeves ending in large rolls, the fabric, where it touched her body, soft and soothing to her skin, she sat facing what she knew to be a dressing table mirror, wondering how many other women had used it.

She debated asking Marta and decided it wasn't a proper question. It wasn't any of her affair. Instead, she asked if Robin were covered.

"*Ja,*" Marta assured her. "He is covered and sleeping sound."

Eve returned to her thoughts. When Robert, if he was Robert, called her honey, touched her, pressed her fingers to his face—her cheeks burned remembering it. That other had been so long ago. She had been so young, so inexperienced. This was, seemingly, so different. Was, or wasn't he, the man whom she had known as Robert Stanton?

Marta finished combing her hair and her capable fingers began to fashion the thick strands into braids. "The Frau Stanton has lovely hair," she complimented.

In the adjoining room, Robin said, "Bang, bang," distinctly in his sleep.

"The little one," Marta chuckled, "is dreaming. All he could talk of was horses while I was giving him his bath."

Eve asked her what time it was.

"Is early morning, almost day," Marta said. She consulted the watch she wore pinned to the stiffly starched fabric stretched over her ample bosom. "Is twenty-five minutes after five."

Guided by Winston Churchill, Eve crossed the room and stepping out of her borrowed mules sat on the edge of the bed with her bare feet dangling. She wished she dared ask Marta to stay with her. She didn't want to be alone.

Seeing Eye dogs were new to Marta. "The dog stays in or oudt, Frau Stanton?"

"Out then in, please," Eve said meekly. She started at a knocking on the door.

"Are you in there, Marta?" Stanton called. Marta said she was.

"Is Eve decent?"

"Decent?" Eve repeated.

"He means are you dressed," Marta told her. Reading the frightened girl's mind, she patted her shoulder. "Is nothing to be afraid of. Mr. Stanton is a gentleman." Her lips compressed slightly. "Besides, Marta will stay. *Ja.* She is decent," she called.

The room door opened. Changed into a gray tweed suit, Hi Lo at his heels, Stanton walked directly to the bed. The pink and white of her small oval face accentuated by the thick twin black braids hanging down to cover her breasts, the English girl looked disarmingly young.

Stanton sat on the edge of the bed beside her. "Stop trembling, honey. No one is going to hurt you. I know you must be dead for sleep. But this can mean my neck unless we straighten it out." He pressed an object into her palm. "Can you tell me what this is?"

She said, "It feels like my locket." Her sensitive fingertips found the engraved E. "It *is* my locket."

Hi Lo told her, "Bob found it in the pocket of his trench coat a few minutes after that newspaper gang arrived, minus the picture it contained when you turned it over to Hanson."

Marta asked if the newsmen were gone. Hi Lo said they were. "We just got rid of the last one and locked the gate."

Eve asked Stanton if he had phoned inspector Treech and told him he had found the locket.

"No," Stanton said flatly. "He wouldn't believe I found it in the pocket of my trench coat. In fact, if Inspector Treech knew the locket was in my possession I would be inside of a cell in an hour and indicted for both the Turner and Hanson murders before the day is over. I don't know why he has held off as long as he has. But finding out who put the locket in my pocket is my job. I mean to try. All I want you to do is identify it."

"It is my locket."

He bent her fingers over it. "Take care of it for me, will you, honey?" He hesitated briefly, added, "Now, about this other matter."

"What other matter?"

"When we were in the living room you told me that you have our original marriage license or registration or certificate, or whatever they call it in England."

"I have."

"Where is it?"

Eve hesitated. She wanted to believe him. She wanted to trust him. But the paper was all she had to prove she was married. The curate who had married them was dead. So was Grace Turner. The other witness had been a stranger to her, a friendly charwoman in the chapel.

The pressure on her hand increased. "I'm not trying to pull a fast one, believe me, honey."

There it was again. If only he wouldn't call her honey. The word and the way he said it made her stomach do tricks. *I must be a very bad woman at heart,* Eve thought. She could almost wish Marta and Mr. Hi Lo weren't in the room. Then maybe he would take her in his arms and kiss her.

Stanton continued. "What I am doing I am doing for the two of us. I think you're a grand kid. In fact, believe it or not, I'm crazy about you. I want to help you all I can. But I can't help you if I'm in a cell or standing trial for murder. And I'm free on borrowed time. Inspector Treech may decide to have me picked up and thrown behind bars any minute.

"And the only possible way we can clear this up is to find out who married you under my name."

"Our marriage registration will tell you that?"

Hi Lo said, "The signature should help. And there must be one."

"Of course there is," Eve said. "You'll find the certificate in an envelope in the pocket of my hat box along with my passport."

"And your bags are at what hotel?"

"The Hollywood-Highland Hotel. I chose that because it was the name on the stationary Grace Turner used to write me."

"Now think. Does Inspector Treech know you have a room there?"

"Yes. He does. He asked me where I was stopping."

"Oh, oh," Hi Lo said.

Stanton shrugged. "We'll have to chance it. And it won't matter too much if he has beaten us to it. It isn't my signature on that license. What is your room number, Eve?"

"Room three twenty-four."

Stanton released her hand. "Thanks. Thanks a lot, honey."

He rose from the bed. "Take good care of her, Marta. Hi Lo and I may not be back for some hours, possibly not until tonight. But both gates leading into the house grounds are locked and I will leave instructions with Eddie not to let anyone in but Dr. Schaeffer."

The housekeeper puzzled, "Dr. Schaeffer?"

"A *landsmann* of yours," Stanton grinned. "A dub golfer to me but reputed to be quite an eye specialist. I just got him out of bed and while he did some fancy swearing, he said he would try to drive out here some time this morning."

Eve repeated the name. "Dr. Schaeffer. My doctor in London mentioned an American doctor by that name. But he said he was frightfully expensive."

Stanton snapped his fingers. "That for his fee. Who am I to haggle with a man who may be able to save me from the gas chamber." His voice was glib but his face was haggard with the strain of what he had been through and what he, undoubtedly, still had to face. "Besides when it comes to wives of mine, money is never an object." He stooped and kissed Eve on the lips. "And that is what you are going to be if we ever get this mess straightened out. Now think that over while I'm gone."

The door snicked shut solidly behind him. Eve sat touching her lips. She had wanted him to kiss her. He had. And bad woman or not, she liked it.

Marta insisted she get under the covers before she caught cold. Then she drew up a chair and sat patting one slim shoulder.

Eve began to relax, to feel warm and secure. "What sort of a man is he, Marta?"

"What sort of a man is who?"

"Mr. Stanton."

Marta was getting on in years but she had had her moments. "Well, I'll tell you," she told Eve. "Mr. Stanton is a man...."

There was little traffic on the highway. Spotted in between long stretches of open country and walnut and citrus groves and night clubs and roadhouses and hot dog stands and filling stations and real estate offices, the little outlying towns some thirty miles distant from the center of the city but still a part of Greater Los Angeles were still yawning in the tardy winter dawn as the speeding wheels of Stanton's car ate up the decreasing miles. Past Studio City traffic began to thicken and he was forced to slow his speed.

"Who?" Hi Lo demanded.

Stanton shook his head. "I'll be damned if I know. It could have been Johnny, or Lou, or Ed, or Lyle, or even Marty Manson, for that matter. They were all in the room."

Hi Lo immediately absolved Marty Manson and Lyle Ferris and gave his reasons. Both men were well known in their own identities, Ferris as an actor, Manson as a producer. And while Ferris, self-admittedly, had been in London during the summer of 1941, he doubted Manson had ever been out of the country. Given to boasting, the producer had never spoken of foreign travels.

Stanton said, "Then Ed or Lou or Johnny. I know they were in London. What's more all three of them were at the table in the Silver Pheasant when Grace Turner phoned."

Hi Lo agreed that any of the three could have slipped the locket in the pocket of the trench coat. "It wasn't there before? I mean when you put it on?"

"N-no," Stanton said. "I'm almost positive it wasn't. I am positive."

Drumming on the ledge of the car door, Hi Lo suggested, "Let's work from another angle. Why should anyone use your name to marry Eve?"

Stanton sighed. "You have the college education. You matriculated. The termites had to masticate the schoolhouse to get me out of the eighth grade." He bore right on the freeway down Highland Avenue and turned right on Hollywood Boulevard. "Maybe he had a wife. Maybe he wanted to pose as a big shot. Maybe he wanted to get me into trouble. He could have if Eve had gone to the military authorities and demanded a dependent's allowance. An officer and a gentlemen doesn't desert his wife and child. It says so in the book."

"You like her, don't you?"

"That," Stanton admitted, "is a masterpiece of understatement. I like her so much it gives me goose pimples to think about it. And this is the only time I ever felt that way. You heard what I said before we left the house."

"But what if Schaeffer can't help her eyes?"

"Let's not worry about that now. But even if he can't I ought to be able to compete with a Seeing Eye dog, even one named Winston Churchill."

"Yes. You should," Hi Lo laughed. "Boy, what a liar that guy must have been. He felt *self-conscious* wearing his uniform." He began to quote from memory. "An officer will at all times—"

"Yeah. I know," Stanton cut him short. "I used to work there, too." He braked the car and backed into an open space at the curb across from the Hollywood-Highland Hotel. There were few cars and fewer pedestrians on the street. Hollywood Boulevard was gray with dawn and thick with fog. Neither man noticed as they crossed the street that Matt Kelly was lounging in the doorway of the drug store on the corner.

Except for a bored bell-captain, a porter screening the sand in the ash urns, and the room clerk, the hotel lobby was deserted. His heels clicking on the freshly scrubbed tile, Stanton crossed to the desk. "My name is Robert Stanton," he identified himself. "You have a Mrs. Stanton and her son staying in Room three twenty-four. That is, they *were* staying there. They moved out to my ranch last night." He took his wallet from his pocket. "And I would like to settle their bill and collect their luggage."

The clerk glanced sideways at the headline of the morning paper that he had been reading. There hadn't been time for many details in the early edition but thanks to Leatrice May's bathroom scoop an alert city editor had managed to headline his paper—PROMINENT L. A. ATTORNEY SLAIN

The sub-head read—

Attorney's Death Linked to Attempt by Robert Stanton, Highly Paid Movie Writer Engaged to Joy Parnell, to Conceal Fact He Is Father of Son of Pretty Blind English Girl.

Stanton swung the paper around so Hi Lo could see it. "Tasty, eh? A good thing I'm not writing for radio." Stanton extended his hand to the clerk, palm up. "All right, chum. Let's go. You can see by the paper I haven't got much time. If you will give me Mrs. Stanton's key and tote up her bill while I'm upstairs, I'll phone down for a bellboy when I'm ready."

The clerk laid the key on the counter and turned away without comment.

At the elevator bank, Hi Lo asked if he wanted him to accompany him to the room.

Stanton nodded at the nest of house phones. "No. Stay close to one of those and tip me if Treech or any of his boys show up. They'll probably claim I am trying to steal Eve's luggage."

Room 324 was a large front room with twin beds. The shades were drawn and, despite the fact that both windows were wide open, a strong smell of cigar smoke permeated the room. Stanton swore under his breath. Inspector Treech had beaten him to the marriage certificate. Even now the signature was probably undergoing scrutiny at headquarters.

He looked around the littered room. Either Eve was very untidy, which didn't seem likely, judging by the appearance of her person, or the police hadn't followed their usual routine of carefully repacking her bags after they had searched them. Intimate garments lay scattered on the unmade bed in between heavy-ribbed black stockings and shorts and small undershirts that could only belong to Robin. All were pathetically shabby as were the bags that had contained them. He sought for and found Eve's hat box. It was on the luggage rack near the open door of the bathroom.

Raising the lid of the box, Stanton felt in the shirred inner pocket for the envelope of which Eve had spoken. The envelope was still in the pocket. That in itself was strange if the police had searched the room.

The room was gray with morning but not enough light filtered under the drawn shades to permit him to read print. The thick envelope in one hand, Stanton stooped to find the switch of the lamp on the table between the beds. It was his last conscious act for some minutes. Calm with cold desperation, the man whom Stanton had interrupted in the bedroom, and who had taken refuge in the bathroom, took a quick step forward and brought down the barrel of his gun on the back of Stanton's head.

Breathing heavily, the man who had slugged him tiptoed to the door and cracking it open looked down the hall. Sergeants Gieger and Swen and Kelly were emerging from the freight elevator. In blind panic he closed the door and locked it and retreating to the windows drew one of the shades aside. There was no fire-escape but there was a narrow ornamental stone ledge just below the window. White with fear, he crawled out onto the ledge and clinging to the small rough surfaces of the building with his fingers he walked the ledge to the next room. His luck, bad as it was in some respects, still held. The window of the adjoining room was open. The bed was unmade and unoccupied.

He stood a moment, clinging to the sill, making certain the occupant of the room wasn't in the bathroom, then crawling in through the window he lay on the floor gasping for breath as a heavy pounding began on the door of the room he had just quitted.

When he could breathe again he walked into the bathroom, took a piece of stiff paper from his pocket, tore it into minute scraps and flushed the scraps down the drain.

Now he was almost safe. All that remained was the boy. And Robin had recognized him. He was certain of that. He should have killed him last night when he had the chance. He would never be safe again as long as Robin lived. All the boy had to do was point a finger and say, "Why, that is my father there." He had to do something about the boy. He had to do it fast. And this time he wouldn't weaken....

"Open up. We know you're in there, Stanton."

The shouting and the pounding beat on Stanton's ears like a hammer. Lifting his nose from the nest of intimate garments in which it was resting, he sat up feeling the back of his head, the fog lifting as abruptly as it had descended. Score another one for the killer. He had not only been slugged, he had been outsmarted. The killer had beaten him to both the certificate and the punch. He knew the value of his signature.

The shouting and pounding continued. Stanton growled, "Come in. The door isn't locked."

"The hell it isn't," Gieger called.

Still holding the envelope, Stanton opened the door. "I didn't lock it," he puzzled. "It must have been the guy who slugged me." He asked hopefully, "You got him?"

"Sure. Right in my vest pocket," Gieger said. He took the envelope from Stanton's fingers and switching on the ceiling light emptied the contents of the envelope on the dresser. It contained a passport, Eve's and Robin's birth certificates, and a much-handled clipping from the London *Times* stating that First Lieutenant Robert Stanton, an accredited observer from the United States Army Air Forces, had failed to return from a night bombing mission over Bremen and both the crew of the ship and Lieutenant Stanton were presumed to be dead as other members of the flight had seen the plane go down in flames. "It isn't here," Gieger told Swen and Kelly. He sounded disappointed. "All right. What did you do with it, Stanton?"

"What did I do with what?"

"Your wife's marriage certificate."

"I haven't seen it."

"Don't give me that."

"I mean it. I found the room like this. I thought you fellows had been here. I had just found the envelope in her hat box when some guy stepped out of the bathroom and slugged me."

Swen looked into the bathroom. "You say there was a guy in here?"

"Taking a bath no doubt." Kelly was disgusted.

Stanton protested, "I mean it. There was someone in here and he slugged me. Look at the back of my head."

Sergeant Gieger pushed at the contents of the envelope with his finger. "You sure you didn't see us coming up the hall and bump it hard after you destroyed the certificate?"

"I'm positive. There was a man in here."

Kelly raised one of the shades and looked down at the street three floors below. "Baloney. If there was a guy in here he must have had a helicopter parked outside the window. He certainly didn't pass us in the hall. Maybe you'd better phone down to the lobby and give that big Indian of yours a chance to earn his merit badge by trying to follow the spoor of the little guy who wasn't here."

Stanton asked how they had gotten by Hi Lo.

"We didn't," Gieger said. "We spotted him standing by the house phones so we came in via the boiler room door and up the freight elevator." Gieger considered the situation. He didn't like what he was going to have to do. The certificate had been in the envelope. He knew. He had returned it to the envelope himself after a photostatic copy had been made. This had been the Inspector's idea, not his. "I'm afraid you're it, Stanton," he said finally. "This was your last foot of rope. The Inspector knew that, innocent or guilty, the first thing you would do would be to try and get your hands on that certificate. My orders were to bring you in for a little talk if you had the certificate on you and it was agreeable to you to have it examined by a police handwriting expert."

"And if I didn't have the certificate?"

"That changes everything. If you had destroyed it, or tried to do so, my orders are to bring you in with cuffs on."

Stanton protested, "But I didn't destroy it, Gieger."

Gieger took his handcuffs from his pocket. "Come on. Let's go, Stanton. You don't seem to be in a very co-operative mood but you may feel more like talking after a little session in one of the back rooms of the Bureau. And this time we won't invite Ernie Goetz to be present. We held Hale. And we can hold you."

Stanton backed a step away from him. "No. Now wait just a minute, Gieger." He knew what a session in the back room would mean. He had seen other men go through it.

"Oh, but yes," Sergeant Gieger insisted.

Stanton backed still another step and felt the jamb of the open hall door hard against his back. He had written the scene perhaps twenty times, thinking each time as he wrote it what a fool a man in real life would be to attempt to escape from an armed officer of the law. But this was different. He had Eve to think of. A killer was on the loose. And Inspector Treech thinking he was the killer would end his investigation.

"No. I'm sorry. I'm really awfully sorry, Gieger," he refused the detective's invitation. Then, before the detective realized his intention, Stanton punched him out of his way, slammed the door behind him to gain a few seconds' time, and raced for the stairs beside the elevator bank.

The pretty colored girl was waiting with the door of her cage open. "You might as well ride as use the stairs," she called. "It's quicker."

Stanton veered toward and into the cage just as Swen burst from the room shouting, "Stop!" For fear of hitting the girl, the detective held his fire briefly. Then it was too late to shoot. The steel door had slammed shut. The cage was beginning to descend.

There was so much to do, so much to see. Robin had never dreamed any one place could contain so many or such exciting things. He insisted on seeing and doing them all, then starting all over again. By nine o'clock Eddie was willing to swear that his legs were two inches shorter. He knew the seat of his pants was sore and he had a crick in his back.

He stole a brief respite by begging a cup of coffee from Marta. "Not that I'm complaining, understand," he told her soberly. "It's nice to have a kid around the place. It makes it sort of wholesome like." He sighed. "But since seven o'clock this morning we've been for eight rides on Danny Deever looking for bad Indians who might just have happened to get through our outposts and are creeping up on the corral. We've halter-led each colt around the corral sixteen times. We've built two forts out of packing cases. We've been swimming three times. We've picked and et a box of oranges. We've cracked and et a bushel of walnuts. We've picked two bouquets for his mother. We've combed the hen house for eggs. We've fed the chickens until I'm afraid they're going to have the pip. And we've walked, and we've walked, and we've walked."

"Is good for you," Marta laughed.

Eddie wasn't so certain. "That could be. But I sure wish that Mr. Stanton or Mr. Hi Lo would get back. Keep an eye on the boy, Mr. Stanton tells me. And how can I keep an eye on him unless I go where he does?"

"Is exercise. Is good for you," Marta repeated.

His nose white against the screen door of the kitchen, wearing a faded flannel shirt and a pair of turned-up dungarees left behind by the slightly larger son of a former married employee and washed and saved by the thrifty Marta, Robin wanted to know, "When Eddie finishes his coffee, may he come out and play again, Marta? I see smoke signs in the hills and I think the Indians are going to attack."

Eddie groaned.

"*Ja*," Marta assured Robin. "Eddie is finished now." She made certain by removing his cup from the table. " Oudt. Indians is aboudt to attack."

Eddie limped to the door. Coating a doughnut liberally with powdered sugar, Marta handed it to Robin, then held a finger to her lips. "But *shh* when you are around the house. The little mother is still asleep."

Munching at his doughnut, Robin tucked a trusting hand in Eddie's fist. "Which shall we do, Eddie? Spy out the Indians on Danny Deever, or creep up on them through the bushes?"

Unable to decide which part of him was sorest, Eddie sighed, "Whichever you say, Robin. We'll do whatever you want to do just as long as you stay inside the fence. But remember. Over the fence is out. If you go outside one of them newshawks might get you. And we wouldn't want that to happen, would we?"

Robin wasn't quite certain what a newshawk was but he agreed with Eddie emphatically. "Oh, no. We wouldn't want that to happen."

"And you aren't to go outside the fence with anyone but your mother or your father or maybe me or Marta. You're sure you understand that now?"

Robin said he was but wanted to know, "How about Chief Hi Low?"

"He's all right, too," Eddie said. "It's just your father doesn't want them newshawks to get at you. Boy! They'd eat you up alive."

It sounded exciting. Robin wondered if newshawks were anything like buzzards. If they were it might be fun to look at them through the stout woven wire fence if there didn't happen to be any Indians. The day, so far, had been perfect. There was only one minor flaw. It wasn't a bit nice of his father not to come out and at least say good morning. He asked, "Eddie—"

"Yeah?"

"Is my father at home this morning?"

Eddie shook his head. "No. Not since just before six o'clock. Him and Mr. Hi Lo had to go into town on some business." His voice was wistful as he limped into the box stall and prepared to saddle Danny Deever. "But they should be back almost any time now. I hope...."

Slumped in the back booth of a cheap Santa Monica bar with his hat brim pulled low over his eyes and an untouched glass of beer in front of him, Stanton felt like a shady character out of one of the dozens of B gangster pictures he had ground out. "This is where we part company," he told Hi Lo. "Together we're too easy to spot. You take the car. I'll use cabs. And the first thing I want you to do is to drive in to L. A. and alert Ernie. Tell him to be ready to try and spring me on a writ if I'm picked up. I doubt if he can. But it's nice to know someone is out there trying."

Stanton tore the list of names he had written in half. "Then you check on these guys, concentrating on Ed Wilcox and Johnny Hass."

"Right."

"I'll check on Lyle and Marty and Lou Saunders. It *has* to be one of the boys who were in my living room and I'd sell out right now for one of the four men who were at the table when Grace made her phone call." He sipped his glass of beer. "It can be that Inspector Treech will put out a general radio pick-up on me. But I doubt it. He's depending on a back room session to give him the club he needs. And he needs it now more than ever. If Eve's marriage certificate with its forged signature is destroyed, and it undoubtedly is by now, this thing could resolve itself into a Mexican stand-off. Treech made a lot of noise last night and did a lot of talking but when you boil it down to cold fact I have an alibi for one murder and on the Hanson deal he has nothing on which to ask for an indictment but 'alleged' motive and circumstantial evidence. On the other hand, I can't prove someone else used my name or that I'm not married to Eve."

Hi Lo beat the table softly with his fist. "If only—"

Stanton felt the bumps on the back of his head. "Yeah. If only. But unfortunately gun barrels don't leave fingerprints."

Alone on the street a few minutes later, Stanton allowed two cabs to go by, then flagged down a third cab with an obvious lug at the wheel. "Take a good look at me," he ordered the driver. "Do you know who I am?"

The driver was bored. "Naw. Maybe I should. And maybe be I should also ought to take a memory course. But I pick up so many big shots I don't know one from the other. You look kinda like Pat O'Brien. But you could be his sister Margaret for all I care. Now do you want a cab or not?"

"I want a cab," Stanton said. He gave the driver the first address on his list. "18345 Ensenada Drive. That's over off Coldwater Canyon. I think your best bet from here would be to cut over to Sunset and—"

The driver was hurt. "Look, Mister. Please. I may not know you but I know my business. You pay the fare. I'll drive."

CHAPTER 12

The house was small and white and modest. Despite the large salary Ferris earned, he was known to be careful with his money. He employed only one servant, a man. His name was Tate and he had been with the actor for years. In answer to Stanton's question he shook his head. "No. Mr. Ferris is not at home. He hasn't been home since sometime yesterday evening, Mr. Stanton. I believe he was going to a party at your ranch."

"Well, thanks anyway," Stanton said He thought he knew where he could find Ferris.

The Manson home and grounds were more elaborate. Every inch of the five-acre plot was expensively landscaped. The huge white-pillared Georgian-type house he had given his daughter and his new son-in-law as a wedding present was reputed to have cost J. V. Mercer a half million dollars. He considered it a small price to have Lili happily married and settled. He had spent far more bailing her out of other messes, most of them titled and male.

As his cab braked in the drive, Stanton saw Lili in one of the upper front windows but a French maid in a perky lace cap informed him, without qualification, that neither Mr. nor Mrs. Manson was at home.

So saying, she closed the door politely but firmly in his face. Baffled, Stanton returned to the drive and looked up at the window in which he had seen Lili. There was no way he could force an entrance without creating a scene. And he couldn't afford a scene. Moving Marty Manson down on his list, he gave the cab driver Joy's address.

The gates were closed. He had to give his name but he was admitted almost immediately and directed to the pool. The scene might have been a technicolor movie set. The lawn was a vivid green against the grey of the castle. The pool was blue. Tall date palms dwarfed the whole end against a background of scarlet salvia and hibiscus, Lyle in swimming trunks and Joy in an abbreviated swim suit were lounging in striped canvas deck chairs, a portable bar well-stocked with bottles convenient to both chairs.

Ferris greeted him cordially but with reservations. "Hi, old man. I just ran over for a drink and an early morning swim. Why not strip down and join us?"

Ruefully, Stanton shook his heed. "No. But thanks, Lyle." He sat in a chair near Joy. Her well-cared for body was lovely. She looked youthful and happy again. "I would like a drink. But it seems I am playing Tom Harris to a peck of old Massa Treech's bloodhounds and I have to keep my head clear in case I come to ice." He took an ice cube from the container on the table and sucked it.

Joy studied his face. "There's not much use in trying to fool you, is there, Bob?"

"Not much," Stanton grinned. He petted her hand. "God bless you, my children. This is the way it should have been from the start. I hope you both will be very happy. I don't know any other two people to whom I would rather see happiness happen."

Leaning over, Joy kissed him. "You are nice."

"Besides," Stanton pointed out. "It would seem I already have one wife."

"I thought so last night," Joy admitted. "And I was furious. But I don't think so now. You wouldn't treat any women that way, you couldn't, let alone a baby like that blind child. It's a frame-up of some kind, isn't it, Bob?"

"Of a very definite kind," he told her. "I don't suppose either of you saw anyone put anything in the pocket of my trench coat last night?" Stanton questioned them.

Both said they had not. "Put what in your pocket?" Joy asked.

"A small gold locket. A locket that once contained the only known picture of the man who married Eve, using my name."

Ferris said what he thought of such a trick. Joy wanted to know where the girl was. Stanton said she was at his ranch, then added doggedly, "What's more she's going to stay there, both she and the boy." He got to his feet, then sat down again and asked the actor, "I wonder if you would give me a straight answer to a possibly embarrassing question, Lyle?"

"That," Ferris said, "depends on a number of things."

Stanton worded the question as diplomatically as possible. "Let's put it this way. If it should become necessary, can you prove where you were last night a half hour either side of the time that Hanson was killed?"

"I can," Ferris said promptly. He looked at Joy. "After all, you were engaged to Joy. And not knowing that between the two of us she was going to choose me, I—"

"Please," the blonde star stopped him. "I would rather not know about her." She smiled and she was beautiful. "Remember? We started all over. We both were born again at six o'clock this morning."

Ferris kissed her.

Stanton said, "You're nice people, Joy. I envy Lyle. And I know you're going to be very happy." He looked at his watch. It was noon. The morning had frittered away.

Both Lyle and Joy insisted on walking him back to his cab. Enroute, Joy laid her hand on his arm. "Now, don't forget, Bob. I'm going to marry Lyle.

That's definite." She wrinkled her nose at the actor. "I have to make an honest men of him. But if Inspector Treech gets tough with you and you need money or a good lawyer—" She left her offer open.

Stanton patted her in farewell. "Thanks. I'm currently filthy with both. But if I should need a character witness—"

The star's laughter followed him into the cab. "Not with my character.

The cab driver was goggle-eyed. "Say. You *are* a big shot. That was Joy Parnell. You *aren't* Pat O'Brien, are you, chum?"

"No," Stanton told him soberly. "I'm his little sister, Margaret." He gave him Lou Saunders' address.

It wasn't far from the Union Station. Both the carpet and the wood of the stairs were commingled into a spongy pulp that gave under Stanton's feet. The hall was filled with the sour smell of stale beer and the odor of cooking things, most of them highly spiced. The reporter opened his door, sleepy-eyed, smelling strongly of good whiskey, wearing nothing but shorts. "What," he demanded, "do you want at this ungodly hour of day? Haven't they executed you yet?" He stepped aside ungraciously. "Well, you're here. Come in."

"I didn't kill Hanson, Lou." Stanton sat in a raddled overstuffed chair and poked absently at the springs that were trying to escape from one arm. "And I didn't kill Grace Turner."

The reporter was indignant. "What are you trying to do, make a liar out of me? Didn't you read my story in the nine o'clock edition?"

"No," Stanton admitted. "I didn't. Why? Did you pin it on me?"

Saunders lighted a cigarette and sat back on the unmade roll-away bed. "Did I pin it on you? I practically have you in the gas chamber. Wait until you hear the pellet drop. Inhale deeply three times—and say hello to Hanson."

Stanton studied the other man's face. He never before had realized the superficial resemblance between so many men. Saunders, too, was six feet tall, light-complected, brown-eyed, and weighed around two hundred pounds. He came to the purpose of his call. "You were in London in August '41, weren't you, Lou?"

The reporter poured himself a drink. "Oh, no. You're not tagging me with your peccadillo." He grinned. "But that little English chickadee could if she wanted to. I would be very pleased to be the father of any sons she might have, present tense or future indicative. How come you let a gorgeous piece of flesh like that cool off for seven years?"

It was an effort for Stanton to keep his temper. "You have me all wrong, Lou. I never saw Eve before last night. It was one of four other men who married her, using my name. You, Lyle Ferris, Ed Wilcox, or Johnny Hass. I would even include Marty Manson but he wasn't at the table when

Grace called and I don't believe he ever was in London."

Saunders laughed where the cuff of his shirt would have been if he had been wearing a shirt. "Why be upstage with me, Bob? You know I never betray a trust or a confidence, unless it suits my purpose, which it usually does."

"Shut up, Lou," Stanton said wearily. "This thing is serious. I mean it. I didn't kill either Hanson or the girl."

The reporter pointed out, "That's only one man's opinion." He poured more whiskey in his glass. "I'm sorry I can't offer you a drink. But this is really very bad whiskey. I doubt if your stomach, accustomed to rarer fare, could assimilate it. As I pointed out to Marty Manson one night in a little Limehouse pub, the rich get richer and the poor get indigestion."

Stanton said sharply, *"Marty was in London? In what year?"*

For once Saunders wasn't glib. "In the fall of 1941," he said thoughtfully. "That was before he married the Mercer money. He was an assistant director with some fly-by-night outfit making a blood-and-intestines quickie and they came over to pick up some bombed-ruins shots." He continued, talking to himself, "On this night I mentioned he was crying in his beer because he was a failure. He wanted to know why you and Lyle Ferris should be big shots, what you had that he didn't have. And I told him— talent."

The reporter ran down like an unwound clock.

And there it was. A lot of things were suddenly clear to Stanton. He had been using his feet instead of his head. Marty was his alibi, and he was Marty's. He didn't know how it had been done. But it had to be Marty Manson. During the whole of Inspector Treech's long questioning, Marty had scowled and nodded and grunted. But he hadn't spoken one word.

He hadn't dared to speak. Not with Eve in the room. Eve was blind. She couldn't see him. But she might recognize his voice.

Stanton's mind raced on.

Lili hadn't fainted because she feared that Hanson's records might reveal some indiscretion on her part. She had been afraid for and of Marty.

Lost in almost identical thoughts, Saunders said, "I will be damned. And I call myself a newspaperman!"

Stanton dialed the Silver Pheasant and asked if either Ed Wilcox or Johnny Hass were there. Both were. Ed Wilcox answered the phone. "This is Bob Stanton, Ed," Stanton identified himself. "And this phone call can be very important. Think back to the day I got that phone call from Grace Turner. Where did you go after you left the booth? And to whom did you mention the phone call?"

"I went to my office," Wilcox said. "And I didn't mention it to anyone. At the time I thought it was a rib. Why?"

"Ask Johnny," Stanton said.

Hass came on the phone. "Why, I went over to the Consolidated lot. I'd made the appointment with Marty not twenty minutes before."

"In the Silver Pheasant?"

"Yeah. Sure. Marty was here. He walked out just before you came in."

"And during your appointment you told him of the phone call that had come after he'd left?"

Hass thought a moment. "Yes. I think I did. I know I did. We had quite a laugh about it."

"Thanks, Johnny," Stanton said quietly. "Thanks a lot."

Saunders said, "The dog. It was Marty the Turner dame saw through the window, but knowing him as Bob Stanton she phoned him by that name." The phone rang as Stanton set it down. "Saunders speaking," the reporter said crisply into the mouthpiece. "Yes... Yes... Yes. Well, it's news. Put it on the wire. What do you want me to do, crochet an epilogue on it?" Hanging up, he told Stanton, "The was the lad I left haunting your gate. A Dr. Schaeffer just left the place and when my lad slugged him for an interview, Schaeffer said, quote, Mrs. Stanton's complete recovery of sight is almost a medical certainty under proper therapeutic treatment, plus a minor operation to relieve the pressure now paralyzing her optical nerves. But it will be a gradual process. It may take a year, even longer, for normal vision to be restored. Unquote."

Stanton reached for the phone again and gave the operator the number of his ranch. Eddie answered. "Yeah. It's straight stuff, Mr. Stanton," he assured him. "We're all tickled pink about it but if you want to speak to Mrs. Stanton I think you had better call back a little later. She's kinda having happy hysterics and Marta is letting her cry it out on her shoulder." He added, "But if I might make a suggestion, Mr. Stanton. Why don't you forget the white pony for now and drive the boy home? You two are the first ones Mrs. Stanton wants to speak to after the doc gives her the good news and Marta and I are forced to tell her that neither of you are here at the moment."

Stanton gripped the phone so hard his hand hurt. "White pony? Drive Robin home? What the hell are you talking about, Eddie? Robin isn't with me."

Eddie sounded as if he were about to weep. "He isn't with you, Mr. Stanton? But he *has* to be. You were going to buy him a white pony on account of Danny Deever being too big for him to ride on alone."

Sick with growing apprehension, Stanton told Saunders, "I think Marty has the boy." He spoke into the phone again. "I haven't been within twenty miles of the ranch since Hi Lo and I left it at six o'clock this morning. Talk fast. What made you think he was with me?"

"He *said* he was going with you. We had been playing all morning, see, Mr. Stanton, scouting out Indians and building forts and riding on Danny Deever. And I am kinda tired out like. I am sitting under the big pepper tree in back of the stable hoping you or Mr. Hi Lo will show up pretty soon so I can go back to my own work and Robin is scouting through that sage and greasewood thicket near the back road when I hear a car pull up and stop. When it didn't pull on again I got to my feet to go see who it was but just then Robin shows up grinning from ear to ear and tells me you want him to go for a ride and look at a white pony you have seen. Then he runs back into the thicket again and a minute or so later I hear the car pull on but I don't think anything of it because I know Robin is safe with you."

"He said I wanted him to go look at a pony?"

"He said his father."

"You didn't see the car?"

"No I didn't, Mr. Stanton. The road is sunken right there and you know how that thicket is."

Stanton slapped the table. "The locket. The picture in the locket. The boy naturally has seen the picture many times. And while his mother is blind, he isn't. He knew his father when he saw him...."

Later, asked how he happened to think of the Mercer lodge at snow-bound Lake Arrowhead, Stanton admitted he didn't know. He didn't. The five minutes following his phone conversation with Eddie were always confused in his mind. He remembered phoning Inspector Treech and being very surprised when instead of laughing at him, the Inspector thanked him soberly for the information and assured him he would put out an immediate radio alert for Manson and the boy.

He remembered phoning Ernie Goetz and being told that Hi Lo had just entered the office with a report that cleared Wilcox and Hass. He remembered asking Hi Lo to drive out to the ranch and stay with Eve until the boy had been found. Still more vividly he remembered arguing with Lou Saunders that Marty wasn't all bad, that he couldn't do this last terrible thing. He also remembered reasoning Marty would not dare take the boy home because of Lili and the servants, nor would he dare remain in the Los Angeles area with the living proof of two murders in his car. He would head for some lonely spot. One of the loneliest spots in wintertime that Stanton knew of was the Mercer summer lodge high on the Rim-of-the-World Highway. So, possibly, he came to his deduction.

The Mercer lodge was between Lake Arrowhead and Big Bear, set in a quarter of a mile from the highway on a privately paved lane. The orange and olive groves and vineyards were far below them now in the early winter dusk. This was another world, a world of snow and cold and towering pines. From the moment they left San Bernardino behind them and began the six thousand-foot climb in Lou Saunders' souped-up Ford with the big PRESS sticker on the windshield, snow fell in great soft clinging flakes that threatened at times to clog the over-worked windshield wiper completely.

When they finally reached the Mercer lane, a single set of car tracks wound back through the snow-burdened pine. Following them, rounding a bend, Saunders almost rammed the car for which they were searching. Fast being obliterated by the falling snow, two sets of footprints, one large, one small, led from the car to the lodge.

Saunders wanted to know if Stanton had a gun. When Stanton said he hadn't the reporter got a tire iron from the back of his car.

"You take the back. I'll take the front," Stanton said. He followed the mismated footprints up the stairs and across the drift-whitened porch. Through the small pane of glass in the door he could see the interior of the living room. Manson wasn't in it. Robin was.

As Stanton watched him the boy looked apprehensively at a closed door that Stanton knew led into the rumpus room and bar. The door was unlocked. Stanton opened it and walked in, putting a finger to his lips in warning.

Ignoring the warning in his relief, Robin dropped the blanket and raced across the room to him. "Oh, I *am* so glad you came. Please take me home to my mother." He tried hard not to cry, and failed. "I don't want a white pony, I don't."

His thin arms clasped Stanton's legs as the door of the rumpus room opened. Marty Manson stood framed in it, a filled glass in one hand, a revolver in the other. "It would be you," he said. Without taking his eyes off Stanton, he ordered Robin back to the fire. "And you come in here," he told Stanton.

Under the menace of the gun, leaving the way clear for Lou Saunders to get the boy out, Stanton did as he was ordered.

"Now close the door," Manson said. He had been drinking heavily but he wasn't drunk. "How did you find me? How did you know?"

Stanton leaned one elbow on the bar. "It finally dawned on me. As to finding you, I tried to put myself in your place. You couldn't do it, could you, Marty?"

The producer shook his head. "No. The girl was one thing. Hanson was another. You were still another. But the boy was a different matter. He's my son. No. I couldn't do it. You came alone?"

Stanton told the truth. "No. Lou Saunders drove me up. But the police are looking for you. They know you have the boy."

"How? No one saw him get into my car."

'That's right," Stanton agreed. "But when I told Inspector Treech what I thought had happened, for some reason he believed me." More a vibration than a sound, Stanton sensed Robin's lifted voice, heard a sibilant answering "shh," then muffled snick of the closed front door.

If Manson heard it he made no sign. "You fool. Treech has known all along but he couldn't prove it. He's been using you for a cat's-paw, hoping you'd pull his chestnuts out of the fire."

"But his theory—"

Manson repeated, "You fool. Inspector Treech wouldn't know a theory if he met one face to face. He works with facts. And I made one bad mistake, as he rode me the other night. I got the wrong blood in the wrong place."

"Blood?"

"Your blood. In the back of your car. You were in the luggage compartment when I killed Grace Turner. I doped your drinks at Sherry's, walked you out and into the trunk. Then I kept your date with the girl." He shuddered at the recollection. "I damn near died when Johnny Hass told me about that phone call. There could be only one explanation. Grace Turner was in town and she had seen me in the Silver Pheasant. She *thought* she was speaking to me when she laid down the law to you. If the truth came out, I was sunk. Then I saw how I still might wiggle out of it. I would have if it hadn't been for Hanson. I sent that bottle of rye to the poker game at the studio, knowing your drinking habits. Then, picking up Lili, I trailed you from one bar to another. She thought it was a lot of fun. Then I sent her on home and kept your date with murder. And out of the two million people in L.A. it would have to be Shad Hanson who saw me at the wheel of your car."

"Lili knows?"

"She knows I killed Hanson. She knows he phoned me yesterday afternoon. She knows that enroute to your party I left her parked in a bar while I took care of a little business." He poured a drink with his left hand. "Manson kills Hanson. Hell. I couldn't even pick out a guy to kill whose name stood out from mine." His lips twisted in a bitter smile.

"And after killing Grace you drove me home?"

"Yes. And I tucked you in bed with an empty Scotch bottle that would have sent you to the gas chamber. It had the Turner girl's fingerprints all over it. But when Shad put the bee on me I foolishly told him about the bottle and he sent one of his stooges out to your ranch for it. If you were tagged for the murder, he couldn't blackmail me."

"And that fire at the hide-out?"

"I set it. I tried to kill you to get Hanson off my back. If you had died in that fire the Turner investigation would have been dropped. I could have told Hanson to go whistle. No," Manson corrected himself. "The investigation wouldn't have been dropped. But I thought so at the time. I didn't know that while rounding one of the curves on the canyon road you had stupidly bumped your head on one of the supports and bled all over the back of the car."

Looking at the gun in Manson's hand, Stanton computed his chances of successfully closing the gap between them before Manson could fire and decided it couldn't be done. As Marty had said, Robin was one thing. He was another. Manson would pull the trigger any moment now. He stalled for more time. "It was you who slugged me at the hotel?"

"It was. I had to get that certificate. Treech's men were watching the front but I sneaked in the back way and opened the room door with a skeleton key."

"And you left the room, how?"

Manson shuddered at the recollection. "On a damn ledge about two inches wide." He sighed. "It isn't fair. Other men do worse things than I did and it doesn't bounce back in their faces." He seemed anxious to have Stanton believe him. "I didn't know there was a child, Bob. I swear it. As that fellow Hale told Grace Turner, I thought it was just one of those things."

Stanton edged a step closer to him. "But why use my name to marry Eve?"

Manson considered the question. "That was seven years ago. I was tired of being a nobody, a failure. I met Eve at a dance one night right after I'd been talking to Lou Saunders and he'd told me the difference between you and Lyle and myself was that you both had talent. I was still angry when I met Eve. She made me angrier. She thought all Americans were big shots and wanted to know what I did. What was I to tell her, that I was an errand boy for a fly-by-night movie outfit? No. I let her think I was a big shot. You were everything I wanted to be, successful, an officer, a gentleman. So I borrowed your name and reputation. You were a hero. Because of a punctured eardrum I couldn't even get into the Army and get myself decently killed."

Stanton asked, "But why end the masquerade so soon?"

Manson was frank about it. "You know the facts of life. You know why I married her. I couldn't get her any other way. Then, to complicate matters, the fly-by-night outfit that I was working for folded and I ran out of money. Besides, early in November you got yourself shot down and I couldn't very well impersonate a dead man. So I dropped Eve cold and came back to Hollywood and punked around in small jobs for three years." His laugh was bitter. "Then I met Lili in '44 and we were married and I was suddenly a big shot."

The revolver in his hand all but forgotten, Manson leaned his forehead on the back of the hand holding the gun and despite what he had done to

Eve, Stanton couldn't help but feel sorry for him. Success had come to Marty too late.

He moved another step closer to him. "Look, Marty. You're not entirely a heel. You've proven that. Why not put that gun in your pocket and come on down the hill with me?"

"And stand trial for two murders?" Manson jeered. "No, thank you." He waved his gun at the expensive wood paneling. "I like being a big shot. I like money and servants and cars. I like to live in places like this. And I'm not going to trade it for the lethal chamber or a cell at San Quentin." He was silent a moment, then said in a lower tone, "Look. You like Eve pretty well, don't you, Bob?"

"I do."

"And you like my boy?"

"I do." Stanton nodded affirmatively.

Manson motioned him from the room. "Then get out of here. Go on back down the hill and straighten things out for both of them as best you can. By the time you get back to the ranch Eve should be free to marry you."

Stanton protested, "But, Marty—"

Manson uncorked a bottle and gulped a stiff drink from its neck. "Do as you're told and don't argue. Let me do one big thing. This is the story as I see it. I didn't kill Grace Turner because of Eve. I'm the guy who never saw Eve before. I killed Grace because I had an affair with her in England. And I killed Shad because he knew I killed her. Both of them were threatening to tell Lili and her father and I couldn't have that happen." He pulled the phone on the bar toward him and made certain the line was open. "Shortly after you leave here I'll phone Inspector Treech and make a full confession." He leveled the gun at Stanton. "Now get the hell out of here before being so noble chokes me and I change my mind. I'm going to count to three. One... two...."

Robin watched, enchanted, as the big man on the edge of his bed rolled a brown paper cigarette with one hand. "That must be difficult to do. Do you think I could learn how?"

Hi Lo reminded him, "You're supposed to be trying to go to sleep. Remember?"

"Yes sir." Robin stretched luxuriously, then curled up into a ball. The day had been long and full. It was warm and cozy in his bed. Marta had stuffed him with good things to eat. His mother had wept over him and hugged him. The nice man who it seemed was his real true father had promised him Danny Deever for his very own. There was no reason he shouldn't sleep except for the loud voices on the other side of the wall separating the bedroom from the living room.

Hi Lo scowled at the wall as Inspector Treech's voice rumbled, "Don't give me that, Stanton. So you didn't kill either Hanson or the girl. Manson was right about me using you as a cat's-paw. I couldn't buck the Mercer power and money until I was certain. But neither you nor Manson can make me swallow him having an affair with the Turner girl. He could tear up the marriage certificate but he couldn't tear up the photostatic copy I had made. And the signature is Manson's."

Saunders asked, "How do you know? Are you God? Did you see him sign it? I am willing to kill the biggest story I ever had, what's your beef? The city of Los Angeles pays you a salary to keep the homicide rate at a norm and, failing that, to ferret out a killer. Well, you have one with a full confession. At least you have his body. What more do you want, bananas on your corn flakes?"

His mother said something Robin couldn't hear and he asked Hi Lo, "What's homicide?"

Hi Lo evaded the question. "You aren't even trying to sleep."

Robin closed his eyes and as promptly opened them again as the man who was his real true father said:

"I think you sympathize with what we are trying to do, Inspector—minimize this thing with as little heartache possible to everyone concerned, especially Eve, Lili, and the boy. Marty wanted to do one big thing in his life. He did it. Lou is willing to kill his story. I want to marry Eve. She's willing to marry me for the boy's sake. That's the way Marty wanted it. That's why he was willing to save the State the expense of a trial. Why not let it ride at that?"

Robin asked Hi Lo, "If the nice Mr. Stanton is really my own father and the other man was just pretending, why should he want to marry Mother again?"

"Because," Hi Lo skirted the truth, "that other marriage was in England. And the laws in this country are different."

"Oh."

Robin slid his hand under his pillow and brought out the small gold locket his mother had given him. Opening it, he studied the picture it contained. No matter what anyone said it wasn't the same picture that had been in it before. He was positive. Well, almost positive.

Robin snuggled a cheek into his pillow. Well, maybe he was wrong. Maybe his memory had tricked him. Mother said the nice Mr. Robert Stanton was his father. The nice Mr. Stanton said so. Chief Hi Lo said so. And anyone who went to the cinema knew that good Indians never lied. He was glad it had turned out this way. His real father was much nicer than the man who had tried to fool him. His real father hadn't promised him a pony. He had given him Danny Deever outright and had thrown in a saddle just like Roy Rogers' to boot.

His eyes grew gritty with sleep, then popped wide open again as a door slammed and the man who was a newshawk but not at all like a buzzard laughed heartily. "It was a tough fight, Ma, but we won. Well, having helped fix Treech's clock, I will be on my way. But, remember, Bob. If you want me for your best man I'll be glad to fly to Las Vegas with you in the morning."

Then his mother said, "You've been wonderful, Mr. Saunders. You all have been wonderful. I'll never forget it—"

Saunders made a peculiar sound with his mouth. Robin tried to imitate it and a fairly credible Bronx cheer escaped his lips.

"You learn fast," Hi Lo complimented him. He turned off the lamp by the bed. "But now you get to sleep."

Robin bargained, "Will you leave the door open just a little bit?"

"Just a little bit." Hi Lo tiptoed out and a deep silence settled on the room. Robin lay staring out the window at the sky. He had never seen so many stars nor had they ever seemed to hang so low. This was really a very nice place to be. Then the stars became confused with horses and the horses, in turn, became confused with ducks and cows and chickens and a mile-long swimming pool suspended in the sky. He was about to plunge in with Eddie and swim up through the milky way when he felt Winston Churchill's cold muzzle nuzzle his hand and sleep receded instantly.

"You bad dog," Robin reproved him. "You know you shouldn't leave Mother alone."

Climbing out of bed, he tugged the reluctant dog to the door of the bedroom, then stopped short in the hallway looking into the living room.

He might have known. Winston Churchill, as usual, knew what he was doing. Mother wasn't alone. Standing on her very tiptoes, her hands cupped on the back of his father's head, she was kissing his father, hard. And both of them seemed very pleased about it.

Trudging back to bed and snuggling Winston Churchill under the covers with him, Robin lay wondering sleepily if there were any bees on his father's farm. He hoped so. It would be nice to have a baby brother or a sister. Perhaps some day he would.

THE END

My Flesh is SWEET

BY DAY KEENE

CHAPTER 1

Heat lay a prickly, flower-studded, blanket on Mexico City. In an hour or so it would rain. At this season of the year it always did. After the rain the city would come to life again. Now, in the hour before *siesta*, pedestrian traffic was thinning. The cries of the beggars lining the Avenida Juarez had grown less shrill. Small merchants yawned in their doorways, eager to roll down their shutters. Sleeping Indians were already sprawled on the grass or nodding on the tree-shaded benches dotting the Alameda.

Hurrying across the east end of the Alameda to the post office to pick up a check for sixty-five thousand dollars in payment for the seven part serial he'd written for the Saturday Evening Post or, failing that, still be able to reach the National Pawn Shop before it closed, Ad Connors thought—

This is it. One way or another, I'm getting out of here. Today.

A big man, in his early thirties, his last clean white suit was sodden with perspiration. The *frijoles* he'd eaten for lunch lay heavy on his stomach. He had a sudden and a fierce nostalgia for the sight and smell of Broadway and a kosher corned-beef on rye. If he ever got back to New York he'd never again go farther south than 42nd Street. By hocking both his typewriter and his watch he should be able to raise the fare.

He was rounding the Palace of Fine Arts when he heard the crash. By the time he reached the corner the usual post-office-corner-crowd of petty thieves, sidewalk merchants, and male and female lottery ticket vendors, were gathered around two cars in the intersection of Tacuba and Teatro Nacional. One of the cars was a '50 gray Ford coupe with Illinois license plates. The other was a soldier-chauffeured army Cadillac.

In the back seat of the dented Cadillac a fat-faced, one star *generale,* the neck of his uniformed shirt unbuttoned, sat picking his lunch from his teeth as he admired the anatomical topography of the little brunette *turista* climbing out of the Ford coupe.

Connors didn't blame him for looking. She was a little honey. She was a breath from home wearing Indian straw sandals on bare feet, white slacks so sheer the rolled hem of her scanties showed, and a V-necked bolero to match that left her tanned mid-riff bare. More, she was so mad she was willing to dig up Santa Anna's bones and start the Mexican War all over.

Connors pushed his way up closer so he could hear what she was saying.

Eleana forced herself to be calm. After all accidents did happen. It wouldn't do a bit of good to follow her first inclination to kick the chauffeur in the shins. Both of the policemen shouting at her in Spanish wore small American flags on their sleeves. According to the automobile club guide book that meant they spoke English.

She gave them her best school teacher look. "Stop that shouting right now. And if you want me to listen to you, speak English. It wasn't my fault. I had the right of way."

The policemen stopped shouting but neither of them spoke. Despite the *Estados Unidos* flags on their sleeves, both had lost their English. They wanted no part of the *generale*. All they wanted was to get the little *turista* and her car out of the intersection.

The chauffeur got into the argument. The light might have just changed, true. But he had blown his horn and *Generale* Estaban was in a hurry. If the *señorita* hadn't been driving faster than the law permitted she could have stopped. He shrugged his contempt. Besides, from the manner of her dress, she was obviously nothing but a *Norte Americano* baggage.

It wasn't any of Connors' business but it burned him to hear the chauffeur stamp the girl as something he doubted she was. Pushing the man in front of him aside, he stepped into the small opening around the two cars. "Now, just a minute, soldier. Let's watch our language."

Eleana clutched his arm. "You're an American?"

"I am."

"And you speak Spanish?"

"I do."

The fingers on Connors' arm tightened. "Then tell the police it wasn't my fault and I demand they arrest the officer who owns the car unless he agrees to pay for the damage he's done."

Connors attempted to disillusion her. "Honey, you're in Mexico and the guy is a general."

She insisted. "Please."

Connors set his portable typewriter case on the street and repeated what she'd said in Spanish.

The policemen looked at the *generale*. Taking the toothpick from his mouth he leaned both arms on the window sill and patted Eleana with his eyes. Then he turned on his Spanish charm. The fault was entirely that of his stupid chauffeur. He would be pleased to have her automobile made as good as new. More, if the beautiful young lady would be so kind as to give his chauffeur the name of her hotel he, *Generale Estaban,* would be happy to escort her to her room where they could discuss the matter further over a few drinks of something cool.

The onlookers laughed knowingly.

Eleana wanted to know what he'd said.

The back of his neck red, Connors gave her part of it. "He admits it was his chauffeur's fault and he's willing to pay the repair bill on your car."

A wide smile on his fat face, *Generale* Estaban opened the door of the Cadillac. The palms of his hands sweating, Connors stuck his neck all the way out by closing the door. It could be he was wrong. It could be the little brunette would enjoy being tumbled by a Mexican *generale*. But he was damned if he would be a party to it.

'The *señorita*," he told Estaban, "thanks you from the bottom of her heart. But as she has no one to whom she may entrust her car she must refuse your gracious offer to escort her to her hotel."

The army man gave him a sour look. Eleana said, "Be sure to get his name and where to send the bill. And tell him my name is Eleana Hayes and I'm stopping at the Flamingo."

One of the policemen wrote the name and address on the back of a charge slip and handed it to *Generale* Estaban. He stuffed it in his shirt pocket and ordered his chauffeur to drive on.

Connors inspected the Ford. Outside of a broken bumper and a crumpled fender it seemingly was undamaged. He wrenched off the broken bumper and put it in the turtle back. "You're all right now?" he asked the girl. "You can drive?"

Eleana smiled, "Of course." She slid in behind the wheel and killed the motor three times just trying to put the car into gear.

Connors looked at her lips. They were quivering. Reaction was setting in. With traffic as thick as it was, he doubted she could drive a block without getting into another jam. He told her to slide over, reached for his typewriter and found that it was gone. Sighing, he slipped into the seat Eleana had vacated.

Eleana was concerned. "Weren't you carrying something?"

"Yes," Connors said. "I was. A ride on the B.M.T. and a kosher corned-beef on rye."

The crowd cheered as they drove away. Eleana was puzzled. "What are they cheering about?"

Connors told her. "Love."

There was a parking space in the chained-off area in front of the Palace of Fine Arts. Connors parked in it. "Now look, Miss—"

"Hayes," Eleana smiled. "Eleana Hayes."

Her smile was as nice as the rest of her. Connors introduced himself. "My name is Ad Connors." He waited a moment hoping she might recognize it. When she didn't, he continued, "I'm an American citizen, reasonably respectable. And you're still pretty shaky. So if you don't mind waiting while I pick up my mail, I'll be glad to drive you wherever you want to go."

Eleana's smile brightened. "You're very kind, Mr. Connors. And if you don't mind, I'll take you up on that. I did have the green light. Believe me. But after driving those mountains between Laredo and here—"

"Yeah. I know what you mean," Connors said.

He climbed the steps of the post office whistling. There were three letters for him but none of them meant a thing.

On the bottom of the rejection slip from the Post his agent had scribbled a few kind words. Shad still thought the novel was the best piece of work he'd done so he was sending it on to a book publisher. He mustn't feel discouraged. The thing for him to do was sit right down and write another book. He was as good as the best. Sooner or later he couldn't help but break into the big money.

Fingering the three *pesos* in his pocket, Connors was pleased to hear it. The other two letters were from lads still running pulp mills. Business was bad with them, too.

He dropped the letters in a trash can and walked back to the Ford. Eleana was applying lipstick. "I wonder, Mr. Connors, if—"

"If what?" Connors asked.

"If having imposed on you this much I could impose on you still further." Digging into her braided straw purse Eleana handed him a letter. "I wonder if you would help me find this address? It's really much more important than having my car repaired."

Connors glanced at the address. It was on Tacuba, less than a block away. "Why not?"

He locked the car and helped her across the street, hoping the fact she was being escorted by a fairly husky male *Norte Americano* would spare the seat of her well-filled slacks from too many lemon-colored fingers with a habit of nipping what they admired.

The address on Tacuba wasn't good. It wasn't bad. Attorney Caesar A. Santchez's office was on the second floor rear. A plump Mexican girl who looked like she had been crying was typing at a flat-topped desk in back of a varnished railing. She got up and came to the rail as Connors opened the door for Eleana.

"*Si, señor?*"

Eleana said, "Tell her I'm Miss Hayes and Attorney Santchez is expecting me."

Connors repeated what she'd said in Spanish but the name didn't mean a thing to the secretary. She was sorry but Attorney Santchez wasn't in his office. In fact he wasn't in Mexico City. At four o'clock that morning, Attorney Santchez had received a phone call from an old *amigo* in Uruapan and had departed almost immediately to effect a reunion. His secretary didn't know when he would return. Neither did she bother to explain what she had been doing in her employer's apartment at four o'clock in the morning.

Connors translated what she said. "Attorney Santchez is out of town. He left for Uruapan this morning."

"Uruapan?"

"Yeah. It's over on the west coast. Well, not exactly on the coast. It's near Paricutin. You know. The volcano that pushed up out of a corn field back in 1943."

Connors thought Eleana was going to cry. Instead her lips compressed and green drowned the gray in her eyes. "But that's impossible. I wired him I was on my way. He can't be out of town. I *have* to see him."

Connors repeated what she'd said in Spanish.

The secretary shrugged. Connors doubted she approved of Miss Hayes. He knew she didn't approve of the outfit Eleana was wearing.

"Ask her," Eleana said, "if she knows the address of Mr. Donald Hayes."

The girl had never heard, or claimed she'd never heard of anyone by that name. Connors told Eleana so and Eleana pounded her fist on the railing. "She's lying. She has to be lying." She screamed at the secretary. "You give me my father's address."

The secretary screamed back at her. Then, recovering her dignity, she assured Connors *he* was a gentleman. *He* had removed his hat when he entered the office. *He* had spoken softly and in a considerate tone of voice. *He* hadn't doubted her words. It desolated her to have to ask him to leave. But unless he did so, immediately, and took his *Norte Americano* baggage with him she would be forced to call the police.

Connors asked her if Santchez was really in Uruapan. The girl said he was and Connors believed her. Lighting a cigarette, he told Eleana, "I don't know what this is about. It isn't any of my business. But Attorney Santchez' secretary is plenty sore about something. And she says unless we leave she's going to call the police. Do you want them in on this?"

Eleana shook her head. "No. This is a private affair."

Down on Tacuba again, Connors guided Eleana into a small restaurant and blew two of his last three *pesos* on coffee and pastries. The little brunette protested she wasn't hungry but she ate three pastries and allowed the waitress to refill her cup. Connors let her mention the affair in the attorney's office. Eleana began by asking how far it was from Mexico City to Uruapan.

Connors said he thought it was around two hundred and fifty miles.

"Over what kind of roads?"

"Good. That is, good for mountain roads."

Eleana accepted a cigarette. "Damn and double damn."

Connors offered her a light. "I take it you don't like to drive mountain roads."

"It gives me goose pimples to even think of it."

"Still you *have* to see this Attorney Santchez?"

"Either Attorney Santchez or my father. This isn't a pleasure trip. It's business. It could mean a lot of money to me."

Connors did some mental arithmetic. The rent on his apartment was paid for another two weeks. But a man couldn't eat an apartment. Now, with his typewriter stolen, he couldn't raise train or bus fare back to New York. On the other hand if he could get as far as Laredo he could pick up a newspaper job for a month or two to tide him over until he could bat out a few pulp yarns. So he couldn't write serious novels. He could still write whodunits.

"Why??" Eleana asked. "I mean why are you so interested?"

"I was just wondering," Connors said, "if we couldn't be of mutual benefit to each other. How long do you intend to stay in Mexico?"

Eleana sucked hard at her cigarette. "Not a minute longer than I have to. In fact I'd hoped to start back tomorrow morning."

"That," Connors said, "would suit me fine." He laid his last *peso* on the table. "Look. That's my bankroll. One *peso*. You want to go to Uruapan to see this Santchez. But mountain driving terrifies you. I want to get back to the States. I was on my way to hock my typewriter to raise the price of a ticket when you smacked into *Generale* Estaban. While I was giving you a hand someone swiped my machine and now I'm stuck. So I'll make you a proposition."

Eleana's eyes narrowed slightly. "What sort of proposition?'

"I'll drive you to Uruapan to see this Santchez and then on up to Laredo for the ride and my expenses."

The waitress assumed the *peso* was her tip. "*Gracias, señor.*"

Eleana asked Connors if he was serious.

"I was never more serious."

She protested. "But I don't even know you."

Connors pointed out few employers knew their employees before they engaged them. He gave her a thumbnail sketch of himself. "I'm a fairly well known former pulp writer who thought he could write a serious novel. I came down here to write it because I thought I could live cheaper. Now the novel has flopped and I'm broke. But I can give you good references, including a sub-secretary over at the American Consulate. What do you say?"

He watched the little brunette wet her lips with the tip of her tongue and knew what she was thinking. People just didn't do such things. Still, she was afraid of mountain driving. He had been kind to her. He seemed respectable. A new, deeper, shade of green crept into her eyes as she asked, finally, "It would be strictly business?"

Connors raised his right palm shoulder high. "Strictly business." He hoped, suddenly, that he was lying.

Eleana smoked a long moment in silence. Then she temporized, "Well, I *have* to see Attorney Santchez and I've had all the mountain driving I can take. Let's talk to this man you say you know over at the Consulate."

The sub-secretary's name was Demming. He gave Connors a big send-off. Ad Connors, Demming swore, was both a gentleman and the best damn detective story writer in the entire United States. More to the point he showed Miss Hayes a tall stack of pulp magazines with Connors' name on their covers.

Connors grinned at Eleana. "Which ought to prove while I may be broke, I'm not exactly a bum."

Back in the car again, she asked, "But if you're such a successful writer, how is it that you haven't any money?"

Ad explained, "That's the hell of it. I'm not successful. I'm merely one of perhaps two dozen hacks in the pulp detective field on whom the editors can depend to stuff the seven basic plots with suspense and give them fresh reader appeal."

Eleana accepted another cigarette. "And just what are the seven basic plots?"

Grinning, Ad admitted, "I'll be damned if I know. But I read in a book once that there are seven of them."

CHAPTER 2

The Ford Agency was closed but Connors found a garage not far from his apartment that agreed to go to work on the car immediately. He elected to stay with the car while the work was being done. Miss Hayes thought it a good idea. She cashed two fifty dollar travelers' checks and gave him enough for the bill plus thirty *pesos* for expenses. Connors felt like a fool but he took it. The understanding was he was to call for her at six o'clock the next morning ready to take off for Uruapan.

Then, hoping she might call and suggest they spend the evening together, Connors gave Eleana the phone number of his apartment.

The Mexican mechanic watched her into a cab and drew out the word in absolute approval. "N-ice."

Connors had to put his hands in his pockets to keep from hitting him. He had no right to be jealous. So far he was just a hired hand. Except for a few minutes in the restaurant when the air had grown decidedly sticky he had no reason to even hope it might be otherwise. But a lot could happen in a thousand miles, especially in Mexico.

It was after six when the fender was dry. The body man had done a good job. Unless one looked close, and that under a bright light, the fender looked as good as new. He paid the bill, got a receipt, and drove the car up the street and into the woven-wire protected parking area beside his apartment building.

By seven his grips were packed and he'd locked them in the car. Then he sat down and waited for the phone to ring. When it hadn't rung by ten o'clock he knew that Eleana wasn't going to call and walked down to Louie's to eat and buy a bottle of rum.

It was two o'clock when Eleana called. Ad sat up mouthing cotton that the rum had seeded. "Ad Connors speaking," he said into the phone.

Eleana sounded worried, also a little high. "Come right over to the hotel, please," she begged him. "As fast as you can make it."

Connors spat out a mouthful of cotton. "I'll be right over," he told her.

After returning from Louie's he'd lain down on the couch without bothering to undress. All he had to do was lace his shoes and put on his hat and topcoat. He got as far as the hall then went back for the remaining half litro of rum. A man never knew when a little rum might come in handy.

The Flamingo was on Insurgentes not far from the Paseo De La Reforma. Connors parked the Ford at the curb and went in. The hotel night clerk brushed him with his eyes then returned them to the paper he was reading.

Two-A was in the front of the building at the end of a long hall. Connors could hear the *generale's* voice while he was still twenty feet from the door. Eleana had been smart enough to leave it cracked. Connors pushed it open and walked in. It was a two room suite, bed and sitting room. Her back to him, Eleana was standing in the doorway of the bedroom superimposing in English her opinion of the *generale* on his hiccup punctuated flow of gutter Spanish. She was wearing a pastel green backless evening gown and from the angle at which her elbows were jutting Connors had the distinct impression she was cupping her breasts in her hands. When she heard him, she turned. What there was left of the front of her dress was in tatters. He'd been right about her being high.

"Get him out of my room, please, Ad," she begged.

Connors looked into the bedroom. *Generale* Estaban was making himself at home. He'd already removed his dress tunic and his shirt and was sitting on the edge of the bed busily tugging at one of his boots.

"Get him out of here," Eleana wailed.

Connors asked her if she had ever tried to throw a Mexican general out of a lady's boudoir deep in the heart of Mexico City at two o'clock in the morning.

"Please, Ad," she begged. "I didn't know what I was getting into. I was about to call you and suggest we have supper together when General Estaban phoned and—"

"Yeah. Sure. I know," Connors said. "He wanted to discuss the damage to your car."

The army man continued to tug at his boot, too pleased with his graphic recital of past performances to realize his two-some had become a crowd.

Eleana began to cry. "I can't leave the room like this. And every time I try to get some clothes, he grabs me."

Connors asked why she hadn't phoned the desk instead of him.

Eleana said, "I was afraid they'd send for the police and I can't afford any scandal."

Connors walked on into the bedroom and sat on the bed beside Estaban. The *generale* wasn't pleased to see him. He opened his mouth to say so. Before he could, Connors took the bottle of rum from his pocket, swigged a quick drink from the neck, and handed Estaban the bottle. "*Saludos.*"

Theoretically, the *generale's* hands were tied. A gentleman had to respond to a toast. He also wanted a drink. He took a big one. "*Saludos.*"

Still not entirely convinced that Connors was friendly to his cause, the army man washed the first drink down with a second. Then looking from Connors to Eleana, his eyes lighted in comprehension. Of course. Not all the best things in life were free. The reason the little *turista* had played coy was to give her bully time to arrive and discuss terms. Estaban was a sport about it. Fishing a fat wallet from his hip pocket he spilled a heap of ten- and twenty-*peso* notes on the bed. Then leaning forward he breathed rum in Connors' face. *"Quanto?"*

Connors wished he knew how much English the army man understood. He took a chance and asked Eleana if she had another bottle in the suite.

"No," she sniveled. "I haven't." She took advantage of the diversion to slip into a house coat and for a moment her breasts were exposed. They were nice breasts.

It didn't, Connors decided, matter greatly about the bottle. It hadn't been much of an idea. He doubted if he could pass Estaban out. His kind didn't pass out. They just got uglier and he was on the verge of being ugly now.

"How much?" Estaban repeated in English.

Connors stalled for time. "Well, the damage to the car came to two hundred and forty-five *pesos.*" He laid the receipted bill on the bed.

Estaban counted two hundred and forty-five *pesos* on top of it. Then, after a moment of drunken consideration, he added five twenty-peso notes to the pile. "Okay." He kicked off his boot and fumbled with his belt. "You go now."

Eleana gasped, "Don't you dare leave me alone with him."

"I don't intend to," Connors said.

He wished he knew what to do. This far south of the border the military, especially in General Estaban's brackets, ranked one star short of God. Taking a deep breath he separated the five twenty-peso notes from the rest of the money and tucked them back into Estaban's still bulging wallet. Then, as diplomatically as he could, he broke the bad news.

He was sad the young lady's manner of dress and willingness to accept a supper invitation from a total stranger, even a military man as distinguished as himself, had led him to false conclusions. But they were false. Despite appearances to the contrary the foolish little *señorita* didn't commercialize her affections.

It was a good sales talk. But Estaban wasn't having any. Getting up from the bed he wove a few feet toward Eleana. Thinking he meant to grab her Connors stood up and balled his fists. But the army man had forgotten Eleana for the moment. He was after the holstered revolver he'd laid on the dresser.

Pointing it at Connors, he said, "Get out. Get out or I'll shoot."

He was drunk enough to shoot. Connors shrugged and turned as if to leave the room. In getting the house coat Eleana had trapped herself near the closet. Sobbing she tried to follow Connors and Estaban threw out his gun hand to block her. As he did Connors turned back and brought up his balled right hand.

It was like hitting a stone wall. All Estaban did was grunt. Then, furious, using the gun barrel as a club, the general lashed out at Connors and Connors caught at his gun hand and wrestled him down on the bed. The shot was muffled between their bodies. The fat man went, suddenly, limp. Connors got to his feet drenched with sweat. Blood was staining Estaban's white undershirt. He lay on his back with his mouth open. As far as Connors could tell, he was dead.

"Good," Eleana panted.

"No. Not so good," Connors corrected her. The surface was thinner down here and easily scratched. Down here they still stood you against a wall and shot you for a lot less than shooting *a generale.*

Fighting down a desire to be sick he tiptoed to the hall door and looked out. No one seemed to have heard the shot.

Turning back he asked Eleana, "Did you tell him you were going to Uruapan?"

Eleana shook her head. "No." She was completely sober now.

"Then pack your things," Connors said. "Neither of us can afford to be here when they find him."

It took Eleana less than five minutes. She'd packed the same as he had, earlier in the evening.

A film of cold sweat on his palms, Connors locked the door behind them. It might be minutes. It might be an hour. It might be morning before the body was found.

As Eleana paid her bill, Connors winked at the clerk. 'The *generale* is tired and requests he not be disturbed until morning. *Comprendo?"*

The clerk patted Eleana with his eyes. *"Si, señor."*

Connors carried Eleana's bags outside and put them in the car. Then he asked the driver of one of the taxis parked near the hotel where he could pick up the Laredo road.

"You're on it, chum," the taxi-man told him. "Only you're headed the wrong way."

The *generale's* car with the chauffeur asleep at the wheel was parked in front of the taxis. Hoping the driver wouldn't wake up, Connors swung the Ford in a wide U turn and pointed it north on Insurgentes.

According to the road maps he'd studied in the garage, the Paseo De La Reforma led into the road to Morelia where he could pick up the road to Uruapan. Not that he intended to stop. Not now. Now it was a race for the border. But when road blocks were erected the chances were they would be on the main highway to Laredo.

Passing Chapultepec Castle, Eleana spoke for the first time since leaving the hotel. "Thank you. I don't know what I'd have done if I hadn't met you, Ad."

Connors laughed harshly. He'd killed a man for her, and she thanked him. Now the immediate danger was over, reaction was setting in. He was so cold that his teeth chattered. He asked if there was a heater in the car. Eleana said there was and turned it on.

"What gave him the impression I was a tramp, Ad?"

Connors told her. "You."

Another girl might have kicked it around. Eleana left it there. She was twenty-one and attractive. She'd had the same trouble before. But not in Mexico. North of the border the combined letters n and o meant nothing doing. But there was a policeman on every corner to back up Funk and Wagnalls.

The heater helped a lot. The night air was cold but it was warm inside the car. Connors drove in silence until they were well into the mountains. Then he asked Eleana what she did in Chicago. She said she was an elementary school teacher and Connors realized for the first time she had a faint suspicion of a drawl.

"But you weren't born in Chicago."

"No," Eleana admitted. "I was born in Blue Mound, Missouri."

Connors lighted cigarettes for both of them. "Now suppose you tell me what this is all about. I've stuck my neck way out for you. And I'd like to know where I stand. What's this Attorney Santchez business? Why do you have to see him?"

She said, "I'm trying to locate my father. He has something I want."

"Your father is this Donald Hayes you mentioned?"

Eleana's drawl was even more apparent. "That's right."

Connors drove glancing from time to time in the rear vision mirror. "And what is it he has you want?"

"My mother's marriage license."

"Your what?"

"My mother's marriage license." Eleana's cigarette tip described a fiery arc. "It's such a mixed up affair I don't know where to begin. But I'm engaged to be married this Fall. And I want proof he and mother *were* married." The lights of a car traveling in the other direction gilded her face briefly. Her voice was wry. "In other words, certified proof I'm out of Celeste by Donald in the manner as prescribed by law so if I should bear an heir apparent there will be no possible stain on his or the Lautenbach escutcheon."

Connors asked, incredulous, "You mean you're marrying old man Lautenbach the multi-millionaire meat packer?"

Eleana laughed. "Don't be silly. Of course not. I'm marrying his son, Allan."

"Oh," Connors said. "I see." He drove, trying to recall what little he knew about the heir to the Lautenbach money. A man of forty-odd the younger

Lautenbach went in for polo ponies and jumpers and show girls given to breach of promise suits. Somehow he couldn't imagine Eleana married to him. "You love the guy?" he asked.

"Love," Eleana said, "has nothing to do with it. If I don't love Allan, so what? I don't intend to teach school all my life. This is probably the only chance I'll ever have to break into the big money." She sucked the tip of her cigarette to a red glow then exhaled slowly. "Besides, I don't think Allan cares very much whether I love him or not. What he and his father really want is a young, respectable, healthy broodmare to tone up the family blood line."

Connors laughed. "And they insist in this proof of your legitimacy?"

"No," Eleana drawled. "At least they haven't so far. But considering the amount of money involved and the purpose of the marriage, I imagine some lawyer will mention the subject before the wedding bells ring out and I don't want to be caught unprepared. That's why I drove down to see Attorney Santchez and ask him to arrange a meeting with my father."

Connors didn't get it. "A meeting with him?"

Eleana explained. "Yes. You see my father and mother separated when I was four. That is he separated by running off with a Mexican girl who did a high wire act in the circus that my father and his brother owned."

Still puzzled, Connors asked, "But where does this Santchez come in? Why does he have to arrange the meeting?"

Eleana told him. "Because I don't know father's address. And Attorney Santchez does. He's been father's attorney for years. You see, since shortly after he left her, through Attorney Santchez, father has mailed my mother fifty dollars a month for my care. That is he did up until three years ago when I began to teach."

It sounded confused to Connors and he had enough to worry him. "You wouldn't by any chance be kidding me?"

Eleana shook her head. "No, Ad. I mean it. Every word. I don't suppose you ever heard of the Hayes Brothers' Circus?"

"No. I can't say I have."

Eleana snuffed her cigarette in the ash tray. "From what mother tells me it was worth seeing. She was their star equestrienne."

"In other words, bareback rider."

"That's right. And they had three rings and four elephants and all sorts of acts and clowns and sideshows. The show wintered in Blue Mound where I was born. And father and Uncle John made lots of money. That is they did until the depression hit them. Then father had to go to some man in California and mortgage the show for fifty thousand dollars. I've read the letter he wrote mother saying he'd gotten the money and was starting back. And he did come back. A half dozen people in Blue Mound saw him.

But the stinker didn't go near either mother or Uncle John. Instead he picked up this Mexican girl and skipped with her and the money."

Ad asked, "What happened to the circus?"

"The man who held the mortgage took it over. Mother didn't even know where father was for two years. Then I guess father's conscience hurt him and she began to get the monthly letters and checks from Attorney Santchez."

Connors glanced up at his rear vision mirror. "Your mother divorced your father, I suppose?"

"Years ago."

"And now you're down here to get her marriage license from your father?"

"That's right."

"Why didn't you write for it?"

"I did. A dozen times. And Attorney Santchez always replied that he would take up the matter with *Señor* Hayes. And that would be the last I'd hear of it."

"*Mañana*, eh?"

Despite the strain she was under the heat and the motion of the car was making Eleana sleepy. She curled sideways on the seat and rested her left cheek against the cushion. "*Mañana*, my eye. It went on for months."

"Then why didn't you or your mother write to the city clerk of whatever town she was married in and get a duplicate?"

Eleana closed her eyes. "Because mother had only been over from France two months. And all she knows is that she and father were married in some little town in the midwest and they had to drive all night to get there."

"You wrote your father you were going to be married?"

"Urn hmm."

"And he didn't ask for an invitation to the wedding?"

"Uh-uh. You see, the girl he ran away with had a husband."

"Even so. After all these years."

Eleana opened her eyes again. "You still don't understand, Ad. Father can't come back to the States. He killed his sweetheart's husband the night they ran away. That's why he does all his business through Santchez." She laid her hand on his arm. "I'm scared, Ad. Do you think General Estaban is dead?"

"I'm afraid so," Connors said grimly.

"And what will happen if they catch us?"

Connors gave it to her straight. "I don't know what they'll do to you. But they'll probably shoot me."

CHAPTER 3

There were a number of good hotels and restaurants in Morelia catering to tourists. Connors passed them up in favor of a combination hotel-restaurant patronized chiefly by local trade. If the police hadn't fallen for the off-to-Laredo gag, it wouldn't be smart of them to show themselves in the places in which they might be expected.

While Eleana went to the washroom to freshen up, he gassed the car and had the oil and the tires and the battery checked. Then he ordered breakfast for both of them.

Eleana looked like a sale to *Colliers* when she sat across from him. She'd taken one of her suit cases into the washroom with her and changed into a two piece gray nylon suit with snakeskin purse and shoes to match and a sheer chartreuse blouse for contrast. She knew how to make up, and had.

Connors grinned at her. "You don't look much like a school teacher to me."

Eleana was cramped from sleeping in the car. The strain was beginning to tell on her. She wanted a cup of coffee. "And just what's wrong with being a school teacher?" She found her glasses in her purse and picked up the grease splattered menu.

"Nothing," Connors said. "And I've ordered for both of us."

Eleana returned her glasses to her purse. "Oh. And all this for just the ride and your expenses."

It was both what she said and the way she said it.

Connors pushed back his chair and stood up. "And to hell with you, too, Miss Hayes."

He walked out and got in the ear and pointed it back toward Morelia. He hoped she thought he was stealing it. Eleana told him later, she did. But when he got back to the filling station she was still sitting at the table mashing green sauce into her eggs as if she had a grudge against them.

Eleana spoke before he could. "I'm sorry. Please believe me, Ad. I didn't mean to be bitchy."

Still standing on his dignity, Connors showed her the fistful of *pesos* he'd gotten for his watch. It looked like a lot of money. It wasn't. There were only one hundred and thirty-two *pesos* in the roll and he'd had to sell the watch outright to get that much.

Eleana asked where he'd gotten the money.

He told her, stiffly, "I did what I was on my way to do when I met you. I sold my watch. From now on you pay your way and I'll pay mine."

Eleana's smile wasn't bitchy this time. It was cute. "Okay." She held out her hand palm up. "But if you don't mind then, Mister, will you give me the two hundred and forty-five *pesos* you euchred out of the *generale* so I can pay my check?"

Connors put his hand in his left coat pocket and brought it out filled with *pesos* he'd forgotten were there. It wasn't that funny but they both laughed until the little Indian waitress thought they both were crazy. After that they got along fine.

Back in the car, Connors wanted to head directly for Guadalajara but Eleana pointed out, not illogically, that if Estaban was dead and the police were searching for them the larger cities would undoubtedly be alerted before the small towns would and they would be as safe in Uruapan as they would be anywhere.

Connors agreed with her. "Uruapan it is then. Maybe I didn't kill the guy after all."

Eleana talked as he drove. As Connors got the picture, shortly after her father had deserted them, Eleana's mother had moved to Chicago and they had lived there ever since.

"Except for vacations," Eleana said. "Summers we go back to Blue Mound and live with Uncle John. He's been grand to us ever since father ran out. How well do you know Chicago, Ad?"

"Quite well," Connors admitted. "I spent five years in it."

"Writing detective stories?"

He grinned at her. "No. Dreaming up soap chip operas to fill in the deadly lull between commercials on how to wash one's panties in which soap and who won't smell any more if they listen to Gertie's Life Is Beautiful and remember to send in twenty-five cents and a box top for a bottle of genuine *Affair de Passion* as rubbed into the armpits by some of Hollywood's loveliest stars."

Eleana laughed. "Mother listens to those things all day long. I don't see how you could write them."

"There came a time when I couldn't."

"But it did pay well?"

Connors lighted cigarettes for both of them. "In the five years I was in it I averaged eight hundred dollars a week."

"And you quit that kind of a job?"

"Alas."

"And now you're broke?"

"No," Connors corrected her. "I have one hundred and thirty-two *pesos*. A good job. And prospects."

He glanced sideways at Eleana. There'd been a Slav in some bed in her family. Her cheeks under high bones were slightly hollow. Her lips were full and parted. From time to time she ran her hands over her breasts as if they were hurting her. She met his eyes and looked away.

"Hoot. Listen to the man."

Connors' pulse beat a little faster. He had Eleana classified now. She was neither naive nor a tramp. She was neither a prude nor a virgin. She did what she wanted to do with whom she wanted to favor but only in a manner and under circumstances that befitted the innate qualities of a lady. If *Generale* Estaban had been a gentleman about it, the chances were that he would have gotten what he wanted.

Uruapan was just another town. There was the inevitable market place and plaza and a pretty public garden with a river flowing through it. There were the usual local police in the Square but none of them seemed in the least interested in either Connors or Eleana. Connors began to feel better. The chances were he'd only wounded Estaban and the army man was keeping his mouth shut to save face.

Attorney Santchez wasn't checked in at either of the big hotels but his secretary had been telling the truth. Connors found the attorney registered at the Morelas, a small hotel catering to the better class Mexican trade.

Connors drove the car into the fenced-in parking lot back of the hotel. Then, still thinking of Estaban, he registered himself and Eleana as *Señor* Schmidt and *Señorita* Braun of Vera Cruz and requested two rooms with a connecting bath.

Both of the rooms were huge with tall French windows opening on a flower-filled patio. For the sake of appearances Connors ordered the bellboy to take his bag into the far room. Then, when the boy had gone, he took Eleana into his arms and kissed her. Eleana wanted to be kissed. She kissed him fiercely in return. But she was practical.

"Please, Ad. Not now. I came here to talk to Attorney Santchez."

He said, "To hell with Attorney Santchez."

Eleana shook her head. "Maybe later, Ad. After I've talked to him."

She came into his arms again but the fire was gone. It was nice just holding her. Brushing his lips with hers, Eleana smiled, "You *are* nice. I like you." She pinched the lobe of his ear. "Now you get a few hours sleep."

"And after that?"

"We'll see."

Connors patted her and walked through the bathroom to his room. The boy had opened the windows, but the room was still hot and stuffy. He took off his coat and shirt. Then he stripped to his shorts and lay down on the bed thinking:

The damndest things happen to me.

He heard Eleana phone the desk clerk and asked to be connected with

Attorney Santchez and assumed the lawyer was on the ground floor with them, not far away. At least a phone bell rang for a long time in one of the rooms across the patio. Then it stopped and Eleana said, "Two dirty words."

Connors asked her what was wrong.

She called, "Santchez doesn't answer his phone. And the clerk thinks he must have driven out to see *El Monstruo*. Would you like to see a volcano?"

"No thank you," Connors called back. "I've seen one."

The cool and quiet of the tree-shaded patio crowded into the room. The bed was soft. Connors felt a breeze ripple the hair on his chest. His sense of immediate need had dissipated. It was a long way to the border. He lighted a cigarette and lay listening to the muted sounds in Eleana's room.

For some reason, having nothing to do with General Estaban, he felt depleted and a little sad. Perhaps because at thirty-five he was still tom-catting around, still not amounting to a damn any way a man looked at success. Other men his age had homes and families and a good job or a business. But somewhere along the line he'd missed the boat. He'd been lured on by a dream, spending life as if it was money.

There was a scuff of mules on the tile of the bathroom floor. Eleana closed and latched the door leading into his room. A moment later he heard running water and the intimate, homey, bathroom sounds of a woman preparing to—shop, attend a P.T.A. meeting, offer her fair white body as a Kinsey Report statistic. The thought amused rather than aroused Connors. The splashing in the tub went on for a long time. He closed his eyes for a moment. He had no intention of sleeping. He slept.

It was cool and much darker in the room when Connors awakened. The splashing in the tub had stopped. The door was unlatched and open. He got up and looked in the bathroom. A dropped towel lay in a drying puddle on the floor. There was a lingering fragrance of bath powder. Eleana's bed had been slept in, or rested on, but she wasn't in her room.

Connors padded back into the bathroom scowling. Then he saw Eleana's note and caught on fire again. Scrawled in lipstick across his bare abdomen were the words, 'Alas. Poor Romeo. Will be back by five o'clock.' It was signed with a broken heart bleeding lipstick.

Connors' grin hurt his ears. "The devil. The cute little devil."

He started to dig a dressing gown out of his bag. Then, changing his mind, he dressed and left the hotel.

The flower market was less than two blocks away. He bought as many long stemmed gladioli as he could carry for six *pesos*. Then a *litro* of rum and a carton of cokes. The *rebozo* was in the window of a Japanese curio shop. Connors knew he was going to buy it as soon as he saw it in the window. Most *rebozos* are coarse and made of cotton. This was black silk appliqued with big white flowers. It looked like Eleana. The Japanese started at eighty-five *pesos*. Connors gave him the old tourist *esta mucha* and got him down to seventy-five. Then he let him have it in Spanish. The Japanese grinned and came down to sixty and he'd bought a shawl for his love.

Back at the hotel he sent an Indian maid for vases while he spread the silk shawl on the bed. Along with the flowers it brightened the room immeasurably. He had more trouble getting ice. As a compromise he put the cokes in the bathroom basin and let the cold water run.

He heard Eleana before he saw her. But she wasn't in her room or in the hall. She was in the patio and there was an imperative ring to her voice. "Ad."

Connors opened the French window wider.

It was almost dark in the patio now and the room light reached out to meet her. Eleana was still wearing the gray suit and chartreuse blouse. Her arms were filled with packages. She'd even bought a cheap sombrero. It dangled by its cord from her arm. As Ad took the packages from her, she said, worried, "I think he must be sick or something, Ad. I watched through the window a long time. And he didn't even move."

"Who didn't move?" Connors asked.

Eleana laid the sombrero on a chair. "Santchez. I got his room number from the clerk and looked in the window." She pointed across the patio. "And he's over there, lying on his bed but he won't answer his phone."

Connors walked with her across the patio. There was barely enough light left for him to see the figure of a man on the bed in the room she pointed out. "You're positive that's Attorney Santchez's room."

Eleana said, "I'm positive."

Connors stepped in through the French window. The man on the bed was tall and thin and not unhandsome. He was also Caesar A. Santchez. At least that was the name on the sheaf of letters spilling from the mouth of the brief case on the dresser. But he wasn't sick. He was dead. The handle of the knife that had killed him protruded three inches from his chest.

Eleana followed Ad into the room. "What's the matter with him, Ad?"

Ad told her the truth. "He's dead." He felt the flesh with the back of his fingers. The body was still warm. "And recently."

Eleana said, "Oh, my God."

Connors looked around the room. The bed was unmade and rumpled. A chair was lying on its back. A waste basket was overturned. But the chair and the basket were the only sign that the dead man might have fought for his life. His hair was neatly combed. His clothes were in order. Both would seem to indicate he'd known and trusted the person who had stabbed him.

A gleam of metal caught Connors' eyes. He'd used the gag in murder yarns a dozen times but it seemed such things did happen. In falling back on the bed, Santchez had made a last grab and hung on to a piece of gold chain supporting an old fashioned heart-shaped watch charm. Connors struck a match and could read the initial D engraved on one side of the bulge.

Then, before he could stop her, Eleana reached over his shoulder and pried at the locket with her thumb nail. It popped open, exposing the picture of a smiling young woman. Eleana's hand shook so badly she dropped the locket and it swung back and forth on the chain firmly anchored in the dead man's hand. In the last flare of the match, Connors saw the initial H was carved on the other side of the bulge.

"You know her?" he asked Eleana.

She gasped, "It's a picture of mother when she was about my age."

The ague extended to her knees. Connors stood up and slipped an arm around her waist. He knew what she was thinking—D. H.—Donald Hayes.

Tightening his arm around her waist he walked her out into the patio. A paunchy Mexican business man was smoking a last cigar before his supper. He took the cigar from his mouth and bowed graciously.

"*Buenas tardes, Señor, Señora.*"

Connors returned the bow. "*Buenas tardes, Señor.*"

Back in his room he sat Eleana on the bed and closed the windows. Her face was as white as the flowers appliqued on the *rebozo*. He opened the bottle of rum, splashed some in a glass and offered it to her.

Eleana shook her head. "No thank you."

Connors drank what he'd splashed in the glass, then took a big drink from the neck of the bottle. He needed it. His knees were as weak as Eleana's. No one needed to tell him what could and probably would happen. A man was dead, just across the patio. And they had inquired for him.

Now he had two dead men to worry about.

CHAPTER 4

N ight continued to fill the patio until it absorbed even the trunks of
the trees. The smell of the flowers was sickening. Some color
returning to her cheeks, Eleana asked Connors if he didn't think they
should report what they had found to the police.

He said, "And find they're already looking for me for killing General
Estaban? No thank you. Besides as soon as the body is found the police
will come to us. The first thing we did when we checked in was attempt
to contact Santchez."

"Damn and double damn," Eleana swore.

"All of that," Connors agreed. He wiped cold sweat from his forehead.
"I'm going to wind up against a wall yet. And after the police will come
the reporters. What are you going to tell them?"

Eleana gave him a dirty look. "You got me into this."

"Not me. All I tried to do was get a free ride to the border."

"You think my father killed him?"

Connors lighted a cigarette. "I haven't the least idea. The locket with
your mother's picture would seem to indicate he did."

When Eleana was excited her faint drawl was more pronounced. "But
why?"

Connors said, "There could be a dozen reasons. Maybe Santchez had
something on your father he didn't want Santchez to tell you. You say your
father is wanted for murder in the States. That in itself is ample reason for
him to want to keep his present identity and whereabouts a secret."

Eleana changed her mind. "Please mix me a drink, Ad."

Connors added cola to the rum, trying to evaluate the situation. There
was no light in Santchez's room. Unless the lawyer had made an evening
appointment with the old friend his secretary had mentioned, the chances
were his body wouldn't be found until morning. And by morning they
could be miles away.

Eleana asked, "How far is it from here to Guadalajara?"

Connors picked the road map from the dresser. "Two hundred and twenty miles. And it's four hundred and thirty miles from Guadalajara to El
Mante. And three hundred and ten miles from El Mante on up to Laredo.
But if we run, once Santchez's body is found, every federal, state, and city
cop along the way will be looking for a '50 gray Ford coupe with Illinois
license plates."

"You mean they'll think we killed Attorney Santchez?"

Connors pointed out, "Mexican police aren't any different from other police. They like their jobs. Consequently they're going to try to find out who killed Santchez. Maybe it was your father. Maybe it was someone else. If the Uruapan police can find him and convict him, fine. But if they can't they're going to try to pin this thing on anyone who could have done it. And if we run we're going to look guilty." He shrugged. "On the other hand, for all we know, they may be looking for us now."

Eleana nibbled at her lower lip. "Then run or stay, we're stuck."

"Yeah. Run or stay we're stuck."

Eleana asked for another drink. "And a cigarette if you please."

Connors mixed a drink but the cigarette pack was empty. "Sit tight. I'll get some," he said.

Eleana caught at his arm. "Don't be long, Ad. Please."

It was the first surface sign she'd shown of fear. Connors admired her for it. She was people. He stooped and kissed her. "Know something, honey. I like you."

"I like you, too," she told him.

There was no cigar counter in the hotel. There was a *cantina* a few doors up the street. Connors bought some cigarettes and paused in the doorway to light one before returning to the room.

The Cadillac parking in front of the hotel was black and familiar looking. So was the chauffeur's face. As Connors watched it through the flare of the match, *Generale* Estaban got out. He hadn't killed him after all. Estaban hadn't been dead but unconscious. All he had done was wound him and the shock of the slug and the liquor he'd consumed had done the rest.

Two big men followed Estaban to the walk. The tribe looked the same the world over. They could only be plainclothes police. One of them walked into the hotel. Sweat trickling down his spine, Connors left the lighted doorway and pressed his back against the adobe wall next to it. Estaban was out for blood, and he had found them. His face hadn't been as important to him as getting even. But how had he found them? Then Connors thought of the receipted repair bill. He had discussed Uruapan at length with the mechanic who had repaired Eleana's car.

Connors snuffed out his cigarette lest the glow of it call attention to him. The small of his back ached. Knots developed in his calves. He hadn't the least idea what Estaban had meant to charge him with. Attempted murder probably. It didn't matter now. The general had a better club. A dead lawyer.

The plainclothes man came out of the hotel grinning. He and his partner and Estaban promptly went into a huddle. Connors seized on the opportunity to slip into the dark patio.

Eleana was still sitting on the bed nursing her second drink. She looked up as he came in the window.

"Estaban's alive and outside," Connors told her. "He just drove up with two detectives and they've already confirmed the fact we're here." He slipped into his coat. "I'm going to run. You'd better stay. As far as I'm concerned this is a shooting matter. But nothing much worse than Estaban is apt to happen to you."

Eleana said, "I'm going with you."

Connors didn't have time to argue. He expected, momentarily, to see the light in the room across the patio go on. The first thing the detectives would do would be to contact Santchez to learn Eleana's business with him. He snatched the *rebozo* from the bed. "Then let's go."

"But our bags?"

"We'll have to leave them. And remember this. I don't know where I'm going. I don't know how I'm going to get there. Maybe you'd better stay."

Eleana picked up her purse, folded the *rebozo* over her head as if she'd worn one all her life and walked out into the patio.

The last window on their side opened into the lobby. Through it they could see General Estaban and the two detectives talking to the desk clerk. Connors tightened his grip on Eleana's arm and stopped her under a giant live oak just the dark side of the bright yellow runner laid down by the street lamps and the headlights of the passing cars. A drawn revolver in his hand the chauffeur was leaning against the front fender of the Cadillac, watching the front door of the hotel.

It was evening and warm. The walk had its usual evening complement of giggling girls walking with their arms entwined and admiring knots of strolling young men. Connors waited until three particularly pretty girls walked by in the opposite direction from the one in which he wished to go. As he'd hoped, the chauffeur's eyes patted their plump buttocks up the street.

"Now," he told Eleana.

They moved out into the crowd on the walk. His eyes filmed with sweat, the muscles of his back tensed against the shout or shot he expected to hear at any moment, Connors forced himself to stroll.

So far, so good. They were out of the hotel.

Then he realized Eleana was crying. Tears might attract attention. He told her to stop or he'd slap her. She stopped crying and asked:

"Now what are we going to do?"

"I want to get the car if I can," Connors said.

He didn't hope to drive out of town in it. They wouldn't get far if they did. All hell was due to pop in a few minutes. But if he could get the Ford out of the lot and under cover it might help confuse their trail.

He told Eleana what he was going to try to do and left her on a bench in the Plaza with instructions not to move or talk to anyone. Then, walking around the block, he came at the hotel from the rear. The parking lot was dark and silent but Attorney Santchez's body had been found. The patio was filled with excited voices and bright with a portable trouble light.

Connors eased the car out of the lot. Then he parked on a dark side street while he tried to figure his best move.

There was a car with Federal District license plates parked a few yards up the street in front of a building under construction. Finding a screw driver and a pair of pinchers in the back of the Ford, Connors took the plates off both cars, put the Mexican plates on the Ford and hid the Illinois plates under a pile of used lumber.

Then he drove on to the market section in search of a second hand store. He got the kind of a black suit he wanted for twenty-eight *pesos*. It was threadbare and none too clean but it looked as though it might fit him. A broad brimmed black hat cost eight *pesos* more. He bought new things for Eleana, a black full skirt and a ruffled white off-the-shoulder blouse. The shoes she was wearing would have to do. He didn't know her size.

Then rolling the things in a bundle he drove back to the bench on which Eleana was waiting. Eleana was in the car almost before he'd stopped. Connors laid the bundle in her lap. "I'm going to drive out a way and we're going to put these on. From now on we're strictly Mex. I do all the talking. And no argument."

"I'm not arguing," Eleana drawled. Her voice sounded as if her throat hurt her.

Connors stopped at the first secluded spot he came to, stripped off the suit he was wearing and put on the black one. It smelled and it bagged at the knees and elbows but it didn't fit him too badly. With sufficient dirt under his nails he could pass as one of the letter writing scribes that infest every plaza and market place in Mexico.

Eleana struggled out of her smart gray suit. Some of her tension had left her. "If my pupils could see me now."

Connors wished he could see her better. Keyed up as he was, just catching glimpses of white flesh excited him. He took her in his arms and kissed her.

Limp in his arms, Eleana asked, "Are you certain you aren't sleepy?"

Connors sat back on his side of the car. Then when Eleana was dressed, he drove back into town. To reach the bus station he had to pass the Morales. There were two local police cars in back of the Cadillac now. He drove on and parked across from the bus station.

"Now what?" Eleana asked.

"We're going to try to get out by bus," he told her.

Satisfied his own clothes would pass, he inspected Eleana in the yellow pool of a street lamp. Both the teacher and the *turista* were gone with the gray suit. The *rebozo* brought out the green in her eyes. The full skirt was short enough to show her legs to good advantage. Just enough of the round of her breasts showed to focus male attention away from the lightness of her skin. He told her to smear on more lipstick. She did. It gave her a bold look. She was still pretty enough to eat but her smeared lips dropped her down into the class of the sentinels prowling the street in front of the bus station, trying to pick up some two-*peso* trade.

A bus for Guadalajara was scheduled to leave in fifteen minutes and was waiting on the apron of the station. Connors bought two tickets and put Eleana in the unlighted bus with instructions to hold a seat for him but not to dare speak one word of English.

"I'm frightened," Eleana said.

Connors swallowed the lump in his own throat. "That's odd. But come to think of it, I've felt better myself."

He walked back to the Ford, unscrewed two of the spark plugs, cracked them with the handle of the screw-driver, and screwed them in again. The Ford bucked and chattered and back-fired when he pulled away from the curb. He barely made the garage he'd spotted up the street. Once inside the big door the coupe gave a realistic shudder and pooped out.

The lone mechanic on duty wasn't pleased to see him. This was Saturday night. As God was his judge he had been on his way to close the door when Connors had driven in. He couldn't possibly work on the car until Monday, possibly Tuesday morning.

Connors said that was all right with him. And that took care of the car. It would be days, perhaps a week, before the police would think to check the local garages for the car that wasn't turning up at any of their control points or inspection stations.

He made the bus with minutes to spare. It was packed with women and children and drunks and home-bound Indians carrying the live chickens and fruits and melons that they had been unable to sell. Eleana was holding a seat for him but it was the last one on the bus and she was having trouble with two drunks who. were making remarks about her that Connors was just as well pleased she couldn't understand.

Departure time passed by five minutes, ten. Connors began to sweat again. He wondered if he had underestimated the Mexico City plainclothes men General Estaban had brought with him. It was just possible the two detectives had ordered all traffic out of Uruapan stopped.

Still more people crowded into the bus. Then the driver appeared out of nowhere, slammed the folding door shut in the faces of still other would-be passengers, and engaged his clutch with a jerk that would have sent all the standees sprawling if they hadn't been packed in so tightly.

Eleana's fingers bit into Ad's wrist. He put his arm around her. Twice on their way to the outskirts of Uruapan police cars with wailing sirens passed the bus. Out fifteen miles where the highway made junction with the new road leading to Paricutin Volcano, another police car was stationed. But the policemen standing beside it merely looked at the bus. They were waiting for a 1950 model gray Ford coupe with Illinois license plates.

The night grew old and darker. Now and then the bus stopped in a pool of blackness to allow a passenger to disembark at some invisible group of huts or lonely crossroad. The rest of the time Connors had to hold Eleana in his arms to keep her upright in the seat as the bus swayed around curves and scampered down down-grades with its gas pedal pushed to the floor.

It was hot in the bus and smelled of unwashed bodies, overripe melons, and chickens. Connors took off his coat and loosened the knot in his tie. Eleana kicked off her shoes and sat with her feet curled under her.

Once at a lonely outpost near a bridge they caught sight of a rifle-armed sentry. A dozen times faster traveling cars passed the bus. Connors hoped they weren't police cars.

It was two o'clock in the morning when the bus rolled into Guadalajara. There was a fat policeman on the walk in front of the bus station but he paid no attention to them. The hue and cry hadn't spread this far as yet. The police were still confident they had them bottled up on the spur that led to Uruapan.

Both Eleana and Connors were hungry. They ate in an all-night lunch-room a few doors from the bus station, neither of them saying much. Then Connors located a cheap hotel with a flashing red neon sign. There was no nonsense this time about rooms with a connecting bath. Connors registered as *Señor* and *Señora* Gomez, Mexico City, D.F.

A sweet-faced Indian woman called Eleana a pretty child, took the eight *pesos* she asked for, and showed them to their room.

It was more a cell than a room. The walls were white plaster, unpainted. There was a three-quarters bed, a wash stand, and one chair. The light was an unshaded bulb in the ceiling. The flashing neon sign was directly outside the window.

When the Indian woman had gone, Connors switched off the ceiling light and walked to the window and raised the shade. The sign would give all the light that was needed.

The sign flashed off as he turned. Across the small room, Eleana's eyes were cat-green in the dark. Then the sign flashed on again. Eleana's clothes lay in a black and white pool at her feet. The only thing she had on was lipstick.

There was a great roaring in Connors' ears. He found it difficult to breathe.

Then Eleana ran her hands over her breasts. In the flick on and off of the sign hard pink nipple tips found their way out from between her splayed fingers. Connors could see the muscles in her groin move.

They had no need of words.

There were big bells, little bells, loud bells, mellow bells, cracked bells. They pealed on for what seemed like hours, tolling the faithful to church. Her passion spent, Eleana lay content to have Ad hold her. "I still like you, Ad."

"I still like you, Eleana," he told her.

Connors' respect for Eleana had grown immeasurably.

There were no tears. No regrets. No false shame. What was done was done. It had been beautiful. But they couldn't stay where they were. They had to move on. Today. A man named Caesar A. Santchez was dead in Uruapan. Every policeman in Mexico was, or would be, looking for them.

It seemed to Connors the best thing for them to do would be to continue by bus. A plane or a train would be faster. But questions might be asked. And there still was the border to cross.

He asked Eleana if she had her motor club guide book in her purse. Eleana said she thought she had and got up to get it and her glasses. Before returning to the bed she stopped and looked out the window. There wasn't much to see. It was the usual early morning big city scene near almost any bus station; old buildings, narrow dirty streets, trash cans and debris.

Sitting on the edge of the bed she adjusted her glasses, then wanted to know what Ad was laughing at.

He told her. "You. This is the first time I've ever been in the same room with an elementary school teacher whose only article of dress was a pair of rimless glasses."

Eleana looked at him over her glasses. "You don't like the effect?"

Ad said, "I think it's cute as hell."

Her eyes had been smiling. They sobered. She laid the guide book on the bed, took off her glasses and leaned over him, one arm on each side of his chest. "Let's talk a little sense for a change, Ad. What are we going to do?"

Having her so near excited Connors. He tried to fondle her and Eleana put his hand back on the bed. She was worried. She had reason to be. Even if they made it across the border without being stopped she still would have plenty to explain.

"You still figuring on marrying Lautenbach?" Connors asked. He was sorry he'd brought up the subject. It left a sour taste in his mouth.

"Yes," Eleana drawled. "I am." She brushed his lips with hers but her eyes were all gray now. "You see, sweetheart, this is it. I mean the last time. And while I'm not sorry it happened, this sort of thing isn't ever going to happen again."

"Not with anyone?"

"Not after I'm married to Allan."

Connors picked the guide book from the bed and found the page with the main numbered highways on it. They were closer to Laredo or Brownsville than they were to El Paso. But for that very reason the border watch would undoubtedly be intensified at those two points.

If possible, he wanted to stay off Mexico I. Even if the police found Eleana's car and knew they were using public transportation the police would expect them to head out through Laredo. Against that, there wasn't a sign of a road, at least in the guide book, between Guadalajara and Torreon which would be the logical take-off point for Ciudad Juarez and El Paso.

Eleana took the guide book away from him. "I asked you what we were going to do."

"Head out through Juarez if we can," he told her.

Some of the green came back into Eleana's eyes. She made a little mountain peak by twisting a tuft of hair on his chest between her fingers. "The how is up to you. All I have to do is pay the expenses. Remember?"

Connors lay silent a long moment, thinking. Then he asked, "How much money have you, Eleana?"

"I don't know," she admitted. "That is, exactly. But I had five hundred dollars when I started and I must have over three hundred of it left."

"In cash?"

"No. In travelers' checks. I doubt if I have more than a few *pesos* in cash. I spent a lot in Uruapan."

Connors did some mental arithmetic. He'd had one hundred and thirty-two *pesos,* plus the two hundred and forty-five he'd gotten from General Estaban. Gas and oil and breakfast in Morelia had cost twenty-four *pesos.* He'd spent six for the flowers, eleven for the rum and coke, sixty for the *rebozo.* His suit and hat had taken twenty-eight and eight, or thirty-six. Eleana's skirt and blouse had come to almost eighty. Then there had been the bus fare. Their night lunch had cost six *pesos.* He'd given their landlady eight more. He totaled up the money he'd paid out, subtracted it from the sum he had, and, if his mental arithmetic was correct, they had around ninety-six pesos or seventeen dollars American to feed and shelter themselves and buy two bus tickets to the border.

Connors checked his arithmetic against the money in his wallet. He hadn't made a mistake. They had ninety-four *pesos* in bills and a handful of assorted *centavo* pieces, plus what little Eleana had in her purse.

He tossed the money on the bed. "That's it."

Eleana started to contradict him. Then she realized what he meant. They didn't dare cash her travelers' checks. As far as she and Ad were concerned, they were the hottest pieces of paper in Mexico.

They had her name on them.

CHAPTER 5

Connors lay back on the bed. "There's no use kidding ourselves. We're in a bad spot. By now our names and descriptions have been broadcast and the police in every little town on the way to the border have been alerted. You haven't anyone you could wire for money?"

He offered Eleana a puff of his cigarette. She drew the smoke into her lungs then drawled, "There's mother and Uncle John. But they wouldn't wire any money to *Señora* Gomez. Besides I don't want them to know about this."

Connors reclaimed his cigarette. They had registered in Uruapan as *Señor* Schmidt and *Señorita* Braun. But Estaban knew Eleana's right name and there had been plenty of old letters in his bags. Then he thought of Shad.

It was just possible Shad might wire him another advance if he put on plenty of pressure. He could call Shad long distance in the morning. That way he wouldn't have to give his name. But whether Shad would stand for a bite, at least as big a bite as was needed, was another matter.

"I think I've got it," he said. "I'll call my agent in the morning and have him advance me some money."

"He'll do that?" Eleana asked.

There was no need for both of them to worry. "Of course he will," Connors assured her.

He dressed and walked up to the lunchroom in which they'd eaten the night before and bought a sackful of cold chicken *tacos,* a paper container of hot *frijoles,* and two quart milk bottles of coffee.

Enroute back to their room he met their Indian landlady and gave her another eight *pesos,* saying that he and the *señora* would require the room for at least one more night.

"*Si, Señor,*" the woman beamed.

The breakfast tasted good. Eleana and Connors ate everything in the sack and could have eaten more. After eating, they slept. It was early evening and the church bells were pealing again when Eleana opened her eyes and snuggling closer to Connors, kissed the lobe of his ear.

"Know something, Mister?"

Connors held her even closer. "What?"

"I still like you."

Eleana stopped kissing his ear and began to nibble at it. Then their bodies met and sleep was out of the question.

When it was dark they dressed and went out to eat. Connors doubted that anyone would pay any attention to them so long as they stayed away from the tourist traps and Eleana didn't try to speak Spanish. He'd suggested she wear her hair in twin braids that hung down over her breasts. It made her look younger than she was and plenty Mex. But the moment she opened her mouth, her trace of a Missouri drawl gave the show away.

After eating they window-shopped. Then, shortly after eight o'clock on a narrow picturesque back street they came on a street carnival and Eleana insisted on riding the carousel. Connors bought her a strip of tickets and stood leaning against a warehouse, fanning himself with his broad-brimmed hat, as he watched her go around and around, big-eyed with delight.

Eleana wasn't pretending to have a good time. She was having a good time. The little brunette wasn't immoral. She wasn't amoral. She wasn't merely uninhibited. She was *Woman, naked and unashamed, before man,* starting with the serpent, had attached a penalty and a stigma to a perfectly natural appetite.

The same feeling of sadness that Connors had known in Uruapan returned. The hell of it was he didn't know who he felt sorry for, himself or Allan Lautenbach.

The phone booth was hot and small. The connection was bad. The local long distance operator refused to accept a collect call. When Connors did get Shad the other man thought he was drunk and it cost him another five *pesos* to convince his agent he was sober.

Even then Shad didn't go for the bite. He pointed out that Connors was already into the office for fourteen hundred dollars and every other pulp-hack on his string was screaming bloody murder. He'd had lunch with Jack Blade and Maxie Fallow on Friday last. If Connors wanted to put the new book aside, Shad thought he could pick up some quick money for him. Both Jack and Maxie had said they would take a lead novel from Ad if he would put the same old time punch in them.

Connors asked how much the boys would pay.

Shad's voice sounded thin and distorted. "Two and a half pennies a word."

"That's fine with me," Connors shouted into the phone. "I'll get the scripts in the mail as fast as I can turn them out. But I'll have to have some money."

His agent shied away again but finally agreed to wire fifty dollars immediately and advance the balance of the money, minus commission as soon as the scripts were on his desk. He pleaded, "But for God's sake, Ad, make them good. If the boys don't voucher them, I'm sunk."

"I'll do my best," Connors shouted. "Now write down this address. Wire the money to *Señor A.* Gomez, Room 216, Hotel Navidad, Guadalajara, Jalisco, Mexico. You got that?"

The thin voice in New York said, "I have. But what the hell are you doing in Guadalajara?"

"That," Connors said, "is a long story," and hung up while he still had enough money left to buy a bottle of tequila.

He needed it. He was calling from the best hotel in town, one patronized chiefly by tourists. During the course of their conversation, Shad had called him by name not once but several times. He half expected a squad of police to swarm out from behind the potted palms as he stepped from the booth.

Both the armpits and the back of his threadbare coat were sodden with perspiration as he settled his bill with the switchboard operator and walked stiff-kneed through the lobby. He walked and looked as if he was drunk.

An overstuffed Iowa matron drew her skirt aside as he passed. "Disgusting," she said. "Disgusting."

Connors spat, *"Turista,"* and walked on.

Out in the heat of the street again he bought a litro of tequila and took a big swig from the neck of the bottle. It thawed the lump of ice in his stomach but the mild glow the liquor induced faded in the first shop in which he tried to rent a typewriter.

They had three machines with English keyboards, a Royal, an Underwood, and a beat-up Oliver. But they demanded a stiff deposit or three local business references. It was the same in the next two shops Connors tried. He finally found a pawnshop owner who agreed to sell him a battered old three bank Corona for seventy-five *pesos* and he put down a small deposit to hold it until his money arrived. Then, a propitious gesture toward the fates, he spent his last seven *pesos* for paper and a few sheets of carbon. If Shad failed to come through, they were sunk.

When he got back to the room, Eleana was being domestic. She'd washed her stockings and scanties and blouse and now that she had washed the blouse she was wondering how she was going to iron it. Connors went back down stairs, located their Indian landlady, informed her that he and the *señora* would be with her for at least three more nights, and borrowed an electric iron and ironing board.

Eleana thanked him for the iron and board. "When do we leave?"

"Not for three or four days," Connors said. "Possibly not for a week." He outlined the deal he'd had to make with his agent.

Eleana set up the ironing board. "Well, if we can't leave tonight, we can't." She seemed more pleased than worried. "And how much will you get for the stories?"

Connors sat on the bed, admiring her. "That depends."

"On what?"

"On what length stories I do. Because of the paper situation most of the pulp editors have cut their lead novels from fifteen to twelve thousand words. But as long as Jack and Maxie asked for copy from me, I'm going to try them with fifteens. That means I'll get about seven hundred and fifty dollars, minus ten percent and whatever it costs Shad to wire it.

Eleana tested the heat of the iron with a wet finger. "What are you going to write about?"

"The man," Connors said, "is dead. He was stabbed, he was shot, he was pushed off a cliff, he was poisoned. Now who in the world could have done it?"

Eleana ironed her blouse, her skirt, and the *rebozo*. Then she insisted on washing Ad's shirt. He killed the rest of the morning nipping at the tequila he'd bought and trying to dredge up a couple of plots without too much mould on them. At one o'clock they ate on four of the ten *pesos* Eleana had in her purse. The wired money from Shad came just in time for Ad to reach the pawnshop before it closed. Then, what with the telegram, the typewriter, and paying four more nights rent in advance he was able to borrow a fairly steady card table on which to work.

On his way back from the pawnshop he picked up a local newspaper. He and Eleana were on the front page but the press was still calling them *Señor* Schmidt and *Señorita* Braun. More, the Uruapan police were playing it cagey. They hadn't been charged with the murder as yet. Outside of a poor description all that was said about them was that the Uruapan police were very eager to question them concerning the violent decease of Caesar A. Santchez an attorney from Mexico City. But their real identity was known. The tip-off was revealed in a paragraph stating that *Señor* Schmidt and *Señorita* Braun were driving a 1950 model gray Ford coupe with Estados Unidos license plates from the state of Illinois. Anyone seeing them or the car was requested to notify the police immediately.

There was more, but not about them. The newspaper story described Santchez as a successful lawyer and quite a ladies' man. There was no mention made of the chain or locket but some prominence was given to a bellboy's testimony that a beautiful, heavily veiled *señora* had spent the preceding night in Attorney Santchez's room.

Eleana was every bit as smug as Attorney Santchez's secretary had been. "Hmm. I wonder who his girl friend was."

"I wish we knew," Connors said. "Maybe it wasn't your father who killed him. Maybe her husband did."

He put a piece of carbon paper between a white first and a yellow second sheet, rolled them into the Corona and wrote—

Ad Connors   (Approx. 15,000 words)
Guadalajara,
Republica Mejicana

KILL ME, MAÑANA

Eleana laughed. "So that's the way it's done."

Connors grinned at her. "At least it's the way I do it." He clicked the carriage across the frame of the old three bank, fiddling for an idea. "Okay. I have a dead man. He was a Mexican attorney."

Eleana was shocked. "You're not going to use Attorney Santchez in your story?"

Connors shrugged. "Why not? He's dead." He continued to think aloud. "He was stabbed. His room was on the first floor and his window was open so how the killer got to him isn't of any importance. The thing that matters is who killed him, and why? The first half of that one is easy. He was killed by a former North American circus owner who skipped the States twenty years ago with a bundle of Mexican fluff and fifty thousand dollars, half of which rightfully belonged to his brother. No. I'd better make that one hundred and fifty thousand dollars. Fifty thousand is peanuts nowadays. But why did the former circus owner kill the attorney? And where to begin and how to complicate it and what to use for suspense and counter plot?"

He took a sip of tequila and waited for lightning to strike. It was hot in the room. Eleana took off her blouse so she wouldn't wrinkle it and lay down on the bed in her skirt and bra. "Is there going to be a girl in your story?"

"Um hmm."

"Me?"

Connors shook his head. "No. The pulps were raided once and they've been afraid of sex ever since. You can have a girl in your story. You have to have a girl in your story. She has to be the most beautiful little bitch whose mammary glands ever graced the dust jacket of a best seller. And you can beat her or break her legs or stab or poison or shoot her. But nothing but murder and mayhem can happen to her. She can be cooped up for thirty days and thirty nights with an escaped con who hasn't seen a woman in twenty-two years until he went over the wall. But you don't dare let him lay a hand on her. He can't even think evil thoughts." Connors amended his statement. "Well, maybe he can leer a little. But even then she doesn't know what he means. She still believes the stork brought her and wonders why everyone laughed when the little boy seeing the groom kiss the bride, asked, "Mama, is he putting the pollen on her now?"'

Eleana laughed until she had to get up and get a glass of water.

Connors ripped out the title page he'd written, rolled a yellow second sheet under the platen and wrote:

Bill Brown: Hardboiled, expatriate, oil man and former circus owner who killed the husband of the Mexican girl with whom he skipped to Mexico, (twenty years before) deserting his American wife and infant daughter. (Has been sending fifty dollars a month ever since for said daughter's support.)

Conchita: Former high-wire artiste. (Now a trifle stout at thirty-nine but still a beautiful woman.)

Sabines: Mexico City Attorney through whom Bill Brown has been contributing the fifty dollars a month to his daughter's support, lo, all these many years.

Connors stuck there. By killing Attorney Santchez as he had, if he had killed him, Eleana's father must have known he was putting Eleana on a spot. So it was necessary for him to shut Santchez's mouth. It seemed, at least to Connors, a man with as well-developed a sense of responsibility would have handled the matter differently. Still a man pressed to the act of murder was seldom in a position to observe the niceties. "What sort of a man was your father?" he asked Eleana.

She said, "I don't remember him. Mother says be was nice."

"She knew he was in love with this girl?"

"I don't know."

"Had there been any other women?"

"I don't know that either," Eleana drawled. "Mother never talks much about father. And every time Uncle John or someone else mentions him she cries."

"She's still in love with him, eh?"

"I suppose so. At least she's never married again."

"What sort of a looking man was he?"

"Good looking. Tall. Gray-eyed with little laugh wrinkles around his eyes. High cheek bones like mine."

"I thought you said you didn't remember him."

Eleana wrinkled her nose at Ad. "Smarty. That's a description from one of mother's pictures of him. But why all the questions about my father?"

Connors lighted a cigarette and offered her a puff. "I'm trying to talk myself into believing it wasn't Donald Hayes who killed Santchez."

"Why?"

"I think I could make a better story with another killer."

"But that locket?"

"The locket could be a plant." Connors enthused slightly. "Hey. How about Conchita? She's still presumably living with your father. Why couldn't Conchita have intercepted Attorney Santchez's letter to your father saying you were coming to Mexico. Then, after intercepting the letter, she lured Santchez to Uruapan with the promise of an assignation and shoved her knife in him to keep him from getting in touch with your father and your father from getting in touch with you?"

Eleana's bra was binding her. She sat up and unhooked it. "And just who is Conchita?"

"The Mexican high-wire walker your dad ran away with."

The school teacher in Eleana came out. "With *whom* Dad ran away. Only her name wasn't Conchita. It was Tamara."

"Tamara isn't a Mexican name."

Eleana shrugged. "It was the name of the girl with whom father ran away. But why should she want to kill Santchez?"

"I just told you. To keep your father from getting in touch with you." Connors built his story in his mind. "Twenty years have passed. Tamara's getting old. Her once beautiful body has begun to sag. She has a double chin."

Eleana took the cigarette from his fingers. "Which should be a big inducement to a ladies' man."

Connors ignored her. "She knows your father is tired of her. She's afraid if he saw you it might awaken old memories and he might decide to go back to the States."

"Where he is wanted for murder."

"I'd forgotten that," Connors admitted.

Eleana puffed on the cigarette and returned it. "No. That won't wash, Ad. Besides, Tamara is dead. In the letter father sent to Uncle John, the one with the draft for five thousand dollars in it, father said it had all been for nothing as Tamara had been killed in an accident shortly after they'd reached Mexico."

"I thought you said your uncle never recovered a penny."

"He didn't." Eleana explained. "That letter came years ago. Mother says Uncle John was raising hob about father sending money for me and not even a thank you, I'm sorry, kiss-the-back-of-my-hand to him. Then the letter and bank draft came along and cooled him down. But mother was having it so tough about then that Uncle John turned the five thousand over to her to make the down payment on the house we're still living in."

"In which we are still living," Connors corrected her. He drew a pencil line around the name Conchita. "I don't suppose you know what type of weapon your father used to kill Tamara's husband?"

Eleana said, "I think it was a knife." She got up and looked out the window.

"All right," Connors said. "The hell with it. Your father killed Santchez." He ripped the yellow sheet out of the typewriter and crumpled it into a ball. Then, kicking off his shoes, he lay down on the bed.

Eleana came back from the window and sat beside him. "I got you into this, didn't I, Ad? You're worried. And so am I. I don't see, under the circumstances, how you expect to think. But what *are* we going to do?"

Connors kissed the tips of her fingers. "I'm going to write two fifteen thousand word pulp novels. Shad is going to wire me six hundred and fifty more dollars. We're going to use part of the money to buy two bus tickets to Juarez and spend the rest of it on room service and champagne in the best hotel in El Paso." He kneaded the back of her neck. "Say. By the way. Did I ever tell you I liked you?"

Eleana breathed a little harder. Her drawl was a trifle more pronounced. "It seems to me I've heard you mention it."

"Recently?"

"Well, come to think of it, not for quite a few hours."

Connors pulled her down until their lips met.

"No, Ad," she protested, not strongly.

The unhooked bra slipped off her shoulders providing more kissable surface. Green crowded the gray from her eyes. The walls of the room expanded. The street noises died away. A train whistled faintly in the distance. Then it, too, faded into the night and they were alone in the world. Eleana compromised.

"At least let me take off my skirt."

CHAPTER 6

It was too early even for the bells when Connors wrote—3o—on the bottom of Page 6o and pushed back his chair. It had been a long time since he had done so much work so fast. He liked what he had written.

The Book-Of-The-Month Club would never buy the story. But it hadn't been written for them. It was good old fashioned pulp with a punch in every paragraph and a corpse on every other page.

He tiptoed to the window and looked out. Both Guadalajara and Eleana still slept. But the city was beginning to stir. He stood watching the growing dawn, wishing he had a pot of coffee. Outside of that, he felt fine. He'd written a good yarn. Turned around the way it was, Connors doubted if Eleana or her mother or her Uncle John, or anyone in Blue Mound, would recognize it. But it was good salable murder.

He'd made the Hayes boys cousins instead of brothers. And instead of them being good fellows, he'd made both of them heels. Eleana's father had started for California but had stopped off in Chicago and had raised the money there. This had returned him to Blue Mound a week before he was expected. He had returned to find his cousin forcing his attentions on his wife. In the fight that followed the wronged-husband had been killed and the cousin had forced the widow to help him dispose of the body.

In his story, Eleana's Uncle John and not her father, had been making a play for the Mexican high-wire walker. Her husband, peering in through the window of the cottage while the fight was in progress had seen the murder committed and had immediately tried to blackmail the killer.

This had given the heel the idea for the perfect cover for his crime. He'd stabbed the Mexican, paid the girl to get out of town, then spread the news that his cousin had committed the murder and run away with the girl. The terrified widow, Eleana's mother, fearing death for herself and her child, had gone along with the story.

Before disposing of the body, John had taken the money from the corpse. But the whole town knew he was broke. To make his story stand up he had to play it cagey. He'd allowed the circus to fold. Then he had contacted a Mexican attorney who, for a fee, had sent fifty dollars a month to the dead man's daughter and, eventually, a letter to himself purporting to be from the dead man. This had a double effect. It salved his conscience and also established the alleged fact Eleana's father was still alive.

The Mexican attorney was the counterpart of Santchez. The immediate conflict began when Eleana, whom he had called Ailine, became engaged to a young prig and insisted on going to Mexico to ask her father for her mother's marriage license (which the dead man had had on his person the night he had been murdered and buried).

All her frantic mother could do was contact the cousin who was now a prosperous business man. His old sin had found him out. Once the girl talked to Attorney Santchez his house of cards would tumble. He'd done the only thing he could do. Packing a few clean shirts and an old locket and chain belonging to his dead cousin he had beaten the girl to Santchez.

But instead of using a writer to crack the mystery, he'd used a handsome young oil man who just *happened* to be staying at the same hotel as Ailine and who was charmed by her beauty and virtue. The young oil man, of course, got the girl. He also got the murderous cousin and once more murder came out and virtue triumphed.

It was corn fresh from the cob. But if Jack Blade didn't like it the pressure of the pulp racket had finally caused Jack to blow his top and he ought to be moved out of his office into the boiler room next to the fifth assistant reader. Gagging a little, Connors separated the white from the second sheets and lay down beside Eleana.

It was late afternoon when he awakened. Eleana was sitting on the window sill being very still. When she saw his eyes were open she came over and sat on the bed. "What did you do? Work all night, sweetheart?"

Connors said he had and asked her for a cigarette. She lighted one and gave it to him and he remarked she must be hungry.

Eleana shook her head. "No. For breakfast I had *huevos fritos* and *tostada*. And both the eggs and the toast were good."

Eleana's Spanish hadn't improved overnight. It worried Connors to think of her going out alone. The police had to be making some progress. The net had to be growing tighter with every hour that passed. One false move would bring the hounds down on them. He laid down the law. "From now on leave the Useful Spanish Words and Phrases in that goddam guide book alone. And don't leave the room without me. If you have to go out and I'm asleep, wake me up."

"My lord and master speaks."

What with the tequila, too many cigarettes, and insufficient sleep, Connors mouth felt like the inside of a sewer. "You read the yarn I wrote last night?"

"I did," Eleana drawled. "And it's a darn good story. But I see now what you mean by the difference between pulp and slick. It's all in the motivation of the story, the subject matter, and the way the characters react. For example, no one in real life would do the things you have them do or act the way you have mother and Uncle John acting."

Connors wasn't in the mood to discuss the finer points of writing. He blew smoke at the ceiling.

"In the first place," Eleana continued, "mother isn't the sweet, crying kind. Mother's a lot like I am. If Uncle John had tried to rape her and then killed dad when he was caught at it, mother would have hit him with an ax."

"Before or after she'd been raped?"

"Before." Eleana ran a finger over the stubble of mustache Connors had left when he shaved. "In the second place, Uncle John—" She used the standard cliches in eulogizing her uncle. He was the soul of honor, a pillar of the church, a substantial business man. "Having father do what he did just about wrecked his life. Why he never even married for fear there might be some taint in their blood."

Connors kissed the finger on his lip. "Now who's getting corny?"

"It's the truth," Eleana insisted.

Connors grinned at her. "Okay. He's your uncle, not mine."

Dressed, he walked up to the. restaurant near the bus station and forced himself to eat some eggs and toast. A policeman came in while he was eating. All he wanted was a small beer. But by the time the policeman had left, Connors' appetite was gone.

Back in the room he took off his coat and rolled fresh paper into the typewriter. The sooner the stories were in the mail, the sooner Shad would wire them enough money to move on. Guadalajara was too close to Uruapan. This wasn't a little scrape. This was murder. A man was dead. He was tagged. When the police blew their whistles this time it was, *"Good morning, God. My name is Ad Connors. I was down in Mexico City trying to write a serious novel. In fact I had written it and mailed it to my agent. Then one morning as I cut across the Alameda to the postoffice I heard a Ford smack into a Cadillac—"*

Eleana sat on the bed and sulked. Connors rolled up his sleeves, opened a vein and began to bleed.

The second story came harder. He called it A CORPSE FOR THE BRIDE and used Mike Herman, one of his series characters, as the chief protagonist.

It should have been an easy story to write. He'd written it in various forms perhaps two hundred times. A man was mysteriously murdered. His widow appealed to Herman for help. Herman promptly got on his bicycle and peddled like hell all over the place with assorted hoods taking pot shots at him and trying to bash in his skull for no particular reason. It was the same stock yat-a-ta-yat-a-ta-yat without a shred of basic emotion or originality in it. He'd hoped he'd gotten away from this sort of thing when he had written the long one the Post had turned down.

It took him two nights and a day and part of the third morning to get it down on paper. Eleana liked it much better than the first one.

Connors mailed both scripts via airmail then spent the rest of the afternoon checking on transportation. It was theoretically possible to get from Guadalajara to Torreon by bus, rather by a series of local buses. If they went by train they could ride the S.P. De M. to Mazatlan, the N. De M. out of Mazatlan to Durango and on up to Torreon, Chihuahua, and Ciudad Juarez. Or, if they dared to risk Mexico I, it would be much faster to take a bus to San Luis Potosi and go out via Monterrey and Nuevo Laredo.

Still undecided, he bought an evening paper. He and Eleana were still on the front page. Newspaper readers were still being requested to report the gray Ford only now they were warned it might be carrying stolen Federal District license plates. That could be good. It could mean the police still expected to pick them up in the car. Still, it could mean they had found the car and didn't want him to know. Estaban knew he spoke fluent Spanish. The police knew it now. It seemed logical to assume they would reason he could also read it and would be watching the daily newspapers. In that case asking the public to look for a car that had already been found could be a ruse to tempt him to try to break out of the country via public transportation.

Before returning to the hotel, Connors walked back to the railroad station, then to the bus terminal. There were uniformed police and men who might well be plainclothes men in both places but Connors had no way of knowing whether they were on regular duty or looking for him and Eleana.

He considered checking into another hotel to confuse their trail in case the police had tracked them to Guadalajara. But there, too, he was stuck. Shad would wire the money to *Señor* A. Gomez at the Hotel Navidad.

Eleana kissed him on his return to the room. "Now all we have to do is wait."

Connors realized the sweat on his forehead was cold. "Yes. Now all we have to do is wait."

He mailed the scripts on a Thursday. They reached Shad Schaeffer in New York the following Monday morning. At five o'clock their Indian landlady rapped excitedly on their door with the information that still another *telegrafiar* had arrived for *Señor* Gomez.

Connors took Eleana with him to collect the money. She wanted to know if they were going on by bus or train.

"I can't make up my mind," Connors told her. "But one way or another, we've moving on. Tonight."

The past three days hadn't done his nerves any good. He knew how Estaban must feel after the shooting in the Flamingo. The Mexican general would make it his personal business to see that they were found. After collecting the money, Connors had walked Eleana almost back to the Navidad when he noticed the commotion in the lobby of the Hotel Progreso directly across the street from the bus station. Men and women were being lined up against the lobby wall by an officious police captain. Connors thought at first that the hotel was being raided. Then he saw a familiar face. It was the hotel clerk from Uruapan. As he watched, the police officer walked the hotel man down the line of men and women and the clerk peered intently at each face.

Eleana's fingers bit into Connors' arm. "What's the matter?"

Connors told her. "The police know or suspect we're in Guadalajara. They're shaking down the hotels. And the clerk from the Morales has been sent along to identify us."

There were two buses waiting on the apron of the station. One was marked Mexico City, the other San Luis Potosi. Connors considered blind flight and resisted the temptation. He would have to buy tickets in the station. Both the agent and the driver would be able to describe them and point a finger in the direction they'd gone. They would be even worse off in Mexico City than they were in Guadalajara. But if they could get out of Guadalajara and board the east bound bus at some small way point enroute they might still have a chance to escape the closing net.

There were two other hotels between the Progreso and the Hotel Navidad. Both would absorb some time. When the police did reach the Navidad and describe them their Indian landlady would take them up to Room 216. He'd said nothing about checking out. The police, certain they had found them, would wait for their return before extending their search.

The palms of his hands as wet as if he had just washed them, Connors said, curtly, "Wait." Then he strode into the bus station and bought two tickets for Mexico City, making certain the agent would remember him by paying for the tickets with a one hundred *peso* note. He studied the road map back of the desk while the agent made change, then returning to Eleana, Connors walked her two blocks back down the street to a taxi stand and engaged a driver to take them to Zapotianejo, the next small town twenty-three miles east of Guadalajara.

Safely out of town and on their way, he handed the bus tickets to Eleana. "Tear them up and throw them out the window."

Eleana looked at the tickets, puzzled. "What are they?"

"Two very slim red herrings," Connors said.

At Zapotianejo they waited for the San Luis Potosi bus and rode it to Lagos De Moreno. Short jumps were the rule from then on. They rode between two towns and spent the night at the local hotel. Most of them made the Hotel Navidad resemble the Waldorf Astoria. But no one tried to stop them. There was no screening of local passengers. And by the time they reached Monterrey, Connors doubted if General Estaban would have recognized them.

Both of them were filthy. His mustache had come out strong and black. He'd bought Eleana a coarse blue cotton *rebozo* to replace the silk one. She wore a flower in one of her braids. Her rumpled white blouse exposed her suntanned breasts almost down to their nipples. The Chicago school teacher was gone. Her cheeks hollowed with strain and with deep blue circles under her eyes, Eleana looked like a little half-breed who had given up the struggle to live up to her Mexican blood. They ate what they could buy in local restaurants and bus stops with an occasional drink of rum to act as a prophylactic.

Both of them were starting at shadows by the time they reached Nuevo Laredo but no one paid any attention to them as they got off the bus. Eleana could have cried. So much had happened. They had come so far. Safety lay just over the bridge. But they still had this one last obstacle to hurdle.

It took Connors half an hour to find the type of a hotel he wanted. It had to be all Mexican during the week but a cheater's paradise on week-ends. He wanted to cross the international bridge on a Saturday night. This was Friday. And during the next twenty-four hours he and Eleana had a second transformation to make. They had to turn *Norte Americano* again.

He registered as *Señor* and *Señora* Seguros of Monterrey and asked for a room with a private bath. The first thing Eleana did was fill the tub. Connors went back down stairs to get a paper and look over the situation. There was nothing about them or Attorney Santchez's murder in the Nuevo Laredo paper. It was dark by the time he reached the dingy customs houses on the south side of the bridge. There were a few pedestrians on the walk. In the west traffic lane, coming into Mexico, an Iowa car was having its baggage inspected and scaled. In the east lane, leaving Mexico, a California car was getting a cursory inspection. Just over the rise of the bridge he could see the American customs buildings. There were the usual uniformed officials of both countries. But walking up to the bridge had been foolish. There was no way of knowing if they could cross without being arrested and sent back to Uruapan until they made the actual attempt.

He picked up a bottle of rum, some coke, and some sandwiches and returned to the hotel. Eleana was still in the tub.

"You know, Ad," she told him seriously, "I think I've discovered the main difference between the inhabitants of the U.S. and a good share of the rest of the world."

Connors peeled off his shirt and ran water in the bowl. "You have?"

Eleana stretched luxuriantly in the tub, then pulled the stopper and reached for a towel. "Um hmm. We *like* to be clean."

"Speaking of being clean," Connors said, "how would you like to have me see if I can find a store open and buy you a complete new outfit?"

Eleana's eyes flecked with green as she stepped out of the tub. "Why the rush? Getting tired of me?" She flicked a few drops of water at him. "Or don't you like what I'm wearing?"

"I think it's cute," Connors said.

He felt the material and one thing led to another. It was midnight when he phoned the hotel desk and asked the clerk to send up another bottle of rum, more sandwiches, and some ice.

They still weren't in the clear. They still had their highest obstacle to hurdle. Trying to forget it they told each other how clever they'd been and what General Estaban and the Uruapan police could do with Attorney Caesar A. Santchez's body.

Leaning on one elbow, Eleana twisted a hairy mountain peak on Connors' chest. "'Imperious Caesar, dead and turned to clay, might stop a hole to keep the wind away.'"

Instead of giving him more of a lift the second bottle of rum acted as a depressant on Connors. He lay listening to the night noises on the street pass in review. He could hear the scuff of sandaled feet, the tap of high heels, the laughter of a drunken woman. For some reason the laughter seemed to symbolize all the sin and sorrow in the world. He wished he hadn't ordered the second bottle.

Eleana wasn't accustomed to drinking as heavily as she had. If it removed all her inhibitions, it also warped her judgment. She was sweet, then bitter, by turn.

"You're the nicest man I ever met, Ad."

Connors held her close.

"I don't know what I'd done if it hadn't been for you." Then Eleana thought of her mother, her uncle, and Allan. They were probably frantic by now, wondering what had happened to her. Even if she and Ad crossed the border safely, she still had the two lost weeks to explain. She wriggled out of Connors' arms. "On the other hand, if it hadn't been for you I wouldn't be in this mess. I'd still have my car an' my clothes. An' I wouldn't have anything to explain."

Eleana sat up on the bed and attempted to look haughty. "I'm sorry now I phoned you in Mexico City. So General Estaban took me. So what?"

Connors slapped her. "You're drunk, you slut. Shut up."

Eleana kneed him in the stomach. "Don't you dare hit me. Just because I've spent two weeks with you is no reason you can treat me like the tramps you're used to sleeping with."

She attempted to claw his face and Connors wrestled her back on the bed and lay with one leg across her. Then, her flesh burning his, he tried to tell her how sorry he was he'd slapped her. He knew now why he had.

She was his love. He didn't want it to be this way. This wasn't just another affair as far as he was concerned. He'd fallen in love with a wide-eyed girl riding a shoddy white horse on a cheap Mexican carnival carousel. If and when Eleana walked out of his life nothing would ever be right again. The knowledge was ice in his stomach that all the rum in the world wouldn't melt.

He tried to explain how he felt and lost himself in words.

Glowering up at him, Eleana scoffed, "Ha. There's no such thing as love. It's all bio-chemical affinity." She used her father for example. "Mother's a beautiful, passionate, woman. I can't imagine her denying a thing to a man she loved. But did father appreciate that? No. When a new biological attraction became stronger than the old, pop went the weasel."

Connors protested no two men were alike.

The sadistic streak in Eleana came out. Drunk and angry as she was it amused her to hurt Connors. She begged to differ. To her personal knowledge all men were alike.

Connors put his head in his hands and wept.

Eleana added, "And I've known quite a few men."

She insisted on telling Connors about them. The first had been a boy in high school. The second a high school teacher. One a man she'd met at a dance. One a married man in Chicago. Once he had driven to St. Charles where she was spending the school Spring vacation with two other teachers. Unable to entertain him in the cottage she had suggested a walk in the moonlight. And because the ground was still wet with melted snow and their need of each other urgent he had taken her against a flag pole on a high bluff overlooking the river.

Connors buried his face in the hollow between her breasts. "Please, Eleana."

Eleana sobered. "I'm sorry, Ad. Really I am." She pressed his face into her breasts. "I'm drunk or I wouldn't be talking this way."

She was suddenly lonely and frightened. Yesterday was dead. Tomorrow was still unborn. All they had was each other. All they knew was now.

After that, everything went.

CHAPTER 7

The night was black and hot and filled with stars. As they approached the bridge, Connors saw a star fall. It could be an omen. The next few minutes would tell. He squeezed Eleana's arm. "Okay?"

Eleana took a deep breath. "Outside of a few butterflies."

They were moving with a boisterous crowd of returning midnight drunks, cheating couples, and tourists on short vacations who were eager to boast to their friends that they had been in Mexico. Even if he and Eleana were recognized, with foot traffic on the bridge as heavy as it was, Connors doubted the guards would shoot. Regardless, he meant to cross.

He made certain for the tenth time that there was nothing about them to attract attention. Eleana's suit was white and similar in cut to the one she'd left in the Ford. With her hair back up on her head and her eyes innocent and wide with interest, for all the night just past and the long trip up from Uruapan, she looked like an American virgin of Lourdes eager to return to her niche.

He'd thinned his mustache and purchased a pair of fawn colored slacks and a gabardine sport shirt to match.

He looked on ahead to the barrier. Two bored customs men were casually screening the returning crowd with their eyes and, from time to time, remarking a pair of pretty ankles or laughing at a drunk. They wouldn't give him any trouble. Then, he saw the dapper little man with the hairline mustache. He had plainclothes man written all over his face. And he wasn't bored. His shrewd black eyes darted from face to face cataloguing and classifying their owners. If his eyes stripped a passing girl it was merely an attempt to ascertain her hair was naturally blond, her padding a part of her person, and she couldn't answer to the description—Hair—*brown*... Eyes—*gray*... Weight—*one hundred pounds*... *when last seen was wearing a chartreuse blouse and a gray nylon suit with gray snake skin shoes and purse to match.*

The end of Connors' spine tingled. They shouldn't have tried to cross at Laredo. They should have gotten to Juarez somehow. He hadn't been smart. He'd been dumb. Still they didn't dare turn back now. It would only attract more attention to them. His spine continuing to tingle, a hard knot in his groin, he walked on with the crowd, watching the plainclothes man. Only one thing gave him hope. The dapper little Mexican seemed to have a decided dislike for drunks. His shrewd eyes dismissed them with contempt.

Connors had taken a couple of quickies to nerve himself for the crossing. He was glad now he had. "We may be in for trouble," he warned Eleana. "I don't know. But when I bump into the little man with the mustache, giggle like you're drunk."

Eleana swallowed the lump in her throat. "Okay."

They were up to the customs men now. Connors hiccuped as he passed them. Then, two feet from the plainclothes man he let his right knee sag and breathed rum in the detective's face as he caught at the other man's coat, ostensibly to steady himself.

Beside him, Eleana giggled shrilly.

Still clinging to the detective, Connors grinned vacuously. "Scuse me, pal. One too many, I guess. Strong stuff, tequila, eh? I don't see how you Mexes stand it as a steady diet."

His face flaming, the officer pushed him erect and on his way. "Dog. Peeg. Dronk. Swine."

Connors staggered on, his neck aching from wanting to look back. Then a big uniformed man with a Texas drawl loomed large in his way and foot traffic diverted around himself and Eleana.

"What you sweatin' so for, chum?"

"He's drunk," Eleana told the immigration man.

A Customs man came up to them. "Is he carrying a bottle, sister,"

"No, sir," Eleana said virtuously. Her drawl matched the Texan's. "He wanted to but I wouldn't let him. An' if I ever give him another Saturday night date, I hope I have my head examined."

The Immigration man nodded approval. "You're too nice a girl to mess around with a drunk. It's guys like him who give Americans a bad name. Where were you born, Miss?"

Eleana gave it the business. "Blue Mound, Missouri, sir." She looked at Ad with contempt. "An' he was born in Chicago."

Smiling, the big man waved them on.

Two hundred feet past the barrier, on American soil, Connors stopped and lighted a cigarette and offered the first puff to Eleana. "Thanks."

"Thank you," Eleana said.

She puffed on the cigarette and returned it and Connors wondered if she was thinking the same thing he was. This was the end of the line. She'd made that plain in Nuevo Laredo. He hailed a cab and helped her into it. "On into town." he told the driver. "No particular address. And now?" he asked Eleana.

Eleana rode looking out the window of the cab. "I'm leaving for Blue Mound on the first plane or train I can get."

"Just like that."

"Just like that." Eleana continued to look out the window. "I'll wire mother and Allan from Blue Mound. Uncle John will cover for me. He'll think of something. He'll tell them I've been sick and in Blue Mound all this time."

"Then you still intend to marry Lautenbach?"

"Why shouldn't I? Wouldn't you marry twenty million dollars if you could?"

Connors tried to think of something to say but none of the thousands of words he knew seemed to fit the situation. Silence filled the cab and built a wall between them. Then Connors thought of money and insisted she take half of what was left of the money Shad had wired.

Eleana protested but finally agreed. "But only as a loan."

Half came to two hundred and thirty dollars. Connors opened the big red purse he'd bought her in Nuevo Laredo to tuck the money in it and found it was stuffed with the carbon-smeared copies of KILL ME, MAÑANA and A CORPSE FOR THE BRIDE. The last he'd seen of them they'd been in the refuse basket in the hall of the Hotel Navidad. He asked, "How come?"

Eleana looked back out the window. "Let's say a souvenir. Something tied with blue."

Connors took her in his arms. "No, baby. You can't do this to me. You can't just walk out of my life."

Eleana refused to look at him. Her lips were compressed. The corners of her mouth turned down. "Not after all we've been to each other?" she drawled.

"It's true."

"It," Eleana countered, "was a biological incident." The cheek Connors could see was wet. Eleana's voice was deep. As deep as it had been the first night he'd seen her stripped and wanting him in an eight *peso* hotel room. "You go to hell, Ad Connors," she said. "And get out of my life. You hear me? Get out of my life."

Connors tilted her chin so she had to look at him. "But, Eleana, sweetheart—"

Her eyes were all gray now. "Why should I waste my life on you when I can marry the Lautenbach money?"

"You may be pregnant."

"I'll chance that."

"Besides you don't love Lautenbach."

Eleana attempted to push him away. "Love has nothing to do with this marriage. It's a business proposition. And I'm *not* going to teach school all my life."

"Then marry me," Connors pleaded. "I promise you, sweetheart. Someday I'll write something big."

Eleana wanted to hurt him. "Not from the samples I've seen."

"You kept the carbon copies."

"I explained that."

Connors tightened his arms and tried to kiss her. "Eleana. Baby. Please."

Eleana squirmed out of his arms and pounded at him with her fists. "You let me go. You keep your hands off me. And don't you ever touch me again."

The taxi man drove over to the curb and getting out opened the door. "What's the matter, Miss? Is this guy trying to get fresh?"

Her lips a thin line, Eleana said, "Yes."

"That," Connors said, "is a hot one. Just how do you get fresh with a dame you've slept with for two weeks?"

"Nix on that kind of talk," the cab driver said, coldly. "You ought to be ashamed of yourself, a big bruiser like you mauling a sweet little kid like that around." He looked at Eleana. "You want me to dump him here, Miss?"

"Yes," Eleana said. "Please."

The driver motioned Connors from the cab. "You heard the lady. Pile out."

Connors debated whether or not to hit him. Then he got out of the cab. "Okay. Good bye, Eleana."

From the darkness of the cab, her voice small, Eleana said, "Good bye, Ad."

Connors walked on without looking back. Eleana sounded like she was crying. He didn't give a damn if she was. He wished he was dead.

CHAPTER 8

The bell boy opened the window and even high up as he was, Connors could hear the song of New York. There was a muted hum of traffic and a distant blare of horns spiced by a police whistle. In one of the buildings adjoining the hotel a workman was using a pneumatic hammer. The combined noises were orderly. They had rhyme and reason to them.

Connors raised his right palm shoulder high. "So help me."

Then, when the boy had gone, he called Shad Schaeffer's office. "This is Ad, Shad," he began the conversation. "And I'm home for good. No more Mexico for me."

Schaeffer sounded more startled than pleased to hear from him. "Where are you calling from, Ad?"

Connors told him. "I'm in 1512 at the Claremont. And look, Shad. To hell with trying to write the big theme. I can't write the sort of stuff the slick paper boys go for. Besides, it isn't worth the grief. So I'm a hack, I'm a hack. The man was dead. That's my story and I guess I'm stuck with it."

Connors expected Schaeffer to laugh. Instead, he said, "I wouldn't say that, Ad."

"What do you mean you wouldn't say it?"

"I mean I've sold the long one that the Post turned down."

"To whom?"

Shad said, "To Tanner Press. As a book."

Connors considered the information. It was as good if not better than a serial sale. Tanner Press hadn't published a book in five years that one of the major book clubs and Hollywood hadn't snapped up at fantastic figures before the galley proofs were dry.

He said, softly, "I love you, Shad."

The other man didn't enthuse. "You say you're in 1512?"

"That's right."

"Then stay there. I'll be right over."

Returning the receiver to its cradle, Connors walked into the bathroom and looked at himself in the mirror. For years he'd told himself he could write something beside detective and western yarns. Seemingly, he could. He'd sold a book to Tanner Press. He'd crashed into the circle of the elite. He was a serious novelist.

Still, he didn't look any different than he had before he'd called Shad. His hair was still flecked with gray. His face was still marked with the deep lines that hours of intense concentration, four packages of cigarettes a day, and uncounted gallons of coffee, had carved in it. Two weeks of lying in the Texas sun had deepened his tan. But Eleana still showed in his eyes.

So what? So he'd had an affair with a green-eyed nympholept, or nymphomaniac, or whatever the current term was. He could get along fine without her. Once his book had sold to the movies and he got out to Hollywood where glamor girls were as common as palm trees—. He stopped trying to kid himself. It wouldn't mean a thing. He was in love with a wide-eyed Eve.

Shad Schaeffer wasn't normally a profane man. He was now. "God almighty, Ad. What the goddam hell kind of a mess have you gotten yourself into?" His brief case under one arm, the agent stood with his back to the door breathing as hard as if he'd walked up the fifteen floors.

"What's eating you?" Connors asked.

His agent told him. "This man who's dead. This Caesar A. Santchez. And this Mexican general you shot." Tossing his brief case on the bed Schaeffer filled a glass with ice water. "I spend ten years building you up. I nurse you through hangovers and the blues. I advance you money I can't afford to advance. I coddle, pamper, and encourage you. And now when I get a chance to cash in, just when I peddle your first book, when we get our first real shot at the Cinderella money, you have to get in a mess." He gulped the glass of ice water. "What happened in Mexico?"

Connors fought a desire to be sick. The two weeks of loafing in the sun hadn't cured a thing. All they had done was incubate cocoons in his stomach. He was afraid to open his mouth for fear a flutter-by would wing out.

Shad sat on the bed beside him and laid a hand on his knee. "Come on, fellow. Tell me what happened. Just when I'm feeling fine for both of us. Just when I'm patting myself on the back for having had faith in you all these years, this man walked into the office."

"What man?"

"The man from the District Attorney's office. He asked if I knew where you were. I thought at first he was from the Internal Revenue Department and there was some beef about your income tax. So I told him why you had little or no income last year. I told him you'd gone to Mexico to write a serious book. Then he told me who he was and why he wanted you."

"Just what did he say?" Connors asked. "Just why does the District Attorney's office want me?"

Schaeffer lighted a cigarette and offered the package to Ad. "Because the Uruapan police, wherever in Mexico Uruapan is, have indicted you for the murder of this Santchez. More, there's a second warrant issued in Mexico City charging you with assault with intentions to kill a General Estaban."

And there it was.

Schaeffer continued. "More. The New York police have been asked to pick you up and hold you. And as soon as you are in custody the Mexican police propose to send an officer to the Attorney General's office with the proper extradition papers."

The butterflies in Connors' stomach fluttered in unison. Such a possibility had been in the back of his mind all along but he had refused to give it credence. He'd tried to convince himself that once he and Eleana had crossed the border everything would be fine, that General Estaban wouldn't bother to try to extradite them. He asked, "Did he, the man from the District Attorney's office, mention any name but mine? Did he mention an Eleana Hayes?"

Shad shook his head. "No. He didn't. Well? Don't just sit there. Tell me. Did you kill this Santchez?"

"No."

"You're not lying to me, Ad?"

"I'm not lying to you."

"Then why should a Mexican grand jury indict you for his murder?"

Connors told Schaeffer the whole story. The telling took the best part of an hour. When he finished, Shad said:

"Well I'll be a son-of-a-gun. And you had the crust to write a story about it. It was this Eleana's uncle who killed Santchez, eh?"

Connors shook his head. "Only in my story. Remember, I said I turned it around. It made a better story that way."

"Then who did kill him? Her father?"

"I don't know," Connors said. "Probably. He's the logical suspect from the viewpoint of motivation although the Mexican papers gave quite a play to a beautiful but heavily veiled *señora* who is reputed to have shared Santchez's bed during his last night on earth."

The agent hooted. "If the dame was heavily veiled, how do they know she was beautiful?" Schaeffer drew another glass of water for his ulcers. "No. I think we can forget the dame angle. That's just some reporter's verbal cheesecake. If the Mex dame this Donald Hayes ran away with was killed years ago, it couldn't have been her. And why would any other Mexican woman, or man for that matter, be wearing Donald Hayes' chain and locket? No. That's asking too much of coincidence. It was Eleana's mother's picture in the locket?"

"Eleana said it was."

"And her father left the United States twenty years ago, one step ahead of a murder warrant?"

"That was the story Eleana told me."

"He went to Mexico?"

Connors nodded. "Right. He went to Mexico. And for the last twenty years he's been sending fifty dollars a month through Attorney Santchez to help support Eleana."

Shad asked, "Then why try to complicate the story? It was her father who killed Santchez. Look at it this way, Ad. He was willing to help support her. But he didn't want even his daughter digging around in his grave. Twenty years is a long time. How do we know but what he's a big shot business man or politician down there now, too big to allow himself to be exposed?"

"That could be," Connors admitted.

Schaeffer patted his knee again. "That's the way it was. What had he to lose? You can only burn once for murder."

Talking had dissipated most of Connors' tension. He lay back on the bed and howled. Shad asked what he was laughing at and Connors said, "That chromo. If I were to use it in a yarn you'd pencil it out so fast the lead would smoke."

"That could be, son," Schaeffer admitted. "I don't pretend to be a writer. You write them and I'll sell them." He opened his brief case and took out a Tanner Press contract prepared in quadruplicate. "How does that look to you?"

Connors skimmed through one of the contracts. "Swell. There's only one fly in the golden glitter. I can't sign it."

Schaeffer uncapped his fountain pen. "Why not?"

"Because of that pick-up and hold request. I imagine you told the lad from the District Attorney's office that you'd try to get in touch with me?"

"I may have intimated as much."

"Then if I sign these and you don't turn me in, you're guilty, technically at least, of aiding and abetting a killer."

Schaeffer handed Connors his pen. "For my cut of a Tanner Press contract, I'll take that chance. Sign on the second line, please. On all four contracts. Besides you didn't kill the guy."

Connors signed the four contracts. "That remains to be proven. And if extradition is granted and I'm taken back to Uruapan I won't have a Republican's chance in South Carolina." He blew on his signatures to dry them. "Well, anyway, it was nice to know I could do it."

Schaeffer scoffed, "Don't be silly, Ad. We'll get the best lawyer in New York busy on this right away. In a case like this who is empowered to grant extradition?"

"I don't know," Connors admitted. "In extradition between states it's up to the governor of the state to which application is made. But with an international boundary line involved, I imagine the Mexican authorities would have to apply to the United States Attorney General. And he, in turn, will request the governor of this state to act. But whether the case would come up before a state or federal judge, I haven't the least idea."

"Fine," Schaeffer said. "Fine." His agile mind was already figuring angles. "So the extradition proceedings come up before either a state or federal judge. All we have to do is have this Eleana Hayes tell her story and no state or federal judge would grant extradition. Now I know the facts, I'm glad it happened. It will make grand publicity for the book. And you can bet the hundred grand or so the contract you just signed will bring you, that the Tanner Press public relation boys will see to it that your trial is spread all over the front page of every newspaper in the United States. This Hayes girl is in New York?"

"In Blue Mound, Missouri."

Smiling now, Schaeffer patted Connors' knee a third time. "Then before I contact the District Attorney's office, before we even engage a lawyer, you grab a plane for Blue Mound and tell her what has happened." His smile faded slowly. "You won't have any trouble getting her to tell her story, will you, Ad?"

Connors lighted a cigarette and drew the smoke deep into his lungs before replying. "Well, let's put it this way."

"What way?"

"From Eleana's point of view. If you were a twenty-three-year-old Chicago school teacher, technically a virgin, and engaged to marry twenty million dollars—"

"Yes—?"

"Just how pleased would you be about having the fact spread over every newspaper front page in the country that you had just spent a delightful, if somewhat harassed and drunken, two week Mexican assignation with an unknown but virile pulp writer who is accused of murdering a respectable Mexican attorney who, alive, very possibly was in a position to prove that your wanted-for-murder father was never legally married to your mother?"

Shad Schaeffer sighed. "Yes. I see what you mean."

CHAPTER 9

Blue Mound was the first country town of its type that Connors had ever seen. It didn't look like a country town. It looked more like a segment chiseled out of Chicago or New York. The station was new and modern. Enroute to the hotel the late-model Yellow Cab in which he was riding passed a good sized movie house, a kosher delicatessen, a bowling alley, two Super Markets, a half dozen smart women's shops, two beauty salons, three cocktail bars, a chop suey palace, and a bank that could have passed for the twin of an uptown Chase National branch.

The cab driver was sixty years old but wearing a loud sports jacket and his white mustache was waxed in two points that extended a half inch from each corner of his mouth. Connors asked him if he knew John Hayes.

"Christ, yes," the driver said. "John owns half the town. He owns this cab, for that matter. And a damn nice guy he is." The driver glanced up at his rear vision mirror. "Who you out front for, chum?"

"I beg your pardon?" Connors puzzled.

The old man shrugged. "My mistake. Forget it. You looked like an advance man to me. Just down for the wedding, eh?"

"Whose wedding?"

The old man's obvious scorn made Connors feel slightly stupid. "Jeez. Don't you ever read *Variety* or the *Billboard?* Eleana's wedding, of course. She's marrying the Lautenbach money. It was going to be next Fall. But it was moved up to next week. On account of they were so much in love, I suppose."

The hotel was on a par with the rest of the town. The desk clerk was as old, if not older, than the cab driver but his hair was dyed a blue-black and he was wearing a smartly cut double breasted white linen suit that built up his frail shoulders. He looked like an old stock actor or vaudeville straight man.

"A room with bath. Yes, sir."

Connors signed his own name on the registry card. The lawyer he and Shad had consulted had been emphatic on that point. The lawyer wanted nothing in the record that could be construed as unlawful flight to avoid prosecution.

The clerk dropped the card into a file, then slipped it out again and did a double take. His aged eyes were bright with interest. "Not *the* Ad Connors who writes detective stories?"

Connors admitted his identity and the old man insisted on shaking hands.

"This is indeed a pleasure. And an honor. Detective stories are my favorite reading. And you are my favorite author."

He proved it by naming the titles of stories Connors had forgotten he'd written. It was obvious the aged clerk wondered what had brought Connors to Blue Mound but he was too much of a gentleman to ask. Instead, he tapped a bell on the desk and a younger edition of Bull Montana bobbed across the small lobby. Then, seeing Connors' baffled look, he laughed. "Blue Mound is a little different than most country towns you've been in, eh, Mr. Connors?"

"Yes,'" Connors admitted. "It is. How come?"

The clerk was pleased to inform him. "It goes back twenty years, Mr. Connors. To the days when the Hayes Brothers' Circus wintered here. The climate is mild. The hunting and fishing good. A good many of the animal men, and quite a few performers, purchased winter homes here for that reason. Then when the depression of the early thirties hit and the circus folded, we were unable to sell out or get out. During the depression other circus, carnival, and tent show people joined us. At least they could eat in Blue Mound and get jobs of a sort, farming, breaking mules, working in the cob pipe factory. With better times we went back to the fair dates, the big tops, and the midways. But a good many of us had come to consider Blue Mound our home. We returned to winter, buy even more homes, and invest our profits in various local businesses and enterprises until, as of today, three-fourths of the merchants and residents of Blue Mound have at some time or other in their lives been connected with one or another branch of the entertainment world."

He laughed. "And as most of us, most of our lives, have been rather scornful of 'towners' and small towns, when we did take root, we've tried to make Blue Mound the biggest small town in the state."

"I see," Connors said. "And you own this hotel?"

The old man smoothed the fit of his coat. "No. I'm one of the boys who forgot to put it away. Just a statement. No regrets." He looked back down the years and his faded blue eyes twinkled. "I had a hell of a time."

The room was on the second floor. With the exception of the window opening onto a fire escape platform instead of a bird's eye view of Broadway it was on a par with the room Connors had had at the Claremont. He tipped the punch-drunk bellboy then got busy with the phone book. There was only one Hayes listed. He was listed as having both a residential and a business phone. Connors called the residential number and a woman answered.

"The John Hayes' residence."

"Eleana?"

The woman laughed. "No. This is Celeste, her mother. To whom am I speaking?"

Connors debated giving his name. "My name is Ad Connors."

Eleana's mother was polite but vague. "Oh."

It was obvious Eleana hadn't told her about him. "Might I speak to Eleana, please."

"I'm so sorry, Mr. Connors," Eleana's mother said. "But Eleana is not here at the moment. She and Allan drove out somewhere, I believe. Could I take a message for her?"

Connors' stomach did a slow turn. He'd promised himself he wouldn't allow Eleana or anything she did to upset him. But he hadn't figured on Allan Lautenbach being in Blue Mound. He didn't want to cause Eleana any trouble. He had too much pride to force himself on any woman. But neither did he intend to be sent back to Mexico in defense of a virginity that, by her own admission was lost in a high school locker room. "N-no. I'm afraid not." he said.

"Then could I have her call you, Mr. Connors?"

"That," Connors said, "would be very kind of you, Mrs. Hayes."

"And where shall I have her call?"

Connors said he was at the hotel and gave Eleana's mother the number of his room. She said she would have Eleana call him as soon as she came in and hung up.

Connors found the bottle in his bag and bought himself a drink. Then he waited two hours for Eleana to call. The room was in the back of the hotel. The afternoon sun beat in the window. There was nothing to look at but the shimmering heat waves rising from the fire escape landing, a high board fence, and the back of a livery stable that had been turned into a garage.

He took off his coat, then his shirt. Then he stripped down to his shorts. The sun dipping to the horizon caught on fire and burned out. The mechanics in the garage put away their tools and rolled down the big back door. With the coming of night a hot black curtain dropped over the window and a pair of amorous cats began to arch their backs along the fence.

They made Connors think of Guadalajara. He phoned the Hayes' residence again. A man answered the phone this time. He said Eleana had not returned. Neither she nor her mother was in. Yes. There was a message on the phone pad asking Eleana to phone a Mr. Connors in Room 205 at the hotel.

Connors asked him if he was John Hayes. "I am," the man said, and hung up.

Connors waited a few more minutes. Then he put on the white summer suit he'd hung in the closet and ate at the Chinese restaurant. The meal was excellent but did nothing to lighten his mood.

At any angle from which he viewed the affair, it was a mess. Kupperman, the lawyer, was reputed to be a top man in his line. But Kupperman admitted he'd never handled a similar case. He *thought* because of Connors' previous good record, both civilian and army, that if Connors could get a notarized deposition from Eleana as to the true facts in the case, plus a signed statement from the local sheriff or county attorney as to her reputation for veracity, any judge sitting on the case would be justified in denying extradition. On the other hand the judge might well and probably would, demand that Eleana appear at the hearing in person. In that case, if Eleana refused to testify for fear of jeopardizing her intended marriage to Lautenbach, Kupperman didn't know what they could do. Connors knew what he intended to do. He was going to blow the whole thing wide open no matter who got hurt.

He'd walked almost back to the hotel when he realized he was being followed. The man stopped when he stopped, moved on when he did, being careful never to close the gap between them or come close enough for Connors to see his face. All Connors could see was that the man was tall and broad shouldered. But there could be no possible doubt. The man was following him.

Connors walked into the hotel lobby. Eleana still hadn't called. There was a new, young clerk on the desk. The old clerk was reading a copy of *Variety* in the lobby. He was pleased when Connors sat down beside him.

"Yes," be said in answer to Connors' question. "I knew Donald Hayes well. I worked for Don three seasons. Two as a spieler for the side show. The last one as ringmaster."

"Describe him," Connors said.

"He was tall. Broad shouldered. Good looking. The type of man women go crazy about."

Connors took his cigarettes from the pocket of his white Palm Beach coat and offered one to the old man. The theory that was building in his mind was far fetched but possible. The whole affair was proof that stranger things happen in reaI life than he had ever been able to foist on an editor. After a lapse of twenty years few of the people Donald Hayes had known, with the exception of his wife and brother, would be apt to recognize him. And even if he was recognized show people were notoriously loyal to their own.

Hayes seemingly had a high regard for his daughter. What if after killing Santchez to conceal his new identity, or for some reason unknown, he had returned to Blue Mound to watch Eleana marry the Lautenbach money? Connors sucked hard at his cigarette. In that case he would have more to deal with in Blue Mound than Eleana's possible refusal to make a deposition.

"Just why," the old desk clerk asked, "are you interested in Donald Hayes, Mr. Connors?"

Connors lied. "I'm not. That is, as a man. But I hear there is still a twenty-year-old murder warrant out on him."

Pleased by his own sagacity, the clerk slapped his bony knee. "I knew it. I knew it as soon as I recognized you. You've come to Blue Mound to write a detective novel based on the facts in the Hayes' case. And there's a story in Don. A good one. I've often wondered why one of your boys didn't write it. How much of the story do you know?"

He continued before Connors could answer. "Anything you don't know, Jimmy Thompson and I can tell you."

Connors asked who Thompson was.

The clerk said Thompson was the local sheriff.

"And he was sheriff when it happened?"

"No. Just a deputy. But old Sheriff Miles was sickly and Jimmy did most of his work." The old man was lonely. He was pleased to have an audience. He winked at Connors. "Look. Why not come up to my room and we'll have a drink or two while I tell you what I know of the story?"

Connors had heard the story from Eleana. He had no desire to hear it again. He didn't want a drink. It was fairly cool in the lobby. He had no doubt the clerk's room would be as hot as his own. He said, "I'd like to. Believe me. But I'm waiting for a phone call."

The old man took it from there. Standing up he called to the clerk at the desk. "When Mr. Connors' call comes in, put it through to my room, Jack."

The clerk said, "Sure thing, Mr. MacMillan."

Connors followed the old man up the stairs. It was as good a way to kill time as any. MacMillan's room was on the second floor in front, four rooms down from 205. There was a battered wardrobe trunk in one corner of the room. The old man took a quarter-filled bottle and two shot glasses out of one of the drawers of the trunk and apologized for there not being more. He wanted to go out and buy another bottle but Connors said:

"Forget it. If we run short, there's another bottle on my dresser."

Some of the day's heat had dissipated. The night wind ruffling the drapes on the window was cool. The chair was comfortable. The whiskey was good. MacMillan's version of the yarn was much the same as Eleana's but he knew more of the details. He had always considered Don Hayes a fine man.

MacMillan spread his hands in apology. "After all, Mr. Connors, Don isn't the only man in the world who ever jumped his trolley over a woman. History is filled with them. Samson, David, Paris, Marc Antony, Lord Essex, Louis XV, Eddie Windsor. It might be well to keep that in mind when you're writing the story."

"I'll do that," Connors promised.

MacMillan looked back twenty years. "Don was a right guy, always good for a touch or a laugh. He was also a smart circus man. And if he hadn't chumped off over Tamara the money he mortgaged the show for would have pulled us through. Sure Tamara was pretty. But so was Celeste in those days."

His eyes lighted at the memory. "I remember once when We were making a long jump and the canvas boys struck the side walls of Celeste's dressing tent a little earlier than usual. She'd just stepped out of her ring costume and the drop of the canvas caught her without a stitch on. I can still see her standing there in the work light looking like an ivory statue rising out of a pool of flame."

Connors thought of Eleana in the flick on and off of the Hotel Navidad sign and his groin ached for wanting her.

MacMillan chuckled. "But even with a bunch of us standing here gaping at her like yokels, was Celeste embarrassed? She was not. She just smiled that superior, bitchy smile of a woman who knows she has what it takes to set a man on fire. Then she ran her hands over her breasts and down over her hips and asked in that French accent of hers, 'You like?'"

"What happened then?" Connors asked.

MacMillan laughed. "Don came along and gave the canvas boss hell. He also blacked one of Celeste's eyes for being such a little bitch." MacMillan was silent a moment. Then he sighed. "No. I don't know what got into Don with all that loveliness at home. It must have been just one of those things. Hell. I saw Don myself the night he came home from California and he acted perfectly normal."

Connors leaned forward in his chair. "Where was this? I mean where did you see him?"

MacMillan said, "On the station platform. We didn't expect him for another week but he came in on the two o'clock milk train. He wasn't in much of a mood to shoot the breeze but I thought at the time he was just eager to get home. In fact it wasn't until I went into the cook house for breakfast the next morning that I learned what had happened."

"But you did talk to him?"

"For a few minutes. I asked if he'd been able to mortgage the show. He said he had and seemed very pleased about it. As I recall, he told me, 'With what I have in the money belt, Mac, we're going to pull through in fine shape.'"

"He had the mortgage money in cash?"

"I imagine so. Most circus business involves cash transactions. At least it did in those days."

"Then what?" Connors asked.

"Then Don walked off down the road whistling." MacMillan refilled their glasses. "I mean it, Mr. Connors. You could have knocked me over with the breeze from a tent stake when I learned what had happened."

Connors sipped his drink. "You knew, that is the circus knew, Hayes was carrying on with this Tamara?"

The old man considered the question. "Speaking for myself, I'd say no. Oh, Don kidded with Tamara a lot and Tamara kidded back." MacMillan shrugged. "But when a man climbs into another man's saddle, unless he's a complete damn fool, which Don wasn't, he's usually fairly careful where he mounts the mare."

"And how long after you saw Hayes was it when he killed this Mexican high-rope walker's husband and skipped with her and the money?"

"Sometime between then and morning." MacMillan defended Hayes. "And I don't think the killing was premeditated. I imagine Don hoped to eat his regular meals and still nibble at his cake from time to time but Pablo caught them cheating and Don was forced to kill him. Then, with a dead man on his hands, all he could do was take a powder."

"Pablo was Tamara's husband?"

"That's right." MacMillan snuffed his cigarette. "And if you want your yam to be strictly accurate, Tamara wasn't a Mex. She was Gypsy."

Connors sat up in his chair. "She was what?"

"She was Gypsy. Along with walking the high wire she ran a mitt camp on the midway."

Connors considered the information. He'd wondered about the name Tamara. "You say she was pretty?"

MacMillan kissed the tips of his fingers to the ceiling. "Mmm."

"And married."

"Very much so."

"What was her husband like?"

"He was a Mexican Gypsy. A big man, six feet two or three, weighing maybe two-twenty. We had to build a special coffin. Then we had to squeeze him in. Pablo was a good looking devil, too." The old man grinned. "Not disparaging Don, understand. But I wondered at the time what he could give Tamara she wasn't getting at home."

"And you're sure Tamara was Gypsy?" Connors asked.

"I'm positive. She used to boast her blood was pure Tsigani. Why?"

The room was suddenly hot again. Connors' shirt collar was too tight. He asked the question that was bothering him. "Look, Mac. You were in show business a long time. You must have known a lot of Gypsies."

"I have. Hundreds of them."

Connors leaned forward in his chair. "Then tell me this. Think back. How many Gypsy women have you slept with? How many Gypsy women have you known who ran away with another man? How many Gypsy women have you ever met who would let any man but their husbands touch them?"

The old man thought a long moment. Then he shook his head. "None. Chastity is a fetish with them. Gypsy women will lie and steal and raise hell. They'll laugh at a dirty joke and kid and drink with you. But you slip a hand between their knees or cup a titty and they'll go for a knife and try to cut your heart out." He was silent another long moment. "Hmm. Yes. I see what you mean. Funny I never thought of that before."

MacMillan looked at the bottle. It was empty.

"I'll get the one in my room," Connors said. He got to his feet as the phone rang.

MacMillan answered the phone and handed Connors the receiver. "It's your call."

Connors gave him his room key. "The bottle's on my dresser." The old man straightened the set of his coat and left the room. Connors spoke into the phone. "Eleana?"

She sounded both angry and frightened. "Yes. Eleana. What are you doing in Blue Mound?"

The phone was on a table near the door. Connors glanced out into the hall to make certain MacMillan wasn't listening. The old man was standing in front of Room 205, inserting the key in the door. Connors spoke into the phone again. "Something's come up we didn't expect. I have to see you. Now. Tonight. As soon as possible."

"I won't see you," Eleana said fiercely. "I told you to get out of my life."

Connors cut short a hot retort as a dull double roar filled the hall. When he looked into the hall again, MacMillan was no longer standing in front of Room 205. The door swung open into the unlighted room and the blast had hurled MacMillan against the opposite wall. The set of his smart white coat was no longer important to him. The front of it was sodden with blood. As Connors watched, the old man's knees gave away and he pitched forward on his face.

Other doors along the hall opened. A fat man said, "GeeSus KeeRist." The frightened face of the youthful desk clerk rose over the head of the stairs. Somewhere a woman was screaming.

Then Connors realized the screams were coming from the receiver in his hand and returned it to his ear.

"Ad," Eleana screamed. "What's happened?"

He told her. "Someone just tried to kill me."

CHAPTER 10

There was, Connors thought, something indecent about death. Alive the old man had known a measure of pride and privacy. His past, his future hopes, his mind, his body, were his own. Now he was so much cooling flesh, an inanimate, inarticulate object of morbid and official curiosity. Dust returned to the test tube.

There was no doubt MacMillan was dead. His frail body had been blown almost in two. Connors hung up on Eleana's demand for details and was, mildly, surprised to find his hands were shaking so badly he had to strike three matches before he could light a cigarette.

The silence in the hall deepened, then was broken by a blue-bottle fly that appeared out of nowhere and began to buzz noisily. A moment later the excited voice of the desk clerk informed someone in the lobby, "It's old man MacMillan, sheriff. Someone blew him in two with a double-barreled shotgun."

A man in his late fifties flanked by a younger man appeared at the stairhead and walked down the hall. Both men wore fawn-colored riding pants with shirts to match, expensive white sombreros, and silver-studded gun belts.

"I'm Sheriff Thompson," the older man announced. "Who saw it happen?"

No one answered him.

He looked from the body to the open door of Room 205. Then stepping over the spreading pool of blood he entered the room and switched on the light. Whoever had fired the two shots hadn't bothered to take the gun with him. It lay where it had been dropped near the window.

The younger man asked if he should check the fire-escape and the yard.

"Do that, Macey," Thompson said. He picked up the shotgun and laid it on the bed. Then he returned to the door. "Which one of you men is checked into this room?"

"I am." Connors said.

"What's your name?"

"Ad Connors."

Sheriff Thompson pushed his hat back on his head. "Oh, yes. You're that detective story writer Mac was all steamed up about. Kinda bumped into the real thing, didn't you?"

"So it would seem."

A tall thin man wearing a crumpled seersucker suit pushed through the group in the hall and set the black bag he was carrying beside the body. "Old Mac, eh? Who shot him, Jimmy?"

Thompson shook his head. "I just got here." He looked at Connors. "Mind answering a few questions, Mr. Connors?"

"Not at all," Connors said.

"Then suppose you start by telling us what you're doing in Mac's room and what he was doing in yours."

Connors told him the truth. "We were talking and we ran out of whiskey. I offered to get the bottle in my room but just then I got a phone call and MacMillan went for the bottle."

The thin man squatted down beside the corpse. "Poor guy. He never knew what hit him."

The youthful deputy returned to report the killer had scuffed a few flakes of rust from the fire-escape but no one had seen him come or go and there were no footprints in the yard.

Sheriff Thompson rolled a cigarette. "Mind telling me who called you on Mac's phone, Mr. Connors?"

The fly continued to buzz noisily. Connors wished someone would swat it. He didn't want to involve Eleana in this but the clerk would tell if he didn't. "Why, no. It was Miss Hayes."

"That's right," the clerk said. "Miss Hayes called maybe ten or fifteen minutes after they came upstairs and I put the call through to Mac's room."

Thompson licked the cigarette he'd rolled. "Down for the wedding, Mr. Connors?"

"No. Not exactly."

"And just what were you and Mac talking about? Anything that might help us?"

The youthful clerk answered before Connors could. "Just before they came upstairs I heard Mac say, 'I knew it. I knew it as soon as I recognized you. You've come to Blue Mound to write a detective novel on the facts in the Hayes' case.'"

Still squatted beside the body, Doc Hanson said, "Oh, oh. John isn't going to like that."

"No," Sheriff Thompson agreed. "Especially at this time. But I doubt if John would try to stuff the family skeleton back in the closet via the shot-gun route." He was suddenly impatient. "All right, Mr. Connors. We've gone through the amenities. Let's get down to business. Who here in Blue Mound hates your guts badly enough to want to blow them out?"

Stalling for time, Connors said, "I don't know that anyone hates me that much." He wanted to talk to Eleana before he told any part of his story. "Certainly no one in Blue Mound. I've only been in town four hours."

Thompson lighted his cigarette. "What color is your suit?"

"White."

"What color suit was Mac wearing?"

"White."

"How tall would you say he was?"

"Six feet."

"How tall are you?"

"Six feet."

"And Mac's hair was what color?"

"Black."

"That's right. The same color as yours, Mr. Connors. And he was killed opening the door of whose room?"

"My room."

"By someone who was waiting in there for you to open the door." Thompson's lean face colored. "Now listen to me, son. I know you're a big shot. Mac told me you were. But stop trying to treat me like a rube sheriff in a trick hat. The gun belt and pants go with the job. But this isn't New York or Chicago. This is Blue Mound, Missouri. And murders don't grow on rose bushes here. It's been twenty years since anyone could possibly have any reason for wanting to kill Mac. Now start talking before I begin not to like you. Who hates you enough to want to kill you?"

Connors shook his head. "I'm afraid I can't help you, sheriff. I'm afraid I'll have to stand on what I've already said."

"Then in that case," Thompson countered, "I'm afraid I'll have to offer you the hospitality of the local pokey."

"On what charge?"

"A perfectly legal one. As a material witness. And I'll see to it that bail is set so high you won't get out until you do talk."

Macey got Connors' straw hat from MacMillan's room and put it on his head. "Go ahead now. Like a nice fellow. Or do you want I should smack you one?"

Shrugging, Connors preceded Sheriff Thompson down the stairs and into the lobby. The lobby was filled with people. More were waiting on the walk in front of the hotel. Thompson propelled him across the walk and started to cross the street only to find his way blocked by a black convertible Cadillac.

"Just one minute, sheriff."

Connors knew the man as soon as he saw him. He was both tall and broad shouldered. His grizzled hair had once been sandy. His eyes were deep set and burned with the inner fire of a fanatic. His drawl was even more pronounced than Eleana's. He could only be her uncle, John Hayes.

Wearing an off-the-shoulder evening gown that matched her eyes, Eleana slid into the seat her uncle had just vacated and held out her hand to Connors. "Hello, Ad. So glad you could come. So nice to see you."

Her voice was friendly but reserved. Connors took his cue from her. "I'm glad to be here, Eleana. But it seems I've run into a little trouble."

Standing beside the car, John Hayes said, "Yes. About that. Eleana told me she heard shots while she was speaking with Mr. Connors on the phone. So we drove into town immediately. Just what happened, sheriff?"

Sheriff Thompson explained what he knew of the story. Hayes listened nodding sagely from time to time. Then when Thompson had finished, he said, "I see. And it is your idea to jail Mr. Connors as a material witness?"

"I thought it would keep him on tap."

"An excellent idea, sheriff." John Hayes smiled thinly. "But a little rough on Mr. Connors. At my niece's invitation he arrives in Blue Mound to attend a wedding and winds up back of bars. Here's a counter suggestion, sheriff. Why not allow us to take Mr. Connors out to the house? I'll give you my personal word he won't leave town until you are convinced he can be of no further aid to you in your investigation of this affair."

God, Connors thought, has spoken. Eleana had been truthful about one thing. Her Uncle John was the local poohbah.

Without waiting for Thompson to answer, Eleana slid over again and opened the other door of the car. "Slip in here beside me, Ad."

Connors hesitated. It could be he would be safer in the Blue Mound jail than he would be as a guest of John Hayes.

Hayes asked, "Well?" a bit impatient

"I guess that will be all right, Mr. Hayes," Thompson said. The back of his neck crimson he turned and returned to the hotel.

Hayes got in the car and drove on down the street. "Someday," Eleana said, "you're going to push Thompson too far."

Connors rode trying to make up his mind whether he loved or hated Eleana. The pressure of her thigh was torture. He wished her bare shoulders weren't so close.

A mile out of town, Hayes swung the convertible in between two stone gate posts. Then driving onto the shoulder of the private road he stopped the car. "All right. Let's have it, young man. Why have you come to Blue Mound? And what's this nonsense about someone trying to kill you?"

Connors looked at Eleana.

She made a gesture of distaste. "It's all right. You can talk. Uncle John knows all about Mexico. I had to tell him so he could help me think up a plausible story to tell mother and Allan."

John Hayes voice was as thin as his lips. "And let's understand each other, young man. I appreciate what you did for Eleana. But I'll stand for no nonsense from anyone."

"So I observe," Connors said.

Hayes ignored the flippancy. "In my opinion the whole affair could have been handled much differently. There was no excuse for either you or Eleana to give away to your carnal appetites. But feeling as I do about her, I can't and won't allow her to suffer for her foolishness. If this is a matter of blackmail, come to the point. How much money do you have in mind?"

"There's no money involved," Connors said.

"Then why did you come to Blue Mound?"

Connors told him. "Because it seems our little Mexican interlude didn't end at the border. A jury in Uruapan has indicted me for the murder of Attorney Santchez and the Mexican authorities have requested that I be arrested and confined pending extradition proceedings."

Eleana gasped. "Oh, no."

"Oh, yes," Connors said.

A car bound into Blue Mound swept the convertible with its headlights and the night seemed darker when it had passed.

Hayes said, "I see. Hmm. That does complicate matters. And just what is it you want of Eleana?"

"The truth." Connors lighted a cigarette and offered first puff to Eleana. "My lawyer says if Eleana will make a deposition as to what really happened in Mexico City and in Uruapan he doesn't think a judge will grant extradition."

"She wouldn't have to go into court?"

"That I don't know and can't promise. If the judge who hears the proceedings refuses to accept the deposition she'll have to appear in person."

Eleana puffed the cigarette to a red glow. "I absolutely refuse. I won't go into court and admit I'm the kind of a little bitch who would—well, do what I did do."

"Eleana. Please," John Hayes said. He shook his head. "No, Mr. Connors. Either such a deposition as you propose or Eleana appearing in court to testify for you is impossible. To do so she would have to admit two weeks of carnal intimacy with practically a total stranger. And I won't allow her to do that. It would break her mother's heart. Besides, I have my position in the community to think of."

Connors opened the car door. "To hell with your position."

Eleana caught at his arm. "No. Wait, Ad. What are you going to do?"

He said, "I'm going back into town and ask Sheriff Thompson to lock me up. Then I'm going to ask him to wire the New York authorities and blow this whole thing wide open."

"No," Hayes said. "You can't do that."

"Why can't I?"

"I'll lie," Eleana said. "I'll lie my head off. If you make me go into court I'll testify against you."

Hayes said, sharply, "Keep quiet. You're being hysterical, Eleana." He answered Connors. "You can't because I won't allow you to. Eleana has told me the whole story, including a vivid description of the locket and chain you saw in this dead lawyer's hand. And it was Don's locket beyond question. Celeste bought it for him shortly before he left for California. Don't you see what will happen if Eleana is forced to go into court. Not only will her own reputation be destroyed but her father will be stamped—"

Connors finished the sentence for him. "As a man who has committed murder on both sides of the border."

"That's one way of putting it."

"So to protect a double killer I'm to be made a sacrificial goat."

Hayes protested, "No. Nothing like that. Believe me, Mr. Connors. We'll work this out some way."

"How?"

"I don't know."

Connors found the ashtray on the dashboard and snuffed the cigarette he was smoking. "How long has it been since you've seen your brother, Mr. Hayes?"

"Approximately twenty years."

"You're positive of that?"

"I am."

"But you'd recognize him if you saw him?"

"Of course I would."

"And he isn't in Blue Mound now?"

"Not to the best of my knowledge."

"What are you getting at, Ad?" Eleana asked. "What makes you think father might be in Blue Mound?"

"MacMillan," Connors said. "Because of the attempt on my life. The killer mistook MacMillan for me."

Eleana took a deep breath and drawled, "I don't believe it."

"Because you don't want to believe it." Connors tried to keep the bitterness out of his voice. "Have I ever lied to you, Eleana?"

"Not that I know of."

'Then believe me. Before I allow myself to be extradited and stood up against some bullet-pocked wall as a sop to General Estaban's unrequited libido, I'm going to bring this whole thing out in the open. Your father is a smart man. He must be. Being smart, he knows what my defense will be. He also knows with me dead and out of the way the Mexican authorities will drop the whole affair and the name of Señor Donald Hayes need never be mentioned."

Eleana began to cry softly. "I can't believe that of my father."

John Hayes' voice was bleak. "You never knew your father. And a man capable of doing what Don did to Celeste and myself is capable of doing anything. But tell me this, Mr. Connors. Have you anything but theory to support your supposition it was my brother who shot MacMillan, mistaking him for you?"

Connors said, "No. Nothing except for the fact a tall, broad shouldered man whose face I was unable to see followed me from the restaurant to the hotel."

"And you have no known enemies who might have followed you to Blue Mound?"

"None."

Hayes broke the long silence that followed by sighing. "Well, the decision is yours, Mr. Connors. Viewed in the light in which you put it, it's possible my brother is in Blue Mound. Attempting another murder to conceal the two he has already committed is the bold sort of a thing of which Don would be capable. Naturally he wouldn't dare to show himself to either myself or Celeste."

John Hayes studied the night enveloping the car. "I'd hoped we'd finished with Don these many years. Now this." He started the car. "Well, what must be faced, must be faced. So, if you wish, I'll drive you back to town. There you may do as you please as to informing Sheriff Thompson of your suspicions. You'll find him a capable officer, if somewhat subservient to my wishes."

Connors asked, "And the alternative?"

"Continue on to the house as my guest and we'll discuss this at greater length."

Eleana said, quickly, "But not in front of mother or Allan."

Connors flipped a mental coin. He had the same feeling he'd known in Uruapan, that he was wrestling with shadows. Beside him Eleana's perfume and the gleam of the bare shoulders he'd kissed added to the tissue of unreality with which the whole fabric of the affair had been interwoven from the start. He hesitated. "Well—"

Eleana laid her hand on his arm. "Please come to the house, Ad."

He shrugged. "Okay. Let's go on to the house."

CHAPTER 11

It was the sort of a house a former showman with money might build. The living room was huge, mostly natural field stone and rough-hewn timber beams. The room was two stories high. A five foot wide balcony, off which the sleeping rooms opened framed it on three sides. On the fourth side a great stone fireplace rose unimpeded to the shadowy, cathedral ceiling. The waxed wide-board floor was bare except where it was splashed with colorful Navajo rugs, anyone of which would have been too large for the average living room.

The out-jutting balcony formed a natural gallery and Hayes had used the over-hang to bizarre advantage. The space under it was filled with mementoes of the circus he'd once owned.

The walls under the over-hang were papered with faded one and two and three-sheets, playbills, throw-away, dodgers, all bearing the legend HAYES BROTHERS' CIRCUS and eulogizing its attractions. Between them hung framed professional pictures of now aged, or long dead, aerial artists, actors, spielers, bull men, cat men, kinkers, fire-eaters, clowns, dancing girls, riders, musicians, freaks. In front of them stood gilded wagon wheels and chariot tongues. There was even a moth-eaten lion and a stuffed baby elephant labeled—Happy.

The entire east wall was devoted to colored lithographs and pictures of Eleana's mother. There were pictures of her pirouetting on the back of a white horse, riding one horse and driving six, diving through a hoop of flame. She came into the room with John Hayes as Connors was looking at her pictures.

At forty-two the former equestrienne was still beautiful. Her face was unlined and animated. Her chin and throat muscles were firm. Her uncorseted figure was as slim as Eleana's. She had even more inner fire than Eleana. How any man in his right mind could have deserted a twenty year younger Celeste was beyond Connors' comprehension. Except for the silver streak time and tragedy had brushed into her black hair, and her work-worn hands, Celeste Hayes could pass as her daughter's sister.

Eleana took a deep breath. "This is Ad Connors, mother. An old friend from Chicago who's come down for the wedding."

The fact that Celeste still spoke with a trace of a French accent almost as elusive as Eleana's drawl only added to her charm. "So nice to meet you, Mr. Connors." She pinched Eleana's cheek. "Eleana has told me all about you."

So saying, she walked on into the dining room and called for a maid to bring her a bowl for the short-stemmed white roses she was carrying.

Connors looked at Eleana. Her smile was wry. "Don't flatter yourself. I haven't mentioned your name. Except to Uncle John. Celeste says that to all the boys. It's merely mother's way of making you feel welcome."

"Oh," Connors said. "I see."

Eleana's fingers bit into his arm. "Please, Ad. Mothers worked so hard. She's so happy about my making what she calls a good marriage. Let's not tell her what you suspect. I mean about father. At least not 'till we're certain."

"I think that's wise," Hayes said. "There's no need of alarming Celeste. Why not let Sheriff Thompson nose around and see what he finds out. There are three dozen men in town who worked with and for Don. And if it was Don who fired those shots, if Don is in Blue Mound, one of them is certain to recognize him."

Connors asked if there was any chance of Donald Hayes coming to the house.

"Here? Don come here? After what he did to me?" John Hayes was vehement about it. "I'm not fond of running a cob pipe factory and a bank, young man." He indicated the playbills. "That was my circus. It was my life. I loved it. And Don sold me down the river for a hot pants Gypsy tramp and less money than we often took in on a good two-day stand."

Hayes walked up the stairs to the balcony on some errand of his own. Alone with Eleana, Connors took her by the elbows. "Baby, please. You have to listen to me. You can't go through with this marriage."

He attempted to kiss her and Eleana slapped him. "I told you to get out of my life." Then, twisting free, she joined her mother in the dining room.

Supper was at nine. Celeste did most of the talking. Connors and Lautenbach were the only guests although Connors gathered from Celeste's conversation that a good sized crowd of Eleana and Lautenbach's friends was expected for the weekend.

The dining room opened on a well-kept lawn that sloped down to a river. From time to time as he ate, John Hayes looked thoughtfully out the tall French windows. Once when he dropped his napkin and stooped to retrieve it, Connors saw the black butt of a gun under John Hayes' left arm pit.

"And what is your business, Mr. Connors?"

The question came from Lautenbach. "I write," Connors said.

Eleana added, "Adventure and detective stories. Mr. Connors has a wonderful imagination."

Connors let it go at that. His recent conversation with Shad and the news of the Tanner Press sale seemed very remote and unimportant. He'd expected to dislike Lautenbach. He didn't. He didn't feel anything toward him. A lean man with a wisp of a sandy mustache, Lautenbach was a gentleman, burned out in his middle forties. If he was curious as to why Connors was in Blue Mound he was too well bred to ask. From time to time during the meal his watery blue eyes appraised Eleana without heat.

Connors doubted the marriage would last. The man had nothing to give Eleana. Marrying Allan Lautenbach would be equivalent to marrying a piece of limp toast. The man had spent everything but his money.

They had their coffee and liqueur in the living room. At ten o clock the phone rang. When he returned from answering it, John Hayes sat on the sofa beside Connors.

"That was Sheriff Thompson. There were no fingerprints on the shotgun. The gun is an old one that was kept in a downstairs back closet of the hotel. Thompson thinks it originally belonged to me. He thinks it's the gun I gave MacMillan five years ago when the old man wanted to go rabbit hunting."

He kept his voice down. So did Connors. "Anyone could get at it?'

"Anyone."

"You mentioned the fact we think your brother may be in town?"

"No," Hayes said flatly. "I didn't."

Across the room, Allan Lautenbach's voice droned on in a chukker by chukker, hoof beat by hoof beat description of an international polo match in which he'd played. Only Celeste pretended interest. Slumped on the end of her pretty spine, Eleana was candidly bored. Shortly after the phone call she suggested she and Allan drive out to a roadhouse called the Barn. They left a few minutes later without inviting Connors to accompany them.

With Allan and Eleana's departure conversation became even more desultory. It was obvious to Connors that his presence in the house both puzzled and worried Eleana's mother. But, as with Allan Lautenbach, she was too much of a lady to ask personal questions.

At ten thirty she supplied herself with magazines, excused herself graciously, and said goodnight.

John Hayes watched her up the stairs. Connors watched John Hayes. If ever a man was in love with a woman Hayes was in love with Celeste. Connors thought of the twist he'd written for Jack Blade and began to wonder.

John Hayes had known he was in town. John Hayes was tall and broad shouldered. John Hayes owned Blue Mound. John Hayes knew where the shotgun was kept. Hayes House was only a mile from town. After firing the two shots, Hayes could have reached it in ample time to return with Eleana. The small veins in Connors' temples began to throb.

What if *his* version of the story had been the correct one? What if Donald Hayes had returned to Blue Mound a week early to find his brother, John, making love to Celeste? What if in the fight that followed John Hayes had killed his brother and used a similar cover to the one he'd schemed up in his story? What if John Hayes had killed Attorney Santchez?

Against that was the fact that Hayes had armed himself.

Connors waited for the other man to drink, then poured himself one from the bottle Hayes set out. Murder destroyed and distorted values. When one dealt with it, anything was possible. It was even possible, considering Eleana's vehement refusal to make a deposition or appear in court, that *she* had killed Santchez. Eleana had a temper. She wanted the Lautenbach money. She had discovered the body.

What if while he had slept Eleana had talked to Santchez? What if she'd learned the marriage license she wanted didn't exist? What if in her fear of losing Allan, or of possible future blackmail, Eleana had taken the most expedient way of sealing Caesar A. Santchez's mouth.

Her pretended fright and shock could have been an act. She was a clever actress. As soon as her need for him was finished, she'd dropped him at the border and ordered him out of her life. Still, the locket didn't fit into that picture. It was an over-complication of plot. And Eleana wasn't a fool. If she'd stabbed Santchez she wouldn't have left anything behind to call attention to herself or any member of her family.

In the car John Hayes had offered the alternative, 'Continue on to the house as my guest and we'll discuss this at greater length.' Now they were alone Connors waited for him to begin. Instead Hayes drank in silence, scowling at the floor. At eleven thirty he stood up and wound his watch. "I'm going to bed. If I were you I'd lock my door tonight."

Connors got to his feet. "I intend to. But before you leave would you answer two questions? First, were your brother and Celeste legally married?"

Hayes said, "I have no reason to believe otherwise. They left after we dropped the top in Omaha and rejoined the show in Des Moines, saying they had been married. Celeste says they were married in a small town. But in those days she knew very little English and Don had the license on his person the night he ran away with Tamara. What's your second question?"

"Do you approve of Eleana's marrying Lautenbach?"

"No," Hayes said flatly. "Lautenbach is marrying an aphrodisiac. The chances are what manhood he has left is in his head. Marriage to him will revolt and disgust Eleana." Hayes shrugged. "But I've nothing to say about it. I'm her uncle, not her father."

Connors watched him up the stairs then walked out on the lawn. The moon was full and low. At the foot of the hill the river winding off into the night to disappear behind a clump of silhouetted trees looked like silver foil.

Connors walked down to the river and threw stones in it for a few minutes. Then he climbed the hill back to the house. Seen from the rear Hayes House was even more impressive than it was from the front drive. For a bankrupt former circus owner, John Hayes had done well.

To reach the other side of the house Connors cut through a grape arbor and found himself in the vicinity of a recently lighted trash fire. The fire had almost burned out. He glanced at it incuriously and started on when a last flickering tongue of flame illuminated a familiar looking piece of paper. Stooping, Connors rescued it from the fire. It was the charred title page of the carbon copy of KILL ME, MAÑANA.

He walked on around the house. Two of the second floor rooms were lighted. The shades on one were drawn. Through the open window of the other room he could see John Hayes kneeling beside his bed in fervent prayer.

His nerve ends tingling, Connors lighted a cigarette. He had a hunch if he was to enjoy the money and prestige the Tanner Press contract could bring him, it was up to him to find out what the poohbah of Blue Mound was bothering God about.

CHAPTER 12

It was a whistling morning. The robins and meadowlarks sang. The sparrows cheeped. A soft west wind shepherded a flock of gamboling white clouds across the sky. Connors felt like hell. He wished whoever had tried to kill him would drop the other shoe.

He parked the car John Hayes had insisted he use and sent a wire to Shad. Then he drove to the hotel to get his bag.

The youthful clerk was sorry. "Gee. That's a shame, Mr. Connors. But Sheriff Thompson took your bag last night. Why don't you go over to his office and get it?"

"I may do that," Connors said.

He asked to see the closet where the shotgun had been kept. It was in a small hall in the back of the hotel, sealed off from the lobby by a fire door.

"It's a kind of a catch-all," the clerk said.

A door led from the hall to the service yard enclosed by the high board fence. The door was wedged open.

"It was that way last night?" Connors asked.

The clerk nodded. "It's always open in summer. Excepting when it rains."

A walk led to a wide areaway between the hotel and the building next door. Anyone in Blue Mound so minded could have walked back through the areaway, taken the shotgun from the closet, then walked up the fire escape to the landing outside Room 205.

Connors offered the youth a cigarette. "Mr. Hayes wasn't around last night, was he? I mean shortly before the shooting?"

The clerk shook his head. "Not that I know of."

Out on the walk in front of the hotel again Connors felt the bristles on his chin and decided to be shaved before calling on Sheriff Thompson. The sun felt good.

He stood a moment longer looking in the window of the smart florist shop next to the hotel, admiring a corsage of short-stemmed white roses and sweet peas. He wished he could buy it for Eleana. He felt the cheek she'd slapped.

"I told you to get out of my life."

All right. He would. Connors moved on up the street. He'd get out of Eleana's life, and get her out of his, as fast as he possibly could. But he didn't intend to make his exit on a stretcher.

There was a hardware store in the middle of the block. He bought a revolver and a box of cartridges and loaded the revolver before holstering it in his coat pocket. Then he looked for a barber shop.

The barber shaved him in silence until the second go-over. Then the scrape of razor stopped briefly. "You're that writing fellow in whose room Mac was killed last night, ain't you?"

"That's right," Connors said.

The barber scraped a stubborn whorl of beard. "You figure the guy was trying for you?"

"At least Sheriff Thompson seems to."

"Funny," the barber said.

"What's funny?" Connors asked.

"The guy turning loose both barrels so fast. I mean before he made certain it was you. Doc Hanson says even at the distance he almost missed with one barrel. Must have been nervous."

"Or in a hurry."

The scrape of the razor resumed. When it paused again Connors asked casually, "Say. By the way. Wasn't Mr. Hayes out of town about four weeks ago? I thought I saw him in New York."

"That could be," the barber said. "I wouldn't know. John's in and out of town a lot on bank and factory business."

"He's out of town a lot, eh?"

"Quite a bit," the barber said.

Shaved, Connors walked across the street to the sheriff's office. Thompson was sitting with his feet on his desk. He didn't bother to lower them. From the smell of his breath and the office, he'd been drinking heavily. "Well," he greeted Connors. "One of the privileged class come to tell the rube sheriff what it's all about. That's why you did drop in, isn't it, Mr. Connors?"

Connors sat on the edge of the desk. "Let's understand each other, Thompson. If I knew the score, I'd tell you. I may know it within the next hour. If I do, I'll tell you then. But right now all I've dropped in for is my bag. You do have it, I believe?"

Thompson nodded at the traveling bag Connors had bought in Laredo. "There it is. Take it. Or, you being a guest at Hayes House am I supposed to carry it out to the car for you?"

Connors ignored the sarcasm. "No progress since last night, I suppose? No one in town has reported the usual mysterious stranger?"

Thompson took a bottle from one of the desk drawers and bought himself a drink while he considered the question. Then, returning the bottle to the drawer without offering a drink to Connors, he said, sourly, "On a transcontinental highway you don't have mysterious strangers. But no stranger to Blue Mound killed Mac. No one just passing through would know where that shotgun was kept, know you were in Room 205."

There was a crumpled package of cigarettes on the desk. Connors slipped a cigarette from the pack and straightened it. "No," he agreed. "They wouldn't. And while we're on the subject. The barber across the street just gave me something to think about. Whoever killed MacMillan was in a hurry, nervous, or both. In fact I hear he almost missed with one barrel. That at a distance of a few feet. The chances are, in that case, he wasn't holding the gun tight to his shoulder and it kicked hob out of him."

"So?"

"So his shoulder is probably black and blue this morning."

Sheriff Thompson was alcoholically enthused. "Fine. Leave it to a detective story writer and a barber to figure out a way to trap the dastardly criminal before the dumb rube sheriff even knows what all the shooting's about. Now all I have to do is strip the shirt and undershirt off every male in Blue Mound. And when I find a man with a black and blue shoulder, presto. I have the lad who had a try for you and wound up killing Mac. I'll get busy on it right away."

He took the bottle from the drawer again.

"I just thought I'd tell you."

"Thanks. I appreciate it, fellow."

Connors picked his bag from the floor. "You have every thing you want out of here, I trust?"

"Everything," Thompson said. He lighted his dead cigar and puffed on it with relish. "All I wanted was a little information. And I got it. I learned from your copy of the contract that you just sold a book to some outfit called Tanner Press and that your agent is a man named Shad Schaeffer with offices at 580 Fifth Avenue, New York. I also learned from a pair of receipted hotel bills that you recently stopped at the Hotel Claremont in New York and before that spent two weeks at the Plaza Hotel in Laredo. And I incorporated all of it in my wire."

"Your wire?"

Thompson was pleased with Thompson. "That's right. To New York. I wired the District Attorney's office telling them what I knew and asking them what *they* knew about you and if they knew of anyone who had reason to want to blow you in two."

That tears it, Connors thought. He didn't know the exact legal procedure. New York would probably wire back and ask Sheriff Thompson to hold him. And Sheriff Thompson would be pleased to accommodate New York.

"I don't think," Connors said finally, "that John Hayes is going to approve of what you've done."

Thompson put his feet back on his desk. "Pee on John Hays. This is a murder case, son. The electorate voted me in. And until they vote me out, I'm the sheriff."

Decidedly the worm had turned.

Connors walked out of the office carrying his bag, the revolver sagging his side coat pocket. He put the bag in his borrowed car. Then looking at his watch he found he still had half an hour before his eleven o'clock appointment with the local poohbah. He killed it drowning butterflies in coffee but there were still a few fluttering sodden wings in his stomach when he walked into the bank.

The girl back of the railing opened the gate. "Right this way, Mr. Connors. Mr. Hayes told me to expect you."

Hayes' office was large but plainly furnished. Eleana was before him. Connors admired the small of her sun-tanned back as Eleana pounded her small fist on Hayes' desk.

"But what am I going to do?" Eleana demanded. "What am I going to do?"

John Hayes looked older than he had the night before. The lines in his face seemed deeper. Nodding to Connors, he said, "Pull up a chair and sit down, Mr. Connors."

Connors drew a chair up to the desk and smiled pleasantly at Eleana. "Before I unburden my soul, what new rain has fallen to dampen your young life?"

Eleana bit at her lower lip. "The Lautenbach lawyers will be here tomorrow to draw up the marriage contract. And if one of them asks for mother's marriage certificate, what am I going to tell him?"

Connors hazarded a guess. "That you're afraid you may be a little bastard?" He moved his legs to one side as Eleana kicked at his shins.

"That," John Hayes said, "will be enough of that. Sit down, Eleana If it wasn't for Celeste, I'd wash my hands of both of you."

Eleana sat scowling at Connors.

Connors said, "I'm afraid you can't, Mr. Hayes. Your pet sheriff has slipped his leash. He's wired New York for information on me. You know what their answer will be. And I'm not going back to Mexico to protect your reputation or Eleana's chance of marrying a millionaire. As soon as a cell door closes on me I'm going to start talking. I'm going to talk loud and long. I'm going to tell the whole thing just as it happened from the minute Eleana smacked her Ford into General Estaban's Cadillac in the intersection of Tacuba and Teatro Nacional up to, and including, our tender parting in a cab in Laredo when Eleana told me to get out of her life after clipping me for a last two hundred and thirty dollars."

"I clipped you?" Eleana said. "Ha." She took a check from Hayes' desk and used his desk pen to fill it in.

Hayes picked up his phone and asked the operator to connect him with the railroad station. When the connection was made, he said, "This is

John, Charlie. You're going to receive a wire from New York for Jimmy Thompson in reply to the wire he sent. When it comes in bring it up to the bank. And if Jimmy inquires about it tell him there hasn't been any answer as yet."

Hayes cradled the phone and lighted a cigar.

His grin tight, Connors said, "At the risk of sounding corny, you can't get away with that. No man can play God."

Hayes puffed at his cigar. "I can, in Blue Mound."

Eleana handed Connors the check. "There's your two hundred and thirty dollars. Thank you very much."

Connors put the check in his wallet. "Thank *you*, Miss Hayes."

John Hayes continued. "For example. I know you asked the clerk at the hotel if he'd seen me before the shooting last night. I know you purchased a .38 caliber, five inch barrel Smith and Wesson revolver and a box of cartridges for it. I imagine that's what's sagging your pocket. I also know you asked the barber if I was out of town four weeks ago."

Connors put his hand on the gun in his pocket. "You must be psychic."

Hayes' smile was thin. "Things come to me. But not in a supernatural way. It just so happens I own the hotel. I advanced the money for Joe to start his hardware store. Bill used to run the barber concession on my circus. Charlie is an old friend. We're all ex-showmen in a small town. And we still come running when one of us yells, 'Hey Rube.' Now let me ask you a question. What makes you think it might have been I who shot MacMillan last night?"

Eleana gasped. "But that's ridiculous."

"Utterly," John Hayes agreed. He spoke without emphasis or heat. The lack of either made his statement that much more deadly. It was just that, a statement. "I assure you, Mr. Connors, if I wanted to take your life I wouldn't be nervous or in a hurry about it. And I would kill you, not an old man whom I liked. Well, I asked you a question."

Connors didn't know what to say.

Eleana said, "He's thinking of that silly story he wrote in Guadalajara. I told him about father and Tamara and Pablo. But because father sent me money every month, Ad said he had a well-developed sense of responsibility and wouldn't have killed Attorney Santchez the way he did and gotten me into a jam. So he turned the story around. In his story father came home unexpectedly and caught you making love to Celeste. So you killed father and buried him. Then you killed Pablo when he tried to blackmail you and paid Tamara to leave town so people would think father had run away with her. Of course you took the money father was carrying. But your conscience began to hurt you so you made an arrangement with Attorney Santchez to send me fifty dollars every month purporting to come from father. Then last month, when I drove down to Mexico to look up father and take care of the license business, you were afraid Attorney Santchez would expose you. So you flew down to Mexico, lured Santchez to Uruapan, killed him and left father's locket in his hand. I don't recall if Ad explained *where* you got the locket."

Connors said, "He took it from his brother's body when he killed him twenty years ago."

Hayes looked at Connors with fresh interest. "Is that the story as you wrote it?"

"Substantially."

"And someone bought it?"

"They did."

Hayes removed his cigar from his lips. "I'd like to read it sometime."

Connors loosened his tie with his left hand. "Are you certain you didn't read it? Eleana had a carbon copy. And I found the title pages in a rubbish fire back of Hayes House shortly after you said goodnight and I'd walked down to the river."

Hayes' voice was flat. "No. I didn't read it. I don't have much time to read."

"Oh, that," Eleana said. "I threw the carbons of both stories away just before supper last night. I threw them in the kitchen trash can." Her drawl with the lilt at the end of her words was more obvious sometimes. This was one of the times. "I was so darn mad about you showing up in Blue Mound."

Connors asked her, "And before that, where did you keep the carbons of the stories?"

"In one of the drawers in my vanity." Eleana twisted the knife. "Nestled in sachets of lavender. Against my old age."

Hayes smoked in silence a moment. Then he said, "I begin to see your point of view, Mr. Connors. I understand why you're keeping your hand on the gun in your pocket. If I had murdered my brother over Celeste's affections I might have followed a similar course to the one outlined in your story. I undoubtedly would have covered the murder somehow. Undoubtedly my conscience would have bothered me and I'd have made some arrangement to send money for Eleana's support. I certainly would have killed this Mexican attorney to keep from being exposed. And, matters transpiring as they have, I certainly would kill, or attempt to kill, you to keep from being returned to Mexico and executed."

He's cool. He's shrewd, Connors thought. I underestimated the man.

CHAPTER 13

His cigar protruding from between his fingers Hayes put his elbows on his desk and rested his forehead in his hands. The silence in the office became almost unbearable. Then, lifting his head, John Hayes said:

"Unfortunately the only thing true about your version of the story is that I am in love with Celeste. I was in love with her when she and Don ran away and were married."

Connors asked, "Why haven't you married her then?"

Hayes said, as flatly, "Because she won't have me. She's still in love with a dream. Despite what he did to her and Eleana, Don is still her man. She still keeps their first cottage as a shrine. She still hopes someday Don will return to her."

Connors took his hand from his pocket. "It's a good story," he admitted. You could get five cents a word for that from *True Confession*. But I still incline to the theory Don Hayes is dead and buried somewhere here in Blue Mound. Over sixteen hours have passed since MacMillan was killed. If your brother is in town, alive, someone would have seen him."

"Not necessarily." Hayes returned his cigar to his lips. "Don was born in this country. He knows every tree, every hill, every cave. We played in them as boys." He pushed back his chair and stood up. "Frankly, I don't know what to do or what to think. We can't stall this thing forever. I'm not simple minded enough to think we can. It has come at an inopportune moment."

Connors lighted a cigarette and offered the first puff to Eleana. "No, thank you," she said sweetly. "I'm not certain it's sanitary."

Hayes ground out his cigar. "If it was Don who killed Mac the whole thing will have to come in the open regardless of how it may affect Eleana's wedding plans. But while there's a possible chance of some other solution, I'd like to spare Celeste if we can. How about it, Mr. Connors? How about giving me twenty-four more hours to work on this?"

Connors' grin was wry. "What with you having the sheriff, Western Union, and the railroad station in your pocket I don't seem to have much of a choice."

"Suppose I could prove to your satisfaction I didn't kill my brother?"

"That would be something else."

Hayes took a folder from a filing case. "It was on the night of March 28, 1931 that Don returned from California, killed Pablo, and ran away with Tamara. You can check the date with two dozen men in town." Taking a letter from the folder he handed it to Connors. "Where was this letter written? On what date?"

Connors glanced at the letter. "Mexico City, 9/5/36."

"Read it."

The letter was written in a bold masculine hand on Hotel Geneve stationery. It read:

Dear John:

So I'm a heel. I couldn't help myself. But it was a mess for nothing. Tamara was killed in a car accident near Acapulco shortly after we reached here. Enclosed find draft for five thousand dollars on the Banco Nacional De Mexico. It's a small part of what I owe you but I'm in on an oil deal that looks promising. If it develops, I'll send more. It won't bring back the show but at least we'll be square as to cash. Meanwhile, tell Celeste I'll continue to send money for Eleana's support through my attorney here. I can be reached through him. Address Attorney Caesar A. Santchez, Calle Tacuba 23, Mexico City, Mexico.

Don

Connors handed the letter back to Hayes. "That seems to shoot my theory. Eleana told me about the letter but I didn't know it was handwritten. It's in your brother's handwriting?"

"I'd swear to that in court."

"That was the five thousand dollars you gave Eleana's mother to pay down on a house?"

"It was."

"And your brother never sent any more money?"

"Not a penny."

"Then Hayes House, the cob pipe factory, the hotel, this bank, Blue Mound—"

John Hayes worried his now sodden cigar. His voice was bitter. "Were all built on hard work. Dirty eighteen-hour-a-day hard work and a desire to make up to Celeste the misery Don caused her." He returned the letter to the folder and the folder to the file. "For all the good it did. Outside of the payment on the house in Chicago, and she had to have shelter, Celeste has always refused to accept any money from me. To eke out Don's fifty a month she's clerked in stores, sold corsets and cosmetics and magazine subscriptions. She's sung in dingy night clubs, waited table, scrubbed floors, to keep herself and Eleana going. Why, I practically had to use force to get her to accept enough of a loan to cover Eleana's four years at Normal." Hayes' voice was as gray as his face. "Why? Because Celeste hopes someday Don will come back and she doesn't want to be obligated to any other man. She wants to be able to say, 'Here I am, Don. Just as you left me, twenty years ago.'"

Hayes turned and looked out the window. Eleana looked at Ad, her eyes pleading with him to understand. "That's the main reason I'm so determined to marry Allan. I don't love him. I know what I'm getting into. But I'm tired of being poor. I'm tired of counting pennies. And while mother won't take any money from Uncle John, she will take money from me. And I want to be able to give her the things I'll never he able to give her otherwise."

Eleana dabbed at her eyes with the back of her hand. Connors handed her his breast pocket handkerchief. "Here. Blow hard." The pleasant pain was back in his groin. The sluggish beat was gone from his pulse. Eleana looked more than ever like a starry-eyed adolescent riding a merry-go-round much too big and swift for her.

I love you, Shad, Connors thought. He considered telling Eleana about the Tanner Press sale. It wasn't the place or the time. He didn't want to buy her. That would put him in a class with Allan Lautenbach.

Eleana wiped her eyes and put the handkerchief in her purse. "Now even if Allan's lawyer doesn't make a fuss about proof of mother's marriage to father all this will have to come out." A tear trickled down her check. "And the only reason old Mr. Lautenbach likes and put his stamp of approval on me is because I've never been in any scandal. I'm just a healthy little mouse of a public school teacher in whom his beloved son Allan will plant the sacred seed that will germinate into a spoiled brat, heir to the Lautenbach millions, here-in-after to be known to the financial and horsey set as Allan Lautenbach III. This, of course, after appropriate ceremony, the burning of incense and sprinkling of attar." Eleana wiped the tear from her cheek. "If Allan II is still able to plant a seed."

Connors laughed.

John Hayes was shocked. "Eleana."

Eleana opened her purse, took out Ad's handkerchief, and blew her nose. "Well, it was nice having money while it lasted. Now I'll probably even lose my job."

Hayes asked Connors, "Okay on twenty-four hours?"

Connors shrugged. "What have I to lose? But what about Sheriff Thompson?"

"I'll take care of Thompson," Hayes said. He lifted the switch of the inter-office annunciator. "I'm leaving for the balance of the day, Miss Harris. And I won't be available to anyone."

Connors asked if he could be of any assistance.

"Yes," Hayes said. "Stay alive. I've enough to worry about now. I don't want you on my conscience." He added, "And you stay close to Mr. Connors, Eleana. Your father is much less apt to take another potshot at our guest if he's in your company."

After the air conditioned bank the street was like an oven. Eleana blew up at a lock of hair the heat had plastered to her forehead. "How," she asked, unsmiling, "would you like to buy me something tall and cold and filled with gin?"

Connors played along with the gag. "Be careful. You are speaking of the woman I love."

Eleana looked at her watch. "Then we'll have to drive out to the cottage and get mother."

"The cottage?" Connors puzzled.

Eleana explained. "Where I was born. Where she and father lived. Mother works in it or the garden almost every morning we're in Blue Mound."

The relief afforded by the gin bucks was temporary. It was cooler driving than it had been in the cocktail lounge. Connors thought of a thousand things to say but couldn't isolate any one. It was familiar and normal being with Eleana. It brought back pleasant memories.

Eleana felt the same way. But she was articulate. "I'm sorry, Ad. I'm sorry it has to be this way. You've put me in exactly the same spot mother's in. I'll never forget you. I couldn't. Corny or not, we've been too much to each other. We've been through too much together. I've tried to put you out of my mind. And I can't. It isn't all physical. It's the *rebozo* and the flowers you bought me. It's your never once scolding about me being so foolish as to go out with General Estaban. It's the fun I had on the merry-go-round. It's window shopping in Guadalajara. It's the electric iron you borrowed, watching you while you slept, after working all night—for me."

Connors wondered why so many people were so ashamed and so afraid of corn. It was the gossamer fabric of which dreams were woven, the bedrock on which lives were built. He slackened the speed of the car while he waited for Eleana to continue.

Eleana laid her hand on his arm. "I'll always remember and treasure the time we had together. You are nice, Ad. I like you. I only wish I'd never met you."

They were in open country now on a tree-shaded road. Pulling over on the shoulder, Connors reached for the ignition key to kill the motor and Eleana blocked his hand.

"No, Ad."

He protested, "But I just want to tell you something."

Eleana transferred her fingers to his lips. "I don't want to hear it. I still intend to marry Allan if I can. I think I can. As far as you and I are concerned the boat sailed in Nuevo Laredo. And there's no sense in both of us just getting upset again."

"Well, we'll see," Connors said. He kissed her fingers and, for the time being, let it go at that.

Hayes Cottage was white, a story and a half. It looked substantial but unlived in. The shed and outhouses were in poor repair. Four or more acres of nettle and milk-weed separated it from the fringe of willow and cottonwood that bordered the river. There was a half-dead elm tree in the yard. The garden was beautiful. Back of a blue alyssum border vari-colored portulaca formed a base for a riot of gladioli, golden California poppies, petunias, snapdragons, marigolds, zinnias, and cosmos. A flowering vine of heavenly blue morning glories, closed now against the heat of the day, completely covered the small front porch. The front door of the cottage was open. So were most of the first and second story windows. A hot west wind billowed stiffly starched curtains out of what must have been a stifling interior. Wearing a halter and shorts and a pair of no-longer-white gardening gloves, a smudge of dirt across her nose, Celeste sat on the front stoop surrounded by trowels and weeders and spray guns and insecticides.

"What love does for a woman," Eleana said. "Mother keeps that darn cottage just as if she expected father home for supper. She even used to tack a card with our address on the door when we left for Chicago. She's compromised on that now. She just leaves a key under the mat and a note on the kitchen table."

Celeste waved gaily as Connors stopped the car. "So soon?" she asked Eleana. She appealed to Connors. "Where has the morning gone, Mr. Connors? I am not half finished with what I hoped to do." She looked at the garden. "You like?"

"Very much," Connors said. He was referring to both the garden and Celeste. In her green shorts and halter she was lovely as Eleana. He didn't blame John Hayes for being in love with her.

Eleana studied the garden critically. "You know, mother, you ought to pull up some of those California poppies. They're spreading all over and crowding out everything else."

Celeste added another smudge of dirt to her nose as she pondered the matter. "I like them," she decided. She peeled off her garden gloves. "But lunch will be waiting. You both are probably starved." She smiled at Connors. "I will be with you as soon as I resume a skirt and blouse."

Blowing a kiss to Eleana she disappeared into the house.

"She's pretty," Connors said.

Eleana nodded. "Celeste's a sweetheart. And she has a few good breaks coming to her. I mean to see she gets them. Uncle John wasn't kidding about her scrubbing floors to bring me up."

Connors returned his attention to the garden. "I see what your uncle meant when he used the word shrine. Your mother and father planted the garden together?"

"I don't think so," Eleana answered. "In fact I'm certain they didn't. At first there were just a few poppies growing wild. Then Celeste added the other flowers."

"Do you think he might come here?"

"My father?" Eleana thought a moment then shook her head. "It's possible. But I doubt it. I doubt it very much, Ad."

"Why?"

"Because I'm inclined to agree with you as to his character. Pablo caught him in bed with Tamara. Father had to kill him and run away with her. Attorney Santchez threatened to expose him and father closed his mouth in the most expedient manner. But I don't think he could be enough of a heel to break Celeste's heart again by deliberately dragging her into this second mess."

"That," Connors said, "would seem to me to fall into the category of being a moot question."

"What is a moot question?"

"Whether her heart would be broken or whether she would consider the physical return of his love sufficient compensation for any possible involvement in his latest escapade."

He lighted a cigarette and offered it to Eleana. She started to reach for it, then shook her head. "No, thank you," she drawled primly.

There was the squeak of a rusty pump inside the house and the splash of water in a tin sink. Then the billowing curtains were pulled in and the windows closed. A few minutes later Celeste appeared in the front doorway again wearing a sheer white blouse and having trouble with a wraparound skirt. "Is not nice to be a woman, no?" she smiled at Connors. "One must be so modest while a man can wear anything." She closed and locked the front door and put the key under the mat. "A woman can show her legs on a beach, yes. But in the town, no." Celeste laughed. "And of course on the back of a horse as it used to be in the circus."

Eleana laughed with her. "Silly." She inspected her mother's face. One of the two smudges of dirt was gone but Celeste had missed the other one. Eleana took a piece of tissue from the glove compartment and wet a corner with her tongue. "Here. Let me get that dirt off your nose. And you'd better use my lipstick. Yours is smeared all over your mouth."

Celeste submitted meekly to the cleansing and accepted Eleana's lipstick and mirror. She used the tissue to wipe the outline of her lips. Then between strokes of the lipstick she appealed to Connors. "Eleana is hard on me. No, Mr. Connors?"

Grinning, Connors started to turn the car around. Catching sight of a billowing curtain, Eleana stopped him. "And you've left the front upstairs window open. Want me to run up and close it, mother?"

Celeste continued to apply lipstick. "No. That will not be necessary."

"But what if it rains?"

Celeste shrugged her slim shoulders and returned the lipstick and mirror to Eleana. "It will not rain in the next few hours. And I intend to come back this afternoon." Celeste touched her hair to make certain it was in order and Connors saw her fingers were trembling slightly. "We were apart so long this time, my garden and I. I still have so much to do. Drive to Hayes House, Mr. Connors."

Connors backed the car to turn it around. As he did he glanced up at the window casually and a hard, invisible fist hit him in the pit of his stomach. He opened his mouth, then closed it.

A gray spiral of smoke that could only be coming from a lighted cigarette or cigar was wafting lazily out of the open second story window.

CHAPTER 14

Allan Lautenbach forked a piece of avocado. "Then in the second chukker, Fleetwind sprained a tendon and I had to substitute a decidedly inferior mount. As I recall, it was Bayrick out of Cakra by Red Valiant. Yes. I remember now. I'd purchased him the week before from an English colonel. The colt had good blood. Definitely. But he hadn't lived up to either strain. Nevertheless—"

Connors wished Lautenbach would choke on the piece of avocado. Horses and women seemed to be the only things he knew. And the women he had known, undoubtedly, made better barroom than table conversation.

Connors shut Lautenbach out of his mind and looked across the table at Celeste. Celeste was eating little. From time to time she smiled at some inner thought and ran the tips of her fingers over her cheeks or touched her lips. When spoken to she answered. But only her physical body was present at the table.

Connors transferred his attention to Eleana. Eleana refused to meet his eyes. Her small jaw took on a decided set as she forced herself to pretend interest in what Lautenbach was saying.

It would serve her right, Connors thought, if I let her marry him.

He wished he knew what to do. He couldn't confide in Eleana. He was afraid to confide in John Hayes. Both of them worshiped Celeste. Either of them would throw him to the wolves for her. He was glad when lunch was over.

Celeste fluttered around the living room for a few minutes, then insisted she had to get back to her garden. "I have so much to do."

Eleana suggested, "Why don't we three go swimming? We can all pile into Allan's car, drop mother off, then go on out to the club pool."

"We three?" Lautenbach puzzled. He turned his watery blue eyes on Connors. "Oh. Yes. Of course. Mr Connors."

"You can count me out," Connors said. "But I will accept a ride back to town."

Eleana began a protest, then changed her mind. "Suit yourself. It's too hot to argue." She smiled at Lautenbach. "We'd better dress here, Allan. The locker rooms out at the club are rather antiquated and Uncle John hasn't got around to having renovating them."

"Right," Lautenbach said. "Right."

He and Eleana went upstairs to put on swimsuits. Celeste continued to flutter around the room. Connors wished she would light somewhere. She was beginning to make him nervous.

Celeste fluffed a cushion then began to rearrange a perfectly good arrangement of the white roses that had been the supper table decoration the preceding night. "Mr. Lautenbach is nice. Don't you think so, Mr. Connors?"

"No," Connors said flatly. "I don't."

"No?" Celeste was momentarily perturbed, then she laughed. "I see. You are one of Eleana's former suitors. I begin to understand. You came to Blue Mound hoping she might change her mind. I am sorry. Believe me, Mr. Connors." Celeste gave his cheek a motherly pat. "But love is sometimes cruel. A girl must marry as well as she can. And I am very happy about this. It is a good marriage for Eleana. She will be secure for life."

Yeah, Connors thought. Also up to her neck in horse chips.

He looked up as Eleana came down the stairs wearing a wisp of a bathing suit and trailing a white silk dressing gown behind her. The bitchy smile was back on her lips as she drawled, "Certain you won't come with us, Ad?"

"Certain," Connors said.

Lautenbach followed close behind Eleana. And no matter what his lawyers might say, Eleana would have no trouble in marrying him. His eyes bugged every time he looked at her.

Celeste picked up her purse. "If we are ready."

Connors rode in the back seat with Celeste. The hot dry wind had died. The curtain no longer billowed out the second floor window of the cottage. It sat asleep in the sun. Even the flowers looked drowsy. Connors helped Celeste out of the car with a wary eye on the open window.

Eleana kissed her mother. "Have a good time, dear."

"I will," Celeste assured her. Taking the key from under the mat she entered the cottage and a moment later the routine of opening windows began.

Lautenbach turned his imported car around. "A charming person, your mother, Eleana. As I understand it from your uncle, she keeps this cottage as a shrine in memory of your father. He has been dead some time?"

"Twenty years," Eleana said.

"How touching."

Neither he nor Eleana spoke again until they were entering Blue Mound. Then, visibly relieved Connors wasn't to accompany them, Lautenbach was gracious to him. "Any particular place in town you care to be dropped, Mr. Connors?"

"Any place," Connors said.

Lautenbach glanced over his shoulder. "Interesting profession, yours. I've often thought I'd like to take up writing. I've had so many interesting experiences. Know I could write a book about them if I tried."

He stopped the car in front of the hardware store and waited for Connors to get out. He was hot. He was worried. Being patronized annoyed Connors. He'd had about all he could take of Allan Lautenbach. Getting out of the car, Connors said, "As I see it, there would only two drawbacks in your writing such a book."

Lautenbach fell into the trap. "And what would they be?"

"Horses can't read," Connors said. "And you'd have to write the other half on bathroom stationery."

Eleana said, "Ad," sharply.

The car was a right hand drive. Lautenbach stepped out on the walk and faced Connors. His sallow face was mottled with color. "Now just one minute, Mr. Connors. I don't like that remark. I don't like you. In fact I more than dislike you. I'm curious. Just what is your standing at Hayes House? Eleana tells me she didn't invite you. I'm certain that I didn't. Just what is your business in Blue Mound?"

Eleana said, "Ad," again. There was a pleading note in her voice this time.

Connors rubbed the knuckles of his right hand with the fingers of his left. The chin a few inches away was a tempting target. But fighting with Lautenbach wouldn't help anything. The other man was well within his rights in asking the question he had. Connors compromised. "Let's say it's a matter of business. Why?"

Lautenbach wasn't a coward. "I just thought I'd ask on the chance you might care to take the question personally."

A small group of curious had formed. Connors felt suddenly shamed. He felt like one of two dogs yapping over a bitch in heat. "Okay, Lautenbach," he said. "You've impressed Eleana with your rugged manhood. Go on and have your swim."

Rounding the car he walked across the street and into the bank. Hayes' secretary was pleasant, but no help. She said, "No. I haven't seen Mr. Hayes since he left with you and Miss Hayes this morning."

"I just thought I'd ask," Connors said.

He was relieved not to find Hayes in. He still wasn't certain it would be wise to confide in him. He wished he knew what to do.

The smoke he'd seen had been real. It hadn't been a figment of his imagination. If Celeste was concealing some man in the upper front room of the cottage it was logical to assume the man was the husband for whom she'd waited twenty years. But what to do about it?

That morning, leaving his borrowed car in front of the hotel, he'd rolled up the windows and locked it. It had sat in the sun all morning. The wheel was so hot it burned his hand. The interior was unbearable. Connors rolled down the windows and walked back to the cocktail lounge where he'd bought Eleana a gin buck.

Sheriff Thompson was sagging on one of the stools. His drunk was obviously progressive. He had trouble sitting erect. Some of the film left his eyes as he saw Connors. "Well if it isn't my old friend Mr. Connors the bigshot detective story writer."

Macey explained, "Jimmy's drunk." The deputy looked worried.

"So I see," Connors said. He sat a few stools away.

"Not that I blame him much," Macey added. He included the barman in his scowl. "Me and Jimmy were both born here in Blue Mound. And just because we've lived here all our lives, the show fellows who run the town treat us like we're a pair of rubes."

"I wanna drink," Thompson hiccuped.

The barman hesitated and Macey said, "You heard him."

The barman shrugged and refilled Thompson's shot glass.

Then he asked Connors, "What will yours be, Mister?"

Connors told him. "Beer."

Ignoring his drink, Thompson turned on his stool to scowl at Connors. "Bigshot ain't you?" It sounded like one word.

"I never made any such claim."

Thompson ignored the statement. It was doubtful he heard it. "But bigshot or not I'm going to throw your pants in the clink as soon as I hear from New York." He located his deputy with an effort. "Call the railroad station."

"I just called, Jimmy," his deputy assured him. "And Charlie says there's been no answer yet."

"Inefficient. Inefficient," Thompson said. "Wired 'em nine o'clock this morning." He lifted his shot glass to his lips and put it down. "Something damn funny going on. 'Minds me of the gag about the whore an' the guy with lace on his shorts. What I wanna know is who's doing what to who an' who's getting paid for it."

Macey kept glancing at the door. "Come on. Drink your drink and let's go. You gotta get some sleep and sober up. Be a good fellow, Jimmy. If Mr. Hayes sees you in this condition we'll both be out of a job."

Sheriff Thompson was luridly explicit about what Mr. Hayes could do but he drank his drink and allowed his deputy to lead him out of the lounge.

Connors watched them leave. It had been in the back of his mind to blow the whole thing wide open and confide in Thompson. That was obviously out of the question. Sober, the sheriff was intelligent, if somewhat frustrated and dominated by John Hayes. Drunk, he was a moron.

The barman picked Thompson's glass from the bar and wiped up the spilled liquor. "A nice lad, Jimmy," he said. "But he pulls one of these about once a year. Feels he has to express himself, I guess. Then Mac getting killed last night has hit him hard. We all liked the old man."

"I'll buy a drink," Connors offered.

"Thanks. I'll go you a brew," the barman said. He drew himself a short beer then put it down as the phone at the front end of the bar rang. A moment later he turned back to Connors. "Your name is Connors, ain't it? Ad Connors?"

"It is."

The barman laid the receiver on the bar. "New York. Long distance. The operator says she's been calling you all over town and someone just told her they seen you come in here."

Connors walked up to the front of the bar and took the call. It was Shad. "You can talk?" the agent asked.

Connors glanced down the empty bar. "Within reason." Then he thought of the operator. If John Hayes had the sheriff, western union, and the railroad station, in his pocket it wasn't likely he'd overlooked the local phone exchange. "But I wouldn't mention any names if I were you." It was a good connection. Schaeffer might have been in the next room. He said, "Well, the same man I told you about came back just a few minutes ago and wanted to know if I'd seen you. Naturally I said no. Then he said they'd had a wire from, well, where you are now asking for information. And he said they've wired back a pick-up and hold while they refer the question to the Attorney General's office."

"Why the Attorney General?"

"Because now they aren't certain who has jurisdiction. They've never had a case just like it before. And they don't want to send a man out there until they've had a ruling."

"You contacted K?"

"I did."

"What did he say?"

"He says it's in our favor. He says he thinks this throws it back into the party of the first part's lap and they'll have to start all over if they want your company."

"I see," Connors said. "You got my wire?"

Shad said, "This morning. That's where I called, Hayes House. But when the maid said you'd gone into town I asked the operator to trace you." The agent's enthusiasm bubbled over. "Look, Ad. I've got more good news."

"Yes—?"

"While I can't state for a positive fact they're going to pick it up, one of the three judges who make the decision for one of the major book clubs read your book in manuscript form and called me this morning."

"Yes—?"

"And he said it was certain of one vote. He said it was one of the most powerful and concise pieces of writing he has ever read and we both should be proud of it. I told you, boy. We're in the Cinderella money now."

"I love you, Shad."

"Now I love *you*," Schaeffer said. "How are things going out there?"

"They stink," Connors admitted.

Some of Schaeffer's enthusiasm faded. "Well, keep me posted, boy."

"I'll do that, Shad," Connors said.

He hung up the receiver and went back to his beer. Damn John Hayes. Damn Donald Hayes. Damn Celeste Hayes. Damn Hayes Cottage. Damn Allan Lautenbach. Damn Eleana. Right now after all these years of dropping sweat and talent in the slot just when he hit the jackpot something like this would have to happen.

Finished with his beer he picked his change from the bar, walked back to the borrowed car, and drove slowly out of town in the direction of Hayes Cottage. He slowed the car almost to a crawl just before he reached it. Celeste wasn't working in the garden. Neither was she sitting on the porch. All of the windows, including the second story front, were open but the front door was closed. Closed and locked, Connors imagined.

He drove on a few miles up the road and turned around in the driveway of a lane leading back to a farm house. Then he drove past the cottage again. There was still no life in the garden or the yard but this time he caught a flash of movement in the window.

Nearing Blue Mound he turned down a rutted lane that led past a fair grounds to the river. There was a huge oak tree on the bank of the river. Parking under it Connors sat watching an old man patiently training a three-gaited walking horse.

He supposed the thing to do was to go back to the cottage, bang on the door with the butt of his gun, and demand a showdown. Somehow he didn't feel equal to it. It was one thing to write about a man breaking in on a triple killer. It was another thing to do it.

He tried to bolster his ego. He didn't know the man in the room was Donald Hayes. Connors realized the palms of his hands were wet and wiped them on his thighs. If John Hayes was making a fool of him it could be John Hayes in the room. Hayes could have told Celeste the real reason for his being at Hayes House and sold her a bill of goods. Hayes could have convinced Celeste that, at this late date, it would do no good to have the truth come out. He could have convinced her it was better for still one more murder to be committed than to destroy Eleana's illusions and her plans to marry Allan Lautenbach. Celeste approved of the marriage. Celeste loved Eleana. Mother love was as fierce as it was tender. In that case the wisp of smoke, Celeste's smeared lips, the trembling of her fingers, had been bait to lure him into a trap. If he walked into Hayes Cottage and was shot, after what happened at the hotel, even Eleana would think that her father had killed him. Hayes could take care of the local angle without any of the background of the story coming to Lautenbach's attention. Donald Hayes would still be a wanted man. And his and Eleana's Mexican 'interlude' would be wiped off the record.

The old man training the walking horse hitched her to a rail in shade. Then coming over to the tree under which Connors was parked he took a waterbag from one of its lower branches.

"Howdy." Recognition lighted his face. "Say. You're that—"

Connors finished the sentence for him. "Detective story writer, aren't you?"

The old man grinned. "Hear it on all sides, huh?"

His grin was infectious. Some of Connors' sour mood left him. "Well, at least this is one town in which I'm recognized."

The old man thrust his arm in the window. "Name's Carson. No relation to Kit. Mac was a great admirer of yours. Glad he got to meet you. The sheriff made any progress on who killed him?"

Connors said, "Thompson's drunk."

Carson didn't seem surprised. "It's about time for one of Jimmy's periodics. Jimmy's a good hand when the going is smooth but he's not much of a hand in a tight one. John Hayes has done his thinking for him so long that Jimmy's high up in the blues without a prayer whenever a big top blows down." The old man put a pinch of fine cut in his cheek.

Connors asked a flat question. "What sort of a man is John Hayes?"

Carson thought a moment. "I could say, salt of the earth. But John has his faults along with the rest of us. He's a good friend, a bad enemy. He'll go through hell and high water to make his point. But I feel sorry for John. I always have. The one thing he really wants he's never been able to get."

"And that is—?"

"His brother's wife. John's always loved her. Loved his brother, too. That's why Don doing what he did hit John so hard." Carson spat tobacco juice at a beetle zig-zagging through the dust. "You know though, Mr. Connors, there's always been one thing about that affair that puzzled me."

"You mean Don running away with Tamara?"

"Um hmm. Pretty little thing, Tamara. Shy, too. Not like most Gypsies. Of course through the years it's been talked about Tamara's been made out to be a little tart who'd slept with everyone on the lot before Don ran away with her. But you pin any of the old timers down and it's always some other gilly who'd bedded her. I don't think any of 'em ever did, except Don and her husband. But what I'm getting at is this."

"Yes?"

Carson spat at the beetle again and hit it this time. "Jennie Silvers was postmistress in those days. Her husband was station agent. Curious souls, both of them. And between 'em they had Western Union and the United States Mail sewed up. Now mind this. Don came home a full week before he was expected. If he'd wired Tamara to expect him, Silvers would have passed it on. If Don had written to Tamara, Jennie couldn't have waited to put a bee in Celeste's ear." The old man looked expectant. "See what I mean?"

"No," Connors admitted. "I'm afraid I don't."

Carson spat with the impatience of the aged. "Could be Mac was wrong about you. Sure you're a detective story writer? Look. Don got in on the two o'clock milk train. Come in unexpected with neither John nor Celeste down to the station to meet him. The last Don was seen he was hoofing it down the road toward his cottage. To reach it he had to pass the shack in which Pablo and Tamara lived. So far, fine. But now tell me this. *How did Tamara know Don was coming?* How was Tamara alerted so she could get Pablo out of the way? Or did Don just turn in off the road and climb into her bed at two o'clock in the morning? That don't seem logical to me. He had to expect Pablo to be gone. And Pablo had to come back before he was due and catch Don in his saddle. Pablo going for a gun or a knife is the only reason for Don to have killed him. Don wasn't the sort of a man to go around sticking knives in people for fun."

"Pablo's body was found in the shack?"

"On the floor of the bedroom with one knife in his hand and another in his ribs. The sheets on the bed had been slashed. A wash bowl, a pitcher, a chair, even the chamber pot had been smashed. Oh, it was a hell of a mess. Although I remember remarking at the time about there being so little blood."

Connors sat looking at the river, sensing rather than hearing the ripple of the water as it cascaded over a small falls. And there it was. He knew who had killed Attorney Santchez. He knew who had killed MacMillan. He knew who was waiting for him on the second floor of Hayes Cottage. Keeping his voice casual, he asked, "Who found the body?"

Carson said, "John. The next morning. Along with doing a knife act, Pablo handled the rigging for Tamara's highwire act and John wanted to see him about some new guy wires he was figuring on buying as soon as Don came back with the money."

"I see," Carson said. He felt his way. "Say. Along the same line. MacMillan told me something the other evening just before he was killed, something I've thought of a dozen times. Were you with the show the night it was making a long jump and the canvas boss dropped the side walls of Celeste's tent before she'd finished dressing?"

"I was." Carson's aged eyes lighted at the memory. "It was one of the prettiest things I ever saw. And I never did hold Celeste was bitchy about it like Don accused her. Well, not very bitchy. She was young. She was pretty. She knew it. She knew what the sight of her body was doing to every man within eyesight. Being a woman, it pleased her. If I'd been a woman the knowledge would have pleased me. Believe me, Mr. Connors, it was beautiful. What with the night and the wind and the glare of the work lights and the whinnying of the horses and the snarling and cough of the cats and the trumpeting of the elephants it was like being present at the Creation. After that side wall hit the ground, and before Celeste put on her wrapper, every man present felt like Adam must have felt the first time he knew Eve."

"John Hayes was in the crowd?"

"He was. John raised hob with Don after Don blacked Celeste's eye and called her a little bitch. John said there was nothing bitchy about it, that Celeste had carried off an embarrassing situation well. And John said if Don ever laid a hand on her again, brother or no, he'd—kill him." The old man's voice trailed off like the final ticks of an unwound clock. His eyes looked sunken and worried. "Well," he said finally. "Well," he pushed himself away from the car, "I guess I'd better get back to my training."

Connors sat a moment longer watching the old man. Then he drove on into Blue Mound.

The west side of the street was shady now. There were more people on the street, more cars and farm trucks at the curb. He parked in front of the drug store and went in. The pharmacist was putting up a prescription. The soda clerk was washing glasses. Two high school girls were sitting at the counter giggling over their chocolate malted milks.

Connors got change for a quarter from the soda jerk, then, walking back to the phone booth he dropped a nickle in the coin slot and gave the operator the number of Hayes House.

"This is Connors calling," he told the maid who answered. "Has Miss Hayes returned yet?"

"No she has not," the maid said.

"Is Mr. Hayes there?"

"No. He isn't here either. I'm sorry."

"It's quite all right," Connors said. "But would you take a message for Mr. Hayes. Tell him I'm driving into St. Louis on a matter concerning the business we discussed in his office this morning and I won't be at the house for supper. It may be quite late before I return. Possibly not until tomorrow morning."

"Yes, sir. I'll tell him, Mr. Connors," the maid said.

Connors continued to face the phone after he'd hung up the receiver. At this point, in a pulp story of his, his hero would turn to find the guilty party eying him with a murderous gleam over the barrel of a revolver.

Connors turned and looked through the glass. The status quo hadn't changed. There was no one in the drug store but himself, the pharmacist, the soda jerk, and the two high school girls giggling over their glasses of chocolate malted milk.

CHAPTER 15

It had been hot too long. It had to rain. It did. Leaving the florist shop next to the hotel, Connors drove out the road to Hayes House. It was a few minutes after nine when he parked his car a few hundred feet beyond the stone gates and walked through the grounds to the house. His clothes were sodden by the time he'd gone twenty feet. Rain cascaded from the brim of his hat. It beaded on his cheeks and the backs of his hands. He liked the feel of it. It was cool and soft and clean.

There were four cars in front of the house. John Hayes' Lincoln sedan. Allan Lautenbach's imported Jaguar. Eleana's new Buick convertible. A '39 Plymouth coupe.

The French windows that opened on the lawn were partly closed against the rain. Standing back of a small blue spruce, Connors watched the family at supper.

The scene was much as it had been the night before. Lautenbach was doing the talking. Celeste pretended interest. Eleana was candidly bored and seemingly worried about something. She touched her lips, her forehead, ran her hand over her hair. John Hayes was equally as jumpy. He divided his attention between Celeste and the partly opened windows. Once he got up and opened them a little wider. There was still a bulge on the left side of his coat.

Leaving the vantage point of the spruce, Connors crossed thirty feet of wet lawn and stood with his back against the house next to the first French window. In his new position he could hear but not see. Lautenbach was still talking.

"A dirty old hole, Monte Carlo. Hardly worth bothering about, especially since the war. Oh, of course we'll drop in. But most of the crowd goes to Biarritz. That is, the crowd we'll travel with."

Eleana's voice sounded as if she was wrestling with some knotty problem. "What did you do in the war, Allan?"

Lautenbach seemed surprised by the question. "Why, worked with father, of course. You know, gave parties for the right people in Washington. Snagged our share of Army and Navy contracts. Helped keep the boys well fed."

"Oh," Eleana said flatly.

Careful, honey, Connors thought. Don't get thinking thoughts like that. You're going to marry the guy. Remember?

Celeste broke the awkward silence that followed with a pleased exclamation. "Oh. Walt Disney's new picture is at the Playhouse. In Technicolor. Would you like to see it, Eleana?"

"No, mother," Eleana said. A chair scraped on the parquet flooring. "If you'll excuse me, Allan, I think I'll go up to my room. The swim, or the drinks, or the rain, or something, has given me a headache. You don't mind awfully, do you, if we don't go out to the Barn tonight?"

There was the scrape of a second chair. "Not at all, Eleana. You go up and rest." Lautenbach laughed. "And don't worry about me. I'll drive out to the Barn alone later on and give the tables another whirl." He added, probably to John Hayes. "Did quite well out there last night. Eleana lost a few dollars but I came away with almost two thousand."

Hayes spoke for the first time since Connors had taken up his listening post. "I'll have to speak to Mickey. If you won, he let you win. He must be building you up for a killing. Mickey used to be the crookedest three-card monte man in the business. I'll bet I've run him off my lot a dozen times."

Lautenbach laughed. "It's only money."

Eleana said, "Good night, mother. Good night, Uncle John. Good night, Allan."

There was a brief pause between each good night and Connors could visualize Eleana kissing each in turn. When she came to Lautenbach his stomach turned over. Love was indecent. What it did shouldn't happen to a man.

After Eleana had left the room, Celeste asked, "How about you, John? Would you like to see a movie?"

Hayes sounded tired. "No. Not tonight. But I have to drive back to town to take care of some unfinished business and you're welcome to ride in with me."

"That," Celeste said, "will not be necessary." Her French accent was pronounced tonight. "When Allan and Eleana picked me up at the cottage this afternoon I had them stop at the garage to see if my car was ready, and it was. All it needed was new pistol rings, or something." She added with French thrift. "That is why it burned so much oil. Now we shall see."

Lautenbach laughed again. "You're charming, Mrs. Hayes. If I wasn't in love with your daughter, I think I'd fall in love with you."

"Shall," John Hayes asked, "we go into the living room?"

Connors walked back through the rain to his car. He knew what he wanted to know; where the occupants of Hayes House would be for the next few hours. At least where they proposed to be.

As he drove through Blue Mound he saw a light in Sheriff Thompson's office. Thompson's feet were on the floor. He was apparently sober and still waiting for the wire that had been sent and John Hayes had ordered the station agent to bring to the bank.

The windows of Hayes Cottage were closed except for a two inch crack between sill and frame of the front second story window. The shade on the window was drawn but the light seeping out around the edges of the shade could only come from a lighted oil lamp.

The light puzzled Connors. Then he thought he understood. The problem he presented had to be disposed of tonight—or never. When Sheriff Thompson didn't acknowledge the answer to his wire, the D.A.'s office in New York would inquire into the matter. They might even send a man to Blue Mound.

Connors drove a quarter of a mile past the cottage. Then he parked just off the road and slogged back through the rain. There was no need of striving for silence. The rain drowned out all sound but its own.

Reaching the cottage he stood a moment in the shelter of the stoop to get his breath and to allow the rain to drain from his hat before he tried the front door. It was locked and the key was no longer under the mat. More bait, he supposed. Make it difficult for the fly to walk into the spider's parlor. A fly wouldn't expect a triple killer to leave his front door unlocked.

Rounding the house, Connors found an unlocked kitchen window. Opening the window he pulled himself up and sat on the sill until his eyes became accustomed to the even darker interior.

The kitchen had a dry and unused smell. There was a table under the window. Connors eased his weight onto it. Then, sitting on the table he took off his wet shoes before stepping down to the floor. There was always the chance he was wrong and Donald Hayes was waiting for him in the lighted room.

The rain heard from inside the house was louder than it had been out in the night. It beat in angry frenzy on the roof, pounded against the clapboards, and gurgled noisily down the tin rain spouts.

Connors tried to light a match but both the book and his hand were wet. He threw the matches away and took the revolver from his pocket. It didn't matter if it was wet.

The kitchen opened into a small dining room. The dining room opened into a parlor. The yellow runner laid down by the lamp in the upstairs bedroom gave sufficient light for Connors to see the appointments of the parlor. The furniture was well-chosen. The chairs looked comfortable. The magazines he could see were yellowed copies of *Billboard*, *Variety*, and *Field and Stream*. A battered Teddy bear, undoubtedly Eleana's, sat in a small red rocking chair with one fuzzy arm around a girl doll. A lump formed in Connors' throat. Celeste had kept the parlor exactly as it must have been on that night twenty years before.

He walked to the foot of the stairs and listened. There was no sound on the floor above but the pound of the rain on the roof. He put tentative weight on a step. The stairs were well built. They didn't creak. It might have been better if the carpenter hadn't been so thorough.

Keeping close to the rail he climbed the stairs and stood in a small upper hall. Two bedrooms opened off it. The doors to both rooms were open. There was a small bed in the back bedroom and a mate to the red rocking chair.

The lamp in the front room was on a table, just inside the door. There was a double bed on the opposite wall and a night table in front of the window holding a butt-littered ash tray and a Bible. The bed was made but there was the outline left by a body on the spread and the spread was deeply indented where it covered the pillows.

Connors examined the butts in the ash tray. Half of them were smeared with lipstick. Through the open curtains of a closet alcove Connors could see a row of men's suits. Donald Hayes hadn't had time to pack as thoroughly as Tamara.

He sat on the bed and picked up the Bible. It was old and often used. It fell open in his hand to Genesis IV. The verses VIII, IX, and X were smudged as if they had been traced many times by a moving finger. Connors laid the revolver on the bed and read the verses:

VIII And Cain talked with Abel his brother; and it came to pass, when they were in the field, that Cain rose up against Abel his brother, and slew him.

IX   And the Lord said unto Cain, Where is Abel thy brother? And he said, I know not. Am I my brother's keeper?

X   And He said, What hast thou done? the voice of thy brother's blood crieth unto me from the ground.

Connor laid the Bible back on the table and picked up the revolver. Then, too nervous to sit still, he got up and prowled the small room, looking out into the hall from time to time to make certain no one was ascending the stairs.

He found the bundle of letters in the bottom drawer of the dressing table. They were tied with a blue ribbon and then made him think of the carbon copy of KILL ME, MAÑANA that Eleana had kept.

"Let's say a souvenir. Something tied with blue."

Connors sat back on the bed and slipped the ribbon from the letters. The first one he read was a letter that Donald Hayes had written to Celeste shortly after they had been married. The writing was bold and masculine.

The handwriting looked the same as that of the letter John Hayes had shown him in the bank.

Connors laid it on the bed and read another letter. It had been written the night after Eleana had been born. In it Donald Hayes laid bare his soul and hopes for his wife and baby daughter. Both letters were well-spotted with tear stains.

Connors laid the second letter on the first and was reaching for the third when he thought he heard a door open and close. Picking up the revolver he walked out into the hall, then, cautiously, down the stairs.

There was a sweet, fresh smell in the parlor but the front door was still locked and closed. There was no one in the parlor. His hair ends tingling, Connors walked back through the dark dining room to the kitchen. There was no one in either room. The sound he'd thought he'd heard had been due to his nerves. Breathing hard, Connors returned to the upstairs front bedroom.

The next two letters were inconsequential. They touched on nothing with which he was concerned or familiar. The eleventh and next to the last letter was an abject apology for having so lost his temper as to strike Celeste and pleading with her to forgive him. It was written on Oklahoma City hotel stationery but as there was no postmark or stamp on the envelope, Connors concluded that Donald Hayes had either slipped it under the door of his wife's hotel room or left it on her dressing table on the circus lot. As the other letters it, too, was spotted with tear stains.

Connors put it with the letters he'd already read and picked up the last letter. It was written on Biltmore Hotel stationery and the envelope was stamped and postmarked Los Angeles, Feb. 16, 1931. Connors slipped the letter from the envelope and read it. It began on a cheerful note—

Sweetheart:
It looks like it's in the bag. I had lunch with McGivney at the Hollywood Brown Derby this afternoon and he seemed very favorably impressed with our collateral...

The letter went on to discuss the proposed mortgage and the amount of interest he and John would have to pay. Then Donald Hayes began to generalize. It was his first trip to California. He was impressed by a number of things and he described them in detail to Celeste. There was a trip to one of the movie studios, a fishing jaunt to Catalina, an evening spent in China Town and on Olivera Street. He'd been to the Hollywood Bowl. He'd rented a car and driven out to Thousand Oaks to see old circus friends. The last trip had impressed him the most. He wrote glowingly of the small towns along Ventura Boulevard and of the film celebrities who were beginning

to purchase small ranches in and near Sherman Oaks, Encino, and
Tarzana. Hayes was particularly impressed by the California flora.

I want you to see this country, Celeste. It's all mountains and valleys,
green now for this is their summer. I drove past miles and miles of climbing red roses and flowering eucalyptus and acacia trees. There is also a
species of yellow poppy peculiar to this region, but which I am assured
will grow anywhere the soil and climate is favorable. One of our friends
was in Thousand Oaks, Jim Kelly. (You remember Jim. We met him at the
Muehlebach in Kansas City. He was out ahead of Ringling Brothers and
kidded me about trying to cut into their take.) Well, anyway, Jim's wife has
given me a small packet of poppy seeds to try in our garden. I have it in
my pocket now. And Jim says if they grow he'll see what he can do about
sending us a seedling eucalyptus and acacia.

Connors re-read the paragraph then pushed his wet hat back on his
head and sat holding the letter in his hands. There it was. There it had
been all these years for all of Blue Mound to see. And not a soul in Blue
Mound had been the wiser.

The pelt of the rain increased in intensity. Connors started to lay the letter with the others and got to his feet instead. This time it wasn't his
nerves. And the sound hadn't been outside the house. There had been a
distinct thump, then the sound of heavy china-ware shattering. Jamming
the letter in his pocket, Connors picked the lamp from the table and
walked to the head of the stairwell. At the end of the yellow runner laid
down by the lamp lay a heavy shattered china pitcher that hadn't been
there before.

Taking a firmer grip on the revolver and holding the lamp the length of
his arm from his body, Connors stepped down one stair. Then a rush from
behind knocked the lamp from his hand before he could turn and a short
length of heavy pipe began to batter his head with blinding, murderous
blows.

The revolver followed the lamp. The first sound he'd heard had been
real. It had been the killer of Pablo, Santchez, and MacMillan, entering the
front door. Seeing him start down the stairs the first time, the killer had
hidden behind a chair or perhaps the parlor drapes. Then when he'd gone
on into the dining room and kitchen, the killer had climbed the stairs to
wait in what had once been Eleana's room.

A red tongue of flame from the dropped lamp crawled across the floor
and licked at one of the parlor drapes. Blinded with blood, stunned by the
suddenness and fury of the attack, Connors turned on the stairs in a sub-
conscious attempt to grapple with his attacker and knew a moment of

intense sadness. He had been right after all. The bare flesh under his hands was soft and yielding. Donald Hayes was dead. He had been dead for twenty years. And if John Hayes was wielding the length of pipe that was beating him to his knees the poohbah of Blue Mound had suddenly grown breasts.

They held Connors' fast-numbing fingers like magnets. They were bare, wet, firm, familiar breasts. Breasts for a man to dream on. Breasts like Eve might have had.

CHAPTER 16

The cottage vented by the open front door burned rapidly. It was his constant coughing that roused Connors to consciousness. He was lying face down on the landing. Clouds of black smoke were billowing up the stairs. The parlor was one large flame. The heat was already intense but the air a few inches from the floor was still pure.

Connors backed the length of the hall and into the room that had been Eleana's. Before he reached it the flames were licking the stairhead. In another few minutes the inferno on the lower floor would eat away a supporting wall. When that happened the second floor would fall into the first. Holding his breath, Connors got to his feet and tried to open the window. The lock was stiff. The window stuck. Then it slid up.

The added ventilation gave impetus to the flames. The crackling became a roar. There was a screen on the outside of the window. Connors kicked it out. Then he was astraddle of the sill with the rain pelting at his head and shoulders.

Connors twisted in the window and dropped. A lilac bush cushioned his fall. As he struck the earth he rolled away from the house. Fifteen feet from the building he got to his hands and knees and crawled, sucking in great lungsful of fresh air, until the wet darkness covered him. Then he lay with a cheek pressed to the wet earth looking back through the rain at the burning cottage.

Flames were leaping through the window out of which he'd dropped, licking up at the leaf-filled gutter and setting the eaves afire. As he watched, fire bored through the roof in three places and fought the rain for the shingles. Then the front wall of the cottage fell in and the roof fell into the flames and the matter was decided.

Somewhere out on the road, Connors heard the whine of a car starter and lifted his head an inch. A motor turned over stiffly, caught. There was a grind of gears. A pair of car headlights flicked on and moved rapidly in the direction of Blue Mound.

Connors turned over on his back and let the rain wash his face until he felt strong enough to get to his feet. When he did, he found he was standing in Celeste's flower garden. Stooping, he snapped the stem of a poppy. Then, chewing on the stem, he limped through the rain to his car.

The fire siren in Blue Mound was wailing now. Wailing, Connors thought grimly, twenty years too late.

When he reached Hayes House, the Lincoln and the Buick were stand-

ing on the drive. The Jaguar and the Plymouth were gone. Parking his borrowed car, Connors walked through the huge living room and up the stairs
to his room, meeting no one en route.

In his room he switched on the lights and stripped off his sodden clothes.
Then picking a pair of clean shorts from his bag he padded on into the
bathroom wondering where he was going to get a pair of shoes. He'd only
brought the one pair with him. And they'd burned up with Hayes Cottage.

Closing the bathroom door, Connors examined his face in the mirror.
The length of pipe had done more damage than he'd realized. There was
a nasty gash on his right temple. Despite the pelt of the rain his hair was
still matted with blood. Only the fact he'd been wearing his hat had kept
the damage as relatively minor as it was.

He adjusted the shower to lukewarm and washed the blood from his hair
as best he could. Then, through the closed door of the bathroom, he heard
the room door open and snick shut and the sick feeling returned to the pit
of Connors' stomach. He hadn't been smart in returning to Hayes House.
He'd been dumb. He'd been seen crawling away from the cottage. He'd
asked for it. And now he was going to get it.

Then Eleana called through the closed door. "Is that you in the bathroom, Ad?"

Connors leaned against the tile wall. "Yes. Why?"

"I want to talk to you," Eleana said. She waited a moment, then added, "I
thought I heard you come up the stairs." Her voice sounded as if she'd been
crying. "I—I've been waiting for you for hours. Where did you go, Ad?"

Connors put on his shorts. "What's it to you?"

Eleana said, "A lot. Please. Come out, Ad. I want to talk to you."

Connors toweled the hair on his chest. "One last oat, eh? Well, I'm sorry,
baby. The boat sailed in Nuevo Laredo."

"No," Eleana wailed. She hadn't been crying. She was. "No. Please, Ad.
Don't be mean to me. I was wrong. I admit it."

Connors leaned against his side of the door. "You were wrong about
what?"

"Us. Allan," Eleana drawled. "I can't marry him. I won't"

"And when did you come to this decision?"

"This afternoon. Tonight. At supper. I almost died when you didn't show
up. I thought maybe you were never coming back." Eleana sounded as if
she was standing with her cheek pressed to the door. "I will die if you ever
leave me again. I love you, Ad. I fear me? I love you."

"Oh. I thought it was all bio-chemical affinity."

Eleana sniffed. "That helps. But there's more to it than that."

"Now you tell me," Connors grinned. "How about the Lautenbach
money?"

"I don't care," Eleana said. "Mother had her life. I'm sorry it was tragic. I'm willing to do anything I can for her." Eleana was emphatic about it. "But I'm going to marry you."

"That's a proposal?"

"It is."

"I love you, baby," Connors said. "I think I have since I saw you standing in the intersection of Tacuba and Teatro Nacional."

Eleana was practical. "Then come out here and kiss me."

Connors opened the door and Eleana came into his arms. Then she saw his face and backed a step. For a moment he was afraid that she was going to scream. Then her voice fiercely possessive, she demanded, "Who did this to you, Ad?"

Connors kissed her gently. There was no heat, no passion in her lips. Even spiced with the salt of her tears they were sweet and clinging and a promise. This was the kiss with which they should have started.

Connors held her close for a long time. When he spoke his voice was as gentle as his love. "You'll have to know in a few minutes, Eleana. But to save me telling an unpleasant story twice, would you mind waiting until I dress? Then we'll go look up your uncle."

Eleana raised her eyes to his. "It was Uncle John who had this done to you?"

"No," Connors said. "It wasn't. I did John Hayes an injustice. He's everything you said he was." Connors picked his rain sodden coat from the floor and transferred the letter to his other coat. Then he put on a clean shirt and the suit he'd worn into Blue Mound.

"Where are your shoes?" Eleana asked.

"They're part of the story," Connors said. Dressed, he walked Eleana down the hall to John Hayes' door.

Connors was lifting his fist to knock when Hayes opened the door. He saw Eleana and said, curtly, "You'd better slip out of that negligee, put on a dress, and come with me, Eleana. The incompetent fools. They let it burn to the ground. And then they call me."

"Let what burn to the ground?" Eleana asked.

Connors told her. "Your mother's cottage."

Seeing him, Hayes stopped struggling into his coat. "Oh. You're back." He looked at the younger man's face and the lines in his own face deepened. "Don or a truck?" he asked.

The rain was distant here. It was merely a patter on the thick slate roof. The silence on the three-sided balcony deepened. Then Connors said, quietly, "Neither. Your brother Don is dead, Mr. Hayes. He's been dead since the night he returned to Blue Mound from California."

Eleana's fingers bit into Connors' arm. "How do you know? How do you know it was Hayes Cottage that burned?"

"I just came from there," Connors said. "The shoes you inquired about are still there. I imagine they burned with the cottage."

John Hayes took a cigar from his pocket, rolled it between his fingers, then crumpled it in his palm. "You can prove my brother is dead? That Don has been dead for the length of time you say?"

"I can."

John Hayes looked at his clenched right fist. Then he opened his lean, hard fingers and allowed the crushed tobacco to trickle to the carpet. "I was afraid of that," he said finally. "I've been afraid of it for some years." Squaring his shoulders, he pushed open the door to his room. "Come in. Come in, please, Mr. Connors."

CHAPTER 17

John Hayes put down his glass as the car stopped on the drive. Eleana said, "It's mother." She allowed the drape to resume its fold and sat in a chair by the fireplace.

Celeste brought a breath of fresh air with her. A few jewels of rain had fallen in her hair. She brushed the moisture from her palms then came directly to John Hayes. "I've bad news for you, John," she said. "They called me out of the theatre to tell me Hayes Cottage had burned. There is nothing left but rubble."

Hayes looked at his dead cigar.

A bit impatient with him, Celeste said, "Well, why don't you say something, John? You know what the cottage meant to me." Celeste looked at Eleana. "You and your uncle have been quarreling?"

"No," said Eleana. 'We haven't been quarreling." She might have been speaking to a stranger.

Celeste was hurt. "Eleana." She removed her transparent rain-cape and turning to lay it on a bench, saw Connors and all of her brightness left her. "Oh," Celeste moaned. "I see."

She passed her fingertips over her face and weaved as if she was about to faint. John Hayes got to his feet and steadied her. "You should have told me, Celeste. You should have allowed me to help you." He guided her to a chair and filled a wine glass with brandy.

Celeste shook her head at the glass. "No thank you. I'm glad," she told Connors. "I'm glad. You won't believe it, Mr. Connors." Her smile reflected her inner sickness. "Neither will Eleana. Loving you, she hates me. That is as it should be. But I'm glad, very glad to see you. I'm glad you got out of the cottage."

Then Celeste put her face in her hands and rocked her shame. "These awful things I have done."

"You killed Don, too, Celeste?" The question came from Hayes.

Celeste raised her eyes to his. "Yes. I think you could say I did, John. I have always considered it so although it was not my hand that used the knife." She drank the brandy she'd refused. "But how did you know, Mr. Connors? That is what has worried me the most. That is why I make no futile attempt at denial. It all had to come out sometime, I suppose."

"I didn't know," Connors admitted. "If you're referring to the story I wrote in Guadalajara based on what Eleana told me, I merely transposed the motivation because it seemed truer to life that way."

"I almost died when I read it," Celeste said. "I have wished I might die so many times." She passed her fingers over her face again. "Of course, in your story, you made John my lover." She patted John Hayes' arm. "I have often wished for that, too. I am bad, no?"

"No," Hayes said loyally.

Celeste looked at Connors. "So it was just a story. I thought you knew. When you called from the hotel and asked to speak to Eleana, I was certain." She spread her hands in a futile gesture. "And I had no money to buy your silence. No money left at all. So, to cover my old sin I did what I thought best."

Hayes knelt beside the chair in which Celeste was sitting. "It was you who shot Mac, Celeste?"

She nodded. "When I went for the flowers for the table. I knew about the fire escape. I knew the gun was in the closet. I thought MacMillan was Mr. Connors. And when I saw it wasn't, I couldn't undo what I'd done."

Hayes' voice was surprisingly gentle. "I followed you. I followed you, too, Connors. I was the man you thought was Don. That's why I was almost certain he wasn't in town. Still there was the possibility."

"You knew it was I who killed MacMillan," Celeste puzzled. "Still you said nothing John?"

Hayes shook his head. "No. I didn't know until you just told me, Celeste. I merely wondered why a call from the man with whom Eleana had been romancing in Mexico should so upset you. But when I saw Connors go into the hotel and you go into the florist, I damned myself for a jealous fool and drove back here to Hayes House just in time to drive Eleana to Blue Mound."

"I took the roses up to the room with me," Celeste said. "I am very sorry about Mac. I am very sorry about it all. I have caused you all much trouble and much heartache."

Connors studied Celeste's face. She was sane in the legal definition of the word but years of emotional upset and physical self-denial had eaten away the foundation of her emotional balance and conditioned her to act on impulse.

"But why try to kill Ad?" Eleana demanded of her mother.

"He knew," Celeste said. "Oh, maybe not at first. Maybe at first it was just a story. But he knew. And I knew he knew when John stopped at the cottage this morning and told me he was looking for Don, told me he'd shown Mr. Connors the letter in Don's handwriting that it took me so long to write."

Celeste was silent a moment. Then she continued. "So, when you came with Eleana, Mr. Connors, I set a trap for you. A small one. I smeared my lipstick. I left a lighted cigarette on a tray. I acted nervous. And it worked. While I waited this afternoon I saw you drive by twice and knew you would come tonight." Celeste smiled wanly. "I am a good actress. No?"

"Yes. You're a good actress," Connors said.

Eleana accused, "You tried to kill Ad to hush up the past so I could marry the Lautenbach money."

"No." Celeste shook her head. "The money didn't enter my mind. Many men have wanted me. Several of them wealthy. One had almost as much as Allan Lautenbach." The strain in her eyes crept into her voice. "But except on two occasions when it was forced on me by circumstance, out-side of the one time, I have always been true in mind and body to your father. Poof. That for Allan. Remember? It was you who were determined to marry him. It was you who insisted on going to Mexico to talk to your father and obtain our marriage license." There was a note of hysteria in her laughter. "I tried to dissuade you. Remember? I begged you not to go."

Eleana looked at the floor.

Celeste continued, "Knowing Caesar, I knew what would happen. He'd taken all the money I had. It cost me a hundred dollars every month for the fifty I sent you. It cost me ten thousand dollars to have him send five thousand dollars to your Uncle John." Celeste spread her hands. "And there is the money for which your father mortgaged the circus, plus what I made singing, selling corsets and cosmetics, waiting table. I, Celeste, who had been an equestrian star. I was in a trap and I couldn't get out." She wanted confirmation of the one thing in her life that had been beautiful. "I could ride, couldn't I, John?"

Hayes steadied her with his arm. "You were beautiful on a horse."

Celeste's smile faded. "I never rode again." It wasn't a plea for sympathy. It was a simple statement of fact. "I think I died with your father, Eleana. This is only a shell that lived on. Of course, when you were young there was you to care for. But once you were grown, I would gladly have gone. Then you met Allan Lautenbach and it started all over again."

Celeste asked if she might have another glass of brandy. Sipping it, she confided:

"The day you left I called Caesar and asked him to meet me somewhere in Mexico. Anywhere out of Mexico City. It was he who suggested Uruapan."

"Ah," Connors said. "The beautiful veiled *señora*."

Looking at Eleana, Celeste said, "I pleaded with Caesar. I gave myself to him. He took me and laughed. He was always greedy that one. He want-ed more money. Whether your father and I were married was unimpor-tant. He knew how your father died. I had to tell him that first night in Mexico City before he would agree to do what I wished him to, keep Don-ald alive through money sent to you. And he meant to use that knowledge after you were married to Allan. He even boasted he would possess you, that you would be afraid to deny him for fear of losing so many millions." Celeste's eyes flashed. "For that, I killed him.

"I had no idea you were in the Morelas. I did not then know this business about a General Estaban. I do not know it now except what I have overheard whispered between the three of you. I'm sorry, my child, if I have cursed you with my passion. I had hoped you might be cold. Such women are much more happy. Not so much happens in their lives to tear their hearts and bodies to pieces." Celeste smiled wryly at Connors. "But perhaps Mr. Connors can resolve that problem for you."

"I'm certain he can," Eleana said coldly. "There's never going to be any other man in my life, Ad."

Celeste handed the brandy glass to Hayes and wiped her fingers on the handkerchief he offered. "I thought that once about your father. I meant it to be that way. See that you keep that pledge, my child. Good is like a stone thrown in the water of the river. The ripples spread out from it until there is no end and everything they touch is benefited. Evil is the same way. Starting with one mistake, the ripples befoul everything with which they come in contact. So it was with me and Pablo."

Celeste wiped hot tears from her eyes. "It all started, I suppose, that night Spike Mallen dropped the side walls of my dressing tent and caught me *au naturel*. I was embarrassed but also, I suppose, what it pleased Don to call "bitchy." There were so many men staring. All had but one thought. It made me drunk with power. It made me realize that within me I had the source of life. I passed it off with a laugh and a remark. And then Don called me the name and struck me and John told Don he would kill him if he ever struck me again."

Celeste leaned her head on John Hayes' shoulder and cried. "I'm sorry, John. I didn't mean to cause his death. I loved him, too." She sat up and wiped her eyes. "Women are so full of tears. And tears are such futile things. I forgave Don, naturally. I loved him. But in the back of my mind was the thought he once had been mean to me." Celeste shrugged her exquisite shoulders. "And that's how Pablo happened. In my right mind I detested him. But he was a man. Don had gone to California to raise money for the show. I'd begged him to take me with him. But he insisted we couldn't afford it. And there he was in California and I was home doing housework, taking care of our child. All I had of interesting places, I had to get from his letters. All I knew was resentment. I didn't expect him for a week. And that night Pablo came to the house on some minor matter. I've often tried to remember what it was. I can't. But it must have been about a snake."

Celeste looked at Eleana. "I'd just put you to bed. I was sitting in the kitchen when Pablo knocked on the door. He came in and took off his hat and stated his errand. I had to pass him to get whatever it was he'd come for. And as I passed him he touched me, there, deliberately. I tried to slap him and couldn't. As much as I detested him the pressure of his hand paralyzed me with desire. Then he had me in his arms and was kissing my lips, my neck, my breasts, whispering how beautiful I had been in the work light and how he had wanted me ever since. I was young. Don had been gone a month. In the back of my mind, I suppose, there was the idea of being even with Don for striking me. I let Pablo have his desire. And after that time lost all meaning. There was no right. There was no wrong. There was only a red sea of passion and a trumpeting of distant bugles in my ears. I was Eve at the birth of Creation. I was Jezebel and Messalina. I was the mother of all whores. I was Woman. Not all the men in the world could have fulfilled my needs that night."

Celeste gripped John Hayes' hand for support. "I didn't even hear Don on the stairs. He walked into our bedroom and found us, Pablo and me. There was a gun in the vanity drawer. Don meant to shoot us both, I think. But when he turned to get the gun Pablo leaped from the bed, snatched his knife from his clothes, and stabbed him."

Celeste was past tears now. It was a recital of fact. "Then Pablo laid the bloody knife on the table and stood there, panting. When I realized what had happened, I picked up the knife and served Pablo in a different manner.

"All the fire was gone. The roaring had died away. I was alone with two dead men, one of whom I loved. I sat on the bed for hours. I didn't know what to do. Then I dressed and drove Pablo's car down the road and told Tamara. I think I hoped she might kill me. She didn't. She drove back to the cottage with me and spat in Pablo's face. Then she suggested, for Eleana's sake, that I take him to their place and she would go away. But she wouldn't help me. I had to dress Pablo and drag him to their car. Don's wallet had fallen from his coat. I tried to give Tamara money and I thought she was going to spit on me. Then she did what was done to their bedroom and drove away. I never saw her again." Celeste looked at Connors. "Someone described that bedroom to you, didn't they? That was one of the reasons why you knew."

Unable to speak, Connors nodded.

"Then I walked home," Celeste continued. "You were crying, Eleana. You wanted a drink of water. I got it for you. Then I went back in the bedroom with Don. I still wasn't thinking clearly. I had some wild idea if I buried Don in the garden I could keep him with me always. And I did. But Mac and some of the boys had seen him come in at the station. And the next morning when John found Pablo and it was discovered Tamara was gone, all the evil minds in town jumped to the wrong conclusion and I wasn't blamed at all. You never knew. You never suspected, did you, John?"

Hayes shook his head. "Not for years. Then it was only a wonder. The steady fifty a month wasn't like Don. If he'd made good in Mexico, he'd have sent Eleana thousands. If he'd pooped out, there'd have been no fifty. Then there was the letter with the money in it for me. The letter that came so opportunely. Just when I was threatening to go to Mexico and look Don up. Then once in a while it was the way you looked at me. I was tempted to believe you loved me and the reason you wouldn't have me was because there was some wall between us you couldn't, or wouldn't, explain."

Celeste put her hand in his. "I have loved you a long time, John. I loved you when I married Don. It was just I loved him more. But while I could and did betray the living, I couldn't bring myself to be faithless to the dead." Her voice barely audible, Celeste added, "Except on two occasions with Caesar A. Santchez. Once when I arranged to have the money sent. And in Uruapan when I killed him. I couldn't give the money to you without telling you what had happened. I couldn't do that. And then after I'd made the deal with Caesar, there was no turning back."

Connors asked, "How did you first contact Santchez?"

Celeste shrugged. "I was selling cosmetics then. One of my trips took me to Laredo. While I was there I thought of this thing of sending money for Eleana's care. So I went on down to Mexico City and asked a man at the consulate to recommend a Mexican lawyer who spoke either English or French. He recommended Attorney Santchez. The man said Caesar was a smart lawyer. And he was. He got the truth out of me and has lived well all these years on Don's money. Even then it might never have come out if Eleana hadn't insisted on trying to obtain the license I buried with Don. I might have known though. I might have known when the poppy seeds Don had in his pocket that night began to blossom." She cried for a moment or two. "It was Don telling me he forgave me. It was Don trying to warn me."

Celeste got up and walked across the room and back.

Connors cleared up the last detail. "And the locket that Eleana and I saw in Santchez's hand? You put it there?"

Celeste shook her head. "No. I tried to take it away from him. Don hadn't worn it when he'd gone to California. He was wearing a new wrist watch I'd given him for Christmas and his old watch and chain were in my purse that first time I went to Mexico. And Caesar took them away from me and had worn them ever since. He said he wanted to remember his *Norte Americano* goose." Celeste turned to Hayes. "Well, you'd better call Sheriff Thompson, John."

Hayes was still kneeling by the chair in which Celeste had been sitting.

He got to his feet and looked thoughtfully at Connors.

Celeste bared enough of her shoulder and the round of her right breast to reveal an ugly purple bruise. "I carry the proof on my body it was I who shot Mr. MacMillan. I admit to burning the cottage and the attempt on Mr. Connors' life. Oh, I was so clever there. I went to see a movie. Right through the front door and out a fire door. And I took off my clothes in the car when I reached the cottage so I wouldn't leave any clue or get them spotted with blood. Killing three times makes you so wise. Then the lamp fell from Mr. Connors' hand and set the cottage on fire. And I was frightened and fled and didn't do as good a job as I did on the others." Celeste buried her face in John Hayes' shoulder and sobbed, "Well, why don't. you call Sheriff Thompson? I confess. I caused Donald to die. I killed Pablo and Caesar and MacMillan. I am a bad woman. I must be punished."

Hayes stroked her convulsing shoulders and looked over Celeste's head at Connors. The indecision was gone from his face. He was a man with a plan. "Would you consider giving us a forty-eight hour start?" he asked.

Connors shook his head. "You're crazy to think of it, Hayes. You can't get her away."

"I can try. There's an international airport in St. Louis. And in forty-eight hours we can be a long way from here."

"Possibly. But Mexico still wants me."

"You don't need Celeste. You've Don's body and Eleana to support your story."

Eleana refused to look at her mother. "When I'm questioned I'll tell the truth."

Celeste raised her head from Hayes' shoulder. "But of course. I want you to, Eleana." She lifted her hand as if to touch her daughter's arm and changed her mind. "You love Mr. Connors very much?"

Eleana still refused to look at her. "Very much."

"I'm glad."

"Well?" Hayes demanded of Connors.

Connors attempted to dissuade him. "It's insane, Hayes. They'll find you. You'd have a few weeks, a few months at the most."

Hayes said, "A few weeks are a few weeks. I've loved Celeste for twenty-four years. I may get her away entirely. And if we stay they'll send her to the chair or lock her up for life."

"She's killed three men."

"Only one of them wasn't a heel."

"There's Blue Mound."

"To hell with Blue Mound," Hayes said. "I've carried it almost as long as I've loved Celeste. Let someone else play God. Why don't you play God and give us a forty-eight hour start?"

Connors looked at Eleana. "It's up to you, Ad," she said.

He said, "Celeste's your mother."

"She tried to kill you. I hate her."

"No, John, please," Celeste begged. "I don't care what happens to me."

Hayes said, "I care. I know now why I made and saved money. I know why I've kept most of it at the bank in cash. We can fly from St. Louis to Miami. From Miami we can fly to Bogata, or possibly Quito in Ecuador. From Quito—"

Connors turned his back on him. "Don't tell me. I don't want to know."

"Then you'll give us forty-eight hours to disappear?"

"I'll give you forty-tight hours. But you can't get her away."

"I'll chance that. And I won't forget this, Connors."

"She's Eleana's mother," Connors said.

There was a terse, whispered, conversation behind him, Hayes urging, Celeste protesting. Then Celeste said, wearily, "All right. If you say so, John. I'll put a few things in a bag." Celeste went upstairs and returned in a few minutes carrying an overnight case.

Hayes helped her into her transparent raincape and opened the door. It still was raining, hard. Celeste started out without speaking, then turned back. "Thank you, Mr. Connors. Good bye, Eleana."

Her face buried against Connors' chest, Eleana said, "Good bye, mother."

Then the door closed and they were gone. Connors waited until the sound of Hayes' car had died away. Then he sat down and held Eleana in his lap. She wiped her eyes with his tie. "Uncle John can't get her away, can he, Ad?"

Connors settled Eleana more comfortably in his lap. "That's something I wouldn't know. At least with Hayes' money they have a chance. A much better chance than we did."

Eleana nuzzled her nose in his neck. "And look what happened to us?"

Connors lighted a cigarette and offered Eleana first puff. "And look what happened to us."

Eleana puffed the cigarette to a glow before returning it. "One cigarette, one man." She lifted her lips to be kissed.

Connors glanced at the front door. "How about Lautenbach? He's still out."

Eleana crinkled her nose. "Oh, him."

It's fun to play God, Connors thought.

Then except for the faint pat of the rain on the thick slate roof there was no sound at all and they were alone in the world and the all enveloping roar of the universe.

THE END